DOWN MEXICO WAY

Book 4 of the Lone Star Reloaded Series

A tale of alternative history

By Drew McGunn

This book is a work of fiction. Names, characters, places and incidents are the product of the author's overactive imagination or are used fictitiously. Any resemblance to actual events, or locales is coincidental. Fictional characters are entirely fictional and any resemblance among the fictional characters to any person living or dead is coincidental. Historical figures in the book are portrayed on a fictional basis and any actions or inactions on their part that diverge from actual history are for story purposes only.

Copyright © 2018 by Drew McGunn

All Rights Reserved. No part of this this publication may be reproduced, stored in a retrieval system or transmitted, in any form or by any means, electronic, mechanical, photocopying, recordings, or otherwise, without the prior permission of the publisher and copyright holder. Permission may be sought by contacting the author at drewmcgunn@gmail.com

Newsletter Sign Up/Website address:
https://drewmcgunn.wixsite.com/website
V1

ISBN: 1723143081
ISBN-13: 978-1723143083

ACKNOWLEDGEMENT

Down Mexico Way wouldn't have seen the light of day without the support of my wife, the lovely Mrs. McGunn. This surreal journey came about because of her faithful support and encouragement.

Table of Contents

The Story So Far	1
Chapter 1	4
Chapter 2	19
Chapter 3	29
Chapter 4	45
Chapter 5	61
Chapter 6	72
Chapter 7	83
Chapter 8	96
Chapter 9	112
Chapter 10	125
Chapter 11	141
Chapter 12	157
Chapter 13	170
Chapter 14	180
Chapter 15	192
Chapter 16	200
Chapter 17	214
Chapter 18	232
Chapter 19	243
Chapter 20	256

Chapter 21	268
Chapter 22	277
Chapter 23	290
Chapter 24	303
Chapter 25	319
Chapter 26	333
Chapter 27	344
The Texas Cession: A Short Story	356
About the Author	370

The Story So Far

In 2008, SSGT Will Travers couldn't have imagined how wrong a routine supply run could go, as he counted down the days until his National Guard unit would rotate back stateside. That is, until an explosion overturned his Humvee and propelled him through space and time.

When he woke, he was trapped in the body of William Barret Travis, with only a few weeks to go before his fateful death at the Alamo in 1836. Trapped in the past, and with no desire to become a martyr for Texas liberty, Will could have fled. With nearly two centuries of history to exploit, the possibilities were endless. Instead of fleeing or dying at the Alamo, he chose the impossible. He rallied every Texian volunteer between the Rio Grande and San Antonio and met Santa Anna at the Rio Grande where he stopped the dictator with the help of David Crockett, Jim Bowie, James Fannin and seven hundred more patriots. After decisively beating Santa Anna twice, Will and David Crockett captured the wily dictator and much of his army, and won independence from Mexico.

Having won the war, Will was determined he would win the peace. As a student of history, he knew without changing direction, Texas was headed towards a constitution trapping thousands of slaves and freedmen in one of the most oppressive slave codes in the American South. Indians, like the Cherokee, who were trying to put the pieces of their society back together after President Jackson's genocidal Indian Removal Act, would be driven out of Texas. Thousands of Tejanos, who had lived in Texas for generations, would be forced from their homes, as men like Robert Potter and James Collinsworth strove to make Texas a welcome place for Anglos only.

Will allied himself with David Crockett and Sam Houston to thwart the worst of the pro-slavery faction and passed a constitution that gave the Cherokee a path to citizenship, and allowed for freedmen to remain in the Republic and for slave owners to free their slaves. For a 21st century man, it seemed too little, but it was a start.

In the closing days of the constitutional convention an assassin tried to kill Will. David Crockett used the shockwaves of the attempted assassination to propel Will to command of the Texian army.

Will dives into transforming the army, but he has barely begun before the frontier erupts into violence as the Comanche ride out from the Comancheria, attacking Fort Parker on the edge of the Texian frontier. Will rushes north, pressed by the Republic's congress, to stop the raids. He discovers the Comanches are lords of the Great Plains, and they stay one step ahead of him until he is forced to retreat.

Will learns from the experience and draws upon his background to modernize his army's tactics and develop new weapons. The following year he defeats the combined might of the Comanche war bands and forces the Comanche to seek peace.

DOWN MEXICO WAY

In the years that followed, Will works to develop new weapons, help Texas find its economic footing, and invest in free labor farming and banking, while building a life with the woman who captured his heart, Rebecca, the daughter of the President of Texas, David Crockett.

Mexico looms large to the fragile Republic's south, and as Crockett's term as president draws to a close, he orders Will to take the army and secure the boundary agreed upon by Santa Anna six years before. While Crockett and Will are trying to solidify Texas' borders, unbeknownst to them, Santa Anna has returned to power and is sending an army north.

Total annihilation at the Alamo is only stopped by A. Sidney Johnston's arrival with every army reservist he could scrape together, while Will was still hundreds of miles away with the regular army. After burying the dead, Texas girds itself for an existential war with Mexico.

Chapter 1

Late February 1843

The horse was high-spirited, striking the paving stone with an iron-shod hoof, impatiently waiting on his rider. Thirty-nine-year-old General Raphael Vasquez stepped through the door of the Palace of the Governor in Monterrey into the rising sun. When he saw his prized mount waiting, it brought a smile of pure pleasure to his face. If one must ride to war, he reasoned, there was no better way to do so than on the back of his best steed.

He took the reins from an orderly and swung into the saddle as he scanned the hundreds of *soldados* deployed in long lines in the plaza of the capital city of Nuevo Leon. The men, mostly recruited from central Mexico, stood proudly in their new blue and red uniforms. They were destined to reinforce nine regiments of the 1st Division of the Army of the North, headquartered at Nuevo Laredo, along the Rio Grande. Before the general's arrival, the 1st division constituted the entirety of the Army of the North. These men would go a long way to rebuilding the strength needed to carry the war north of the Rio Bravo del Norte.

His thoughts turned briefly to Adrian Woll, who had been removed from command in the aftermath of his ignoble defeat at the hand of the illegitimate, piratical government of Texas. Vasquez was philosophical about Woll's demise. One man's fall often led to another's rise and that is what opened the door to his own appointment to command the Army of the North.

He nodded at the infantry colonel, who signaled toward a regimental band. A martial marching tune split the air, and the line wheeled into columns as the *soldados* marched out of the plaza. Vasquez's heart soared, watching the men traipse by. His horse sensed his excitement and he pranced in place, waiting for the signal to gallop to the head of the column. When his iron-shod hoof struck a paving stone, the animal stumbled.

His army momentarily forgotten, the general climbed down. He brushed aside the orderly and carefully examined his mount's hoof. Nails were missing, and the shoe had come loose. Worse, the hoof was split. He lowered the leg and patted his mount's neck. "*Hermanito*, it looks like I'll have to ride to war without you."

He sent the orderly to fetch another mount from the stables as he rubbed the horse's nose. The animal stepped forward, nuzzling his neck as though realizing his rider would be leaving. When the orderly arrived with the new animal, Vasquez fumed at the loss of time, while the orderly switched the saddle. But in reality, it only took a couple of minutes before the general mounted the unfamiliar horse and cantered out of the plaza with his headquarters staff in tow, eager to catch up with the column.

As the general and his staff caught up to the marching infantry, they paraded past the 2nd Division's encampment. The regiments attached to it were still assembling, but the large central pavilion belonging to General Almonte was easy to see above the forest of small, canvas tents assigned to the *soldados*. He resisted the urge to swing by General Almonte's tent. Even though it lightened his burden to have another high-ranking officer with experience in the army, he would see plenty of Almonte when the 2nd Division joined his army in the coming weeks.

The young man pulled the new Italian-made binoculars from a leather case. He brought them to his eyes and watched the distant horsemen leap into view. He smirked, recalling the first time Major Hays had handed him the binoculars. The major had sought to trick the young Cherokee soldier, recently transferred from the 1st Cherokee Rifles to Hays' special Ranger force. But Jessie Running Creek was no backwoods warrior. The reason Running Creek had been recruited into Hays' special Ranger command had nothing to do with his accuracy with a rifle, or how fast he could ride a horse, or even how long he could march on the ridiculously long marches Hays preferred. No, the reason he had been recruited was he spoke fluent Spanish. He had learned the language as a child, traveling frequently with his father to trade at Fort Augustine in Florida in the years after the United States had annexed it from Spain.

He grinned slyly as he recalled taking the binoculars from Hays and putting them to his eyes. It was true, the magnification was stronger than anything he'd ever seen, but he played it nonchalantly when he pulled them away from his eyes and gave them back to Hays and said, "I've seen better, sir."

The truth was, he hadn't. But he wasn't going to give the young officer the satisfaction of knowing that.

How he had come to be perched on a rock, overlooking the Mexican column which was marching through the center of the valley below was something he still had trouble wrapping his mind around. The past year had been a whirlwind for the young Cherokee Ranger. He recalled the meeting between his father and Sam Houston, in which the *Raven* had urged the Cherokee to turn out their own militia when word of the Mexican invasion had arrived. His father was not normally a cautious man. A man who had built his wealth on trade took every calculated risk, but as a father with a son of military age, Simon Running Creek had urged caution.

Jesse had been standing atop a heavy freight wagon, verifying the manifest as slaves hauled the supplies from the wagon into the Running Creeks' warehouse. The *Raven* was standing outside his father's warehouse, gesticulating and pointing south, "Simon, I tell you, my fellow Southerners don't have the good sense that God gave to men when it comes to realizing the value of working with the Cherokee instead of working against them."

Simon wagged his finger under Houston's nose, "I've heard it before. It wasn't that long ago that American soldiers showed up on my doorstep and seized my land. I was there at Horseshoe Bend, Sam, same as you. And what did I get for my service to your country? A damned eviction notice."

The slaves and the work forgotten, Jesse listened to the older men. Houston smiled effusively. "Things are different here, Simon. You own your land. You've got a deed to your land that any court in the Republic would honor. But don't think for a second that if Mexico were able to kick the Americans out of Texas that they wouldn't turn their attention to the Cherokee next."

While Jesse's father remained opposed, other tribal leaders, including Stand Watie, rallied the Cherokee militia. Against his father's wishes, Jesse had joined the militia as they marched south, heading toward the Alamo.

All that was now water under the bridge as Major Hays liked to say. He'd been in one of the major's special Ranger companies almost since Johnston's command had lifted the siege of the Alamo last year. That's how he found himself perched on a rock, overlooking the Mexican column.

Like an undulating snake, the column of infantry wound its way through the arid valley below. Jesse remained in place, counting each row of four until the entire army had moved past. He multiplied the number of rows by four and thought his math might be wrong. It was more than he thought he saw. He owed it to the other Rangers to do this right. He swore under his breath as he retraced his steps, returning to his horse. He followed the mountain trail until he judged he was again ahead of the column.

Again, on foot, he moved along a trail overlooking the meandering road through the valley below. He saw the Mexican flag first, then the finely dressed officer, riding at the head of the column, with a few other officers trailing. Jesse didn't like his view of the little army in the valley and shifted himself onto a wide rock just below the trail. A rattling sound startled him as his feet touched the rock.

Lying in the warm sun, curled in the center of the wide boulder, Jesse heard the unmistakable sound of a rattlesnake's warning. Then he saw the brown diamonds on the coiled snake. In his mind, Jesse was hundreds of miles away, eight years earlier, right after his father had brought his family to Texas as part of the Cherokee diaspora of the mid-1830s. He and a couple of other boys had taken off from where their parents were building homes in the new township they were constructing. He and his friends were swimming in the Trinity River, enjoying a break from the construction in the summer heat.

His best friend, Joe, was swimming in the center of the river, when Jesse spotted something that looked like a stick floating in the water. As it approached Joe, Jesse saw it was a snake. He screamed at his friend, pointing at the reptile. Joe turned in time to see the snake, with a large triangular head, open its mouth wide, showing its white mouth and long fangs. Before the twelve-year-old boy could react, the snake struck him on the shoulder.

Jesse raced to his friend and helped him to the shore. He pulled him onto the river bank and turned him over and saw the snake had bitten him multiple times. Jesse and another boy rushed to get Joe back to where the adults were building, but it was too little, too late, and his best friend died while the Medicine Woman attempted to save him.

Since then, Jesse had suffered from herpetophobia. And when he saw the rattlesnake coiled on the rock, every skill he had acquired, every consideration for his mission fled into the recesses of his mind, replaced by pure terror. He clambered back onto the trail as the snake uncoiled and stretched itself out to more than six feet in length.

As Jesse struggled to his feet, his hand bumped against his holster and in the terror that gripped him, he yanked the gun out and pulled the hammer back and fired. Six rounds in the cylinder, and six rounds he fired at the snake, hitting it multiple times. Whether it was simply muscle memory or if the snake was still alive, Jesse didn't know. But when a blast from a bugle down in the valley penetrated his mind, he realized what he had done, and he bolted back down the trail to his horse, cursing himself for losing his presence of mind. He dug his heels into the sides of his mount, racing north toward the Rio Grande. He grabbed his hat to keep it from blowing off, while cussing at himself, and let the horse have his way as he thundered down the mountain trail.

Were it summer, the sun would mercilessly beat down on his army, General Vasquez thought as the cool breeze of late February was channeled through the valley. He swept his hat from his head as the cool wind tousled his still jet-black hair.

Mountains rose on both sides of the valley, and as Vasquez returned his hat to its proper place, a gunshot echoed across the valley. Five more shots followed in quick succession. The general's first inclination was to search the mountainside, looking for gun smoke. But his mount had other ideas as it bucked following the first shot. Part of Vasquez' mind focused on the quick, rapid fire. It could only be the work of one of the Texians' repeating pistols. But the greater portion of his mind was drawn to trying to control the spooked animal, eyes wide in fear, rearing onto its back legs.

Despite his skill with horses, when his mount reared back, Vasquez' boots slipped from the stirrups. The horse slammed its forefeet down on the trail and bucked again.

The general cursed his unfamiliar mount as the terrified animal ejected him from the saddle.

Landing at a different angle would have made all the difference to General Vasquez. A foot to one side or the other and he would have broken bones from the fall. The staff, mounted behind him, instead heard a loud cracking sound as his head slammed into a rock. For want of a nail, Mexico's invasion plans died in a valley between Monterrey and Nuevo Laredo.

Nine months earlier

Brigadier General Juan Nepomuceno Almonte chose to stand in the great hallway in front of his Excellency's office within the castle of Chapultepec. He stood next to a window, staring down into the city where he could see most of the basin in which the capital was situated. In the distance, he watched a group of boys playing tag on one of the city streets. As usually was the case, one of the boys was a bit quicker than his friends as he stayed several steps ahead of the youth who was "it."

The sound of the door at the end of the hall opening broke his attention as the faster boy was being corralled by the growing cadre of boys who were "it." Almonte tore his gaze away from the window as the boy dodged several of his pursuers. General Adrian Woll shuffled toward him as though in a stupor.

"General Woll, are you alright?"

The other officer drew up next to Almonte and deliberately turned, "Ah, Juan. My failure to take San Antonio has been my ruin."

Almonte was dismayed at Woll's admission. "Surely his Excellency wouldn't cashier you from the service,

Adrian." The younger officer shifted to a more intimate address upon hearing of Woll's bad luck.

With a Gallic shrug, Woll said, "Reduced in rank and command of a desk in the capital. I don't know, Juan. Perhaps, I'll return to France. With any luck, I'll find employ in the court of King Ferdinand."

Almonte searched for something that would sooth the sting of Woll's downfall but came up empty as the other officer continued his listless walk down the corridor. Shaking his head at Woll's inglorious fall from grace, Almonte straightened his jacket and tucked his hat under his arm and tapped on the door.

Antonio Lopez de Santa Anna sat behind a massive teak desk. As Almonte marched in and stopped before the desk, he couldn't help but look at his reflection in the desk's wax polish. Santa Anna wore an elaborately embroidered blue and crimson tunic. His desk was tidy, letting the general take in the intricate marble inlay set in the costly wood.

In response to Almonte's crisp salute, his Excellency smiled widely and waved him into a chair. "Juanito, I'm glad you were able to get away from Washington. Were you able to take Maria and Lupe back with you?"

Almonte tipped his head, "Yes, Excellency. The trip back was unremarkable."

"I want you to understand my decision to recall you from that mosquito-infested town had nothing to do with your performance there. I have need of your observations into the Yankees' mind about Texas. What kind of attitude was there in Washington to Woll's misadventures in Texas?"

Almonte ran his fingers through hair which was turning gray at the temples. "There are plenty within the

Democratic Party who agitate for annexation, asserting that Texas should be brought within their union. They believe it is their Manifest Destiny, as they call it, for the United States to stretch from the Atlantic to the Pacific."

Santa Anna steepled his fingers and appeared to meditate for a moment. "But is not the government of President Clay against annexation?"

"As long as Clay is president, his government has made every assurance that annexation is off the table. But you should be mindful, there is yet a constant flow of settlers pouring across the Sabine River or coming in through the port of Galveston, swelling the population of Texas."

Almonte paused as though trying to decide whether to tell more. "Out with it, my friend. I can see something else is on your mind," Santa Anna insisted.

Choosing his words with care, Almonte said, "The way in which Woll carried out the recent campaign in Texas has elicited a strongly worded condemnation from President Clay, Excellency. Their newspapers decry the massacre at the Alamo and the executions at Reynosa."

His Excellency leaned back in the elegant chair and stifled a yawn, "Did you remind him that how Mexico deals with her own insurrections is an internal dispute? The United States has no more business telling us how we should subjugate an unruly province than we would of how they should deal with their Negros."

"Excellency it has been more than six years since we have exercised de facto control over our rebellious northern territory. In that time, even the British have appointed an envoy to Texas. It wouldn't surprise me if they exchange diplomatic missions sooner rather than later."

Santa Anna shook his head, "No, Juanito, they are pirates and as such, my government has dealt with them as the lawless bandits they are. Given the considerable investment by British bankers in our country and the recent purchase of new ships for our navy, the British are firmly invested in Mexico's continued success."

Almonte pursed his lips, "Bandits they may be, Excellency, but if war with them is an inevitability, I recommend caution in how we treat prisoners in the future, if for no other reason than we don't want these pirates killing any of our soldiers they capture."

Santa Anna stared down his nose at Almonte. It was evident from his gaze that his Excellency was of a different mind. After a protracted moment, he said, "The second reason I summoned you from Washington is that you'll have the opportunity to establish our policy, my friend. I require another general officer with experience in the Army of the North. You'll report to General Vasquez in Monterrey, and I'll leave it to the two of you to decide the policy on prisoners. Does this satisfy your sensibilities?"

Almonte ignored Santa Anna's familiar yet patronizing tone. "Yes, Excellency."

"What information have you brought back from the United States that will help us to refine our strategy for the impending campaign?"

"While their army is modest, at little more than a thousand men, it is my opinion they have formed units comparable to our own active militia. My sources are not certain, but it could amount to another three or four thousand men," Almonte said.

His Excellency scowled at the news. "I had hoped to learn Woll was exaggerating, but that matches what he told me. It troubles me to give an inch to any of Mexico's traitors, but I think I'll postpone our land offensive against the Yucatecan rebels for now. In addition to being General Vasquez's second-in-command, I want you to also take responsibility for the division I had intended for our offensive against the Yucatecan rebels. They're currently stationed south of Vera Cruz. Get them on the road to Monterrey as soon as possible. General Vasquez intends to invade before the heat of summer is upon us."

His audience at an end, Almonte rose and saluted. As the noise of his heels echoed off the walls of the corridor, his thoughts shifted to the debacle in 1836 when the Texians had captured much of Santa Anna's army, including himself, after he was severely wounded.

In Woll's campaign the previous year, mistakes had been made. Monterrey was a good-sized town of more than ten thousand souls and should be capable of supporting the coming campaign. He began building a mental list and realized he would require more supply wagons. As his list grew he added surgeons to it. Before he knew it, he glanced up and found himself in the coach, rolling back toward the hacienda at which his family was staying. He had been so deep in thought he didn't recall leaving Chapultepec. He peered out the window and noticed he was rolling down the street where he had seen the boys playing tag earlier. They were still at it. Now, the swifter boy was "it." As the coach rolled past the playing boys, Almonte couldn't help but see how quickly he chased down the others.

About the same time...

Sunlight streamed through the heavily curtained windows into the bedroom, casting light onto the opposite wall. Will Travers slowly opened his eyes and regretted it as his pupils dilated. He listened and heard Henrietta moving around in the kitchen. Within a few minutes the aroma of coffee would drift through the house.

True to form, the freedwoman had the coffee brewing and Will breathed in the fragrance of the beans steeping in the kitchen hearth.

He stretched out, and his hand ran along his wife's still sleeping body. He rolled over, propping his head up with his arm and watched her relaxed breathing as her breasts rose and fell with each breath. He ran his eyes over her sleeping body, admiring it. The pregnancy wasn't showing yet. But when she had been pregnant with Elizabeth, it took four months for Becky to show.

He leaned over and kissed her lips, which curved upwards into a smile and he felt her arms wrap around his neck. "Good morning, my love."

As their lips parted he returned the smile, "Good morning back at you."

Rare were the occasions when Will had time to reflect about the previous six years. But as his wife snuggled with him and her breathing told him she had drifted back to sleep, his thoughts strayed back to the earth-shattering experience which had altered his life forever. When the Humvee ran over the improvised explosive device, and overturned in the Iraqi sandstorm, he thought his life was over. Waking up in the body of William Barrett Travis, a few weeks before he was supposed to die a martyr's death at the Alamo, was something he couldn't have imagined in his wildest dreams.

Even now, as he inhaled his wife's scent while she slept next to him, trying to rationalize it was something he had failed to manage. Being ripped from 2008 to 1836 made no sense whether he attributed it to an act of God or to the fickleness of fate. His mind was more at ease accepting that it was the hand of God, rather some random violation of the laws of physics. He was convinced chasing the contradictions down the countless rabbit holes would drive him mad.

"Dwelling on that, I could gather enough wool to cloth the army," Will thought as he slid out of bed and dressed. He left the thought in the bedroom as he gently closed the door, leaving Becky asleep. He accepted a steaming cup of coffee from Henrietta with a thank you and absentmindedly ate breakfast as he mentally planned his day.

President Zavala had forced a massive funding bill through congress, and Will needed to find out how fast the Trinity Gun Works could increase production. General Ben McCulloch's most recent enrollment estimates for the militia looked promising, but with an invasion to organize, Will needed to know McCulloch's views on how many men were necessary to keep farms, mills, and Texas' nascent industry functioning. Will had already noticed in San Antonio more women were behind the counters of the mercantile stores. There was no question this war with Mexico would take too many men out of the economy. The answer he sought was to find a balance that left enough men on the Homefront, working farms, mills, and factories, while still giving him enough men to defeat Mexico.

In a hurry to get to his office at the Alamo, Will grabbed his butternut officer's jacket and cracked the bedroom door open and saw Becky softly snoring. Despite feeling the burden of the day, the sight brought a smile to his lips. The crib in the corner held his daughter, Elizabeth. Even though Liza was more than a year old, Becky insisted she continue sleeping in their room, at least until the end of the pregnancy.

Along the back of the house, a hallway led to Charlie's bedroom. Will stuck his head in and saw the boy was still sleeping, even as the sun rose in the sky. A few months shy of fourteen, he was growing like a weed and according to Henrietta, eating her out of house and home.

The constant nightmares following the boy's ordeal at the Alamo a couple of months earlier were fewer now. Will still blamed himself for how close the Alamo had come to falling. Had he been at the mission turned fort with his thousand regulars, he was certain he would have been able to defeat Woll's army and no siege would have happened. Instead, he had been securing the western frontier of the Republic nine hundred miles away, bringing Albuquerque and Santa Fe into the fold.

He listened to the faint snoring coming from the boy. He had sworn many times, over the previous couple of months, he would never let his family come so close to being taken from him again. He slipped from the room, closing the door behind, and headed to the Alamo. He had a war to plan.

Chapter 2

Summer 1842

The red-haired officer stood next to the brick wall overlooking Mobile Bay. Were it not for the Secretary of the Army's decision to close the coastal fort at Ft. Morgan, Bill couldn't help wondering if he would have remained in the United States army for the foreseeable future. Recalling the events of the past week, he could scarcely imagine the direction his life would now go. He stared out the embrasure, next to a heavy iron gun. While most of the fort's coastal artillery was to be repositioned at other active forts along the gulf coast, a few, like this one, would remain under the watch of a sergeant's guard, in a mothball status.

Below the fort, waves lapped at the sandy shoreline. As he watched the rhythmic surf pounding at the sand, the sea's motion soothed the trepidation he felt. All this had started only a week ago. He thought back to that fateful day.

Most of the officers had already received their orders for reassignment, but none yet had arrived for him. While he worried about his next assignment, there was plenty on which to focus. He had been cataloging the battery of coastal guns facing the gulf, when a private raced up the stairs, nearly colliding with him.

"Lieutenant Sherman, sir." The private's nasally New Jersey accent grated against his ears, "Captain's compliments, you're to report to his office immediately."

Bill frowned at the interruption and closed the ledger. "Alright, Jones. I'll be there straight away."

As the soldier retreated, taking the stairs two at a time, Bill hid the ledger in the ammunition locker, confident it would be waiting on his return. He was curious about the reason for the summons. As he hurried over to the captain's office, he speculated about where his orders would take him next. Would it be Charleston harbor? Fort Sumter was under construction and Fort Moultrie had several officer billets opening up. Maybe it would be Boston. Fort Warren was also under construction and he had heard they were adding several batteries of coastal guns. As he knocked on the door, an unfamiliar voice called out, "Enter."

Alone in the captain's office stood a brown-haired man of medium height. Apart from a widow's peak that threatened to hide his eyebrows, his hair was receding. Bill eyed the man's clothing, gaging by them, that the owner was well-to-do. Having expected his captain, he was uncertain how to react to the other man, so he came to attention, and said, "Lieutenant William Sherman reporting."

The other man stretched out his hand, "John Wharton, Lieutenant Sherman. I hope you don't mind, but I asked to have a moment of your time." He reached into his jacket and produced a sealed letter which he handed to Bill.

The lieutenant broke the seal and read the letter. His eyes widened when he saw it was from Secretary of War, John Bell. He read then reread the letter before raising his eyes to look at Wharton. "I don't understand, sir."

The stranger leaned against the captain's cluttered desk and motioned for Bill to sit. Once Sherman had settled himself into a chair, Wharton said, "No doubt you're wondering why an agent of a foreign government would request to meet with you alone."

Bill nodded. "The thought had crossed my mind, sir."

"As you, no doubt, are aware, Mexico and Texas are gearing up for war. As part of our preparation, Texas bought several dozen field pieces from the United States. We are creating a battalion of light artillery. But we need trained officers to command it."

Bill could see the trajectory of the conversation. "What does that have to do with me, Mr. Wharton?"

With a faint smile, Wharton said, "President Clay has given his blessing to allow officers who might wish to do so, the freedom of resigning their commissions in the United States army, and to accept a similar or higher rank in the army of Texas."

Bill glanced down at the letter in his hand and responded, "Why would I want to do that?"

Wharton's smile grew broader. "To advance in the United States Army, someone above you has to retire, resign, or die. An officer can spend a very long time moving from lieutenant to captain. Many of your fellow officers retire at that rank, simply because there isn't any opportunity higher. What Texas can offer you is a captaincy in command of a field battery, the experience of commanding men in combat and the opportunity for advancement."

Bill couldn't deny, it was an attractive offer. He had known a few people who had gone to Texas, and the favorable tales they sent back were alluring. But if he accepted the commission, what would that do to his own prospects? His thoughts drifted to Ellen, whom he'd known since they were young children. Of late, he had thought of asking for her hand in marriage. But a lieutenant's pay was paltry. Would she look favorably upon him for accepting a captaincy in the Texian army? The pay would make it easier to provide for her, he was sure of it. Still though, he saw tremendous risk.

With a note of hesitation in his voice, Bill asked, "What are your terms, Mr. Wharton?"

Like an angler setting the hook, Wharton said, "If you accept my offer, Texas will commission you as a captain of artillery. Pay is one hundred twenty dollars per month. Your rations, uniforms and housing expenses will be covered by the army. Also, you'll receive a six-hundred and forty-acre bounty from the Republic if you agree to serve for the duration of the war with Mexico. Upon completion of the war, you'll also receive an additional league of land."

Bill's eyebrows rose involuntarily. As a 2nd lieutenant, he earned eighty dollars each month, but was required to pay for his uniform and rations from that amount. If he lived anywhere other than the fort, he would need to cover rent with his pay, too. From newspapers, he knew that land could be had for as little as fifty cents an acre in Texas. The incentive was worth easily more than three hundred dollars. If he stayed in the Texas army for the duration of the war, an additional league of land was worth at least another two thousand dollars.

As he counted the potential windfall he would receive for service in the Texian army, Bill imagined Ellen accepting his proposal. He offered up a grin as he said, "I believe you've found your man, Mr. Wharton."

The patent clerk raised the window, hoping to let in whatever breeze that might exist as the June morning gave way to afternoon. Dick thought Austin in summertime was hotter than his childhood home in North Carolina. As he filled his lungs with the hot, dry air, he considered it might even be hotter than old Scratch's home. He returned to his desk where he continued reading the specifications of a patent he was tasked with registering. It was the schematics for another modification of a cotton carding machine from the Gulf Farms Corporation. He had accepted the filings for more than a dozen inventions this year alone from Gulf Farms.

He set the completed filing aside and wiped his brow. Most of the inventions which came from Gulf Farms wouldn't amount to much, he thought. But throw enough innovation at a problem, like cotton production, and Dick conceded they would eventually streamline how the South produced cotton. He glanced at his pocket watch which he had earlier set on his desk, and saw it was nearly lunch. He opened a drawer and pulled out the design which had brought him to Texas.

It had started a couple of years earlier when he had submitted his design for a screw propeller for ships, to the United States Patent Office. When he received the rejection letter he was dismayed to find that John Ericsson had filed a patent identical to his own design earlier. When the United States Navy passed on using Ericsson's design, Dick thought nothing would come of it, until he learned the upstart Texas government had commissioned a frigate using Ericsson's screw propulsion system.

When he learned that Texas had purchased technologically advanced pistols from Samuel Colt in Connecticut as well as breechloading rifles from Harpers Ferry, he decided to write a letter to the President of the Republic of Texas. Dick had grown up reading stories about Davy Crockett in dime novels he had bought with the money he earned. In the letter he praised the frontier government for being forward thinking and investing in modern inventions.

He hadn't truly expected a response from President Crockett, so when he received one thanking him for writing and offering him a job with the Republic's Patent Office, he said his good-byes to his family in North Carolina and moved to Texas.

He chuckled ruefully at the memory as he looked in the drawer at the letter from President Crockett. The former president had not been lying, but neither had he told the entire truth. What Crockett had meant was Dick would have the dubious distinction of being the entire Patent Office.

A rushing of feet outside his office announced lunch. The door was thrown open and Dick waved at his friend, Ezekiel Wilson, who clerked for Michel Menard, the Republic's Secretary of the Treasury, and Dick's boss. "Gatling, come on, old boy. Miss Mabry is dining at the Stagecoach Inn for lunch today." Dick smiled. Miss Mabry was, in his estimation, one of the most beautiful single women in Austin. And in a town where single men outnumbered their female counterparts by a wide margin, a man had to make his own opportunity.

Dick Gatling leapt to his feet, grabbed his jacket and hat and raced out the door, hard on the heels of his friend.

6 August 1842

The wind filled the schooner's canvas sails, taking the ratlines from slack to taut in less time than Mark could have described it. The southerly breeze propelled the ship through the narrow confines of Bolivar Roads, the channel between Galveston Island and Bolivar Peninsula. The fresh breeze carried the briny smell of salt. He grabbed the railing of the ship as he watched the sailors of the British Royal Navy reefing the sails. The schooner slowed. Even the power of the British Royal Navy was no match for the treacherous shoals and shallow water that had been the death of more than a few ships in Galveston Bay and the captain waited for a harbor pilot to continue into port.

His charge, Charles Elliot, stood near the gang plank, apparently willing the ship to move faster. A mooring space was open alongside one of the docks, and the ship was given clearance to berth there. As was proper for a valet, Mark stood well behind Mr. Elliot and it allowed him to observe the chargé d'affaires to the Republic of Texas. Elliot had been moody most of the time aboard since leaving from England a few weeks earlier. Even now, as the Schooner glided through the water to her resting place alongside the dock, Elliot frowned.

"*No wonder,*" Mark thought, looking beyond the bustling wharves at the raw town of Galveston. They had been told Galveston was the most developed city in the frontier republic. From a casual look at the town, he held little hope for the rest of the country. This was certainly a step down from Elliot's last posting. No matter how ably he had performed his duty to the crown, being at the center of the debacle the newspapers had taken to calling the" Opium War" in China, was deleterious to one's career.

"Of course, he's not the only one better served by not being in the old country right now." Mark's frown matched that of his charge. Formerly an employee of the General Post Office, Mark Stewart had been a small cog in a much larger scandal when the activities of the Secret Office became fodder for the newspapers and Members of Parliament. Mark's earlier role had been as a decipherer, responsible for breaking French and Spanish codes. In the scandal's aftermath several men were publicly discharged, among them, Mark. In the end, the firings were not enough to stem the scandal, and the office was shuttered.

After the ship was moored to the dock, Elliot strode down the gangway and onto the wooden pier. Mark turned to the ship's purser and gave him the address to which the balance of the diplomat's luggage was to be sent. As Elliot disappeared into the crowd, Mark grabbed a valise, ran down the narrow wooden plank and hurried after the diplomat.

Charles Elliot was in a foul mood as he stormed off the dock and into the teeming mass of men, horses, wagons, and trade goods along Galveston's wharves. A sharp glance behind confirmed his "employee" was following. Hong Kong, while certainly not British in the sense of Surrey or Essex, was still far more civilized and cultured than this crude town. Galveston was home to only a few thousand souls, and as he sniffed the air, each of those souls appeared to have their own outhouse.

Unlike the French, who had moved their own consulate to Austin, the Foreign Office had the good sense to establish Elliot in Galveston. It better suited Her Majesty's government to appear neutral toward the growing republic. Even so, his arrival was a concession of sorts, that Britain acknowledged Mexico was unlikely to subjugate her ill-tempered former northern province.

Even the hotel, which was only a couple of years old, appeared unkempt and rude. As he stepped into the foyer, he made a vow he would buy a house in the town before sending for Clara and the children.

He had finished checking in by the time Mark Stewart had arrived, carrying a solitary valise. "Where's the remainder of the bags, man?"

Stewart returned the frown. "The ship's purser will be sending them, sir."

His valet was another thorn in his side. Having served in the Royal Navy for more than a decade, Elliot was used to clear-cut roles. With any normal valet Elliot would simply tell him what to do and he would expect it to be done. Stewart was a different kettle of fish. The only benefit Elliot had found was at least he didn't have to pay the brusque former civil servant. It still grated on him to have the other man foisted upon him just days before he was to sail to Texas. Stewart's salary was paid for by a consortium of investors with ties to Lloyds Bank and his role was ostensibly that of private valet to Elliot. But with an enigmatic employer, Stewart wasn't his man, and that bothered him.

"Nothing to be done about it now," Elliot muttered as he lay down on the uncomfortable mattress. All things being equal, it was no worse than the bunk he had slept on while on the schooner. Moments later the chargé d'affaires drifted off to sleep.

When Elliot awoke, the sun was sliding below the western horizon. The sound of a door closing had brought him out of his light slumber. He fumbled his watch from his waistcoat and gaged that twilight was still an hour away. The room was unbearably stuffy and warm; he had forgotten to open the window before lying down. He took a step over to the window and raised it. He breathed in the warm, summer air then spotted a familiar figure walking quickly down the road, away from the hotel.

Chapter 3

Will stepped out of his office above the hospital. Even as the sun inched above the eastern horizon, the day promised to be hot. He placed his black, wide-brimmed hat on his head and walked down the stairs. The windows running along the wall of the hospital were open, and he heard Ashbel Smith, Surgeon General of the army becoming exasperated. He paused as he listened to the conversation.

"Dr. Jones, as the surgeon for the 3rd Infantry, I am at a loss as to why you allowed the men to dig latrines as close to the river as you have. I've half a dozen cases of dysentery in the hospital, and by God, if you don't get those latrines moved, there'll be even more."

Will strained to hear Anson Jones' response. Jones had practiced medicine prior to his election to the Senate in 1836. He had resigned his seat to serve as a surgeon to one of the reserve battalions. "Now, Ashbel, you know the boys was just tired when they dug them."

Smith's voice rose, his Yankee accent was thick with emotion, "That's why you're the battalion surgeon, *Dr. Jones.* You're responsible for the health of your men. I don't want to see you in my hospital until those latrines are at least a hundred feet from the San Antonio River!"

As Jones fled the building, Will heard the tinkling of glass breaking, followed by Dr. Smith's voice rising as he swore. Will had been ready to turn around and start back up the stairs. Stranded for more than six years in the mid-nineteenth century had taught him folks could be prickly about issues of honor, and his first inclination was to be somewhere else. But between the sound of breaking glass and Dr. Smith's rising voice, Will swept by Jones as the former Senator stormed out of the hospital.

The hospital was a long room with beds along both sides. Will saw a few men, occupying beds at one end, and Dr. Ashbel Smith at the far end, standing next to a large table.

Will hurried over to the doctor, "You're not hurt, are you?"

Dr. Smith waved his concern away with one hand as he scrubbed the table down with a rag. "No. But that damned fool caused me to drop a couple of vials of acid that shouldn't have been mixed."

Concern stamped on his face, Will said, "What did you break?"

"I had a vial of nitric acid. I use it as a cauterizing agent. I was so mad at that idiot I knocked it against a vial of sulphuric acid. And now I've lost perfectly good bandages wiping this mess up."

Will involuntarily took a step back, regretting he hadn't spent more time paying attention in high school chemistry. "You don't think it'll blow up, do you?"

Dr. Smith draped the soaking rag on the back of a chair, "Lordy, don't even say that, sir. I'll throw the rags out once they're dry, and if need be, I'll lay the blame at Anson's feet."

The odor in that wing of the hospital was strong, even with the windows open. Once the mess had been wiped away, Will walked with Dr. Smith back to the other wing, where he made small talk with the handful of hospitalized men from the 3rd Battalion.

As he stepped out the door from the hospital, Sidney Johnston walked up, "Morning, Buck. I was hoping to find you out and about, and sure enough, here you are."

Will pointed up at his office, "Want to talk up there?"

Johnston waved off the offer, "Have you had the opportunity to inspect the 4th and 6th Infantry battalions, yet? I thought we could take a stroll and see how they're settling in."

Will nodded toward the gate, "Lead the way, Sid."

The 4th Infantry was the last of the reserve battalions to arrive. Recruited from the small towns and farms of Northeast Texas, the men of the 4th had spent a couple of months drilling with General McCulloch's militia units outside of West Liberty before being transferred to San Antonio.

Walking alongside the acequia, Johnston said, "We've got six battalions scattered around the countryside surrounding the Alamo and San Antonio, Buck, and our quartermaster's corps is simply overwhelmed. There aren't enough teamsters between the Sabine River and El Paso to keep our army supplied."

Will frowned, hearing his second-in-command confirm what he strongly suspected. "I know. It's been on my mind for a while now. Do you think we can keep the army supplied through the first week of September with our existing contracts?"

They had come to where the acequia curved around the fort's north wall, and continued across the field, which only a couple of months earlier was covered with the dead and wounded of the Mexican Army of the North. Now, the brutal July sun had baked the field, wilting the flowers and weeds to brown clumps. The field rose until they crested a slight rise. Hundreds of tents spread over the prairie, in precise and orderly rows. As they overlooked the 4th Infantry's encampment, Johnston stopped in his tracks and asked, "Two months? I had hoped to solve our logistics problems sooner than that."

Will kicked a rock and watched puffs of dust where it skipped across the arid ground. "I don't want to stir up animosity among our wealthy land holders in East Texas before the election. No matter what Sam Houston may promise, I fear he'll gut the army once he's in office. I don't want to do anything before the election to cost Zavala even a single vote."

Johnston eyed Will apprehensively. "What have you got in mind, Buck?"

Will's eyes twinkled, "With the expansion of the army, we need more teamsters and wagons. Our wealthy plantation owners back in East Texas possess both the labor and the equipment to fill this need, Sid. Should President Zavala win the election in September, I intend to do whatever is necessary for the government to lease as many bondsmen as necessary, along with every wagon we can lay our hands on."

Johnston stared into the encampment of the 4th Infantry. Will could see his friend and second-in-command contemplating the proposal. Finally, Johnston broke the silence. "They'll squeal like stuck pigs, Buck, especially when they realize the architect of the plan is you, being as you're so popular with Collinsworth and the other planters. But if the government compensates them for the use of their property, I think most Texians, even those fire-eaters will go along with it. It's not like they haven't leased their slaves out before."

Will hadn't planned on paying the slave owners, but as he stood next to Johnston observing the camp, he realized Zavala wouldn't be able to push through an uncompensated use of slave labor, no matter how much Will might agitate for it. He glanced over at Johnston and decided he would let that part die in his mind, even if it left a stench in his nostrils.

After passing through the 4th Infantry's orderly encampment, the two officers came upon the 6th Infantry's camp. The two battalions' encampments were a study in contrast. The 4th had been part of General McCulloch's reserves for a couple of years, while the 6th had been transferred from the militia only recently. Every soldier in the 4th wore a butternut jacket, while the men of the 6th wore a variety of uniforms and civilian jackets.

In one of the companies Will and Johnston were reviewing, a soldier in a surplus US army jacket stood at attention, next to one wearing a gray militia jacket, and on the other side, stood a soldier wearing a brown hunting shirt. Their pants and headgear were even more varied.

The men in the 4th were equipped with Model 1833 Halls breechloading carbines, for the most part. The men from the 6th carried hunting rifles, muskets, and shotguns in every caliber imaginable. As Will inspected each of the men, he was unable to avoid thinking about how much needed to be done before the army could successfully carry the war into Mexico.

He and Johnston found the 6th's commander, Colonel William Ward, sitting under a pavilion in the center of a sea of lean-tos, baker's tents, teepees, and other temporary shelters the men had thrown together.

Ward looked up from a small writing desk he was balancing on his knees. "General Travis, just the man I was writing. If you'll give me but a moment, I'll finish this letter to you."

Will hid his smile. He recalled Colonel Ward had been present at both battles during the Revolution, commanding a small battalion of Alabamans and Georgians. He had proved a capable officer but had taken his land grant after the war, returning to civilian life.

"Morning, Colonel. General Johnston and I are glad to see you and your boys." Will swept his hand around, taking in the encampment.

Ward set the writing desk on the ground and stood and gave the two generals a salute. "Thank you, sir. About that letter, my boys need just about everything, General. We have no proper tents, no uniforms or shoes, and no other guns than the ones the boys brought with them."

Will held up his hands in mock surrender, "Colonel, we're working on all of them. It's just going to take some time," he turned to Johnston, "Sid, what's the latest news about uniforms?"

Johnston looked around the camp, at the hodgepodge of clothing worn by the soldiers and shrugged, "We've received approval from Congress and they've allocated enough money to outfit all the militia battalions to be transferred to active service. The problem is, our normal supplier in New Orleans is completely overwhelmed, and according to our most recent correspondence, is subcontracting some production to other textile mills in Tennessee and Ohio."

Ward was crestfallen at the news. Will and Johnston finished their inspection and were making their way back to the Alamo before the midsummer's sun became too warm.

"I'm glad he dropped it after the uniforms. We won't know for some time yet whether the United States will sell more of Halls' carbines to us," Will said as he took his hat off and used it to fan his face.

Johnston pulled a handkerchief from a pocket and wiped his brow. "Have you received an update from John Berry yet about his production numbers?"

Setting his hat back on his head, Will continued walking back toward the Alamo. As Johnston fell in beside him, he said, "Yes. It is about what we expected. He should be up to ten rifles a day by the end of the summer. A thousand rifles by the end of the year. If we hold off invading until April, he guaranteed a total of two thousand."

Johnston cursed under his breath. "That's a long time to wait and build up our army. Lots of men will leave their fields fallow next year, Buck. That kind of hardship could put pressure on whoever is president to settle. If we haven't dealt with Santa Anna by then, well, all we've done is set up the next war."

As they passed back through the gatehouse, Will said, "I told President Crockett the same thing before he resigned, and I gave Zavala an earful, too."

They reached the Alamo's well, located near the hospital in the plaza. After taking a long drink from the ladle, Johnston asked, "What did our newly minted President say to that?"

Will took the ladle from his friend and as he dipped it in the bucket, said, "The same thing I'm going to tell you. You worry about defeating Santa Anna, I'll worry about keeping the nation going."

Will left Johnston to his duties. He had his own mountain of correspondence to attack. He had just put his boot on the first step when Dr. Smith staggered out from the hospital, wearing a big grin.

"Doc, you look like a tom cat that found a nice, juicy rat."

The doctor beamed, "It exploded, General."

Will was confused. "What exploded?"

Smith continued, "The cotton rags, mixed with the nitric and sulphuric acids. It exploded!"

A light turned on in Will's memory. The two acids, dipped in cotton, like the bandages Dr. Smith had used, may have created guncotton.

Will became almost as excited as Smith. "This needs to be further explored, Doc. Is this something you can work on?"

Smith became hesitant. "General, that was a fluke. I'm sure I could replicate the explosion, but I can think of one or two others who are more gifted with this kind of thing."

"Who?"

"Gail Bordon fancies himself an inventor. He and I are well acquainted, and if anyone can determine the right mix of nitric and sulphuric acids and how to dry the cotton so that it doesn't just self-immolate when it feels like it, Gail is your man."

Will recognized the name. The first couple of years after the transference, he had found Bordon's byline in the *Telegraph and Texas Register*, at least until he sold it to another newspaper man. But even had that not been the case, he thought there was a connection between this Bordon and the inventor of condensed milk and the founder of Bordon Dairy Company. Before joining up after nine-eleven, in a world gone forever, Will had frequently seen the company's trucks making deliveries at supermarkets on his way to school each morning.

The car lurched as the engineer released the brakes and the steam engine began rolling down the tracks, leaving Anahuac for West Liberty. Thick, black smoke slipped by the window and too much found its way into the car. It was too hot to leave the windows closed and the price to pay for the air flow was a fine layer of soot covering his jacket.

In addition to two flat cars and two boxcars, the train pulled a coal hopper and a passenger car. The former President of the Republic, David Crockett dusted the soot from his jacket and watched the handful of men in the car do the same thing.

The nearest traveler to his seat was a couple of rows away. He was finely dressed. Over the years David had become a good judge of people. While the clothes were expensive, the hat was made from straw. A practical choice for a gentleman farmer. David shifted his eyes away, sure that when the train arrived in West Liberty a coach driven by a slave would be waiting at the station to carry him back to his plantation.

Two other men sat next to each other at the opposite end of the car. While they, too were farmers, their clothing was inexpensive and practical. Occasionally, David could hear their voices carry over the rattling of the wheels thundering along the rails. One had a broad Scottish accent while the other's Irish lilt carried over the car's noise. In all likelihood they worked for the Gulf Farms Corporation. Crockett couldn't help but wonder, if they would continue working the company's fields or find their militia company called up.

Letting that thought ruminate didn't sit well with the former president and he turned his attention to watching the coastal plain rush by his window as the train sped along the tracks at thirty miles an hour. He marveled that what used to take two days by shank's mare now took less than ninety minutes.

Construction was underway for a railroad between San Antonio and Austin, but the last he had heard, the investors were conducting another fundraising tour back east. He had also heard the Commerce Bank was partnering with the investors who owned this line and they were surveying a route between Houston and West Liberty. David leaned back in the wooden seat, hearing his back cracking in protest. From Houston, it would only make sense to extend the railroad to San Antonio and Austin. *"When that happens, you'll be able to travel two hundred fifty miles in less than a day."* A wagon laden with supplies, pulled by a team of mules would take nearly two weeks to travel the distance. Even the stagecoaches couldn't do it in less than four days.

The train began climbing a gentle incline and within a few seconds was rumbling across the bridge over the Trinity River. If they could connect San Antonio to

Houston, it wasn't a stretch to image a train that ran from New York City, across the Appalachian Mountains, across the farmland of the Deep South, and even across the mighty Mississippi River, all the way to Santa Fe. Such a trip now took months, but with Railroads, he reasoned, it could be done in just a few days.

David smiled at the thought before allowing the present war with Mexico to invade the happy thought. *"First we deal with Santa Anna, then we build a humdinger of a railroad."*

When he had resigned from the presidency, David thought taking over a militia battalion would be easy. After all, he had the pen in his hand and with a little dab of ink, everything would fall into place. He had expected more opposition from Zavala, but Lorenzo had quickly acquiesced when he had seen Crockett's determination. Even his son-in-law, General Travis had offered only muted opposition after his initial explosive reaction. He shook his head at the memory, it was Liza who had thrown the biggest conniption fit, he'd ever seen.

As he thought about it, the sound of her voice echoed still in his head. "David Stern Crockett, you didn't bring me out here to Texas just to go off a wandering again!" Liza could yell plenty loud when her dander was up. The saving grace was, they had been living in the presidential mansion when this had happened, and there were no nearby neighbors.

He had patiently explained to her that he owed it to the people of Texas to volunteer for service. He'd even gone so far as to remind her that he had never failed to serve when problems came up. He had served under Andy Jackson during the war with the British and the Creek. For once, Liza wasn't having any of it. "David, for heaven's sake, you're not some shirt-tail boy running off for adventure. You're fifty-six years old."

Being reminded of his age, of course had irritated David. *"It's not as if I reminded her she'd been married to me more than a quarter of a century, and she ain't no more of a spring chicken than me."*

David allowed a smile to play across his face, imagining her response, had he been bold enough to remind her she was less than two years younger than he. The smile faded as he recalled her tears after they had moved from the Presidential mansion. He had taken her to San Antonio, where she would stay with her daughter and grandchildren. With Becky's pregnancy, it would be better that way, he thought.

She had clung to him in the front room of the Travis home, the morning he set off for West Liberty. Even after more than a week, he couldn't shake her words, *"David, I've watched you run off to your adventures and I can't watch anymore. You go, if you have to, and I'll be waiting here if you return, but I'm not going to watch you do it anymore."*

He had held her close, running coarse fingers through her graying hair as she sobbed into his hunting jacket. He finally decided it was the way she looked at him, that bothered him the most. Part of him felt there was a finality in the way she clutched at him and when she kissed him, crushing her lips against his, it was as though she was trying to wring from him a final, intimate moment.

Steam escaped from the engine as the train approached West Liberty, slowing down. Thoughts of his wife were replaced by the excitement of being in the field again. As the train approached the town, fields that had previously grown corn, wheat or cotton were blanketed with every type of temporary shelter he could imagine. In front of the camp, a battalion of militia stood at attention as officers purposefully moved from soldier to soldier, inspecting their weapons.

David tore his eyes away from the window as the field slid from view. After a moment, the car jolted to a stop, and he grabbed a carpetbag and his rifle, a gift from the city of Philadelphia, and headed for the exit.

When he alighted from the stairs, he saw General McCulloch, standing under the awning of the station, in an effort to stay out from under the blistering sun. The general wore the black wide-brimmed hat and butternut uniform of the Texian Army. Next to him stood an officer that could have been his twin. With bag and gun in hand, David hurried over to them.

"President Crockett, sir, it's good to see you again." David had known the McCulloch family since Ben had been a little boy. The way in which the General had greeted him caused him to wonder just how welcome the former president would be as another battalion commander. For the briefest of moments, David wondered if Liza was right and this was a mistake. The thought flew from his mind as he sketched a casual salute then shook hands with the General and the other officer.

As he shook hands, he studied the younger officer, and recognized him as Henry McCulloch, the general's younger brother. "I swear, is that Henry, all grown up? Hell's bells, last time I saw you, you were knee-high to a grasshopper."

The younger McCulloch flushed, suppressing a grin. "It has been a few years, Mr. President. When Ben, I mean, General McCulloch asked if I wanted to serve under your command, I told him I'd beat any man that stood in my way."

David followed the McCulloch brothers to a small buggy, which took them to the encampment for the 9th Infantry battalion. The ten militia companies assigned to the battalion had only recently been given their mobilization orders, and the field was empty except for a company already assembled and a few lean-tos surrounding the battalion's headquarters tent.

When David and the younger McCulloch climbed out of the buggy, the general said, "I'll leave you and Major McCulloch to get familiar with your command such as it is as the moment. The rest of the battalion should show up within the next couple of weeks."

With a snap of the reins, McCulloch rolled away, leaving David alone with the young major, on the edge of the sunbaked field.

There was a knock at the door and Will looked up. The door was open, letting in a ghost of a breeze. Colonel Payton Wyatt stood at the door. The expansion of the army from little more than a thousand men, to a half-dozen battalions around San Antonio had created an administrative headache that Will could never have untangled by himself. While Sidney Johnston's skills had come in handy at bridging the gap in Will's knowledge, Wyatt had demonstrated a knack for administration that had led him to become Will's chief-of-staff.

In the years before the transference, before finding himself stranded in Travis' mind, as an infantry grunt, he hadn't had to think tactically beyond the company level. Oh, he had an appreciation for the basics of logistics and combined arms, but since the declaration of war a few months earlier, the army had added the reserve battalions and was now transitioning militia battalions into military service for the duration of the war. If things continued as he anticipated, Will would lead an army of more than seven thousand soldiers into Mexico after the new year. Wyatt's administrative skills were essential. But in some respects, everyone was learning as they went along.

"Sir, Colonel Hodgens and his wing of the 2nd battalion are assembled in the plaza."

Will set his pen down, glad to forget about requisitions for the moment, and joined Wyatt on the landing outside his office. From there, he had a commanding view of the Alamo Plaza. Six companies from the 3rd Infantry were assembled below. Next to them, six 6-pounder guns were limbered and hitched to teams of six horses each, waiting to pull their heavy loads.

As he came down the stairs, Will studied the men of the 2nd Infantry. Many of them had been part of the relief column which had rescued the remnants of the Alamo the previous April. The last four months had been spent turning the reservists into trained soldiers and bringing the battalion up to its authorized strength of seven-hundred-fifty men. Although most of the army was still armed with older rifles, Will had made sure the men under Colonel Hodgens were armed with new M42 Sabine Rifles.

Each of the men, standing at attention wore the butternut uniform of the regulars. Despite chronic shortages of uniforms and rifles, Will was determined to send these men out with the best the army could provide.

It wasn't much, but the six companies of infantry and the battery of artillery were the first strategic move by Texas since Woll's army retreated in disgrace. A single nod from Will to Colonel Hodgens was all it took for the short, stocky officer to swing into the saddle, and call out, "Battalion, by company into columns, right face!"

Like a machine, the four-hundred fifty men smoothly turned from their long line, two men deep, into columns of four men abreast, ready to march.

"Forward, march!"

Will watched the men parade by as they marched through the gates. They were heading south, to reoccupy Laredo.

Chapter 4

15 August 1842

"Somebody in the Foreign Office must really hate me," thought Charles Elliot for what seemed like the thousandth time since arriving in Galveston. The role of charge d'affaires in backwater Texas was a far cry from his earlier posting in Hong Kong, where he was the First Administrator. Apart from assisting a few sailors whose behaviors resulted in their involuntary confinement and occasionally meeting with merchants looking for a favor, Elliot was hard pressed to fill up his day.

On the other hand, he was ahead on his promised correspondence to Clara. The hours of inactivity only accentuated his longing to be with her and the children, but the baby was simply too young to travel. He hoped she and the children would be able to travel to his duty station as early as next year. Galveston was a hardship at the best of times, made all the lonelier by his wife's absence.

A knock at the door broke his reverie, and a moment later Stewart poked his head in the room "Will there be anything else before I go to the market?" The open door created a crosscurrent breeze with the open window. Pages rustled on the desk, threatening to take flight.

Placing a hand on the letter to his wife, Elliot looked up at his enigmatic valet, "Something other than trout, Stewart. And no oysters. I hope you can find some greens available."

"As you say, sir." Stewart closed the door.

"Now there's a riddle of a man," Elliot thought. While the valet attended to the normal duties of a man servant, he was gone far more often than Elliot thought proper for a man of his station. He glared out the window, frustrated with the shackles foisted upon him by the Foreign Office and Mr. Stewart's secretive employers. With a shrug, he tossed the pen down on the page and walked over to the open window, overlooking the street.

The British Consulate was in the central business district on Avenue B, along a stretch the locals had taken to calling "the Strand." It was across the street from the Galveston office of the Commerce Bank of Texas. There were cotton brokers, wholesalers, and attorneys filling up the blocks near the wharves. Much to his dismay, there was also a slave market as well. Before Hong Kong, he had served in Guiana, in South America, in the official capacity as Protector of Slaves. He had taken that position a few years before Great Britain freed the slaves in the colonies in 1833. The experience had converted him into a firm believer in abolition. That brought him back to the present. As if he needed one more reason to hate his new assignment.

He watched Stewart exit the Consulate and head away from the market, deeper into Galveston Island. That was odd. Elliot bit back a chuckle, realizing how odd his valet's behavior had been since the very day he was assigned to him.

If the valet was working on business for the bankers, whose purse strings paid for Stewart's services, then Elliot rationalized, it wasn't really his business.

But he didn't like being lied to or deceived, and his man was definitely not heading to the market. He glanced back at the half-written letter to his wife. It could wait. His curiosity piqued, Elliot grabbed a straw hat from a rack and placed it on his head as he left the consulate and hurried to see where Stewart had gone.

He left the building in time to see his valet turn the corner onto Bath Street, heading back toward the center of the island. He followed as quickly as decorum would allow, reaching the intersection in time to see his valet cross the street. He followed behind for a few blocks until he saw Stewart enter a newly built livery stable.

Elliot came to a stop while he was still more than a block away. *"Do I want to know what Stewart's up to? If he gets caught doing something illegal, what will that do for my career?"* Worried about what he might see, the British charge d'affaires crossed the last block and looked at the livery stable. While there was traffic on the road, the wide doors to the stable were closed.

There was a narrow alley between the stable and the smithy located next door, and Elliot looked to see if anyone was paying attention to him. Seeing folks on the street intent on their own business, he slipped between the buildings. There was a door on the side of the livery stable. As Elliot approached the fresh scent of pine confirmed the recent construction. The door was cracked open, but little light filtered through the door, facing the alleyway.

A lantern hung in the middle of the livery stable, and Elliot could hear stomping of hoofs in the stalls. He ignored them as he slipped through the door and flattened his body against the nearest stall. Sunlight also filtered through several windows set high up along the walls, bathing the wide central aisle in natural light.

Peering around the corner of the stall, Elliot saw Stewart standing next to a wagon, talking to a couple of men. From his hiding place in the shadows, the diplomat did a double take as he stared at a portly man with sallow skin. He had seen the man before in England. The name escaped him, but he was certain he was employed by Lloyds Bank in London. *"What in the blazes is a banker from Lloyds doing in bloody Texas?"*

The third man was a Mexican. His velvet blue jacket and white silk shirt told Elliot all he needed to know about his station. He was a man of importance. But Elliot had never seen the man before and didn't know if the Mexican was one of several thousand who styled themselves as Tejanos, loyal to the Texas government or if he was an agent of Mexico. As they talked, it was impossible to hear what they said.

Elliot eyed the wagon in the center of the building. In the wagon bed there were several heavy boxes, with padlocks on them. He was too far away and couldn't tell if anything was stenciled on their sides. But the way the three men kept looking at them hinted strongly the wagon's contents were the subject of their conversation.

Elliot was unlikely to get closer without being seen, and for reasons he couldn't pin down, he decided he didn't want Stewart to know he had followed him. The diplomat edged back to the doorway to the alley then slipped back into the narrow track between the two buildings. He retraced his steps and had turned back onto the Strand before the livery stable doors opened and Stewart casually slipped out.

A little more than a week remained before the presidential election of 1842. Charles Elliot had taken a ferry from Galveston Island, through the bay and up Buffalo Bayou to a spot between Harrisburg and Houston. Although Texas had yet to develop clearly defined political parties, most men of voting age were split between two candidates, who had agreed to a public debate this day.

Although still learning the ins and outs of the politics of this frontier republic, he conceded that President Crockett was a shrewd judge of his people's character. With the resignation five months before the election, the electorate had become familiar with the new president before turning out to vote, thereby boosting his chances. At first glance, his chosen successor, Lorenzo de Zavala was an outsider. Perhaps one in ten Texians were of Mexican derivation. They called themselves *Tejanos*, and he had read several stories in the Republic's most widely read newspaper, *Telegraph Texas and Register*, about attempts by Americans to invalidate titles to rich farm and ranch land.

Given what Elliot had heard about men from the American South, he had been surprised when he learned the Crockett administration had used the full legal power of the executive branch to defend legitimate land titles, even though it meant frequently siding with Tejano landholders over more recently arrived Americans, with forged titles in hand.

Even without dueling political parties, Texians still found issues over which they were divided. Zavala was campaigning for continued independence, while Sam Houston advocated for Texas to seek union with the United States.

When he arrived, the debate's site was already teeming with people who had arrived from nearby towns as well as from the surrounding countryside. Despite the frontier republic's reputation for being sparsely populated, there were several thousand people settling on blankets or sitting in camp chairs or simply standing around, waiting patiently for Zavala and Houston to take their places on the podium constructed for the event.

Knowing he would need to send a report back to the Foreign Office, Elliot took stock of the crowd. Even though a state of war existed between Texas and Mexico, more than half the crowd were men. An even mix between women and children made up the balance. The number of men carrying weapons staggered Elliot as it seemed to him every man he saw carried a hunting rifle or a Bowie knife. But a closer inspection showed more than half of the men in the crowd were not armed. Even so, Elliot made note of it.

The speech was supposed to start at noon sharp, but a glance at his pocket watch showed it was fifteen minutes after the hour before the two candidates took to the stage, climbing stairs at either end. Both men took their seats as a speaker addressed the crowd, "Folks, thank you kindly for giving up your Saturday for your civic duty. According to the rules agreed upon by Messiers Zavala and Houston, the first speaker was decided by a coin toss, and the president will have the first thirty minutes. Mr. Houston will be allowed to respond for thirty minutes, then each will be allowed another thirty minutes in which to make any final remarks."

Elliot found a nearby tree under which several families had spread blankets and were enjoying the shade. He found a section of grass, burned brown by the sun and claimed it, sitting so that he could make notes in the journal he had brought.

Zavala, whose deep brown hair was surrendering to gray streaks, stood first. He was of medium height and he rested his hands lightly on the podium as he spoke. "Citizens of Texas, I am humbled by the charge to which you elected me six years ago, and I trust that when you go to vote on September 5th that you'll evaluate my performance over the past six years as vice president, and as of late, the president. If you feel that I have faithfully executed my duties, I would ask that you allow me the honor of returning to the Capitol to carry forward the torch of liberty and freedom."

Elliot noticed the crowd listened to his every word. He found Zavala's comments about liberty and freedom ironic. As Texas continued to fight for the right to exist, thousands of Americans flooded across the Sabine River with their slaves in tow. Elliot, ever the abolitionist, briefly wondered how Zavala, by all accounts a staunch Mexican liberal, stomached the odious stench of slavery within the Republic.

Zavala continued addressing the crowd, and Elliot made note when he transitioned his speech. "You have been told the United States will look favorable on Texas' request to join their union, especially if the American presidency should change hands from the Whigs to the Democrats. That may or may not be true. I suppose if Texas were unable to meet her debts or was overwhelmed by Comanche raiding parties, I could understand a desire to splice ourselves into the fabric that is the United States. But neither of these are true statements. Because of our careful shepherding, Texas has a growing economy, a strong currency, and a treaty with the Comanche that has brought a measure of peace to the frontier."

From the center of the crowd a heckler called out, "What about Mexico? They aim to have us back."

Rather than ignoring the voice, Zavala nodded sagely. "What about Mexico? Twice Texians have stood tall and sent Santa Anna's soldiers fleeing from our long rifles. If any man among you thinks that Santa Anna is going to drive us from our land, then, vote for my opponent. While you're doing that, General Travis and I intend to end once and for all Santa Anna's depredations on our fair republic."

Briefly, Elliot wondered if the heckler was a Houston supporter or someone who had provided Zavala the opportunity to rouse the crowd. Most of the folks in the field were on their feet clapping and shouting their approval.

Once Zavala had reached the end of his thirty minutes, Houston replaced him at the podium. Elliot was aware the tall, broad shouldered former general of the Texas army had also been a former governor of Tennessee and had served in the United States congress, at one time.

"Friends, neighbors, and fellow Texians," Houston started. Elliot allowed a brief smile as the speaker borrowed from Shakespeare his opening line. "My esteemed opponent, Mr. Zavala, would like for us to continue puttering along, like one of those newfangled trains climbing a hill, huffing and a-chuffing along, barely making any headway.

DOWN MEXICO WAY

"I'll be the first to support our boys as this latest war with Mexico gets underway. But let's face it, the nigger in the woodpile is that even if we defeat Santa Anna's army, we're still going to be the little fellow between two larger and stronger countries. Mexico is always going to covet our great land, because, let's just be honest, it was the best damned land Spain had managed to claim during their empire."

While the audience laughed appreciably, Elliot shook his head. There was plenty of land in Mexico that rivaled the bounty of Texas, but from someone looking south past San Antonio, Northern Mexico appeared inhospitable.

"What we need is breathing room. Seeking annexation with the United States is the surest way to have the room and freedom to grow our industry and wealth."

The remainder of Houston's thirty minutes were spent detailing the advantages statehood would bestow upon Texas. Elliot noted how the former governor danced around the lack of support from the Clay administration in Washington.

To Elliot's experienced ears, the following hour's rebuttals were simply a rehash of the two men's positions. As they descended the stairs, Elliot listened intently to the applause both men received, and for the life of him, he couldn't decide who the crowd favored more.

The ferry which brought Elliot and several dozen other spectators to hear the speech, took them back to Galveston the same evening. As he stood next to the railing, looking across the bay, he worried that if the Texians voted for annexation by electing Houston to be their next president, his job would become more difficult. It served Her Majesty's government for Texas to exist as a buffer between the United States and Mexico. The boat sliced through the water as Elliot considered what he could do to dissuade a President Houston from pursuing annexation with the United States.

As the boat docked and he saw his valet, Stewart, waiting with the Consulate's new hansom, he disembarked, thankful that two years yet remained before the next presidential election in the United States.

5 September 1842

His stomach rumbled, letting Elliot know he had been watching the men of Galveston standing in line, waiting to vote for most of the day. Tables were set up in front of the county courthouse, where election judges matched the names of the voters against a roll containing the name of every man eligible to vote on Galveston Island. When Elliot asked how they had built their election roll, a judge had told him, Congress made a recent change that required the election roll to be taken from the militia rolls. Men under the age of twenty-one were removed from the list as well as any foreigners who had not yet met the citizenship requirements.

The judge had mentioned there had been some pushback from men who had no interest in serving in the militia when the law was enacted earlier in the year. The judge had referred to them as a bunch of fancy dandies. Elliot took it to mean a few plantation owners. But on the whole, the requirement was met with enthusiasm, especially by many of the poorer farmers and tradesmen in towns like San Antonio and Galveston. "I'll have you know, if a man ain't interested in defending his property, damned if he deserves to keep it." The election judge's admission didn't surprise Elliot. Few men relished serving in the militia to safeguard someone else's property. Elliot made note to send his observations back to London. While Texas might be a backwater frontier republic, he was impressed Texas required militia service in order to vote.

He was growing tired, and Stewart had brought him refreshments from the consulate throughout the afternoon, but it had been more than an hour since he'd seen his valet last. The final voter signed the roll and took a ballot. Elliott turned around, trying to see if his man was close by. Not seeing Stewart, he turned back and watched as the voter slipped the ballot into a large wooden and metal box, with a thin slit across the top, where all the ballots had been stored.

Seeing the ballot box setting on the trestle tables triggered a thought, and he turned around, trying to find Stewart. *"Where in the blazes is that man?"*

As he took his leave of the election judge, several men were hauling the box into the courthouse, where the votes would be tabulated. Elliot would have strong words for his valet when he found him. He returned to the consulate but found the door to the building locked. After unlocking the door, a thorough search of the building turned up nothing. The image of that ballot box kept returning. What was Stewart planning with those other men? The longer he searched, the more concerned he became.

He slammed the door to the consulate and locked it. He hurried down the street and turned onto Bath Street. The livery stable stood, doors wide open, a couple of blocks down the road. He didn't care for people to see him rushing about the town. It was unseemly behavior for a diplomat of Her Majesty's Foreign Office, but he had to find Stewart. Whatever he was up to, Elliot had to find out.

An older teenage boy was shoveling hay into an occupied stall, when Elliot hurried in. The wagon, which had been in the center of the wide aisle, was gone.

"Boy, have you seen an Englishman around here today?" Elliot tried not to snarl as he came toe to toe with the youth.

With a strong Mexican accent, the boy responded. "No, Señor." He stepped around Elliot and shoveled hay into another stall.

Elliot bit off a retort and stormed from the livery stable. Bath Street ran toward the wharves and the harbor to his left, and to his right it ran toward the center of the island. He sucked in air, trying to calm his nerves. Where would Stewart have gone? Whatever the valet had planned, he had kept it from Elliot and that puzzled him. *"Just who is paying the man's bills?"* he asked himself.

One way was as good as another, and he turned and trudged toward the harbor. Elliot pieced together what he knew, and at the moment it was very little. The Englishman he had seen with Stewart worked for Lloyds Bank, of that he was nearly certain. It made sense that whomever that man worked for was probably the one who was paying Stewart's salary. More than that, what could these mysterious men want with this backwater country?

He reached the wharves and looked down the street. Even as the sun was sinking below the western horizon, the docks and the wharves were still teeming with activity. In the milling mass of men, animals, and wagons, he strained to see his valet. In the distance, he thought he saw Stewart, if only for a brief moment. With renewed energy, Elliot began making his way down the crowded street.

Ten minutes later, he found himself standing next to bales of cotton beside a warehouse. The five-hundred pound bales were stacked three high, allowing him to stand behind them without crouching, an act he was certain would make him appear ridiculous. As casually as he could muster, he peered around the corner and saw Stewart standing on one of the docks. A coastal schooner was being tied to the dock's mooring. *"What have we here?"*

A wagon waited on the end of the dock, and from down the gangplank several sailors carried heavy wooden boxes over to the wagon. The man sitting on the seat looked familiar. It was one of the election judges he'd seen back at the courthouse. These were more ballots from other parts of Galveston County. Instead of counting the votes where they were cast, the county chose to assemble all the ballots at one location before counting them.

When loaded, the wagon rolled forward, but went less than half a block before turning from the street and rolling into a warehouse. Followed closely by Stewart. Mystified, Elliot trailed behind. Before he could close the entire distance, the wagon rolled out the door with the judge still atop the seat. Elliot stared, mouth agape, as the wagon turned the corner, heading in the direction of the courthouse.

Where had Stewart gone? Was he still in the warehouse? Intending to find out and put an end to whatever shenanigans his valet was up to, he peered into the Warehouse's dim interior. *"What in the hell?"*

There was a second wagon, close enough in appearance to be a twin to the one the election judge rode out on moments before. Stewart sat on the seat and snapped the reins as the wagon left, rolling into a back alleyway. Paraphrasing Shakespeare as he ran across the floor of the warehouse, Elliot muttered, "Something's rotten in the state of Texas," and he was determined to find out how his valet was involved.

He hadn't gone more than a few hundred feet before regretting not having his own horse. The wagon had continued on a straight route, through the center of the town, heading toward the beach on the gulf side of town. He arrived on the shoreline, drenched in sweat and out of breath. But not more than fifty yards ahead of him stood the wagon, still harnessed to the horses. Were it not for the brilliant moonlight that bathed the sand, Elliot wouldn't have seen Stewart as he pulled a small rowboat back to shore.

As Stewart beached the boat, curiosity overrode Elliot's caution and he strode across the sand, noticing the wagon-bed was empty. "What in the name of all that is holy are you doing out here, Mr. Stewart"

The other man jumped in fright when he heard Elliot's booming voice echo from the darkness. The former decrypter must have recognized his voice. "Lord have mercy, Mr. Elliot." He smoothed his wrinkled shirt and when he spoke again, his voice had returned to normal. "Can I be of service, sir?"

Elliot closed the distance and pointed his finger into his valet's face, "Dammit, yes. What in the blazes are you up to? Conspiring with some fellow from the bank of England and a Mexican? Are you trying to start a war, man?"

Stewart stepped around him and went and checked on the horses. Elliot fumed as the other man appeared to ignore him. *"Who in the devil does he think he is? I'm the goddamned chargé d'affaires."*

The other man climbed onto the seat and finally responded, "Here, sir. Take my hand, and we'll take this wagon back to where it belongs."

Elliot stared at his valet as though he didn't know him. In truth, he couldn't say he did, given that Stewart had been with him for less than three months. He was seriously doubting whether he knew the man at all as he climbed up in the seat next to his valet.

As Stewart guided the wagon back onto the road from the beach, he said, "Like as not, you really don't want to know, sir."

Elliot stewed at the insolence. "If what you did causes an international incident, I damned better be informed."

"There are forces at play bigger than you or me, Mr. Elliot. My employer," Stewart stopped, thinking before continuing, "let's just say that Texas can't be allowed to pursue annexation."

Everything he'd seen over the course of the evening fell into place. The ballots from the coastal schooner had been swapped in the warehouse. The fake ballots had already been delivered to the courthouse, and Stewart had likely dumped the real ballots into the Gulf of Mexico.

Elliot shook his head in dismay. "What have you done, Stewart? If Texas finds out you've tampered in their election, it will undo everything I've been sent here to accomplish."

Stewart coldly stared at him. "Then it would be best if they didn't find out," his voice softened as he continued, "There are two things that matter to my employer, sir. First, anything that keeps Texas out of the United States benefits my employer and Britain. Second, in this election,

Houston's base of support was the planter class and other men who benefit from the slave trade. While there is no guarantee that Lorenzo de Zavala will be a friend to the cause of abolition, the slavers will own Sam Houston should he win the election."

Elliot stared aghast at the deadly game his valet was caught up in. "Who in God's name, is your employer?"

The wagon pulled up in front of the consulate. As he engaged the brake, Stewart gave him a positively feral smile. "You don't want to know."

Chapter 5

From the Telegraph and Texas Register,
Jacob Cruger, Editor
September 16, 1842

Readers will be relieved to know the Election Commission has certified the presidential election results. President ad interim Lorenzo de Zavala has won the election in his own right by a margin of 95 votes, over challenger Sam Houston. 29,048 votes were cast for the office of the president. Below are the results of the count:

13,219 Lorenzo de Zavala
13,124 Samuel Houston
2,705 Robert Potter

The Telegraph and Texas Register received the following telegram from Sam Houston. "I have fought the good fight and would have won the election were I alone to have challenged President-elect Zavala. I still believe that those Texians who favor annexation with the United States are in the majority, but the voters have delivered their verdict, and I wish the president-elect well, and call upon all Texians to support him as he leads our nation through the perilous waters of war."

This paper has it upon authority Mr. Houston claimed that were Mr. Potter a gentleman, that he would challenge him to a duel, but as he is uncertain as to Mr. Potter's provenance, no such challenge could be issued. Mr. Potter was unavailable for comment before publication, but the reader will learn of his response as soon as it is made available to the paper of record.

President-elect Zavala informed this newspaper, he thanks the people of Texas for entrusting him with the authority of the office and he will use every device at his command to seek a just and lasting peace with Mexico and will not rest until the dictator is brought to justice for the vile murder of so many Texian soldiers.

Will looked into the mirror and adjusted the collar of his jacket. It was one of the new jackets supplied by the army's vendor in New Orleans. The blend of cotton and wool was sturdy, extending the life of the jacket while in the field, at least that's what the vendor promised. But the dye used looked less butternut and more of a light shade of brown. He would be attending a working meeting, and apart from the shoulder boards with two gold embroidered stars, his uniform was the same as was worn by enlisted soldiers. As a student of history, he had found nineteenth century officer uniforms to be outlandishly ornate. As the commander of the army of Texas, he had an opportunity to nip some of that in the bud. In the field, officers and enlisted men of the army of Texas wore the same uniform.

Since the declaration of war six months before, the army had been plagued with issues of consistency from the textile mills contracted to provide uniforms. But as he closed the door to his hotel room, he knew there was nothing to be done about it at the moment. As he walked toward the Capitol building, he made a mental note to write to Don Garza at Gulf Farms and ask about the prospects for building a textile mill in Texas. Garza would know if Texas' internal market was large enough for a textile mill to turn a profit.

He reached the second floor of the Capitol and knocked on the door which once belonged to David Crockett.

"Come in."

He found President Zavala sitting at the same desk once used by his predecessor. The two men were as different as Will could imagine. Crockett had kept the room messy, with books and maps strewn about, left wherever he had last used them. Zavala was, by Will's estimation, a neat freak. A few books were stacked on the edge of the desk. His correspondence was organized in several tidy stacks, either waiting for his attention or for his clerk to take away.

As Will settled into a chair opposite Zavala, the President asked, "How was the coach ride up from San Antonio, General Travis?"

Despite liking Zavala, Will missed Crockett's friendly informality. But Will had never grown as close to Zavala as he had to the man who became his father-in-law. Even so, Zavala's easy smile was disarming. "Not bad, sir. Less than twelve hours yesterday to get here. Still though, I look forward to the day when railroads connect our cities."

Zavala nodded with a knowing smile, "From your lips to the Almighty's ears, General."

He grabbed a sheaf of pages from one of his stacks and slid it across the table. "Here's the reason I asked you to come up."

Will flipped through the correspondence, taking a moment to read several of the pages more than once. "Well, that's unexpected, Mr. President. It's not every day you get a letter from General Winfield Scott."

Zavala tilted his head in agreement. "Do you have a problem with the United States placing an observer in our army, General?"

Will looked at the name of the officer referenced in General Scott's letter. *"Captain William Hardee? Why do I know that name?"* While it sounded familiar, he couldn't recall anyone famous by that name. *"Probably a general during the civil war. There must have been close to a thousand generals."*

Will asked, "What do we know of this Captain Hardee, sir?"

Zavala shrugged, "Not much, he's from Georgia and is a West Pointer, like General Johnston. I was hoping you might know more."

Will returned Zavala's earlier shrug with one of his own, "I can ask Sidney. Maybe he knows something. I imagine it would be well received if we allow the United States to place an observer. The thought hadn't crossed my mind before, but if the United States and Britain can't settle their disagreement over their boundary, placing one of our officers as an observer would be a good idea. On that note, it might be worth it to pass along to the British chargé d'affaires and the French minister an invitation to observe the war, as well."

Will didn't much care for making the offer. The world would view his army as using experimental rifles and experimental tactics. The longer he could keep the genie in the bottle the happier he would be, but it wasn't possible to keep the lid on either of them much longer. Better, he thought, to maintain a degree of control on how the Sabine Rifle and his open-order battle tactics were introduced to contemporary armies.

"I'll see to it that we accept their request, Mr. President."

Zavala pointed to the papers in Will's hand. "What do you think of the American terms for selling more of those Hall's rifles?"

Will shuffled the papers until he found the referenced letter. "Two thousand of them at fifteen dollars per rifle is a pretty good price. I wish they had more to sell."

Zavala thumbed through a ledger he pulled from one of the desk drawers before asking, "Remind me again, where we are in respect to preparation for the war?"

Will leaned back in the chair, "Not too bad. Prior to General Woll's invasion, the Trinity Gun works had provided around fourteen hundred of the Model 1842 Sabine rifle. We had transitioned close to two thousand of the earlier breechloaders to McCulloch's reserves at that time. Between March and now, the Trinity gun works has produced another eight hundred rifles. In total, we have close to forty-five hundred breechloading rifles of one design or another."

Will paused, considering all the men mustered into service currently. "Now the problem is that we have six battalions of infantry currently in San Antonio, one of Marines and another of cavalry, all of whom need rifles or carbines. In addition to that, we plan on transitioning up to another six battalions of militia to active reserves between now and next April. That's close to nine thousand men we need to equip and uniform. Against that, even with these two thousand rifles from the United States, our best-case scenario only gives us close to eight thousand rifles."

Zavala frowned, "Is that adequate for your campaign?"

Will had been puzzling over that question since Crockett's resignation six months earlier. "It has to be, sir. I plan on leaving at least one brigade spread across South Texas from the mouth of the Nueces to Ysleta in the west. If they have to use their own rifles and muskets, so be it. Six years ago, we beat Santa Anna's army with nothing better."

The meeting continued for several hours, until interrupted by Zavala's clerk, who reminded the president he had a luncheon scheduled with the Senate's appropriation committee's chairman. Will returned to the Stagecoach Inn, where he ate then retired for a well-deserved nap, confident he had done all that was possible to bring President Zavala up to speed regarding the military's preparations.

"Feliz Navidad!" The door swung open wide as the warmth retreated from the assault by the frigid wind blowing down from the Sierra Madres. General Juan Almonte hastily stepped into the Governor's Palace as the governor of Nuevo Leon closed the door behind him, driving back the frigid night air.

The door closed, warmth returned and Almonte responded, "Feliz Navidad, Governor Llano."

He arched his eyebrows in surprise at finding the governor manning his own door. When he looked around for servants, he saw several bustling to and from a grand hall, carrying platters and trays of food, adding them to tables already groaning under the weight of the platters.

Governor Llano picked up on the reason for Almonte's searching gaze. "It's but a single day, General. The servants are busy in the kitchen. If I can use a military term, sometimes one has to step into the breach, and I'm quite certain they are all the happier that I'm the one bearing the brunt of father winter."

As Almonte shed his cloak, his smile radiated as he patted his host on the back, "Careful, lest the bishop thinks you're doing penance, Governor." At that moment, a fragrant aroma assaulted his senses. "What is that delightful smell coming from your kitchen?"

Governor Llano took the coat and passed it to a servant in the cloakroom and directed Almonte into the well-lit hall. "That's wild pheasant baked in a cinnamon sauce."

He appeared ready to continue describing food being carried into the hall, when a chime at the door announced another guest. "Tis but once a year. If you'll excuse me, General."

As the governor rushed back to the door, Almonte took stock of the richly adorned room. Expensive paintings and tapestries covered the walls depicting important events in the history of Nuevo Leon. Several high-ranking government employees and their wives stood below a tapestry depicting the founding of Monterrey. They were in animated conversation. In one corner of the room, a few musicians were tuning their instruments. In the center of the room, but close to a table laden with food, General Vasquez and several other officers were situated as though defending a citadel from the other citizens of

Monterrey. With a warm smile, Almonte joined them, saying, "We few, we happy few, we band of brothers, for he today who sheds his blood with me shall be my brother."

Vasquez laughed along with several of the other officers. "I hope you brought more than just your Shakespeare, General Almonte. I for one have no interest in shedding blood tonight, unless it happens to belong to that delicious pheasant. If they don't bring it forth soon, I propose we mount an expedition to the kitchen and storm the ovens!"

As the other officers laughed at his wit, Vasquez pointed toward a servant with a tray of wineglasses, "First, though, let's fortify ourselves with more wine." He guided Almonte away from the other officers and as they each took a glass, he continued, "A moment of your time, if you please, General."

Vasquez took a sip before he added, "I'm glad you finally arrived. I trust you had no problems getting here from Vera Cruz."

Almonte swallowed his wine before responding. "Given a choice between winter in Monterrey and autumn in Vera Cruz, I'll take Vera Cruz every time. My *cajones* have yet to thaw."

Given the temperature hadn't ventured above freezing in several days, both men laughed at the mental image. Almonte grew serious. "His Excellency required my service here, and here I have arrived."

Vasquez raised his glass in salute, "Indeed, General. How long before the rest of your men join us?"

Finishing the glass of wine, Almonte set it on a serving tray which was passing by. "Two of the nine regiments are on the march even as we speak. I expect the first of them to arrive by the New Year. The others will arrive between then and the beginning of spring. Additionally, I have good news for you. The levies His Excellency has ordered up to replace Woll's losses in the 1st Division should be here by the beginning of February.

Vasquez's eyes lit up at the news. "Splendid, sir. That will give us an army close to twice the size his Excellency took to Texas back in '36. We'll sweep the *norteamericano* rebels aside, once and for all."

The wine helped to warm Almonte from the inside out. Had he not already had a glass, likely he wouldn't have quirked an eyebrow at Vasquez's bellicosity. Woll's report of his defeat had been sparse on the composition of Johnston's relief column. "What news from the north?"

Vasquez missed the doubt in Almonte's eyes. "My soldiers on the Rio Bravo report that the rebels have rebuilt the fort at Laredo, called Moses Austin. They have reinforced it with a large number of soldiers and light artillery. When it is time to cross the river, removing them will be the first act of our re-conquest."

Almonte frowned. Had neither Woll nor Vasquez thought to occupy the fort? Sensing the question would be poorly received, he shifted his questions further north "What of San Antonio? Do we have any current reports?"

"Travis has returned from Nuevo Mexico with his army, joining up with Johnston's *activos*. Our best guess is there are six regiments of infantry and a squadron of cavalry. Also, if the report is to be believed a regiment of naval infantry."

This should have been news to Almonte. The navy's stinging defeat at Campeche earlier in the fall, had been in the newspapers. As one given to reading Yankee newspapers, Almonte had read detailed reports about the

Texian Marines who had cut out the *Guadalupe*, before the battle had even started. That General Travis had managed to get a few companies diverted to his own army showed forward thinking.

"I have heard their, ah, naval infantry is formidable, General."

Vasquez directed a servant with a drink tray over, before saying, "It would be foolish to underestimate their ability, given their recent performance. But still, they are fish out of water in San Antonio."

Using his wine glass as a pointer, Vasquez added, "When we invade in the spring, Juan, we'll go north with nine-thousand men. Against that, Travis and his rebels won't amount to more than three or four thousand. We are better supplied, and our men are better armed than we were six years ago."

Almonte tried holding his peace, fearing the alcohol which had loosened his commander's tongue might betray him, too. But he knew that Travis had turned the regulars in his army into a truly formidable fighting force. Might he have accomplished the same with his *activos*? If he had, then even if he had four thousand soldiers, they would be formidable.

Against his better judgment he asked, "General Vasquez, have we considered a defensive posture next spring? If we were to take the next few months and develop defensive positions along the Rio Bravo, perhaps we could entice the Texians into bleeding on our fortifications, instead of the other way around."

The second glass Almonte had watched Vasquez drink was empty in the general's hands, and he couldn't help but wonder how many more his superior had drained before his own arrival. There was a glint of sadness in his eyes when Vasquez said, "Juan, like you, I serve at His Excellency's pleasure. It pleases our president to order an attack on San Antonio. Sitting on our hands until Travis decides to try knocking on our defenses, isn't possible."

Vasquez's melancholy response ended Almonte's inquiry, at least on that front. He shifted to a safer topic. "How have you found Monterrey, General?"

"Damned cold," Vasquez replied, "In more ways than one." He pointed toward the hallway, where Governor Llano was still greeting guests. "Don't let Manuel de Llano fool you. I have it on the best of authority he would have joined all these rebellions across our fair country, were it not for the fact that the Army of the North has made treason unappealing to him."

Almonte was alarmed, "You don't think he would throw in with the Texians?"

As though stepping on a bug, Vasquez wore a distasteful look. "He hates the *norteamericanos* as much as you or I. No, I don't think he would. But if he thought he could set himself up as president of a northern republic and make it stick, he would slide the knife of treason in our backs."

Before Almonte could think of a response a bell rang, and he heard oohs and aahs as servants brought in several platters of roasted pheasants. The spicy scent of cinnamon made his mouth water and thoughts of rebellious governors and a rebel province to the north fled as he made his way toward the food.

Chapter 6

Late February 1843

The young man knelt by the bank of the languid Rio Grande, washing the blood from his hands. The water, as it flowed through his fingers, was tinged with red as he frantically scrubbed at the blood. Behind him, perhaps as little as a hundred yards away, he heard footfalls, amid the cottonwoods and cypress trees. "*Aqui!*" a voice called out.

More rushing feet approached. They must have found his mount, where he had been forced to put her down. He wiped his red-streaked hands on his trousers and waded into the muddy river, without a backwards glance. It was too hard. Were he to look, it would have reinforced how far he had ridden, just to come up short, this close to the border.

Everything had been fine the first couple of days after he had killed the snake, but as he had approached the Rio Grande, patrols of lancers had become common, and even infantry patrols were crisscrossing the southern approaches to the river.

"A goddamned gopher hole!" Were it not for that, he wouldn't be stuck on this side of the river forced to swim across.

Recalling how his horse had stumbled and thrown him, he barely avoided hitting a large cypress tree. It was painful as tears threatened to spill down his cheeks at the memory. When he had picked himself up and went back to the mount, he found the mare trying to climb back to her feet, but one look was enough to see her leg was broken.

A soft neigh escaped her mouth as her leg refused to cooperate. He might have found another solution save for the shouts of the Mexican infantry patrol that was following his trail. Still, with no desire to give away his position, he slid his Bowie knife from his belt. With his other hand, he stroked her face, and blinked away the tears as she looked at him with big, solemn eyes. With as much tenderness as he could muster, he turned her face away and used the knife to end her suffering.

Now he was fifty feet into the river, as the current threatened to sweep his feet from under him, voices called from behind, ordering to him to stop. "Like hell!" he muttered as he surged forward.

A gunshot echoed across the river and less than a foot away, the bullet splashed in the water. He thought, *"You don't hear the one that gets you."*

Jesse dived into the still shallow water, and with powerful strokes, drove himself forward. More shots splashed around him. As his strokes carried him toward the Texas side of the river, he saw the shoreline drawing closer. If fate smiled on him and he wasn't struck in the back, he didn't have far to go.

As his feet found the river bottom again, and a bullet plunged into the water only inches away, he realized the downside to the narrow spot in the river. He was still in range of the *soldados* firing away at him.

He crawled out of the water and stretched out behind a rotten tree trunk lying on the shore. Gasping for air, he poked his head over the log and looked back. There were a half-dozen men kneeling on the other bank, still firing at him. His rifle was with his mount back on the far shore, and his pistol was waterlogged. His only weapon was the Bowie knife at his belt.

From behind him, he heard a noise, and whipped his head around, and drew his Bowie knife. A horse was crashing through a stand of mesquite trees. *"I should have listened to my father and ran the warehouse."* With no working firearm, and just his Arkansas Toothpick in hand, Jesse felt naked, waiting to see who would come crashing through the scrub brush and mesquite.

Every few seconds another shot echoed from the southern bank of the river, while Jesse crouched behind the log. He hefted the blade, it was well balanced. With a little luck, he could throw the blade and take out whoever broke through the tree line first. If more than one came through, then it would get ugly fast.

He pulled his arm back, ready to fling the knife, when a horse broke through the mesquite tree's brambles. Atop the mount sat Jethro Elkins, another Ranger from his company. With scarcely a look at Jesse, the Ranger drew his pistol and sent a handful of shots across the river in just a few seconds.

The Cherokee Ranger scrambled to his feet from behind the log and watched the *soldados* scramble for cover. The Mexicans were outside the revolver's range. Jesse put the knife away and ran over to Elkins, who offered his hand. Once the other Ranger pulled him up behind him, they turned and disappeared into the dense tree line as the *soldados* fired at their retreating backs.

A while later, Jesse Running Creek shifted on his feet, waiting for Major Jack Hays to acknowledge him. The major's headquarters was in the bar of Laredo's largest cantina. Hays sat at a round table, a ceramic jug placed in the middle, surrounded by reports, requisition forms and other administrative records. Eventually he set a report down and looked at the young Cherokee Ranger.

"Why don't you tell me how you managed to lose both your rifle and your horse, Running Creek."

The son of a detail oriented Cherokee merchant, Jesse methodically chronicled how he started keeping an eye on the Mexican army in Monterrey, carrying the report through the loss of his equipment and horse just yards away from the Rio Grande, ending with Ranger Elkins' timely rescue once he swam ashore on the Texian side of the river.

Major Hays listened without interruption until the end. "Are you trying to tell me that because you got scared by a snake, a Mexican general is dead, Running Creek?"

Jesse flushed at the absurdity of the situation. Hearing the major say it that way, it did seem implausible. With a shrug, "I think I might have killed the snake, too."

Hays shook his head, "Incredible. I think we might have to start calling you Running from Snake from now on, Ranger."

A glimmer of a smile played across their faces, before Hays returned to his questioning. "With General Vasquez dead, who does that leave in command?"

Jesse said, "General Almonte arrived in Monterrey before the end of last year. As I understand it, he was supposed to be Vasquez' second-in-command as well as commander for the second division."

Hays grimaced at the news. "We'll pass that information along back to the Alamo. They'll want to know, but I was looking forward to facing General Vasquez. He has a reputation for charging straight ahead. Almonte is more of an unknown. The last I heard, he was serving as Mexican minister to the United States. General Travis needs to know this."

Two companies of *Cazadores* were drilling in the valley north of Monterrey, under the watchful eye of General Juan Almonte. The light infantrymen were practicing skirmish drills, armed with British Baker rifles. Each man was trained to use whatever cover he could find, and to fight individually or as part of a larger squad.

Today, they were not practicing their marksmanship. Instead, they were training on small unit tactics. Almonte had been fortunate enough while in the United States to come into possession of a copy of Travis' Manual of Tactics of Riflemen. Part of his time in the United States, he spent translating the manual into Spanish. With command of the Army of the North's 2nd division, he would have the opportunity to apply the enemy's tactics to his own light infantry. By the time he cobbled together his division, he would have nine *Cazadores* companies. Twice that many, if he could talk General Vasquez into adopting the new tactics for the light infantry companies in the 1st division, too.

While he envisioned the equivalent of two regiments of light infantry facing off against the Texians, a rider raced into camp from the north. "General Almonte, sir! General Vasquez is dead!"

Shocked out of the fanciful imagery, Almonte stood dumbfounded, listening to the rider recount General Vasquez's unfortunate demise. The rider informed him the general's body was on its way back to Monterrey by wagon. Vasquez's staff officers had halted the relief column and would wait on General Almonte's orders.

Still in shock at the death of the army commander, Almonte returned to the 2nd division's encampment. Over the previous two months he had come to admire Vasquez. Sure, he was brash and headstrong, but he owned a certain daring that Almonte privately conceded he lacked. Where he was methodical and deliberate in his planning, Vasquez had been decisive and bold. While they were as dissimilar as they could be, Almonte knew he would miss the brazen flare the other officer had brought to his command.

With a sad shake of his head, Almonte sat at his desk and penned a letter, informing Mexico City of the setback. As he finished drafting the letter he considered the circumstances facing his army. The reinforcements for the 1st division would bring the division's effective strength to nearly five thousand men. Getting the reinforcements to Nuevo Laredo was the first priority.

The timetable for the invasion required the 2nd division be assembled by the first of April. Unfortunately, that left Almonte with two regiments in Monterrey at the moment, with the rest arriving over the next month. With the death of Vasquez, he needed to transfer his headquarters to Nuevo Laredo now rather than later. He would leave one of the regiments in Monterrey, waiting for the remainder of the division to arrive. The other, he would order to march north with him.

He finished his correspondence, tossed down the pen. "*Poncho! Ven Aqui.*"

A young officer stepped into the tent. "Yes, sir?"

Almonte handed the correspondence to him. "You've got a long ride ahead of you. Deliver this letter into the hands of His Excellency, the president. Also, see to it these other messages are delivered on your way out of town."

With a crisp salute, the officer took the letters and hurried away.

The next morning, Almonte met Colonel Juaquin Mendoza of the 11th Permanente Regiment along the road north of Monterrey. Mendoza sat astride his mount, and the regiment's five hundred men were strung out on the road, in columns of four men abreast. The two officers exchanged salutes and with little fanfare, Almonte started north.

It took two days for his force to arrive at the temporary camp erected by the 1st division's reinforcements. During the march, as the force moved north, the plain on which Monterrey was founded, narrowed to a rough, narrow valley. The valley ran between two mountain ranges. Almonte noticed narrower points along the line of march that would make exceptional defensive positions. Despite the orders from His Excellency to invade once the army was assembled, Almonte's methodical mind envisioned his army bleeding the Texians in a fighting retreat.

When he led the men of the 11th into the encampment near where General Vasquez died, he found the men subdued. Vasquez had been a popular and gregarious officer and the men under his command had rewarded him with their devotion. The melancholy within the camp was strong, leading Almonte to think, "*I know that level of devotion well. It mirrors the devotion those of us who serve under His Excellency know.*"

During the following week, Almonte led the force northward following the road between the mountain ranges. Even after the column turned back to the northwest, along the road to Candela, Almonte's thoughts returned to the rugged road over which his army had just marched. It was the perfect fallback position, should Travis' Texians invade.

From the dusty, tiny town of Candela, the road skirted the Chihuahuan desert, on its way to Nuevo Laredo. The last five days between those towns was dry and dusty, but the mountains were to their south, and even though it was still late February, the weather was not too cold. As he led the men of the relief column and the 11th Permanante Regiment, he felt that circumstances and Vasquez's orders were contrary to each other.

"If I follow through with Vasquez's orders, I'll be taking this army straight into the jaws of Travis' riflemen. But if I defend the river then fall back to fortified lines In the mountains north of Monterrey, my odds of defeating the Texians are all the better."

After allowing his mind to rationalize the benefits of a defense in depth, he came back around to the problem, "But His Excellency has ordered the army I now command to invade Texas and capture San Antonio."

It was a conundrum that troubled Almonte throughout the two-week march between Monterrey and Nuevo Laredo.

But clarity finally came once he stood in the tower of the little church in the plaza of Nuevo Laredo. He held a spyglass to his eye, studying the star fort Texas had built in the bend of the Rio Bravo. Guns faced Mexico through the embrasures dug into the earthen walls.

Whoever commanded the Texian force in Laredo had done more than simply reoccupy the fort Woll had captured the previous year. Trenches had been dug, extending away from the fort, but facing the river. Spies in Laredo told him there were nearly five hundred soldiers garrisoning the fort and town.

Almonte figured with ten to one odds, his existing division around Nuevo Laredo could overwhelm the Texian garrison, but at what cost? With better weapons and better training, if Texas stayed on the defense, even with both divisions, nine thousand men, a couple of battles like the Battle of the Nueces in 1836 and his army would be ruined. He took an oath to serve His Excellency. His Excellency expected the army to advance and capture San Antonio later in the spring.

"I have no interest in playing King Phyrrus to Travis' Romans."

The guard in the tower looked over at him. "Sir?"

He hadn't realized he spoke aloud. "Nothing, soldier."

He climbed down the ladder, and as he left the church, he knew the surest way to give Santa Anna a victory was to lure Travis to defeat. He untied his mount from the hitching post and swung into the saddle. All the intelligence making its way south from San Antonio confirmed Travis was building an army he intended to use to invade Mexico. Almonte knew there was no time to waste. He had trenches to dig, artillery batteries to position, and an army to train.

DOWN MEXICO WAY

Sergeant Major Julio Leal wore a stormy expression as he stood next to the First Sergeant for Company A, 9th Infantry Battalion. They watched a platoon of thirty-two men deploy into a thin line of skirmishers. "Dammit, Sergeant Jackson, they're coming off the line slower than they should. And *Jesuchristo*! Your rifle teams are as awkward as a group of boys asking girls to dance at a *Quinceanera*."

Sergeant Terry Jackson blushed under the fusillade of criticism from his friend and mentor. "I'm trying, Sergeant. The boys was out in town drinking in the tavern with the colonel and didn't get in until late."

Lowering his voice, Sergeant Major Leal said, "Terry, what Colonel Crockett decides to do with his time is his own damned business. Lieutenant Everett aside, you're responsible for the men in your platoon. If that means the next time the colonel wants to stay out until the sun comes up telling folks tall tales, you will take your ass over to the tavern and get the boys back to camp. Hell, ain't nary a one of them had a pass last night, did they?"

Jackson hung his head in shame. In a battalion full of militiamen, the two sergeants were the only regulars transferred into the unit when it formed a few months before. It grated on Leal that his longtime friend's platoon was underperforming. As far as he was concerned, Jackson's platoon should have been drilling rings around the others.

"Have them start over, and this time, if they don't beat their previous time, I'll assign every last one of them to guard duty for the next week." Leal turned and left Jackson staring at his backside before turning to the men.

As Leal crossed the road between the men drilling in the field and their camp, he smiled as he listened to Jackson chewing at his men for their poor performance.

In the battalion's command pavilion, he found the greying former president crowding over a small camp desk. He was studying a map. As the battalion sergeant major, what Leal's job lacked in leading riflemen, more than made up for it in administrative paperwork. It still bemused him when he thought of the path his life had taken over the past year. A year before, he had been first sergeant for a company stationed on the Rio Grande. When Woll's army had arrived, his captain had sent him and Jackson north to the Alamo, delivering word of the Mexican invasion to Major Dickinson.

He and Jackson had barely managed to survive the siege and only lived because of General Johnston's timely arrival. His friend, Jackson had nearly died and had only returned to duty when they were transferred to Crockett's 9th battalion. Yes, the past year had been more than strange. He eyed his commanding officer who was poring over a map of Texas' newly acquired territory and amended the thought. "Next year looks to be even more interesting."

Chapter 7

24 March 1843

The two men stood in the trench south of Nuevo Laredo, on a rise overlooking the town. Further up the hill another trench had been completed a few days before. Wearing a private's jacket, General Juan Almonte stood next to the captain in command of one of the army's *Zapadores* companies.

Between the Army of the North's two division, they shared a battalion of *Zapadores*. These Mexican sappers were skilled at digging entrenchments. They were the engineers of the army. Several dozen men were swinging pickaxes into the hard soil as others shoveled the freshly turned earth over the lip of the trench, raising a protective barrier against whatever the Texians might eventually throw against them in the coming days.

"How goes the construction, Captain?" Almonte's plain uniform provided a measure of anonymity, especially considering the trench was within extreme range of the riflemen in the fort opposite Nuevo Laredo.

The captain waved his hand in the direction of his workers, "As long as the riflemen in the fort leave us alone, we'll be finished with this trench tomorrow." Seeing a question on Almonte's face, he continued, "Don't worry, General, it will be more than adequate for your *Cazadores* battalion."

A grin lit the general's features, *"Am I that transparent?"* He stepped back and watched the captain instruct his men in their work. Since arriving at Nuevo Laredo more than a month before, he had constructed a ring of entrenchments around and through Nuevo Laredo. The two divisions' eighteen infantry regiments each had a light infantry company. Each of the eighteen *Cazadores* companies had been split from their parent unit and formed into two ad-hoc regiments.

It was quite simple, he thought. The two regiments of riflemen, both armed with British Baker rifles would hold the trench lines closest to the river. There was no guarantee he would be able to deny Travis' Texians the southern shore of the Rio Bravo, but he could make any victory Travis wrestled from him as expensive as possible.

Satisfied the army's sappers were on schedule, Almonte followed the communication trench back up the hill, to where a strong, fortified line had been constructed. These fortified trenches ran for more than a mile, covering the ford at Laredo from all angles. The artillery battalion's thirty field pieces were emplaced along the heights overlooking the town, situated in embrasures, cut in the earth and reinforced by woven gabions full of rocks and dirt. Even if the gunpowder used by the Mexican army was inferior to that bought by the Texians from the United States, he had done all that was possible to give his gunners an edge.

From the fortification on the hilltop, Almonte had a commanding view of the two towns down below as well as the five-sided fort, over which the Texas flag flew. Most of the army was now assembled here and he was as prepared as he could be to defend the line. For a while, he had worried about the Texians attempting to flank his position. Such was always possible, but the other fords nearby were deeper and more treacherous than the shallows across the Rio Bravo at Laredo. Even so, he had assigned most of his cavalry to screen those fords. If Travis decided to flank him, then there would be no battle here, and the effort spent entrenching his army around Nuevo Laredo would be for naught. He had lost sleep over that, until he thought about the four regiments not present with the army. Two of them were fortifying the pass south of Candela while the other two were fortifying narrow points in the valleys that led to Monterrey.

He stared across the south Texas prairie. If the spies in Texas were correct, he wouldn't have to wait much longer to learn of Travis' strategy. Soon, the army of Texas would march across that plain north of Laredo. He tried to let go of the worry, *"If they attack, we defend. If they attempt to flank, then we'll withdraw back to Candela."*

He acknowledged the salutes of the *soldados* in the trenches and returned to his horse. Orders, requisition forms, and other minutiae waited on him at the army's headquarters. As he guided his horse through the encampment behind the fortifications, he wondered what His Excellency would say when he found out that the army was digging in and not invading.

Even now, he had yet to receive any reaction from Santa Anna to General Vasquez' unfortunate death more than six weeks previous. No doubt, His Excellency would demand that he proceed with the planned invasion.

Almonte shook his head, that way would lead to the ruin of his army, he was certain. Over the years of his service to Mexico, he owed every promotion to Santa Anna's patronage. More than slavishly following orders, he owed it to His Excellency to interpret the orders in such a way as to give Mexico a victory over the Texians.

Either he had devised a strategy that would bleed Travis' army, or he hadn't. If he failed, he risked the ire of Santa Anna, and he shuddered at the thought. Maybe their long years of friendship would protect him, maybe it wouldn't. Either way, the die was cast and the cup was in Travis' hands now.

The end of March in Texas was the middle of spring. Winter's last gasp was more than a month gone and the coastal breeze from the south made for pleasant weather as Colonel David Crockett sat astride his mount. He led the column along the road. The men looked sharp in their new uniforms and their black wide-brimmed hats and they were in high spirits as they marched down the Harrisburg Road.

Behind the infantry column came a company of cavalry, one of two assigned to Crockett's little command. The thought of how he had come into possession of them brought a smile to his weathered face.

Less than a month earlier, he had been holding a meeting in his pavilion, doing what his son-in-law liked to call a "debrief," with his officers after a wargame between the two wings of the battalion when General McCulloch had ridden into camp. The commander of the militia had leapt from his horse and strode into the meeting, bellowing, "Everybody but Colonel Crockett, get out of my sight!"

As his officers made like scattering cockroaches, David remained at the camp table, his arms crossed, waiting.

When they were alone, McCulloch only slightly modulated his voice, "What in the hell are you doing going behind my back?"

"I got no idea about what you're talking about, Ben." As the former president, David banked on the familiarity with McCulloch.

Pointing his finger at David, McCulloch growled, "The hell you don't. I just got a letter from President Zavala telling me to cut loose two companies of cavalry for you to play with and to transfer two companies of infantry from another battalion."

David feigned surprise, "I'm sure he didn't say I could play with them, Ben, that don't seem like Lorenzo's style a'tall."

"Yeah, well, same thing." The angry storm now spent, McCulloch collapsed into one of the camp chairs. "What in the hell have you and the President got cooked up, David? Zavala said you're to have a couple of more weeks' drilling, then to report to San Antonio for further orders. Add to that, a fair number of those newly requisitioned teamsters are to be sent along."

David leaned against the camp table, "I ain't like it's going to be a state secret or anything, but I talked Lorenzo into letting me take the 9th to reestablish things in Santa Fe. Couldn't talk him into giving me any artillery but he was nice enough to give me a couple of cavalry troops and a bit more infantry."

McCulloch frowned, "I wish you would have done that through me. We don't have a chain of command for no reason."

David smiled coyly, "Well, I hope it don't play hell with your command here, Ben. Me and Lorenzo just wanted to play it close to the vest."

McCulloch climbed to his feet, with a huff. "Not my problem anymore, David. I've been ordered to bring the 11th Infantry to San Antonio. Buck has given me the 2nd brigade of the army. And I doubt Tom Rusk will miss them."

David's eyebrows raised, "Lorenzo's putting Rusk in charge of the militia again? After the hash he made of it last time?"

"Hell, David, you of all people should know that politics is horse trading. To get Congress to go along with impressment of certain plantation owners' property for the duration, their darling military mind, Tom Rusk, gets to play at being general over the militia again."

As he shook his head, David said, "God save the militia, Ben. Any idea how many slaves are being leased by the government?"

"A few thousand. Maybe a couple of hundred will be teamsters. Most of the rest have been 'leased' to build a railroad between here and Harrisburg and Houston."

David shook his head, "Gonna be hard to get a cotton crop in without them hands," his voice fell, and he grew somber, "It's going to be hell on every family in Texas until this war is won, what with all the men away from their farms."

McCulloch nodded as he climbed on his mount, "Truer words, David, but if those rich dandies have all their labor tied up in the Republic's war effort, then at least they won't be profiting during the war."

Crockett frowned, "How'd Lorenzo manage to avoid paying them?"

Before digging his heels into his mount's flanks, McCulloch said, "War bonds. Redeemable down the road."

Even now, as his command marched toward Harrisburg, the memory made him chuckle. Lorenzo was turning into a damned fine president.

The road ran alongside a graded railroad bed, ready for the iron rails and railroad ties to come. His command made good time marching. The Harrisburg road had been macadamized with crushed gravel and tar as the railroad bed was built parallel to it. It was expensive but weatherproofed the road more or less. Crockett and his men were still another twenty miles from their goal when they stopped for the evening. They had eventually caught up with the crews who were laboring on the roadbed.

The slaves methodically worked, building up the railroad bed. The railroad bed had to be elevated above the ground to reduce the risk of flooding and to keep the grade of the tracks as low as possible. Thousands of tons of dirt had to be moved for each mile of planned tracks. Behind the slaves came teams of Irish laborers using large metal rollers, to smooth and flatten the dirt. Watching over the slaves were men from the militia. As a plantation owner, Rusk had his own ideas about how to keep the slaves working, and as commander of the militia again, he was in a position to make sure the slaves did what they were told.

"Buck must be rubbing off on me," David thought as bile rose in his throat as he watched teams of slaves still working on the rail line. As Crockett's opinions evolved, he

found his son-in-law's abolitionist views making more sense. The labor of free men wouldn't require soldiers guarding them. No longer president, David knew that resolving the conflict between Texas' growing abolitionist movement and her wealthy slave owners would fall upon Zavala or his successor. He hoped that they would be able to find a way to peacefully thread that needle.

That evening, as he sat around a campfire along with several other officers, David pulled out a map he had been carrying. Using the irregular light from the fire he found Santa Fe on the map. Nearly a thousand miles away. But thanks to his son-in-law, the way was much easier than it would have been. Because of the military road and the supply depots, the expedition would take two months or less to get there. That was the easy part.

He hoped the cities on the Texas side of the Treaty line could be quickly integrated into the Republic. There was so much to accomplish and at fifty-six years of age, he was familiar enough with his mortality to know that time was no longer his ally.

The wick burned, causing the lamp's glass chimney to glow. Will strained to hear any noises in the house, but Henrietta, their cook, had yet to stir. He glanced over at his wife. Becky was breastfeeding the newborn. David Stern Travis was only a couple of months old, and he was latched onto his mother, noisily suckling. The sight of mother and child came close to bringing tears to his eyes. As he finished buttoning his jacket, he leaned in and planted kisses on both his wife and infant son.

Becky smiled back, her eyes red rimmed. Their last night together, before leading the army south had been bittersweet. As the night had given way to the predawn, he had held her as she cried, and she had held him as they made love. He never felt good leaving his family, as duty often required, but he had taken every precaution to ensure Texas' victory in the coming campaign, and felt he would be home within a few months. But even feeling confident of victory, it didn't make leaving home and hearth any easier.

As he went to the door, the warmth of Becky's smile nearly broke his heart. When he had become trapped in the body inhabited now for more than six years, he could never have imagined the love he shared with Becky. Now, he couldn't bear to think about riding off to war and leaving her and the children behind.

"I'll be back, I'm going to look in on the children." He closed the door and moved down the hall. One of the doors was ajar, and he slid it open, and saw little Liza sleeping on her small, child's bed. Not quite two years old, normally she was toddling around the house and keeping both Becky and Henrietta on their toes. He still remembered the look on Becky's face when he had suggested child-proofing the house. As he smiled down on his sleeping daughter, his wife's response brought an unbidden smile. "But Will, how in the world will she know not to stick her finger in the fire? One time and she'll figure out quick like that she's to stay away from the fireplace."

As was usually the case, Becky was right. He leaned in and brushed his lips over his daughter's forehead. The day he had arrived back from the fort to find her tearstained face staring up at him as she held up her little fist, where her index finger was wrapped in a linen bandage brought a sad smile to his face.

During the Santa Fe campaign the previous year, he had been gone for only a few months, but she had grown so fast during that time. Now, as the army readied for war, would he be gone for only a few months or would it drag on? He was no stranger to prolonged conflict. When his mind had been transferred to 1836, the United States had been in Iraq for seven years. He shook his head at the thought. Texas couldn't survive a protracted war with Mexico. Seven months might be too long, let alone seven years. For the sake of the republic and for the hope of seeing his daughter soon, he was determined to defeat Santa Anna's armies as quickly as possible.

Charlie's bed was along the other wall. Turning he saw his son sitting quietly on the bed, staring back at him. *"My son,"* he thought, *"Not exactly."* In the months before Will's transference into Buck Travis' body, his wife, Rosanna had divorced him. Not without cause, either. Travis had abandoned her, Charlie, and an unborn daughter. The boy had come as part of the divorce. Fate had played a cruel trick on the young boy. In another world, he would have been orphaned following Travis' death at the Alamo. In this world, he had been left in Will's care when he had replaced the unfaithful Travis. Of all the things Will had changed since the transference, his relationship with the boy he now thought of as his son was one where he was certain his involvement had made the greatest difference.

"Morning, Pa. I was hoping you'd poke your head in before leaving."

Will stepped over to the teenager and tousled his already messy hair. "I had to see my little princess and her valiant and brave brother."

DOWN MEXICO WAY

The boy looked at the table between the beds, where a copy of Scott's *Ivanhoe* was opened face down. "You haven't been sneaking in and reading my book again?"

Will held up his hand, "On my honor, your honor."

The two quietly laughed, trying not to wake the little girl.

Will pulled his son out of bed and was momentarily shocked to find the top of Charlie's head even with his eyes. He was growing up so fast. "You're the man of the house while I'm away."

The boy threw his arms around Will's neck, and said, "I wish to everything, Pa, that you'd take me with you. There's boys younger 'n me serving as musicians in some of the militia companies."

Will returned the hug, "Don't be in too much of a hurry to grow up. Soon enough you'll have all the duties of being a man, and time to read books like *Ivanhoe* will be harder to find."

Charlie stepped back, squared his shoulders and threw Will a mock salute, "Sir, yes, sir." But his smile was wistful. To a fourteen-year-old, it seemed as though the entire nation was going to war, and he was stuck at home. Will hid a smile. He remembered being that age. Too old to be a child yet too young to be a man. Will clicked his heels together and returned the salute.

Charlie lay back down and with a final wave, Will closed the door. He returned to his bedroom and found Becky sitting in a rocking chair next to the crib. She was gently rocking little David. Will looked into the crib and watched his infant son losing a battle to stay awake as his bed swayed back and forth.

Finally, Becky stood and stepped into his embrace, molding herself to his body. Will wrapped his arms around her and pulled her close, she lifted her head, her hungry lips seeking his. When the kiss ended, Becky whispered, "I promised myself I wouldn't shed any more tears, and I won't. But heavens, Will, I'm going to miss you worse than I can imagine."

Will's throat was dry. Despite the duty he had accepted as commander of the Texian army, at that moment, he wanted nothing more than to stay home with his family. When he mentioned that to Becky she playfully slapped his chest, "It's my charms, us Crockett women make ourselves so irresistible that we can scarcely keep our husbands at home."

Will was about to protest, but the glimmer in her eye gave lie to the playful words. She added, "When I married you, General William Travis, I knew that you were a huckleberry above a persimmon. I am the luckiest woman in Texas. I know when you leave out that door, it's not just duty to Texas, but love for your family, your country, and your God, that helps you to do your duty."

Will swallowed any response; none was needed. She followed him into the house's central room and helped him buckle on his sword, then took his black slouch hat from its hook. She set it on his head, and cocked it slightly, giving him a jaunty appearance. She hustled him out the door, and into the cool, predawn air.

He stood on the front lawn, underneath the boughs of a live oak. Instinctively, he knew she was standing in the doorway. The desire to turn around and look back at her was powerful, nearly overwhelming. But he feared if he gave in, he would run back to her arms and to hell with duty and honor.

With every ounce of effort and self-control he possessed, Will put one foot in front of the other. With each passing step, the next became easier until he turned the corner. He exhaled, realizing he'd been holding his breath. With growing confidence, as his feet took him in the direction of the fort, he knew the best way back to Becky and the children was through Mexico.

Chapter 8

Two men pulled on their oars, propelling the skiff across the Rio Grande's murky water. Three more were crowded in the belly of the boat. Jack Hays cast a worrying glance at the sky. Breaks in the clouds increased visibility as the moonlight poked through. *"A little moonlight for us ain't so bad, but what works for us just as easily could work against us,"* he thought. The bow crunched softly into the soil on the river's southern shore. He and the other men leapt from the small boat, rifles in hand. With an efficiency born of practice, they used branches and cuttings from nearby trees to mask the boat from casual eyes.

Hays caught a cautious look from the Rifle team leader, "Sir, are you sure you don't want to wait here? Me and the boys will reconnoiter and let you know what we find."

Matching the other's low pitch, Hays shot back, "Don't start on me now, Sergeant. Might as well see for myself what Almonte's choir boys have been up to, and my eyes are just as good as yours." Without a backwards glance, he started walking through the stand of cottonwood trees, "Let's go."

They had landed a few miles upriver from the ford at Laredo. Hays was betting that Almonte's soldados would be watching any potential low water crossing. They had picked the deepest stretch of river they could find to cross. As they headed south from the river, apart from their footfalls, the night was quiet.

Once Hays and his team reached their intended location, the night clouds had been driven off by the glimmer of sunlight coming from the east. Less than a mile separated them from the little town of Nuevo Laredo. Were it not for the dense copse of mesquite trees, Hays would have felt naked. He chuckled quietly, *"No, without these mesquites, our asses would be as bare as a newborn baby."*

Twigs from the nearby mesquites were tied to their clothing, adding to the natural camouflage provided by their butternut jackets as they settled in to observe the Mexican fortifications. Hays had chosen the spot well, too far away for the typical *soldado* to come foraging for wood, but close enough that a man with a pair of the new model binoculars could see plenty of details more than a mile away.

Hays pulled a notebook from a jacket pocket, and with the team's sergeant acting as a spotter, began making notes.

The sun was high overhead, when the sergeant handed the glasses to Hays and pointed to the south, "Take a gander, sir."

When Hays put the glasses to his eyes, the scene leapt into view. A score of carts pulled by oxen were slowly moving toward the town and entrenchments. Focusing on the convoy, Hays figured the carts were bringing food to the army. In 1836 Hays had missed the battles of the Rio Grande and Nueces, serving at that time under Sam Houston, but he recalled how poorly supplied the dictator's army had been. The strategy then had been to live off the land, and sack San Antonio of the needed foodstuffs. Northern Mexico along the Rio Grande was simply too sparsely populated to allow the Mexican army to forage for supplies. It looked to Hays that General Almonte was doing everything he could to keep his army supplied.

Throughout the afternoon, Hays had watched cavalry detachments patrolling along the road to the south. Maps obtained by the Texian army showed the road connected the town with Monterrey, the largest city in northern Mexico, and according to General Travis, the objective of the spring campaign.

Later, as the sun moved below the western horizon, Hays checked his notebook. He had drawn diagrams of the trenches on the Mexican army's left flank, including much of their artillery. He had identified the standards for ten regiments. He hoped a similar team, scouting the Mexican army's right flank would complete the picture.

He slipped the binoculars into a leather case and muttered, "First we've got to get back to the boat."

"Sorry, Major, what was that?" the sergeant asked.

"Nothing. As soon as that glow disappears from the sky, let's get out of here."

There were fewer clouds in the sky than the previous night. But the quarter moon climbing into the night sky bathed the open ground in a soft glow. Hays didn't like it. A couple of miles separated them from their skiff. If they should be spotted by a Mexican cavalry patrol, those lancers could cut them to ribbons. The thought sent shivers along his spine, and he reached down to his belt, feeling reassured by the two pistols he carried.

Even twilight had faded from the sky before Hays motioned for his team to move out. The Sergeant took lead, and each rifleman followed, leaving a gap of several yards between them. When the last of the other men followed, Hays waited a few seconds, until the Ranger was nearly thirty feet ahead of him, then followed behind.

Two miles, more than thirty-five hundred yards, were between them and their goal. Despite the desertlike conditions of the area, the ground between them and the Rio Grande was still rife with vegetation, ranging from the hardy prickly pear cactus to mighty Cyprus trees. The five men flitted from the copse of mesquite trees to a grove of cottonwoods, and from there through a maze of cacti.

While the smell from the river was never far removed, as they approached the skiff, the earthy smell of sediment confirmed they were approaching their goal.

Between one stretch of cover and another was an open field, sprinkled with scrub brush and a few cactus plants. Hays had just stepped away from cover, when he heard the jingling of saddles nearby. A voice called out in Spanish, "*Hey you, stop!*"

The rifleman in front of him turned and saw riders. He threw his rifle to his shoulder and fired, further shattering the stillness of the night. Rather than standing his ground and reloading, he bolted after the Ranger ahead of him.

When it was clear the horsemen had spotted only one of the riflemen, Hays pulled both of his revolvers and waited. His patience was rewarded when four horsemen loomed out of the darkness, their lances down, racing after the retreating Ranger.

Hays' dander was up, and as the lancers showed him their backs as they galloped after the Ranger, he raised the pistol in his right hand and pulled the hammer back as he sighted on the closest lancer and fired. *"Nothing! Shit!"* he fired twice more and saw the horseman drop the lance as he slid off the horse. While one of the lancers raced after the other Ranger, the other two turned when they heard Hays' shots.

The quarter moon bathed the field in a faint light, but it was more than enough to see the two horsemen as they dug their heels into their mounts' flanks and lowered their lances.

Hays had seen a few of his Rangers who, with plenty of practice, had become proficient trick shooters with their revolvers. Had even seen a few men who could use two pistols at the same time to hit separate targets. Such displays were, in Hays estimation, gimmicks, not something to be attempted under normal conditions. Briefly, he thought it was something a dime novelist would have someone like "Davy" Crockett do in one of those adventure books boys liked to read.

That didn't stop him from raising the second pistol and as the lancers raced toward him, he pulled both triggers as quickly as he could thumb back the hammers. One shot, two shots, and one of the lancers' heads snapped back and he tumbled from his mount. Three, four and on the fifth shot, the second lancer dropped his lance as he grabbed his shoulder. He sawed on the reins, wheeling his horse away from Hays. Before the Ranger Major could decide if he would fire at an injured man's back, a loud boom echoed in the night, and he saw dark mist spray from the lancer's back then watched as he leaned forward, and kept going, until he spilled out of his saddle, landing with a heavy thud.

On the far side of the field the last lancer had been dismounted. Hays ran across the open ground, dodging cactus and thorn bushes. He found three of his men huddled around the Ranger who had been in front of him. The rifleman was prone on the ground, with the tip of a lance piercing his shoulder. "Major, we can carry Gus back to the boat. But the one what did this to him is over there." The sergeant pointed a short distance away, where a body lay on the ground.

"Y'all get on back to the boat. I'll take a gander at the Mexican."

As the three men lifted their teammate and carried him toward their skiff, Hays walked over to the injured lancer. The man groaned and opened his eyes, looking up at the Texian. One of his men had hit the lancer. Hays pursed his lips, eying the wound to the stomach. *"Not even Doc Smith could save him."*

A glance in the direction from which they had come brought only silence. Surely the gunfire would bring other *soldados* to investigate. *"Best to let them find the poor bastard. They can deal with him."*

Hays stood and started after his men. When he reached the tree line, the injured man cried, *"Dios mio! No me abandones!"*

Hays turned, looking back at the figure lying in the field. After the mayhem of the previous few minutes, the silence was unnerving. He swore under his breath and strode back across the field, where he stared at the injured man.

Tears were streaming down the lancer's face as Hays knelt beside him, taking in his pained features. A strong odor filled Hays' nostrils, confirming the bullet had torn the intestines. Left alone in the clearing, how long the Lancer would linger, he couldn't say. The only certainty was the lancer would suffer until he bled out.

In poor Spanish, Hays said, "You will die from the wound. Do you understand?"

The lancer nodded as he clutched at his stomach. *"Dispárame!"*

As a chillness settled over Hays. He lifted one of the revolvers and pointed it at the lancer's head. *"Lo siento."*

He squeezed the trigger, turned, and walked away without a backwards glance.

Captain Bill Sherman rode at the head of his battery, thirty-six horses kicked up a lot of dust, and he had decided long before it was better to ride ahead of the battery than to eat its dust. He glanced behind and his heart swelled with pride, watching his men riding to war. Even though it had been more than six months since he had reported to the Alamo, he recalled his meeting with General Travis like it was yesterday.

Uniforms had been scarce, the Texian army had outgrown its supply system. He hadn't been at the Alamo more than a day when he was ordered to report to the general's office. Rather than go in civilian clothing, he had donned his old blue United States Army uniform to meet with General Travis and Lt. Colonel Carry, commander of the Texian artillery.

When he had arrived, he found lying on the general's desk a heavy, bronze tube. Travis sat behind his desk, while Carry leaned against the back wall. Bill managed to stand at attention and give a salute his West Point instructors would have been proud of, but his eyes kept darting to the weapon.

General Travis had returned the salute then waved him into a chair. "I imagine you've seen one of these before, Captain Sherman."

Bill had nodded, "Looks like a copy of the new mountain howitzers the US army has been working on, sir."

"Not a copy. It's the real McCoy. Texas has acquired six of these beauties. What do you think?"

The smooth bronze barrel reflected his image faintly as he eyed the weapon again. Bill wasn't sure who McCoy was or why he was real, but it couldn't be denied, the bronze barrel was a work of engineering marvel. "Well, sir, she's pretty to look at, but she's an experimental weapon. While the US has manufactured a few of them, they haven't seen combat yet."

The general tilted his head back and laughed. "If you haven't figured it out yet, Captain, this whole army is experimental, with experimental weapons, using experimental tactics. That's why I'm glad that a young man like yourself volunteered. Old men like me have a hard time adapting to new ways of thinking, and a brash, young officer like you ought to have a much easier time adapting than some old goat. What do you say, are you game to work with these experimental guns?"

Thinking back on the conversation still brought a grin to Bill' face. The general was maybe thirty-five years old, and if he chose to believe the rumors, the army's rifle and the pistol had come from him, too. There was no doubt, the tactics used by the infantry were his. After all, the manual had Travis' name on it.

Since then, forming and training his battery was nearly the only thing for which Bill had time. Even though the barrels were less than five hundred pounds and could have been disassembled from their carriage and carried on the back of a horse or pack mule, Bill had opted for a more conventional carriage and caisson configuration. This allowed the battery to take plenty of ammunition into combat, but more than that, each gun crew could ride into battle. Up to six men could ride the team of horses which hauled the guns. Two more could sit on the ammunition caisson and two more on either side of the gun barrel. If the situation arose where he needed to disassemble the guns, he could still do so, and haul the parts on mules.

During war games conducted over the Texas winter, Bill had coined the term, flying artillery, to describe his battery. They could race across a battlefield and position their field pieces where they could do the most good. His men could unlimber the guns and have them in action in only a couple of minutes. The other batteries, some of which were under the command of other American artillery officers, were nearly as well trained as his own battery.

Now, they were but a couple of days away from Laredo and Bill looked forward to taking all the practice of the past half-year and applying it. He was confident not only that his men would perform well, but the guns would meet General Travis' high expectations.

6 April 1843

DOWN MEXICO WAY

General Almonte swatted at a fly as he read from the pile of reports which threatened to upend the fragile camp table. The walls of the tent had been rolled up, letting a faint breeze through, rustling the pages on the table. A small, model cannon cast of brass served duty as a paperweight, keeping the unruly sheets from falling to the dusty ground.

The present report was the most troubling. Four lancers from the Santa Anna cavalry regiment had been found dead near the Rio Bravo. The report was a few days old, but even after expanding the number of patrols along the southern banks of the river, there were few hints about what had befallen the hapless horsemen.

That it was the Texians, there was no doubt, but the soldiers across the river in the fort had only strayed from their defenses to add to the trenchworks north of town. Reports from loyal citizens still in Laredo had told of a mounted company of Rangers operating across the river.

He had also received another report about a raid farther to the northwest, several days away. That one had all the markings of an Apache raid. The usual gristly trophies were removed before the warriors had escaped back into Texas controlled territory. He wondered if the Texians had prevailed upon the Apache to raid into Mexico as part of the war.

No, as close as this one had been to Nuevo Laredo, far better that this was the handiwork of the Rangers. The long running feud between Mexico and her rebellious northern province had bred a level of hatred between the two that had the potential of turning this campaign particularly ugly. But his soldiers feared the Apache almost as much as they feared the dreaded Comanche.

He set the report down and eyed the stack on his desk, trying to decide which one to look at next, when his attention was drawn to the sound of a pair of boots pounding across the hard-packed dirt outside his tent. He looked up when one of his orderlies stumbled to a stop before the table. "General, sir, the Texian army is arriving!"

Any thought of reports was forgotten; he followed the orderly from the tent, grabbing his spyglass as they went. His headquarters was on the obverse side of the main line of fortifications. To reach the top of the trench works was simply a matter of climbing a hill. When they reached the top, he was able to see north several miles. Sure enough, a cloud of dust covered the San Antonio Road, north of Laredo.

He raised his spyglass to his eye and focused on the dust cloud. Cavalry were coming down the road. The blue, white, and red lone star banner floated in the breeze, carried by the lead elements. Almonte strained to make out individual soldiers as cavalry filled up the road bed. Their mud-colored uniforms were the devil to see at this distance.

Almonte had long believed armies needed distinctive uniforms so one could easily tell friend from foe. When two armies stood and blazed away at each other, the space between became choked with smoke from gunpowder. The Mexican army's distinctive blue and red uniforms made it easier for an officer to direct his men in battle. As he stared at the drably colored uniforms worn by the Texians, it was clear General Travis put little stock in colorful uniforms.

Almonte had read Travis' manual. More so, he had trained his own *Cazadores* using a copy he personally translated. Travis wasn't worried about being able to see his men as they marched into battle. His tactics made that clear. He was more concerned with making his men harder for an enemy to see.

At least a battalion of cavalry had materialized out of the hazy dust cloud. They veered off the road and maneuvered cross-country. An infantry battalion came into view, replacing the cavalry in the spyglass's view. They wore the same mud-colored jackets. He stared as hundreds of men, in columns of four, marched toward Laredo. Each battalion carried their own lone star battle flag. After seeing more than two thousand soldiers materialize from the dust cloud, Almonte wondered how many men Travis had been able to raise. For a small country with fewer than two hundred thousand souls, he had been skeptical of reports that Travis had truly raised six thousand from Texas' rural population.

Ten minutes had passed as he watched the infantry march into view. Four regimental flags meant an entire brigade. With long experience estimating troop strength, Almonte figured the Texian infantry brigade numbered close to twenty-seven hundred men. Not even when Woll's army was pushed back had General Johnston brought anywhere close to that many men into battle.

And the Texian army continued to pour down the Laredo Road. Another cavalry battalion crested a ridge in the distance, this time, appearing on the right flank of the approaching army. Almonte raised an eyebrow. The last intelligence received implied Texas had but one regular cavalry battalion.

A second infantry brigade was now marching into view. The lead battalion was the first unit he had seen wearing something other than a mud colored uniform.

These were uniformed in blue jackets and pants. No doubt these were the naval infantry, the Marines, who were serving far away from their ships. They marched under the same lone star flag. No unique banner distinguished the service branches. He made note of yet another of Travis' departures from tradition. As the next battalion appeared behind the Marines, Almonte shrugged. What was one more departure? He was convinced Travis was determined to tear up the rule book.

More than ten minutes had passed since the Marines had appeared on the road, and as best as he could tell, the entire five battalions of Texas' 2nd brigade were nearing Laredo. There were perhaps as many as twenty-eight hundred men in this brigade.

Behind the infantry came a battery of guns drawn by teams of horses. Something was off when he saw them. He eyed them again through the spyglass and realized all the men in the battery were riding horseback on the teams pulling the guns. That was unexpected. One battery, followed by another, and another. Until he counted thirty-six horse-drawn guns. Almonte frowned. He had thought his thirty field pieces would outmatch whatever Texas managed to scrape together. Again, his assumption was wrong.

He slammed shut the telescoping spyglass and frowned. "Of course, no plan survives contact with the enemy." He knew that. But in just showing up on the Laredo plain, Travis was bringing his own rule book.

Early April 1843

Dick Gatling set the brake before climbing down from the wagon. A glance to the east showed nothing more than the rolling hill country. Austin was a half-day's ride behind him. Could he have stayed in town to test the invention? He wasn't sure.

More importantly, he was playing with fire. If he were caught, it could mean his job. As the lone patent clerk in Texas, under normal circumstances, he considered his job secure. But, taking the details from a patent his office had received, and attempting to replicate it, could be seen as stepping over the line. After all, his job was to acknowledge and protect the rights of inventors.

He removed the tarpaulin from the wagon bed and dragged the long, heavy box from the bed, and lowered the end to the ground. He grabbed the rope handles from the end still resting on the wagon's tailgate and gently lowered the other end of the box.

He grabbed a crowbar and began prying open the box as he muttered, "It's not stealing it. I just want to see if Coston's idea really works."

As the nails squealed as they were wrenched from the box, Gatling thought back to the day he was sitting at his desk in the building housing the Treasury Department. The north wind rattled the window pane and he tied the scarf around his neck to keep warm. It seemed almost daily he received correspondence from inventors from the United States, filing the paperwork to have their inventions registered in Texas.

When he had unfolded the application from Benjamin Coston, he perused it. Coston's application was for a naval flare. As Gatling read, he realized the potential went far beyond using flares at sea to signal at night.

He had read accounts of Dickinson's stand at the Alamo the previous year and about General Woll's predawn assault. Had the defenders had flares, they would have been able to launch them and see the enemy before the attack. It might not have made a difference, Gatling conceded. However, it might have. It was that "however" that led the young inventor, who ran Texas' patent office, to stand alone, next to a box of flares he had built using Coston's design, in the Texas hill country.

He pulled the heavy, iron pipe from the box and used a small shovel to dig a hole. He filled it back in once he placed the pipe at the base of the hole. He eyed the long, thin stems atop which sat the flares.

As he waited for the sun to go down, he figured if the test was successful, he would reach out to Coston and request a license for permission to manufacture the flares. Making the flares hadn't been difficult. It was tedious work making them according to the patent application's specifications, because each had been made by hand.

He looked to the west and, as the light retreated from the sky, he pulled a matchbox from his pocket and lit a match. He leaned in toward the flare and lit the fuse. He stepped away to the other side of the wagon and waited.

A few seconds later, with a whoosh, the flare shot into the night's sky, angling away from him. A couple of hundred feet above, a dazzling red light turned the ground below into something Gatling would have imagined from Dante's *Inferno* as the ground was bathed in an eerie red glow.

Instead of plunging back to earth, the red glowing flare drifted across the sky until, spent, it went dark. Had anyone seen him, they would have thought Gatling had lost his mind as he danced across the prairie. "The flare may be all of Mr. Coston's design, but thank you Leonardo Da Vinci for your idea of a parachute." There was no one to hear him, but that didn't keep Gatling from laughing as he lit the second flare.

Chapter 9

7 April 1843

The mountain howitzer's stubby barrel was more than two feet shorter than the 6-pounders which made up the majority of Texas' field artillery. But Bill Sherman didn't care. His guns could, if the demands of the campaign required it, be carried nearly anywhere the army required. *"Carry them over a mountain pass? No problem. I'll get it done."* Sure, most of the artillery could throw their shells upwards of a mile, and his battery's range was only a little more than half of that.

The young captain stood beside the stubby bronze barrel, his hand affectionately resting on it. Most of the army's guns were designed to fire their projectiles at a nearly flat trajectory. But his guns could lob shells over and behind the enemy's position. Soon enough, he would know if the last six months' training had paid off.

Behind the line of guns, the army of Texas was encamped. On one side of the San Antonio Road Johnston's brigade was spread out across the South Texas prairie, and on the other was McCulloch's brigade, respectively the army's 1st and 2nd brigades. Tents covered the ground in a blizzard of white canvas. In the short time in which Bill had served in the United States army before coming to Texas, he had never seen so many soldiers as had assembled behind him. More than six thousand men were encamped across the prairie.

More than once he had wondered how the Republic's government was managing to keep so many men in the field. It had to be horribly expensive. Between the guns, carriages, caissons, and horses, Texas must have spent several thousand dollars just for his battery, and that was before a single soldier received his pay. And there were another five batteries with the army in addition to his. He shook his head. How President Zavala and congress were juggling the bills was definitely above his paygrade. But since he arrived in Texas the previous year, the army's payroll had been regular as clockwork.

From across the river a motion caught his eye. A tiny, blue-clad figure had climbed above the earthen fortifications south of the Mexican town and waved a banner of some kind. It must have been a signal. A moment later dozens of guns opened fire. Bill was tempted to retrieve his new model field glasses to better see where the guns were firing, but as he watched, plumes of earth were flying into the air along Fort Moses Austin's southern ramparts, he could see where the shot and shell were landing without the aid of field glasses.

From the fort his attention was drawn to the town of Laredo, where he could see buildings crumbling under the relentless bombardment. Bill hoped the citizens of the small town had already evacuated. A company of Rangers was still in town. They were there in the event that the Mexicans attempted to cross at the ford, to supplement the six companies of infantry stationed in and around the fort.

Some of the rounds thrown into town were shells, and the resulting explosions set wooden structures afire. From the town, Bill saw more than a half-dozen riders galloping away. Each was guiding a string of mounts behind him.

As more buildings in town burned, a thin line of men in their butternut uniforms fell back. Bill was only passingly familiar with the small unit tactics General Travis had trained the army to use, but he recognized small teams of four men each, acting in concert with each other, as the small company retreated toward a trench extending from the earthen fort. Bill figured it had been too dangerous in town for the Rangers to hold there, when most of the buildings had either been knocked flat by Mexican solid shot or were raging infernos.

As Laredo burned, the whole of the Mexican artillery shifted their fire to the fort's earthen ramparts. Occasionally, shells would detonate over the fort, sending a hail of shrapnel raining down on the men inside. He wondered if they had taken the time to build bunkers protecting against such danger.

A noise behind him brought Bill from his reverie of watching the barrage fall on the Texian fort, and he turned and saw Lt. Colonel Carey's adjutant, Lieutenant Orion Wells riding toward his battery. When the officer arrived, he sketched a hurried salute before handing Bill a folded piece of paper. Bill had barely unfolded it before Wells was already kicking his horse into a gallop, racing toward the next battery.

Bill scanned the note. Every battery was to open fire at the bottom of the hour. A hurried look at his pocket watch showed he had less than five minutes to prepare. Fortunately, the guns had been positioned in a firing line when deployed earlier in the morning, with an ammunition chest set up around twenty feet to the rear of each gun. Bill shouted orders and his men leapt into action, as gunpowder charges were rammed down bronze tubes, followed quickly by shells with fuses set for six hundred yards.

Glancing at his watch, he saw his men had finished loading their guns in about a minute. They had done it faster in timed exercises during training. He made note of it.

When the long hand reached the six on his pocket watch, Bill stepped behind the battery and yelled, "Number one gun, fire!"

On his order, the entire battery fired, one gun after another, like a rolling thunder across the prairie. As soon as the number one gun fired, the gunner shouted, "Load!" and one of the loaders stepped to the mouth of the gun and sponged out the barrel. Steam hissed as he retracted the rammer. Others sprang into action in turn, until the gun was reloaded.

Bill was holding his pocket watch, and when the number one gun was ready to fire, he made note. Just under a minute. Not a record, but it was acceptable. He strode back and forth, behind the battery, directing the gunners to targets along the fortified hill south of the river. At one point, he glanced into the sky. The sun was directly overhead. It was going to be a long day.

"What I would give to trade places with Esteban," the young officer thought as he peered over the edge of

the trench. The ground before him was pockmarked and gouged from the shot and shell the Texian artillery had thrown at their counterparts in the Mexican artillery the previous day. Had the enemy limited their response to just the Army of the North's artillery, the ground before his trench wouldn't have been turned into a pockmarked wasteland.

He glanced down the hill, into what remained of Nuevo Laredo. Not even the church had been spared. Despite the thick adobe bricks, solid shot had pulverized walls and even toppled the church's bell tower. Despite his youth, Javier Morales tried to remain philosophical. The town of Laredo was in even worse shape as tendrils of smoke still climbed into the sky nearly a day after Mexican artillery had turned it to kindling.

Even now, the Texians occasionally fired one of their guns at the Mexican lines. The trench on the slope above the remains of Nuevo Laredo was a favorite target. The young lieutenant ducked below the earthen lip when he saw the puff of smoke a half-mile away. The round shot churned the ground below the trench. He shook his head and wondered how a courier from Mexico City had been placed in command of a platoon of *Cazadores*, in one of General Almonte's light infantry companies.

He had arrived in Nuevo Laredo late in the spring the previous year. He had expected to deliver his dispatches then start the long, grueling ride back through Tamaulipas, to Vera Cruz. He was beyond shocked when General Vasquez informed him that he was being reassigned to the Army of the North. It hadn't been too bad. He had been quick to adapt to carrying messages between the encampment along the Rio Bravo del Norte and the general's headquarters in Monterrey.

As another shot tore into the ground before the trench, he ducked down even further. He would have been happy to have continued carrying messages. But following General Vasquez's unfortunate death in February, General Almonte transferred him to the *Cazadores* regiments formed from the light infantry companies previously assigned to each of the army's infantry regiments. Almonte had unusual ideas about how to use the army's rifle armed *Cazadores*. That was how Lieutenant Javier Morales had gone from courier to commander of a platoon of riflemen. Officers learned how to use the British Baker rifles, the same as their soldiers. And what Morales found even more unusual, he had been using a Spanish translation of the enemy general's manual to drill his riflemen.

"Lieutenant, look!" one of his riflemen called out. Morales stood and looked over the edge of the trench. Something was happening on the Texian side of the river. Passing through the line of artillery pieces, a thin line of infantry was deploying.

As he watched the long, thin line of men in mud-colored uniforms approach in their dispersed, open order, everything in the manual he had read made sense. He focused on a small group that was part of the larger advance, and sure enough, he saw the same teams of four he had been training his own riflemen to become. As he studied the slow advance, he saw that each rifle team was part of a larger squad, which was part of an even larger platoon. He drew his focus out, and saw the platoons were part of their companies. It looked like they were sending only a small part of a regiment forward.

"To arms, boys!" Morales' own captain called out. His own two dozen men formed on either side of him, resting their rifles on the edge of the trench, waiting. He had heard the new model rifles the Texians carried could shoot further than four hundred yards. That was a concern. The Baker rifle was designed to be accurate out to two hundred yards. Although a few of his men had shown they could hit a target at ranges of three hundred yards or more.

Soon, he would see how well his men would perform. Once the Texian riflemen were inside three hundred yards of the river, he watched them use whatever cover they could find even as they advanced. Moments later wisps of smoke appeared. Reflexively, Morales ducked. Like a deadly rain, bullets began to pepper the dirt piled in front of the trench. Down the line, he saw a *Cazadore* tumble to the ground, struck in the head.

Without waiting for the captain's order, Morales cried out, "Aimed fire, boys!"

The battle joined, he tried to shake off his anxiety, and unslung his rifle. He leaned against the earthen wall, pointed his rifle downrange and fired at a flash of light on the edge of the ruins of Laredo. As his men fell into a routine of loading, aiming, and firing, he watched the Texians infiltrate the ruins. Their teamwork kept a steady, yet deadly rain on the trenches. A wailing yelp came from nearby and Morales tore his eyes away from the Texians and found one of his men clutching at his head. Rivulets of blood seeped through his fingers, where he grasped the side of his head.

When the *soldado* pulled his hand away, Morales saw the top of his ear had been torn off. As he pushed the injured man toward the communication trench running between the forward line and the main fortifications at the top of the hill, he marveled at how much blood could leak from a torn ear. But at least the wound wasn't fatal, and while inexperienced, Morales was conscientious about the well-being of his men.

When he returned to the men along the firing line, several of the riflemen were crowded around one of his corporals. The NCO was holding his rifle and wearing a grin. One of the riflemen said, "Lieutenant, Gomez just got one of 'em. Hit 'em at over three hundred yards!"

Morales glanced over the wall and saw the steady flashing of rifles. "Alright, Corporal, show me it wasn't just a lucky shot."

The corporal traded rifles with one of his teammates. He hugged the side of the trench, keeping a low profile and aimed at a target in the ruins below. He fired the rifle and the men around him cheered and pounded him on the back. Another butternut-uniformed soldier had fallen.

Watching the corporal fire at the enemy below gave Morales an idea. "The best marksman from each rifle team shoots, everyone else reloads!" When he gave the order, he had no idea he was echoing the tactics used by the Texians seven years before, when they fought another battle on the Rio Grande.

With only six men firing down on the Texians, the volume of fire coming from his section of the trench dropped off, but the results below were telling. Before, for every few hundred rounds an enemy might have been hit. Now, he saw several men sprawled below, hit by his best marksmen.

When the captain came over to see how his platoon was performing, he spread the news to the other platoon, and they adopted a single shooter per rifle team, too. Like a slow fuse burning across the ground, the change in tactics spread across the entire regiment of *Cazadores*.

After an hour of taking the punishment meted out by the rifle-armed light infantry, the Texians withdrew. Their first effort to test the Mexican line had been turned back.

Will lowered the binoculars from his eyes after watching the soldiers slowing pulling back from the town's shattered remains. He had ordered part of the 1st Infantry forward into the ruins of Laredo. The idea had been to establish a position near the ford where his riflemen could dominate the crossing. Against the musket-armed *soldados* he thought it a solid strategy. The use of the rifle-armed *Cazadores* in the Mexican forward trenches meant a different strategy was needed.

Will slammed his fist into the earthen berm. *"Damn Almonte."* The expectation had been they would be facing General Vasquez. His intelligence on Vasquez had showed a more traditionally minded general. While his plans for the invasion had been to be as flexible as possible, he had expected to meet the Mexican army in an open battle. Defeating Vasquez, sweeping his army aside, and racing toward Monterrey had been a sound idea when he and his officers began planning the campaign months earlier.

Who could have anticipated that Vasquez' death would result in such a radical departure by the Mexican army? Putting trench works midway up the hill south of the ford had been smart. No other low-water crossings were as advantageous as the one at Laredo, at least not within a couple of days' march. Forcing the crossing would have been an unpleasant experience, just facing the Mexican line regiments armed with their muskets but throwing their entire rifle-armed light infantry into their forward trenches was a stroke of brilliance. They had the range to make things interesting for his men before they could get to the ford.

Behind him, he heard someone clearing his throat. Still clenching his fist, Will turned and looked at the men crowding around the small camp table underneath the canvas pavilion. A. Sidney Johnston was crowded next to Ben McCulloch. They commanded the army's two infantry brigades. Juan Seguin sat across the table from them. He commanded the army's three battalions of mounted troops. Lt. Colonel William Carey, artillery commander, stood between the generals, studying the map on the table. The last officer present was Lt. Colonel Elliott West, commander of the Marine battalion attached to the 2nd brigade.

Seeing Will looking at him, Johnston spoke first. "We lost three men in the ruins, along with another seven wounded before pulling back from the town, General. Hadn't expected to run into hundreds of their riflemen."

Will took the one empty chair next to the table and sat. He scanned the map of Laredo and the surrounding land. "Yeah, Almonte isn't singing out of Santa Anna's hymnal anymore."

There was chuckling around the room. "And here I thought we had left the witty comments of President Crockett behind us," Juan Seguin was laughing as he continued, "but General, you've spent entirely too much time picking up your father-in-law's knack for turning a phrase."

"Heaven help y'all If that's the case." Will rejoined before he turned serious, "No, Almonte appears to be taking a page from our hymnal. Putting his riflemen along a front closest to the ford will require we change our strategy."

He turned to Seguin, "What about other fords nearby?"

The cavalry officer ran his fingers along the stubble of his chin, his face wore an uncharacteristic frown. "While there are a few other fords within a day's march, they don't suit our needs as well as the ford here. Also, Almonte's cavalry are watching them like hawks."

Former commander of the Texas militia, now the 2nd brigade's senior officer, McCulloch said, "Couldn't we swing a brigade down to one of those fords and force a crossing there? Catch Almonte's flank."

Using his finger, Seguin pointed at the nearest ford, south of Laredo. "In addition to scouting out the other possible points across the river, we've had some of our Rangers operating behind the Mexican lines over the past few weeks. Major Hays believes Almonte would use his cavalry to slow our advance while his main army here disengages and withdraws south. We don't have the certitude we'd like, but Hays believes that Almonte is preparing a second fortified position much further south and he'll withdraw here if he thinks he's being flanked."

"Then we'd smash them on the desert between here and Monterrey." McCulloch pounded the table, emphasizing each of his words.

Will shook his head. "Perhaps, perhaps not. Where is the most likely spot between here and Monterrey for Almonte to set up more fortifications, Juan?"

The map on the table, drawn by army cartographers, was centered on Laredo and showed only a few miles in any direction. "Around a hundred miles south, after crossing the southern reaches of the Chihuahuan desert, we'll come to the little town of Candela. It's nothing to look at, but just south of the town is a natural choke point.

The road passes between two mountain ranges. That valley might be a mile wide at its narrowest point. But if Almonte is planning a second set of defenses there, whichever battalion draws the short straw will pay the butcher's bill pushing them off that line."

Will's focus was still on the map. "Solid points. If Almonte can't draw us into attacking here, he just pulls back and forces us to fight him where there aren't any choices. He bleeds us either way. We've been pretty good at creating tactical situations forcing Mexico to assault our positions. Now the shoe is on the other foot, and I don't mind saying, it pinches like hell."

He studied the map before continuing. "I'd rather fight Almonte here, where we have a chance, however slim, of decisively defeating him and destroying a sizable portion of his army. If we are forced to fight him in mountain passes, the war may drag out longer than we can afford. Even so, whoever we send in first will pay our pound of flesh."

"Sir, my men can do it." Will looked up, wondering who had spoken. Standing behind the general officers, was Lt. Colonel West. "Give us an artillery barrage until we're on the Mexican side of the river and a couple of other battalions to support our flanks, and my boys will take those entrenchments away from the Mexicans."

West's Marines were, if Will was honest with himself, some of the best fighting men in the army. But there were only six companies totaling a little more than three hundred fifty men. Will eyed McCulloch. There were six companies of the 2nd Infantry garrisoning the fort at the bend in the Rio Grande. They were scarcely more than a rock's throw away from the ford, and they were part of

Ben McCulloch's brigade. "What about Colonel Hodgen's men, Ben?"

McCulloch stroked his well-trimmed beard as he considered the proposal. "It could work. They could anchor the Marines' right flank. What about the Regulars from the 1st on the left flank?"

Johnston offered a thin smile. "My boys would like another crack at those *Cazadores*. With your permission, General Travis, I'd also like to deploy the 4th Infantry close enough to provide support."

Will watched the officers parade out from the pavilion later, in a hurry to make whatever plans were necessary for the next morning. It was one of the oldest maxims that no plan survives contact with an enemy, but it galled him more than he was willing to admit to throw out the playbook before they had even reached the southern shore.

Chapter 10

8 April 1843

The ground beneath him shook Lieutenant Javier Morales awake. Shells exploded over the trenchworks. As he dove into a shelter dug into the rocky ground, he heard the deadly patter of shell fragments raining on the thick wooden roof. It was still too dark to see his pocket watch, but a look to the east showed a glow below the horizon. The sun would be up shortly.

Not everyone had been quick enough to seek shelter and he heard the plaintive cry of one of his riflemen. He swore as he stared into the dark trench. Around him, several of his *Cazadores* crowded under the shelter. He turned to order one of them to go and fetch the injured man, but then saw terror in their eyes. The firefight the previous day, and now the bombardment, were taking their toll on these peasants turned soldiers. As the youngest son of a merchant family in the capital, the lieutenant realized it was his responsibly to set an example for the men serving under him.

Despite the steady rain of shrapnel and shell fragments above the dugout, he raced out into the trench, open to the sky above without a backwards glance. *"I should have traded places with Estevan!"* He found the wounded *soldado* cradling his leg, his rifle lay by his side. He was one of the sentries, who had been keeping an eye on the ruins of Nuevo Laredo below.

"Alright, Fernandez, let's get you out of here." Morales wrapped his arms around the wounded *soldado* and pulled him to his feet. He supported the rifleman as they raced back to the shelter, ignoring the death raining down on the Mexican trenchworks. As they reached relative safety, the other men grabbed their wounded companion and found a spot for him to lay down while one of their number looked at his injuries

The Mexican caste system dictated a man's role in the army even more than in society at large. The *soldados* under his command came from the Mestizo and native populations, nearly all of whom were peasant farmers, or would have been were it not for the conscription laws which swept them into Santa Anna's army. Morales was the youngest son of Creole parents, descendants of Canary Islanders who had immigrated to Mexico several generations earlier. There was a wide gap between the officers, who were typically of Spanish descent and the men they commanded. But when Morales came back from fetching his injured rifleman, those distinctions fell away and for a moment, they were one.

The bombardment continued as the sun climbed into the sky. A few minutes after the yellow orb bathed his world in light, Morales noticed the guns had stopped firing. He stepped out from under cover and peered over the top of the trench. A long, thin line of blue-clad men were racing across the plain east of the remains of Laredo. In their center was a Texian flag, snapping in the wind as the color sergeant carrying it raced toward the river.

Another formation of soldiers in their mud-colored uniforms was entering the town's ruins from the north. More men poured from the trenchworks which ran from the five-sided fort toward the remains of the town. From the fort, a barrage of gunfire erupted along the southern facing sides.

"To arms! They're attacking!" Morales shouted for his *Cazadores* to man their positions along the trench. Out of two dozen present at the beginning of the previous day's battle, now less than twenty were still on their feet. As Morales watched, every one of them raced to their places. He wore a feral grin, realizing he had earned their loyalty. Without waiting for orders, his riflemen used the same tactic from the previous day. One rifleman in four poured aimed fire on the Texian forces moving through the town on the other side of the river, while the other three reloaded.

He looked over the ledge. It looked like hundreds of riflemen were assembling amid the ruins of the town. A bullet buzzed by his ear and he flinched. A nervous smile flitted across his face. Ducking or flinching wouldn't matter. He knew he'd never hear the one with his name on it. Stepping away, he strode back and forth along the trench, encouraging the men to load faster.

When he reached the end of his line, there was a few feet between his platoon and the next company over. He looked and saw that east of town another battalion of riflemen were coming up behind the blue-clad Marines, who were shifting their own skirmish line into town.

The Mexican artillery had been silent until now, and with a roar from their positions on the crest of the hill, they opened fire on the Texians down below. Solid shot and canisters landed amid the foe. Buildings which were nothing more than rubble were further reduced as solid shot turned adobe to dust.

The Texian artillery opened fire again, shifting their aim. And shells began exploding above the fortified positions at the top of the hill.

Within a few seconds, two of his men were knocked from their spots as more aimed fire from below focused on the *Cazadores'* trench. One was wounded, and Morales sent the rifleman toward the rear, following the narrow communications trench. He knelt beside the other. A neat hole was centered in the *soldado's* head, and blood dribbled from it. He didn't need to see the exit wound. Blood and gray matter pooled in the trench under the body. He crossed himself then closed the *soldado's* eyes.

Reloaders stepped forward, replacing the two fallen along the firing line. Despite the continual roar of gunfire below, and the rising casualty count in the trench, the Texians appeared content to hold their position in the ruins of the town. Morales couldn't help but wonder when they would tire of absorbing the losses they surely were taking from the Mexican artillery and the aimed fire of his riflemen.

First Sergeant Julio Mejia watched the gunners loading their field pieces. From his place behind the line of cannon, the glint of the dawn sun reflecting off the bronze barrels caused him to squint. He turned away from the artillery and looked over his company. More than seventy men were ready to move forward as soon as the artillery barrage stopped. Even though the company was under the command of Captain Edwards, Mejia thought of these men as his own. As the ranking non-commissioned officer, Mejia worked with and trained them. Officers could come and go, and often that was the case as the Texian army rapidly expanded in the days following General Johnston's relief of the Alamo. The real measure of a rifle company were the sergeants and corporals that kept things working. Mejia quietly chuckled. At least that's what he told himself.

After arriving back at the Alamo with news of the massacre of his company in Reynosa the year before, he had been surprised when General Travis himself had promoted him to first sergeant. He had helped Captain Edwards rebuild the company lost the previous year.

The guns fell silent. That was the signal. The captain, with his revolver in hand, stepped ahead of the company. With a single word, "Forward," the company advanced through the guns and across the prairie. Their immediate goal was the ruins of Laredo. As he walked behind the rifle teams, spread out across a wide front, he hoped that all the training of the past year would pay off.

When the company reached the town's ruins, each of the rifle teams sought cover behind the mounds of debris as they worked their way toward the ford. The riflemen from the Mexican *Cazadores* regiments opened fire, causing Mejia to drop to the ground behind a short adobe wall. He glanced over it and saw a crucifix lying in the rubble. Crossing himself, Mejia realized he was in the remains of the church. A rifle team was on the other side of the rubble. They opened fire on the trenchworks midway up the hill, south of the river.

To his right, Mejia heard boots crunching under cinders, and turned as he saw a company from the 2nd Infantry working their way through the western side of town. They had climbed out of the trench near the fort and joined the advance.

The ruins of the town ended less than a hundred feet from the shallow ford. A couple of men were sprawled, fallen where they had been hit, when they had attempted to cross the open ground. The distance between the town and ford was a killing ground, well inside the *Cazadores'* range.

As solid shot and exploding shells rained down on the ruins, Mejia saw that whatever shelter the town offered was an illusion. He saw Captain Edwards collapse amid the rubble of the next building over and Mejia left cover as bullets threw up puffs of dirt near his feet. He dove into the rubble, landing next to the captain. The officer's leg was turning red. A long shard of glass had pierced his thigh.

"Don't bother going into the cantina, Sergeant. No drinks to be had. Hays' Rangers have cleaned the place out. All I found was this damned piece of glass."

The sergeant ignored his captain's feeble attempt at humor and pulled a clean handkerchief from his knapsack and covered the wound as he pulled the shard from the leg. Blood turned the white cloth red. "Hold this on the wound, Captain."

Edwards grabbed his arm, "Get the men moving, Sergeant. If you can't get them across the river, by God, get them out of town. This is a death trap."

Leaving his captain behind the wreck of the wall, Mejia joined the handful of men sheltering in the ruins of the church. They were from his company, and they were unnerved by the constant zinging of bullets close by as well as the choking dust from pulverized adobe. He placed his hand on the arm of one of the men, "Nothing good will come of staying here. Who will join me? I'm taking this fight to the Mexicans."

As he leapt over a fragment of the wall, he desperately wanted to look behind and see how many were following him. But whatever he felt, they needed to see his bravery. As he passed by the fallen riflemen in the no-man's land between the town and ford, with every step he braced for the bullet that would lay him low. He reached the ford and was still on his feet, although he had felt more than one bullet whiz by his ears.

As he splashed into the low-water crossing, he couldn't help himself and looked behind. There were dozens of men racing after him. He redoubled his effort, slogging through the shallows. The water never crested his belt, and in the back of his mind, he felt relief, knowing his ammunition box stayed dry.

Even as more bullets plunged into the water all about him, he let loose a primordial shout as the water fell away and his boots landed on dry ground. Behind him, he heard his men echoing the primitive yell. He raced toward the equally devastated remains of Nuevo Laredo, and ducked behind a low, crumbling adobe wall of what had once been a small house. He checked his rifle, saw it was loaded, and rose and fired at the trench in the distance. Shards of adobe rained down on him as he ducked. Bullets tore up the top of the wall where he had stood only a second before.

Along the side of the town facing the river, Mejia saw most of his company had followed him across the ford and into Mexico. But the riflemen above poured a deadly rain of lead on them. Even as his rifle teams infiltrated the broken town and returned fire on the *Cazadores*, he wondered how in the hell he was supposed to close the distance.

Within the army of the Republic field-grade officers were expected to provide their own mount. In theory, it allowed the battalion commanders to issue orders and maintain cohesion among the various companies under their control more quickly than if they were afoot. Lt. Colonel Elliot West had refused, telling General McCulloch, "I'm a Marine. I'll lead my boys on foot or not at all." The truth was, which he would never admit, he was afraid of them. Since being thrown as a young boy, he had avoided the beasts as much as possible.

He strode behind his men as they swept past the Texian field pieces. Their first objective was to secure the river bank east of town, before pivoting into the ruins and across the river. The men deployed smoothly into open-order tactics. They deployed much more smoothly this day than they had a year before when they had driven off the Mexican army under General Woll at the Alamo.

A year's training would do that to any command, he thought, but these were his men and he felt pride as the rifle teams sped across the open ground. They had crossed most of the half mile when the Mexican artillery opened fire. For the most part, the guns tore up the remains of Laredo, as they attempted to drive off the 1st Infantry, which had swept into the ruins a moment before.

But some of the guns on the heights behind Nuevo Laredo targeted his men. Before reaching his line, a shell exploded in the air, raining bits and pieces of iron over the prairie. A couple more shells plowed into the earth before they detonated, throwing dirt and iron into the air. The men picked up their pace and West found himself jogging to keep up.

When they reached the river, two of the companies extended their lines and sought shelter along the river bank and opened fire on the trenchworks halfway up the fortified hill. They would remain in place until the 4th Infantry arrived, providing suppressive fire.

Lt. Colonel West reached the company anchoring his right flank and watched as they poured into the ruins of Laredo, angling toward the ford. When he reached the water's edge, he saw a company had reached the other side of the river and were hunkered down in Nuevo Laredo's ruins. Between the edges of the two towns was a deadly no-man's land. A few bodies were floating in the river and there more were scattered on the ground.

West studied the soldiers sheltered behind the rubble on the Texas side of the river. Several companies were doing yeoman's work returning fire. The problem, as he saw it, was they were supposed to be on the other side of the river. The men tasked with storming the Mexican hill were not supposed to settle into the ruins and return fire. That job belonged to the soldiers in the fort and the 4th Infantry.

A spray of adobe dust blew into his face as a bullet slammed into the partial brick wall he stood behind. He wiped the dust from his face and saw streaks of blood on his hand. *"No, staying on this side of the river won't do."*

The company commander for the lead element of West' battalion was down. He was writhing in the dirt, hit in the abdomen. His second-in-command, a fresh-faced lieutenant, looked expectantly at West.

West snapped at the young officer, "What are you looking for, Lieutenant? You're in command of your company now. You know what to do."

Using his pistol to direct the men in his company, the young officer crouched low and shouted, "Pour it on the side of the hill, boys! Suppress their fire!"

West bit his lip until he tasted blood. The fool of a lieutenant was going to get his men killed if they stayed put. Suppressing his anger, West thought, *"I'll deal with him later. Right now, we've got to get out of these ruins."*

He dodged several gaping holes and craters in the ground as he raced across what had once been a street and reached the young officer. "Lieutenant, I need you take a message back to Captains Simmons and Cooper. Tell them to move our way as soon as the 4th is in position."

It was a meaningless order. The two captains knew exactly what to do when the 4th arrived. But the young officer was a liability.

Gulping in air, the lieutenant glanced briefly at the fortified positions south of the river before he sketched a salute and raced off to find the two companies. For a moment West watched the lieutenant race away before he turned and looked at the men around him. This company should have already been across the river. *"If we both survive I'm going to have a long talk with that boy."*

More men from the next company had made their way forward. Among them was the battalion's color sergeant, carrying the flag of the Republic. West called out, "Do you see that flag, there? That flag and I are going to go take those trenches away from the Mexicans. Who is with me?"

From the throats of several hundred men, a roar of anger and rage boiled forth. West drew his pistol and stepped next to the color sergeant, "I'll see you on top of that hill or in Hell when this is done. Up and at them!"

West raced for the river. Bullets flew by as he reached the water and splashed across. He looked to his left and saw the color sergeant keeping step. Behind him the blue, white, and red banner with its single lone star flapped noisily. Despite punishing counterbattery fire from the Texian artillery, a few Mexican guns fired into the wave of Marines racing across the river. A dozen men were swept from their feet when a cannister slashed into the charging men.

No sooner had his feet reached dry ground than West pointed toward the riflemen from the 1st Infantry who were hunkered down in the ruble. "Up, men! Up! Do you want to live forever? Join us!"

A Tejano with the diamond insignia of first sergeant on his sleeves picked himself up from where he had sheltered and joined him as they raced through the town. Nearly every other rifleman picked themselves up and ran after their sergeant.

Most of the lead element of his battalion had already stormed past as he directed the riflemen from the 1st Infantry forward. Behind him, splashing through the shallows of the Rio Grande, were more Marines as well as more men from the 1st and 2nd Infantry Battalions.

The rubble, that a few days earlier had been Nuevo Laredo, took only a minute to run through, and when West arrived at the other side, he saw his Marines firing and advancing up the hill. The rain of gunfire from the trench full of *Cazadores* had knocked down dozens of men, but still they advanced. The chaos of the battle had broken the cohesion of the rifle teams. But pride swelled within him as he watched individual Marines and riflemen claw their way toward the Mexican line.

He snapped a shot toward the trench, then directed more men forward. Fire and advance. Each foot was gained with bloodshed. But even though it took longer than he thought it should, he watched a squad of Marines leap into the first trench. Their rifles were tipped with their bayonets and a murderous melee broke out as the *Cazadores* reacted by turning their rifles into clubs or drawing their knives.

A line of riflemen who had formed nearby stopped firing at the trench as more soldiers and Marines poured into it "Forward boys." West waved toward the lines with his pistol. "We're not stopping until we get to Monterrey!"

General Juan Almonte looked down at the *Cazadores*' trench. A thick haze of gun smoke hung over it. Rifle fire echoed up the hill as the battle below hung in the balance. Through the haze, he saw a banner waving as it was carried forward, toward the trench line. The lone star left a sinking feeling in the pit of his stomach. He turned to his aide-de-camp, "Ernesto, starting on both ends of our line, I want our guns on the road to Candela within the hour."

Between the earthen fortifications on the crest of the hill and the trenches below, ran a communications trench. Since the attack began shortly after dawn, a steady stream of updates and wounded riflemen had flowed along its narrow channel. But now, as the Texians reached their position, what had been a trickle turned into a flood as the blue and red jacketed *Cazadores* retreated from the hard-hitting onslaught.

DOWN MEXICO WAY

The experienced men of the first division, bloodied in the campaign into Texas the previous year, stood to along the well-placed trenches which zigzagged across the hilltop. As little as eighty yards separated them from the battle on the hillside below. But they held their fire. The smoke and haze reduced visibility. Also, Almonte was clear in his instructions. Until his riflemen were clear of the trenches below, they were to hold their fire.

As General of the army, Almonte's position was in the rear of the fortifications, orchestrating the defensive line. Leaning forward against the earthen wall, staring down at the battle in the trenches below probably wasn't the smartest thing for him to do, but those were his *Cazadores* down there, dying, slowing down the Texian advance.

The communication trench was close by, and he turned and watched his riflemen stream out of it. A few hurried away, beaten. But most carried their rifles and while their expressions showed the exhaustion they felt, these were not beaten men. An officer, wearing the piping of a lieutenant on his shoulders, stumbled out of the communication trench, supporting an injured rifleman. Both his rifle and that of the injured *soldado* were slung on the young officer's back.

Curious about what was happening behind the young officer, Almonte stepped over to the young man. "Lieutenant, what's happening back there?"

The young man looked up and when he saw who was addressing him, his eyes grew wide. "General Almonte, sir. My apologies, I would salute, but…" His arms were full, supporting the injured rifleman.

Almonte waved away the remark, "Never mind that, Lieutenant."

A couple of riflemen, who came from the trench, reclaimed their companion from their platoon leader and the young officer came to attention, "Sir, we're pulling back. The Texian Marines are within our trenchworks and they're pushing us hard. Things are confusing, several of our senior officers are down. I saw my own captain killed with a bullet in his head."

It was as he expected. The fact that most of his *Cazadores* were retreating in good order pleased him. "What's your name, son."

"Javier Morales, sir."

Almonte wrapped a fatherly arm around the young officer and guided him away from the flow of retreating riflemen. "Javier, I want you to get back to your men. All our riflemen need to be on the road to Candela as quickly as possible. Do you understand me, Captain?"

Morales blinked in surprise, "Captain?"

Before he could say anything, Almonte held up a hand, "Brevet, of course. But men that fight like your men are worth a thousand others. I need men ready to resist this invasion and that's men like you. Now, get moving."

He watched the young officer hurry away down the side of the hill where he passed through the men of the 2nd division, held in reserve at the bottom of the slope. As the gunfire behind him grew into a raging crescendo, Almonte decided the best that could be hoped for was to hold the line for the remainder of the day. The 2nd Division would serve the needs of the army by setting up a line a few miles to the rear. He found one of his couriers and scribbled a note, sending the man galloping toward the 2nd division's headquarters.

The *Cazadores* returning through the communication trench dropped to a trickle. The colonel in charge of the section of the line brought up his reserve company. The last of the Mexican riflemen came through the communication trench then sand bags, gabions, and broken boxes were thrown into it, blocking the zigzagging trench.

A *soldado* fell near Almonte's feet. The Texians had wasted no time in following behind the retreating *Cazadores* through the communication trench. A few men leapt forward, aiming their muskets down the blocked trench, and fired into the hazy smoke. Almonte's staff officers reacted, pulling him away from the fortified line.

Many hours later, General Almonte watched the sun slide below the western horizon. The haze of smoke in the air gave it a red hue. It seemed fitting. Hundreds of men had fallen, but at the end of the day, Almonte's command still held their fortifications on the heights overlooking the Texians below. As a testament to the hard-fought battle, dozens of men were splayed in death in the no-man's land between the two sets of trenches. Nearly all of them wore the butternut uniforms favored by the Texians, or the dark blue jackets of their formidable Marines.

But at what cost? Almonte turned and looked into the twilight, hospital wagons were laden down with the day's wounded as they trundled to the south. He turned and walked down the hill. The army's encampment was a ghost town now. The tents were gone and only the detritus common to an army camp remained. His staff were mounted, waiting for him. As he climbed into the saddle, he asked, "Alejandro, what's the status of our *Cazadores* regiments?"

His aide-de-camp said, "Forty-two dead or missing and seventy wounded, General. Per your orders, they'll stop for the night about ten miles south of here where the 2nd division is positioned."

Although the firing had finally tapered off, it would be some time before each of the nine regiments of the 1st Division would be able to confirm their casualties, but Almonte was no stranger to combat, and he had a clear idea the division had likely sustained as much as ten percent casualties. But they had held the Texians for the entire day.

As he led his staff southward, he shook his head, sadly. Historians would look back on this battle as a defeat for his army, but he remained convinced, had he obeyed his excellency's orders to the letter, that his army would have been shattered somewhere north of Laredo. Against that scenario, where the remnants of the Army of the North would be streaming south, leaving the way clear for Travis to sweep in with his army and take Monterrey with hardly a fight, this was far better.

True, his army was battered, but as he watched, the remaining regiments of the 1st division were pulled from the line, one by one, and put on the road southward, toward the next line of defense. Despite the gloom of the night, his *soldados* held their heads high. To them, this wasn't a defeat, it was simply the first battle in the defense of northern Mexico.

Chapter 11

Private Jesse Running Creek inched forward, poking his head over the rocky hill as he clutched the binoculars in his hand. Two other Rangers crouched next to him, studying the long column of Mexican infantry marching southward. The column leapt into view when Jesse put the lenses to his eyes. For an army that had taken it on the chin five days previous they were in remarkably good spirits, he thought as he heard faint voices singing across the desert.

The Ranger to Jesse's right said, "How bad we gotta whip them before they act like they've been beaten?"

Jesse shook his head in response. "Enough lollygagging. The major wants to know where they're going."

The three men slipped back down the hillock and returned to their mounts where another Ranger was holding the reins. They mounted and rode south, swinging wide around the retreating infantry column.

As their horses kicked up dust, Jesse said, "Corporal, any chance we'll run into any lancers this far south?"

"Heaven help us if we do, Running Creek. With any luck, Almonte is using all his cavalry screening his retreating column from Gen'ral Travis' infantry. The plan was to stick to Almonte's army like a tick on a dog."

Jesse glanced north. The arid ground to the northwest was where the Chihuahuan desert gave way to brown, loamy soil. Were it not for the raids by the Apache and the Comanche the land through which the Mexican army retreated would see more farms. As it was, the four Rangers hadn't seen anyone apart from the relentlessly marching column since detaching from Hays' command the previous day.

"We're only a couple of hours away from Candela. Let's see if we can find Almonte's next fallback position." With that, Jesse dug his heels into his mount's flank. The other Rangers followed him at a gallop.

A couple of hours later, Jesse found himself in the branches of a cypress tree, balancing on a thick limb while holding his binoculars to his face. The village of Candela zoomed into view. From below a voice called out, "What's it look like, Running Creek?"

He looked down at his corporal. "It ain't nothing but a one-horse town, where the horse has died."

He climbed down the tree and when he landed on the ground, he said, "There's a few *soldados* on the streets, but nothing of note. I saw a few wagons, along with a company of infantry marching through it. My guess is that they're heading south. A few miles from here, the road runs through a narrow valley. If Almonte is going to make a stand before he gets into the mountains, that's where he'll do it."

To the young Ranger, whose ideas of hills were those found in East Texas, the hills rising in the distance were veritable mountains, rising twenty-five hundred feet above the valley. The road from Candela to Monterrey ran between two peaks before snaking its way around smaller hills, then disappearing to the south.

Jesse and his companions had given Candela a wide berth, stopping a mile or so away from where the road passed between two hills. Jesse retrieved his binoculars and looked southward. "Hellfire, Corporal, there's a little trench dug between those two hills yonder, and it looks like the Mexicans have placed some cannon across the road but check out them hills. It makes what Almonte built on the Rio Grande look like child's play." The glasses were passed around until the corporal grumbled, "The major needs to know about this. I figure we've seen all that's worth seeing for now."

With a backwards glance, Jesse saw a large green, white, and red Mexican flag hoisted above the fortifications on the taller hill. The gun emplacements left little doubt in his mind where most of the enemy's field artillery were now entrenched. He turned, urged his horse to a canter as he hurried to catch up with his companions.

The light had left the sky before Jesse and his companions found Major Hays. He and a company of Rangers were making camp in a dry arroyo a few miles west of the Mexican line of retreat. Several fires burned in the dry creek bed, obscured from any Mexican patrols. Then they heard a voice call out, "That's far enough now. What's the password?"

The corporal gave the password and led Jesse and his other teammates into the flickering light of the campfire. The major was leaning into the light, writing in a journal. When he finished, Hays turned to the them, "Well, how bad is it?"

The corporal nudged him, nodding for Jesse to give the report. The young Cherokee Ranger cleared his throat and said, "We found what must have been a brigade of infantry a few miles outside of Candela, sir, marching that way. The town itself, General Almonte doesn't seem to have any concern for. There were a few *soldados* there, but nothing to indicate they intend to hold it. But, almighty God, Major, they're making up for it with what they've built where the mountains start."

"Are you going to tell me about it or just stand there with your mouth catching flies, Ranger?"

Flushing, Jesse continued, "They've fortified the valley, from peak to peak. It looks like they put a battery of artillery where their trench line crosses the road. But that's not all. On the hill to the left of the road, they have fortified it with more trenchworks and cannons. Where I come from I'd call that a mountain, it's got to be at least two thousand feet high at its highest. It makes the fortifications along the Rio Grande look like a Presbyterian camp revival."

Hays cocked an eyebrow, "I guess Cherokee do their camp revivals different than what I'm used to." The flash of a smile disappeared. "How many men would you say Almonte has moved into those positions?"

Jesse thought about the positions he had seen through the binoculars. There had been plenty of men along those positions, he thought. "I'd guess he's probably got most of one of his divisions already in place. I'd guess his second division is mostly still on the road. Any word from the main force about bringing them to battle?"

Hays grimaced. "Almonte is willing to throw his lancers away, I think to keep us from engaging his infantry. Every time we get within a stone's throw of the rear guard, up come those lancers. General Seguin's cavalry sweep 'em aside, but by that time, Almonte's rear-guard has slipped away. If we can't find a way around the Mexican lines, we'll pay our pound of flesh to push them off those hills."

12 April 1842

The former president held the squalling infant in outstretched hands as he turned, searching for his daughter. "Becky, I'd appreciate it, if you'd stop palavering with your momma and take back David here. I don't reckon he's quite developed an appreciation for his grandfather's stories yet."

Laughing at her father's discomfiture, Becky Travis stepped across the main room of the house and rescued the baby from her father. "I thought you had kissed enough babies to have this down pat, Pa."

David Crockett pretended to scowl at his daughter. "I always had better luck with Whig babies than Democrat babies. Promise me you'll not be raising a Democrat, here."

His wife, Elizabeth laughed. Even after more than a quarter-century of marriage, her laughter was music to his ears. "Leave it to your pa to talk politics even a year after leaving office. Becky, you can take the man out of politics, but you can't the politics out of the man."

Becky lifted the infant into the air, turning his tears into squeals of joy. "If you men would exercise the good sense that God gave you, you'd realize that if women could vote we'd have things fixed right shortly."

David raised his hands, "I surrender, ladies. I will leave my politics in my pocket. Just promise I won't have to listen to petticoat politics."

With a harrumph, Becky turned around, the hem of her dress fluttering up, and exclaimed, "Men."

The three adults broke into laughter when Becky stopped twirling around. Charlie looked up from a book he was reading with a confused look on his face. David saw it and wagged a finger in his direction, "Listen up good, boy. Women talk about wanting to vote, but the truth of the matter is that they let us think we're masters of our house, but it's all a thin coat of whitewash. Your pa might be the general of the army, and I was president. But don't doubt for a second all the power I thought I had ended when I crossed the threshold to my Liza's home."

Charlie couldn't help but giggling at his "Uncle Davy." Becky stuck her tongue out at her father while trying not to laugh. Elizabeth caught him around the neck and gave him a fierce hug. "Don't tell me that's why you stay gone so long, David." The sting of the words was belied by the tenderness in her voice. "But enough of that. Land's sake, I've missed you so much. Are you sure you can't stay with us longer?"

Setting propriety aside, David planted a long kiss on his wife's lips. When they parted, he said, "With kisses like that, I'd forget my duty plum quick."

Elizabeth playfully patted him on the chest, "Liar."

"Caught to the quick I am," David said as he took his wife's hand in his own. "But duty calls me away, my dear. I'll be leaving in a couple of days for Santa Fe."

When his wife and daughter went into another room to change the baby's diaper, David stepped onto the porch with his pipe. He had tamped some tobacco into the bowl and had lit it when the door opened, and Charlie stepped outside.

The boy had grown. His facial features looked more like his father's every day. He stood several inches shorter than David, although he still had a few years of growth to go. "I declare, boy, I do believe you're going to end up taller than both me and your pa."

The teenager shrugged. "Maybe so, Uncle Davy. I reckon that I'm already mostly grown, though." His voice was still settling into a deeper octave. "When you head out to Santa Fe, take me with you, please."

His voice cracked at the end, and he flushed at its betrayal. Crockett used the pipe to point at the boy, "Your pa wouldn't much care for me if I did that, Charlie. I'd have thought after last year, you'd have worked that itch out of you."

The boy's cheeks colored at the comment. "I'm going to join the army when I'm older, I done told Pa that I will. You could use an orderly. I'd be a bang-up good one, too. I promise."

David puffed on the pipe, the pungent smell of tobacco hung heavy in the air. "Why should I let you come, boy? It's dangerous and like I already said, your pa wouldn't rightly forgive me for letting a shirt- tail boy join up."

"I ain't no shirt-tail boy no more, Uncle Davy. I'm near enough a man. You ran away from your pa when you were only thirteen. I'm a lot older than that."

David turned toward the street and blew a ragged smoke ring. It was just like the boy to throw his own past in his face. Crockett groused, "If that's what comes from telling you my stories, I don't think you'll be hearing many more."

He found the taste didn't agree with him. The boy was too smart for his own good. Fourteen and a half wasn't that far removed from thirteen. He had to admit, his own past colored his view and if it were his decision, he wasn't sure he could deny the boy's request. You had to grow up sooner or later.

In all the years he had known Buck, Crockett knew the man loved his family more than life itself. Buck would never forgive him if he allowed the boy to run off from home and join. But as Charlie's favorite "Uncle Davy," he preferred to let the boy down gently. "Tell you what, Charlie. You go inside and write your pa a letter asking him to let you join me, and if he gives permission, you can follow along with a supply train."

As the boy retreated into the house with a hangdog expression, David sighed. Was it really more than forty years since he'd been that age? He shook his head. Where had the years gone? He figured Charlie's chances of obtaining his father's permission were somewhat less than Old Scratch making a personal appearance before dinner. Chuckling at the image, he knocked the ashes from his pipe and went back inside. With so little time before his command was due to leave, he wanted to spend every minute with his wife, daughter, and grandchildren.

The room was dark, the candle on the small table next to the bed was hidden in shadows. He had gone to sleep that night fully clothed and, as his stockinged feet touched the floor, he grabbed his shoes and crept to the door. The door opened without a sound. A little grease on the hinges had solved the problem of a squeaky door. He paused and looked back into the gloom. He could barely make out his sister's silhouette as she tossed fitfully in her sleep.

The idea of not seeing little Liza for a long time threatened to bring tears to his eye. He sucked in his breath. Young men don't cry, he reminded himself. Young men don't blow kisses toward their toddler sisters either, but he couldn't help himself.

He snuck down the hall to the great room. Moonlight filtered through curtains, giving the furnishings a ghostlike quality. Charlie had been planning his escape ever since his Uncle Davy had left a few days before. Everything had been prepared. He slunk over to the kitchen pantry in a corner of the room and rummaged around behind a bag of rice. His fingers closed around a burlap bag. While Henrietta and Becky had been out shopping, he had stored away as much food as the bag would hold. Now, he slung it onto his shoulder then crossed the room to the fireplace. Above it hung his father's rifle. He smirked. "*I've used it far more than Pa ever had*," the boy thought. He took it from the wall and grabbed the ammunition belt. With his hands overloaded, he managed to get to the door, where he carefully set the gear on the floor and unlatched the door. More grease had been put to good use and the door swung inward without a sound.

Now on the porch, he pulled his shoes on and cinched the leather belt holding the cartridge and percussion cap boxes. With rifle in one hand and heavy burlap bag in the other, Charlie hurried down the street.

As he neared the livery stable used by his father, he thought, "*It's not stealing if it's your horse.*" Leaving his things on the side of the livery stable, Charlie climbed into the building through an open window. His father owned a few horses, and except for the two his father had taken with him, they were stabled here. Charlie's favorite, a white and red paint, nickered as he tiptoed into the stall. He rubbed the animal's flank and was rewarded with the animal rubbing its neck against his face. "Hi, Paint. I'm glad to see you, too."

The owner of the livery stable lived next door. Even though his father had given Charlie the horse as a birthday present, the last thing he wanted to do was answer any questions from the stable owner. He raced to saddle the animal and slipped on the bridle. He retrieved his supplies from outside then led the horse to the heavy door. He set the bar aside and with the horse following his lead, stepped into the night air.

The military road crossed the San Antonio River north of town as it wound between the Alamo and the first of four depots between San Antonio and Ysleta, seven hundred miles away. Speaking softly to the horse, the boy said, "Let's cut across country. I don't want to see how close the guards at the Alamo are looking at us tonight."

The well graded road was easy to find, even in the darkness of predawn. The mid-April morning was cool but dry and Charlie leaned back in the saddle and allowed a wide smile to play across his face. He had done it! He had slipped away from home with no one the wiser. And somehow, he would convince Uncle Davy that he just had to let him join the march.

A few days later, Charlie removed his hat and used it to wipe sweat from his forehead. Summer was still more than a month away, but the April sun could still pack a wallop he decided. Bluebonnets and Indian paintbrushes crowded the road and covered the prairie in a blanket of blues, reds, and oranges. He looked to either side and saw a few bees pollinating the flowers. To his horse, Paint, he said, "Those bees make me wish I had some honey right about now."

The fare he had carried off with him included bread, which he had devoured within the first day, and rice, beans, jerky, and dried fruit. The burlap bag had contained more than a week's worth of food. He still had most of it. He had shot a brace of rabbits with his rifle and eaten them instead of his supplies the second evening away from home.

In the distance, he thought he saw the walls of the first depot. Since its construction a couple of years before, the quartermaster's corps had fortified the depots, and even though only a solitary platoon of infantry manned it, Charlie had no interest in making their acquaintance. No, he didn't want anyone who could force him to return home finding him until it was a smaller inconvenience for his Uncle Davy to let him stay with the army than sending him home would be.

From the maps in his pa's office, he had an idea of how far he would need to swing around the depot to reconnect with the military road. He set his hat back on his head and guided Paint off the road. As he guided the horse through the riot of colorful flowers, he recalled words spoken by Jack Hays, the major of the special Rangers. "As a Ranger, your horse is your most important tool, even more important than your guns. Take care of him and he'll take care of you. The single biggest threat to your mount when you're moving across country is prairie dog holes."

He scanned the ground in front of his horse. He was determined to follow everything he could remember from men like Major Hays. Instead of stories, Hays had talked about survival. He spied a hole ahead and steered Paint around it. "That's right, Paint. You and me, we're going to do this the Ranger way."

A couple of days later, Charlie crouched behind a mesquite tree. He used a branch to stabilize the rifle as he pointed it toward a watering hole at a bend in a creek. He had eaten all the jerky, and he really wanted something other than beans and rice, of which he still had aplenty. There were deer tracks leading up to and away from the creek, and he hoped his patience would pay off.

He was well past the first depot and was wondering how long he should wait to catch up to Uncle Davy's column. In a moment of reflection, he marveled at how well things had gone for him since leaving home. He had hunted his own food and had managed to go across country on more than one occasion, still finding the military road when he needed. The first couple of nights camped under the open sky had been scary, if he were honest with himself, but each night away had become a little easier. Thankfully, there were no Comanche riding the prairie around this part of the country anymore. "*I don't know what I would do if I ran into any Indians.*"

Near the creek, he heard something move through the underbrush, and a moment later his patience was rewarded when a white-tailed deer stepped into view. It was a young buck. Charlie counted, there were six points on the antler. His stomach rumbled. Best to make the shot count. He wouldn't get another. He sighted down the barrel, lining the rear sight up with the front sight. He placed his finger on the trigger.

Near the creek several birds scattered into the air and an arrow appeared, protruding from the buck. The animal leapt into the air and raced toward the crossing at the creek. Ignoring an unsettling feeling, Charlie swung his barrel, following the deer and fired as soon as the animal was in his sights. Through the haze of black powder smoke, he saw the animal tumble into shallows of the creek.

He grabbed a paper cartridge as he stood and levered the breechblock open. He inserted the cartridge and closed the rolling block, slicing off the excess paper. Before he stepped away from cover, he crowned the nipple with a fresh percussion cap.

His stomached fluttered nervously as he scanned the area for whomever fired the arrow. From behind a prickly pear cactus plant arose a figure holding a bow. An arrow was nocked, ready to fly. The fear he felt reminded Charlie of the defense of the Alamo more than a year before. He tried not to think about being alone in the wilderness. He kept thinking, "*I'm armed. There's one of me and one of him. I can handle this.*"

The copper-skinned warrior wore no face paint. They were not so far apart that Charlie couldn't discern his features. The expression the warrior wore was one of curiosity and caution. Charlie had grown up talking with soldiers and Rangers who had fought the Comanche, and the man didn't wear his hair in the style common among the warlike tribe. His shirt was a long-sleeved shirt common among the mercantile stores of San Antonio. His pants were durable, and store bought as well, but his feet were clad in doe-skinned moccasins. They looked more comfortable than the sturdy boots on Charlie's feet.

Trying to be brave, Charlie called out, "I don't suppose you're from around these here parts?"

The warrior pointed the arrow toward the ground, although he left it nocked, and closed the gap between him and Charlie. As he approached, Charlie saw the warrior wasn't much older than he was. When no more than a dozen paces separated them, the warrior said, in broken English, "I, son of Flacco," he paused as though searching for another word, "of Lipan."

Charlie had met an Apache warrior by the name of Flacco on a couple of occasions. He was one of the war chiefs for the Lipan Apache. Was it possible he was one in the same? "I'm Charlie Travis. My pa is General William Travis."

The young warrior's eyes registered surprise. "You son of fire hair. He friend of my people."

Charlie allowed a long breath of relief to escape his lips and was stunned to hear the same sound from the young warrior. Both laughed as the tense moment passed. Charlie's curiosity got the better of him and he asked, "What are you doing so far away from your tribe by yourself?"

At that moment, there was a rustling from a bush near the creek and an Apache girl stood, smiling at the young warrior as though sharing a secret. "Not alone. My... sister, Lenna. I am Victorio."

Charlie looked at the girl. She wore a long, blue calico blouse, and skirt made of leather. Her raven-black hair was in a single braid down her back. She looked back at him with the same frank curiosity Charlie wore on his own face. Finally, she pointed into the creek bed, where the buck had fallen, and in Spanish, said, "Are you boys going to do something about the deer? Your mouths will catch flies if you stand around all day."

The young warrior laughed at his sister, and as Charlie translated the words, a smile lit up his features, and he realized it was rude to stare at the girl. He followed the warrior into the creek bed. The boys came to a quick agreement to share the deer. Charlie had helped Henrietta and Becky skin more than a few animals over the past few years and he and the two Apache made quick work dressing down the carcass.

As they cooked the meat over a campfire, he learned about the siblings. Victorio was seventeen years old and Lenna was fourteen. As they shared the campfire they traded stories. Charlie had expected an epic tale of brother and sister on a spirit quest or an epic hunt. Instead he was disappointed to discover that their father, Flacco had decided to send most of the tribe to the west, to land ceded to the Apache in western Texas. The siblings were not sure if they wanted to go with the tribe and were using this hunting trip to make up their mind.

As the meat sizzled over the fire, Victorio confided that he enjoyed working on one of the large ranches near the Nueces River, while Lenna simply didn't like the idea of leaving the land their tribe had lived on for more than a generation. As the evening wore on, Charlie couldn't help stealing glances at Lenna. To him, the way her cheeks glowed in the firelight was alluring. Nor was he blind to the looks she kept giving him.

As the fire died, he crawled into his blanket, confused about the way Lenna had looked at him. On one hand, he couldn't help admitting he had liked it. On the other, it left him feeling confused. It was a long time before he drifted off to sleep.

The next morning, as Charlie saddled his horse, the Apache siblings rode over to him. Victorio waved and smiled widely, while Lenna sat astride her mare in silence. Charlie felt the knot in his stomach tighten when he looked at her, so he redoubled his attention on the young warrior. "Where are y'all off to next?"

Victorio waved his hand to the west, "No hurry. We curious about white chief you follow, go with you for now. See this Crockett."

That wasn't the answer he expected. The road had been lonely, he had to admit, but as his eyes slid over to Lenna, he wasn't sure traveling with the Apache siblings would be any easier. Even so, he nodded and said, "Let's go, we're burning daylight."

Chapter 12

The village was only a couple of dozen mud brick homes surrounding a tiny chapel with a small belfry. The farmers and ranchers who normally made Candela their home had fled when the Mexican troops passed through earlier. Will followed one of the battalions from McCulloch's brigade through the town. No eyes peered from windows and doors creaked on their hinges; only the ghosts of the living welcomed the interlopers. A chill ran down his spine as Will felt troubled by the direction the campaign had already taken.

April was more than half over, and Monterrey seemed further away now than it had at the beginning of the campaign. It was an illusion, he knew. The army had crossed nearly a hundred miles over the past week, always nipping at Almonte's heels, but unable to draw the Mexican army into battle. Almonte's refusal to turn around and fight had not been cheap. He had screened his retreating soldiers with both his cavalry and light infantry units. Using them to delay and harass Will's army had slowed the advance down. Even Seguin's efforts to swing around the flanks had been anticipated and Almonte's lancers were waiting.

In their drive after Almonte's army, the only intelligence he had received had come from a Ranger company Hays had managed to swing far enough around the Mexican line of retreat. The news they brought back had not been good, and now that Will could see the mountains for himself, he wondered just how deeply entrenched the Mexican army had become.

Almonte's skillful retreat, and the use of his cavalry and *Cazadores,* dredged from his memories the cat and mouse game waged in the American Civil War between General Lee and a multitude of Union Generals. That was, until General Grant used the might of the Union army to grind Lee's army into submission. Of course, his memory was the only place that history still lived.

Will took off his hat and slapped it against his leg, watching as dust flew into the air. The problem is that even if Almonte was a Mexican version of General Lee, Will was no Grant. Texas lacked both the population and the resources necessary to grind away at the enemy. He needed a decisive victory that would break Almonte's army.

Once he had passed through Candela's main street, there were no obstacles between him and the mountains to the south, and as he looked through the binoculars he studied the trenchworks on the slope of the nearest mountain. He bit his lip in frustration. *"That would be one hell of a butcher's bill if we have to go straight in."*

No, he may not be Grant, and his army wasn't the Army of the Potomac, but they were Texians, and one way or another he would find a way to dislodge Almonte's army. He turned and ordered one of his staff to find

General Seguin. The first thing was to find a way around Almonte's position.

A short time later, both General Juan Seguin and Major Jack Hays galloped over to him as he continued studying the fortifications. "Gentlemen, take a gander at those trenchworks."

While the two officers studied the slope in the distance, Will continued, "Unless there's no other way, I don't want to send our boys up against those fortified positions. Even with our artillery, pushing the Mexicans off that high ground would prove costly."

Seguin's normally swarthy face blanched at seeing the enemy position for the first time. Hays said, "It looks worse now than it did before. Now their entire army is in those lines. What have you got in mind, General?"

"Jack, send one of your companies to the east. Those mountains can't go on forever. Find a way around or over them. If I'm going to commit our forces to an assault, it's only because we're flanking them."

Hays saluted and dashed down the road toward his Rangers. Will and Seguin shook their heads as they watched his horse kick up dust. The cavalry commander said, "Was I ever that impulsive?"

Will patted him on the back, "Don't get me started. You were ready to take on Santa Anna himself back during the revolution, if you recall."

Seguin chuckled. "I could have taken him, too. Almonte, on the other hand, lacks Santa Anna's brash, 'stick your head in a hornets' nest' way about him. I confess, I'm surprised we haven't brought him to heel yet."

Will asked, "How many men do you reckon he lost in the retreat, Juan?"

"Not as many as I would like. We clashed with his lancers and his *Cazadores* a dozen or more times over the past week and probably inflicted upwards of two hundred casualties over that time," Seguin said, "Against that, we lost a few dozen wounded and ten dead."

Will had read the reports. Taken as a whole, it was nothing compared to the battle at Nuevo Laredo. The army had suffered more casualties in that fight than Will had anticipated. Lt. Colonel West's Marines were the hardest hit. A baker's dozen killed and more than forty injured was high. The Marine battalion was light on men to begin with, at only six companies of sixty men each. The 1st Infantry, composed entirely of regulars, and the 2nd Infantry, one of the longest serving reserve battalions, each had contributed around three hundred men to the assault. They had bogged down in the rubble of the two towns and had taken heavy casualties. Close to a quarter of the men who had gone in didn't come through unscathed. According to the reports Will had received, forty-two men from those two battalions were killed and more than a hundred were wounded.

"Juan, we can't afford to trade casualties with Almonte's army. Make sure Jack knows how important it is that he find a way around those mountains." Will gestured toward the south. "If I'm going to send our boys into battle, I want to make sure that we bag as much of Almonte's army as possible. I'll be damned if I'm going to hound him all the way to Monterrey, one bloody battle after another for the next sixty miles."

April 16, 1843

There was a quiet knock at the door to the study and Lorenzo de Zavala set the book he had been reading down on the end table.

"To have it as easy as Rodrigo Díaz de Vivar," thought the president of the Republic as he turned his attention to the door. "Enter."

His servant, Cesar, a freedman of mixed blood, opened the door, "Señor Seguin and Monsieur Menard to see you, Mr. President."

Zavala suppressed a smile. Not *el presidente*, nor your excellency, but simply Mr. President. He decided it was really David Crockett's fault that the office of president had so little ceremony or grandeur attached to it. He also caught how Cesar was precise in acknowledging Erasmo Seguin's Tejano roots and Michel Menard's origin as a Québécois.

Zavala had been friends with the Seguin family since he arrived in Texas before the Revolution and had worked closely with Menard, who had been President Crockett's Secretary of the Treasury. He counted his good fortune that the wily former French Canadian had agreed to continue serving in the same capacity in his own cabinet.

"Erasmo, Michel, welcome. You wanted to see me? Please, have a seat. What is so important that it requires us to sacrifice our Sabbath?"

As the other two men took seats around a low table, in comfortable chairs imported from France, the elder Seguin nodded toward Menard. The president studied his treasurer. The affable financial wizard's brown hair was retreating from his forehead and comfortable living meant he was losing the battle with his waistline. "I apologize, sir, for imposing upon your time today. But I believe the reason for the intrusion required it."

Zavala raised his eyebrows in response, waiting for Menard to continue, "As you are aware, more than half of the government's revenues for the past year have come from bonds sold both here and abroad.

The president tapped the book he had been reading earlier, in a measured cadence, well aware of the financial situation in which the Republic found itself. Taking the cue to continue, Menard said, "At the end of the coming week, we are slated to issue another round of bonds at auction in Galveston. We've had several representatives from various banks from the United States confirm their intent to attend, but rumors I have picked up are alarming."

Zavala stopped tapping on the book and felt his stomach contract. The pending bond issue was critical. Without fresh specie, paying for the Mexican war would become more complicated. He said, "And?"

"I've heard Edmond Forstall thinks our public debt has left us overextended."

Zavala was alarmed by this. Forstall was probably the most widely regarded banker in New Orleans, perhaps even across the entire southern United States. A considerable volume of Texas war bonds had been factored through his bank over the previous year. "What will this mean for our new bond issue?"

Menard looked like he had bitten into a lemon as he said, "There are a couple of ways this could play out, and neither is to our advantage. We may be forced to increase the interest rate on the bonds to sell them. The plan was to tie the loans to two percent above the Lloyds rate in London, or seven percent. But Forstall is indicating that new bond holders may require both a premium rate above seven percent and a discount from the face value."

As the president digested the information he paled at the implication. "If we're forced to sell at a discount and still pay more than seven percent on the face value, that could leave us dangerously overleveraged, Michel. What about European bond holders? Surely they would pay face value."

Menard gave a typical Gallic shrug. "Maybe. If there are any buyers from Europe in attendance. I have not received any new inquiries from London or Paris."

Shaking his head, Zavala said, "How much are we trying to raise in this round of bond issues?"

"Just enough to carry us for a couple of months, around a half-million dollars."

He had been quiet until now, but Seguin cleared his throat, "I have an idea, gentlemen, that might allay some of the risk. The Texas Land Bank can step in and buy some of the bonds."

Menard swung his head around, surprise etched on his face. "But Erasmo, there's not specie available. If you print cottonbacks to buy the bonds, you'll put the Commodities Bureau in a bind. Buy too many of the bonds and that's going to cause inflation."

Seguin frowned. "I know. But there aren't many arrows in the quiver that we can use to fund the government. I'm sure you've seen the latest property tax receipts. They have fallen by more than a quarter. Too many of our men are in the army and not enough are working their farms and mills. Even the land bank has had to set several hundred loan defaults into abeyance. Our economy is contracting, and people are suffering. We have all agreed the best solution is to give General Travis the tools he needs to win the war, but heaven help us, we're running out of options."

Zavala reached over and patted his old friend on the arm, "We're doing everything we can, Erasmo. As a matter of fact, I had a conversation with James Collinsworth, in the Senate this past week. He said that despite the government 'renting' so many of his slaves, he was committed to growing as much corn and wheat as possible. There are more than a few farms lying fallow, and I fear that by the time the fall harvest is upon us that starvation will stalk some families. I'm glad that even someone as recalcitrant as Collinsworth understands that we're in this together."

As the meeting broke up, Menard added, "There's another possibility, too. The Commerce Bank has not yet participated in any of the bond issues. I will talk with Sam Williams. It may be that I can talk him into buying a substantial number of the bonds."

Less than a week later, the Galveston Customshouse had been turned into an auction house. The crowd was smaller than Menard and Zavala had hoped to see. The largest grouping of men surrounded Edmond Forstall. The Texas Treasurer had registered everyone for the auction, and most of them represented important banks known throughout the United States. There were a few other representatives from elsewhere in attendance.

One of his custom officers stepped to the podium, ready to start the bidding. A rustling from behind them caused the two government officials to turn around. Sam Williams strolled through the door. He came over to Menard and the two shook hands. "You do like to cut things fine, Mr. Williams."

The affable banker hooked his thumbs in his waistcoat pockets and said, "While my duty to my country comes above every other loyalty, Michel, I also have a duty to the bank's other partners." He turned and nodded to Seguin, "Good morning, Señor."

The auctioneer gaveled the room to silence. "The Republic is opening the bond issue for five hundred thousand dollars. The opening bid on the bonds is seven percent, a two percent premium over Lloyds rates. Bonds are available in ten thousand dollar increments."

The room was silent as the banker and their factors considered the bid. As the silence lengthened, Sam Williams called out, "I'll take one hundred thousand dollars at the declared interest rate."

There was a surprised muttering from the men surrounding the New Orleans banker. In one action, a fifth of the entire bond issue was gone. As though waiting for permission, other men began buying the bonds at the same price. Ten thousand in one transaction, fifty thousand in another, until only one hundred thousand dollars in bonds remained.

With a smirk on his face, Edmond Forstall raised his voice, "I'll buy the remainder for eighty thousand at eight percent!"

The room erupted in chaos. Some of the previous buyers were angry while others were shocked at Forstall's effrontery. There was no point in delaying any further. With a sidelong look at Menard, Seguin stepped forward, "The Texas Land Bank will buy the remaining one hundred thousand dollars at face value."

Menard watched Forstall blinking in surprise. The New Orleans banker had expected to take a sizable profit from the auction, and with the last of the bonds purchased, he had come up empty. The Treasurer ambled over to where the Southern bankers stood around the defeated Forstall.

"Well played, Monsieur Menard," Forstall said, offering his hand. "Remind me not to play you in whist. That was a masterful game you played."

Menard allowed an expansive grin to play across his face. But Forstall continued, "What miracles do you plan on pulling off when you issue your next round of bonds?"

The banker turned and left the building. Menard had no response.

Late February 1843

Gail Bordon enjoyed walking barefoot along the beach, watching his children play in the surf as the weather had become unseasonably warm. His wife, Penelope, held onto his arm as she tried to maintain her balance in her shoes.

"You should try it without the shoes, dearest."

She gasped, "What would people think, Gail? It's unseemly. Perhaps we should call the girls back, I don't like them playing in the water. It's not safe. I wish you had continued with the development of the bathhouse you designed." She sniffed as her heel sank deep into the sand.

"Why couldn't you have continued with that? Instead, your current invention is scaring me. You nearly burned down the carriage house today."

Bordon tried to smile at his wife's criticism, but lately, he wondered what he had got himself into. When he had received the letter from his friend, Ashbel Smith, the idea of working with him to develop his nitrated cotton had excited him. But more than six months later, his greatest success had been crystalizing the nitrated cotton.

But today, a small batch had exploded. In addition to damaging the coach house, he had blown out the windows on the backside of his house. Fortunately, one of his neighbors had been available and they quickly put out the fire. But what would have happened had a larger batch exploded?

He looked at his children, playing in the water, and felt his wife's hand on his arm. He had no choice but to relocate where he worked on his experiments. A converted coach house was a poor substitute for a laboratory. He had a few ideas, and when the children tired of the beach, they would return home. He had letters to write.

A few weeks later, Bordon stepped down from the carriage. Steam hissed from the locomotive as other passengers crowded by, intent on the business. "Mr. Bordon?"

He turned upon hearing the voice. A richly dressed Tejano sat in a horse-drawn buggy. Bordon wearily put on a smile. After the boat ride from Galveston to Anahuac then the train ride to West Liberty, he was tired. "Señor Garza? It is a pleasure to meet with you."

After he joined Garza in the buggy, and they were rolling away from the train depot, Garza said, "When I received a letter from my old friend Erasmo that you needed a place to work, I was honored he thought of me."

Bordon was bemused how quickly things had happened, when he wrote to his friend, Ashbel. Smith had written back and introduced him to an inventor of sorts in the Patent Office by the name of Gatling. Gatling, in turn worked for Michel Menard, the Secretary of the Treasury. Menard worked closely with Erasmo Seguin, the Director of the Commodities Bureau. Seguin also served on the board of directors for the Gulf Farms Corporation. And that was how he found himself sitting next to Señor Garza, who was the president of the corporation.

"I'm just thankful that my work is important enough to warrant your interest," Bordon said. And it was true. Even though he had only been working on the nitrated cotton for a few months, the application as a replacement to black powder was too important to not be a priority.

As they drove out of town, they passed by acres upon acres of fallow fields. "Do you expect to plant anything this spring, Señor Garza?"

"Yes. We've set aside some acreage for cotton production, but just a fraction of last year's amount. While I've lost close to half my workers to the army, I've been able to arrange for their families to carry some of the work load. We'll forgo most of our cash crop and focus on corn, wheat, and potatoes this planting season."

Bordon was tired and Garza, like a good host, carried the conversation as the buggy rolled down the road. The road was well maintained, even as the farmland fell behind them. Despite his exhaustion, Bordon picked up on a shift in the conversation when Garza said, "I've talked with Andy Berry about your requirements and he and his folks are prepared to offer you a place to work on your invention. The Trinity Gun Works has been expanding lately, and it so happens they have a building that will allow you to focus on your fire cotton. It's well away from their production facilities, but close enough that you may find it useful to consult with the Berrys as you continue your work."

Bordon was too tired to correct him. He was simply building on Ashbel Smith's discovery. The ride from West Liberty to the Trinity Gun Works was less than a couple of hours, and the last half of it he was asleep. When Gail

Bordon climbed down from the buggy, he was dead on his feet after such a long day's travel. He scarcely saw the small town growing up around the gun works as Andy Berry brought him to his father's house where Bordon fell into the bed provided.

His last thought as he drifted to sleep was his wife and children. His dreams were filled with exploding coach houses.

Chapter 13

Jesse Running Creek eyed the trenchworks on the slope above his position. Since the army's arrival that morning, the four-man rifle team had watched the Mexican trenches. From what he could tell, the men who were gazing down the hill at the Texian army, filling the plain below, were armed with muskets. That likely meant they were armed with the surplus Brown Bess muskets bought from the British in the years following the Napoleonic Wars. Jesse's eyes slid from the trenchworks to his own rifle. The Sabine M42 rifle's design was less than two years old. The Brown Bess had been in service for more than a hundred years.

He would rather face the musket-armed *soldados* in the trenches above than the *Cazadores*. He was heartily sick of the Mexican riflemen and their British-made Bakers rifles. A rustling from behind made him turn and he saw Sergeant Collins, the squad's ranking NCO. "Get your asses moving, boys. Major Hays said we're going on a little ride."

They slipped down the slope to their mounts and cantered across the plain to where Major Hays had encamped his special Ranger companies. Jesse's company, nearly forty men, were crowded around Hays. The youthful officer was talking as Jesse joined the listening men. "We got ourselves a right serious problem, boys. General Travis don't want another battle like what we faced crossing the Rio Grande. That's where we come in. You and me, we're going to see about finding a way around these mountains. If Almonte has left a back door unguarded, I aim to find it."

Jesse looked around at his fellow Rangers and every one of them were nodding their heads and muttering their agreement. Apart from being pushed out of Laredo by the Mexican artillery barrage that leveled the town, they had missed the worst of the fighting. Even during the push from Laredo to Candela they had missed much of the skirmishing between Seguin's cavalry and Almonte's lancers. Jesse found himself nodding, too. Hays' voice interrupted his thoughts, "Alright, collect your gear. We ride in thirty minutes."

Hours later Jesse stood beside his mount as the horse stretched its neck to grab a mouthful of grass. He tipped his canteen up and swallowed lukewarm water. The company had ridden more than fifteen miles, circling around the ridges to their south. The major was still astride his mount, using a pair of binoculars to scan a gap between two peaks.

As he pushed the cork plug into the canteen, Jesse heard the major say, "Captain, have your men mount up, there's a dust cloud to our west. If it's just a few lancers, we can brush 'em aside and have a gander at the Mexican rear."

Jesse grabbed the pommel and swung into the saddle as the captain ordered the men to remount. The young

Cherokee Ranger pulled on the pistol grip, making sure he could free it from the holster quickly. As the Ranger company galloped between the two mountain peaks, Jesse didn't need binoculars to see the dust cloud billowing towards them.

The cloud drew near, and he was able to see mounted men with their steel-tipped lances racing across the arid ground, closing the distance with them. Major Hays drew his pistol and dug his spurs into his mount, "At them, boys!"

Jesse felt his own mount surge forward as he dug his heels into the animal's flanks. Powerful leg muscles kept the horse in the vanguard of the advancing Rangers. The late afternoon sun reflected off the lance tips. Jesse wet his lips as he shifted his reins to his left hand and drew his pistol with the other. The range between the two mounted forces fell as the horses ate away at the distance.

Less than a hundred yards separated the Rangers from the red-jacketed lancers, who leveled their lances, pointing them toward Jesse and his comrades. Fleetingly, the young Cherokee wondered if his own ancestors had felt the same sting of fear when they battled the Creek Indians a hundred years before. The thought was gone nearly as soon as it appeared as he registered the first gunshot. The major's right arm was extended as the puff of smoke slipped behind him.

The hard looks of hatred were engraved on the faces of the lancers, who were close enough for Jesse to see the gleaming buttons on their scarlet jackets. He yanked the trigger and felt the .44 caliber pistol buck in his hand.

He felt a hard tug at his jacket as a lancer sped by. The cloth tore when the lancer's steel blade caught it, and Jesse felt his side erupt with a burning sensation. He glanced down and saw his butternut jacket was ripped open on the side. He turned and saw the back of the lancer, who raced to get through the throng of Rangers. Praying his reflexes were fast enough, Jesse aimed at the retreating back and fired.

The Lancer jerked forward and dropped his weapon. Instead of sliding from the saddle, Jesse watched the horseman swerve to the side, having broken through the line of Rangers. He fired again at the retreating back before becoming aware of the battle raging around him. Smoke from the revolvers hung heavy among the fighting horsemen. Several men had been speared from the saddle, joining many more scarlet-jacketed lancers who had been knocked from their saddles by the Rangers' flurry of gunfire.

Turning his head from side to side, looking for a target, Jesse saw another line of lancers racing toward them from the west. "Look out! There's another company!" someone cried out. As his side burned with pain, any thought of the fear he had felt was burned away. He aimed his revolver at the charging line and waited until they were within range and then emptied his pistol into the oncoming lancers. Even though most of the Rangers were still fighting against the first wave of lancers, those who joined Jesse in firing at the oncoming rush emptied enough saddles to blunt the attack.

From the corner of his eye, Jesse spied a red-jacketed horseman racing toward him, saber raised high. His revolver empty, the Cherokee leaned back in the saddle, and heard the blade sing past his head as the Mexican sped by. He wheeled around and saw the horseman turning, intent to finish the fight. Jesse turned his mount ninety degrees from the oncoming Mexican, which brought the other's horse to a stop rather than colliding with Jesse's horse.

The Mexican leaned forward, slashing at Jesse. He ducked the blade and nudged his horse to the side opposite the other man's sword arm. Bringing the blade across his body slowed the Mexican down enough that Jesse dropped his reins and grabbed the other man's wrist and yanked him forward. Still holding his empty revolver in his other hand, the Cherokee Ranger swung the gun at the Mexican's face. A crunching sound reached Jesse's ear as the barrel smashed into the other man's nose. Howling in pain, the Mexican lurched away from him, tumbling from the saddle.

Digging his heels into his mount's flanks, Jesse escaped the milling mass of fighting men. He retrieved a loaded cylinder from a cartridge box at his waist and engaged the gun's loading lever. He slipped the spent cylinder into a pocket then confirmed the percussion caps were snugly fit on each of the six nipples before locking the new cylinder in place.

He scanned the arid valley and several hundred yards away, he saw a long line of blue-clad infantry marching toward the melee between the Rangers and lancers. He then spied Major Hays dispatch a lancer with a shot to the face. "Major, there's more Mexicans on the way!"

The major stood in his stirrups and gazed toward the west. Jesse repressed a smile as he heard a string of profanity slip from the officer's mouth. "Disengage, boys. It looks like we're not getting through this way!"

With a backwards glance, Jesse saw the rest of the Rangers break off fighting with the remaining lancers, who fell back towards the advancing infantry. A few saddles were empty, and he saw three of his own company lying on the ground. Several more were swaying in the saddle, trying to stay astride their mounts despite their injuries.

The major galloped past him and Jesse fell in behind Hays as they rode through the pass between the two peaks that guarded the rear of the Mexican army. Above the sound of iron-shod hoofs pounding the ground, Hays said, "There's got to be a way around the Mexicans."

April 1843

Since his arrival at the Trinity Gun Works, Gain Borden had made some progress. While the nitrated cotton production continued, he was still plagued with the instability of the product. His laboratory was within a short walk of the Gun Works, but far enough away, to hear Andy Berry tell of it, that should he blow himself up, "the workers of the gun works would know of it right quick."

He was letting several sheets of compressed cotton, which had been soaked in the nitric and sulfuric acid mix earlier, dry. He had several other chemical compounds he intended to use when he milled the cotton into granules.

As if thinking of Andy Berry would make him appear, there was a knocking at the door and it swung open. The younger son of John Berry Sr. stood there holding two parts of a rifle. He saw the cotton sheets drying on one of the tables and set the pieces of the rifle on a separate table.

Bordon raised his eyebrows as he waited for Berry to break the silence. Finally, the young man said, "I don't suppose you've figured out how to stabilize the damned powder?"

Bordon pointed to several flasks which held various chemical compounds. "Working on it. What happened to the gun?"

Berry grimaced. "I've been trying to figure if we can use the nitrated cotton as a propellant."

"How's that working out?" Bordon asked as he looked at the pieces of the gun.

"It would be great if it wasn't so damned unstable. I was able to use the powder and fired a half-dozen shots with it before it blew up the breech-block and broke the gun," Berry said, "but not before I got off one shot that hit a target at more than six hundred yards away."

Bordon shuddered, "Here I thought I would be the one to blow myself up with this invention and lo and behold, you're determined to beat me to it, Andy."

Berry leaned against the work bench, "If Pa raised an idiot, it was one of the other boys. I'm using a shield and a string tied to the trigger to fire the rifle. Even though the nitrated cotton is overpowering our guns, it gives off hardly any smoke. If we can figure out how to stabilize it, then we can figure out how to build a rifle that can use it.'

Bordon, a devout man, said, "I'll pray that neither of us blow ourselves up in the process."

David Crockett watched the men of the 9th Infantry battalion make camp after a long day's march. The sun was waning in the sky, stretching his shadow along the ground. His command had made good time today, he thought, although he was exhausted from so many hours in the saddle. Despite the depot's proximity to a river, the ground was dry and crumbling beneath his feet. *"So much*

for April showers," Crockett thought as brittle grass crunched beneath his boots.

While most of the men under his command were busy setting up camp next to the supply depot, a few were assigned picket duty. Even though the platoon stationed at the depot was responsible for patrols, he believed if his men were vigilant now, then later, when it might really matter, the habit would be ingrained.

Major McCulloch, the battalion's second-in-command, stepped under the canvas pavilion, "Sir, you best come quick, one of the pickets spotted some Indians to our south."

A glance at the nearest campfire showed dinner would be a while. His joints ached as Crockett climbed to his feet and followed the major. Beyond the edge of the camp, a couple of pickets stood, facing southward. The former president followed where they were pointing, and in the distance, he saw several mounted figures making their way across the desolate South Texas prairie toward the camp.

He wished he had one of the new model binoculars as he shielded his eyes from the retreating sun. Six years in the office of the presidency had done nothing for his eyesight. Eventually, the figures became distinct and he saw two Indians and a white man riding slowly toward the camp. Eventually, he could see the Indians' features. "Them Indians look a tad on the young side, Major."

The younger brother of Brigadier General Ben McCulloch eyed the approaching riders. "Yes, sir. The boy ain't eighteen or I'm a ring-tailed panther. The girl is even younger. Hat's blocking the face of the write boy between them, though."

Crockett let his hand fall to his side. He silently cursed his eyes. Two boys and girl, two Indians and a white boy in the middle of West Texas. It was nearly too much. Then they were close enough for him to make out the features and it became too much.

"What in the blue blazes of hell are you doing here, Charles Edward Travis!" The authoritative tone surprised even Crockett as he yelled at his step-grandson.

He watched Charlie lift the brim of his hat, and as he saw Crockett, his eyes grew large. He squared his shoulders and pasted a smile on his face, "Howdy, Uncle Davy."

As the boy climbed down from his mount, his two companions watched Crockett dress him down.

"Becky's got to be out of her mind with worry about you, Charlie. What in tarnation gave you the idea to run away from home and come out here?" Crockett asked as Charlie tied his horse to the picket and began removing the tack.

Despite Crockett's grave tone, Charlie turned back to Crockett and said, "Why, you did, of course. You were younger than me when you ran away from your own Pa. And it ain't like I'm running away from home. After all, I'm with you, now. Pa and Becky can't say anything about that, because I'll just tell them I was taking care of you."

As Crockett's eyes bulged at the boy's effrontery, he was nearly certain he saw a twinkle in Charlie's eyes. "Take care of me? Why you, you..."

There were very few times a situation had left the famous frontiersman, politician, and raconteur speechless; this was one of them.

DOWN MEXICO WAY

Later that night, Crockett sat next to the fire. Major McCulloch stirred the coals with a stick. "You going to send the boy back, Colonel?"

Crockett frowned, "I ought to. But damned if part of me don't think Charlie's right. He's older than I was when I ran off. While I don't need no wet-behind-the-ears pup looking after me, I'm of a mind to let him come along. He sees how tough the soldier's life is, he may be begging me to send him back to Becky."

McCulloch offered, "I was talking with the Lieutenant in charge of the depot. He's not expecting another wagon for another fortnight or longer. If you were of a mind to risk him running off again, you could send him back on the next supply wagon."

Crockett glowered at the young man. "Did your brother assign you to me to be a thorn in my ass, Major? I ain't going to risk Charlie running off to heaven knows where. But now that you mention that supply wagon, I know one thing that will be on it when it heads back east."

The next morning, as the sun edged over the horizon, Charlie found himself sitting on a camp stool with Crockett's writing desk before him. "Two letters boy. One to Becky and another to your pa. We ain't moving until you've written both them letters. I'll pack your ass back to San Antonio on the first supply wagon If you don't own up to this boneheaded choice of yours."

He glowered at the youth. A smile pulled at the boy's lips. Over the years, the boy had come to read his "Uncle Davy" well. Charlie picked up the pen, inked the nib, and starting writing. He was going west.

Chapter 14

20 April 1843

Captain Bill Sherman pulled on the reins of the mule as both man and beast carefully placed their feet along an old trail worn into the side of a mountain. The beast was weighed down with the wheels of one of his battery's mountain howitzers. Another mule, following behind, carried the howitzer's barrel. Several more beasts were burdened with boxes of ammunition for the 12-pounder howitzer. The rest of the battery was strung out behind him as they inched along the treacherous trail.

A couple of Rangers had stumbled upon the trail the previous day, when retreating from a failed attempt to cut the Mexican army's line of retreat. As he stepped over a large rock in the middle of the trail, Sherman allowed his thoughts to wander. Both infantry brigades had arrived and now faced Almonte's well-entrenched *soldados*. He knew this trail bisected two mountains. He prayed the Rangers had gauged the trail correctly.

He turned away from the mule and looked upward. The trail disappeared over a ridge and he saw one of the

Rangers standing, silhouetted against the rising sun. "This way, Captain. I can see tents in the valley below."

Sherman redoubled his effort, pulling on the mule's reins. When he crested the rise, he turned to his right and saw the peak rising twenty-five hundred feet above the valley. It hid the enemy trench lines, but the Mexican camp was spread out below. He abruptly stopped. Thousands of tents bathed the valley in a carpet of dingy white. He pulled his eyes away from the encampment and scanned the slope below until he found a spot halfway down the mountain where he could place his howitzers.

The squad of Rangers who had led the way were already filtering down the mountainside as he stepped off the trail and watched his men lead the pack mules by. Behind his battery came the 8th Infantry battalion. Before General Travis had reorganized the army, they had been known as the 1st Cherokee Rifles. Now, more than five hundred men strong, the Cherokee riflemen flowed across the crest, on the heels of the artillery.

Behind the Cherokee battalion came three hundred men from the 5th Infantry and the remainder of Hays' three Ranger companies. In all, there were close to a thousand men.

With an eye firmly on the camp below, Captain Sherman positioned his guns on the slope. Anchoring his right flank was a jagged peak, jutting several hundred feet into the sky. On the other side of the peak the slope gradually descended into the Mexican encampment. The Cherokee battalion covered the ground between the jagged peak and the steep mountainside a few hundred yards upslope.

"Amazing they haven't seen us yet." The voice behind him startled Sherman and he turned. Major Hays stood behind him.

Recovering from the surprise, he nodded. "Yes, sir. We should be ready to open fire on the camp below in a few minutes."

"That'll give me time to get my Rangers and the boys from the 5th further down the slope. The camp's still a far piece from here. Do you think your guns can hit it?"

Sherman glanced toward the camp. The closest tents were a thousand yards away. "Given our elevation, we should be able to lob our shells into the camp. I figure we're five hundred feet above the valley. We should be able to land shells up to a mile out. Anything we hit at that range will be pure gravy."

Hays stared at the valley through a pair of binoculars, his lips skinned back in a ferocious grin. "No matter, Captain. We're like the boy kicking an ant pile."

Sherman winced at the analogy. "All those ants are going to be focused on our men, Major. It could get pretty hot around here once they see us."

"I hope so, Captain. Let me know as soon as your boys are ready to fire."

A few minutes later, Sherman's six guns opened fire on the Mexican camp and the Battle of Candela began.

Will watched the sun rise over the crest of the mountain to the east. With any luck, Major Hays and his mixed command would open fire on Almonte's rear. The men of Johnston's brigade were positioned in shallow trenches less than a half-mile from the Mexican army's left flank. McCulloch's brigade, that which wasn't with Hays'

flanking maneuver, faced the heavily entrenched Mexican right flank, along the slope of the same mountain that Hays was attempting to circumnavigate.

He went over again in his mind, for what seemed the thousandth time, the plan of battle. Once the flanking attack hit the encampment, Johnston would wait fifteen minutes for Almonte's army to become focused on the threat to their rear, then the rest of Will's artillery would open fire on the Mexican trenches before Johnston's brigade would go forward, targeting the enemy's extreme left flank, which was anchored against a steep hill. Unlike the mountain on the enemy's right flank, this hill wasn't fortified. Artillery couldn't be positioned on its steep slope. A couple of artillery batteries were positioned on the Mexican left, along the valley where it bisected the road between Candela and Monterrey.

McCulloch's brigade would advance up the slope far enough to engage the Mexican right. Their goal was to hold the *soldados* in place along the mountain slope, keeping them from lending support to their troops in the rear or on the left flank.

Once Johnston's brigade broke through, then Seguin's Cavalry would sweep forward, racing toward the encampment, with a goal of hooking up with Hays' flanking force. With a lot of luck, Will hoped he would destroy Almonte's army. The last thing he needed was to pursue the resourceful Mexican general sixty miles through the mountains to Monterrey.

The sun rose above the mountain. There wasn't a cloud in the sky when Will heard the rumble of thunder. The battery of mountain howitzers had opened fire.

The ground reverberated under his feet as General Juan Almonte set the half-eaten tortilla down. His breakfast forgotten, he knocked over the fragile camp chair when he jumped to his feet. Outside the large pavilion, which served as his headquarters, *soldados* turned and looked to the north, toward *Cerro Providencia*, the mountain around which he had centered his defenses.

Across the valley, halfway up the slope, where the mountain merged with a smaller one to the east, he saw puffs of smoke. Several shells exploded hundreds of feet overhead. Part of his mind noted the premature detonations. Whoever commanded the enemy artillery had cut the fuses too short.

Apart from the artillery on the mountainside, he listened and heard no other sounds of attack. At least not yet. Turning, he called to an orderly, "Sound Officers call, now!"

A moment later a bugler belted out a melodic tune. A few minutes later, when shells started landing on the edge of the encampment, Almonte's divisional commanders arrived, followed by several brigade commanders.

"Joaquin," Almonte turned to the first divisional commander, "what word from the trenches?"

The major general in command of the first division said, "The latest is that there is no action from the Texian line."

For the time being, that appeared to be good news. "What about the artillery on the mountainside?"

The other divisional commander said, "I've ordered a company of camp provost guards up the slope. There are riflemen downslope protecting the enemy artillery. I've ordered my reserve regiment to engage their infantry.

With any luck, we'll push their riflemen back against their guns."

Almonte worried the general's confidence was misplaced. The ground shook as a shell exploded nearby on impact. The Texian artillery officer had fixed his problem and was now using longer fuses.

"Take our reserve regiments and, if you're able, turn them back," Almonte told the divisional commander. He scanned the other officers until he found the brigadier in command of the army's cavalry.

"General Sesma, how many lancers can you assemble behind our left flank?"

An officer in an elaborate red and green uniform looked thoughtful before he replied, "We've taken a beating, sir. I can probably move five hundred mounted men over there. If you're worried about the Texians turning our line there, we'll need more than my men. What about one of the *Cazadores* regiments?"

Orders were issued, and one of the *Cazadores* regiments was pulled back from the hillside fortified positions, and another regiment was moved forward, replacing it.

The earth shook again as thirty guns along the Texian front opened fire. Almonte resisted the urge to groan. General Travis was expanding his attack.

Brevet Captain Javier Morales knelt beside two of his riflemen. His company had been pulled from the fortified line earlier and force marched across the plains behind the army's front line, until arriving at their current position, a half mile behind the army's left flank. Most of the army's remaining cavalry were deployed in front of his riflemen.

Even so, he could see smoke rising from the trenches, where Mexican *soldados* were firing on advancing Texian riflemen.

He knew things were going badly when several men leapt from the trench and threw away their muskets as they ran away from the oncoming Texians.

The retreating *soldados* raced by the lancers, and Morales waited to see if General Sesma would order the cowards ridden down. The lancers held their position. A look back to the trenches showed dozens of men retreating now. What started as a trickle of men was turning into a torrent. Through the haze of gun smoke, he saw the lone star flag waving, before whoever carried it leapt into the trench.

A thin line of *soldados* maintained an orderly withdrawal from the trenches as the Texians captured the earthworks. They faced the trenches from which they had just been driven. They might have continued their orderly retreat, except even that island of order broke down when Texian riflemen lined up along the back side of the trench and fired. Several *soldados* fell and the remainder turned and fled.

Nearly eight-hundred yards separated the *Cazadores* regiment from the trenches. The Texians extended their hold by ejecting the demoralized *soldados* from the remaining section of the trenchworks in the valley. Only where the trenches angled upwards to the heavily fortified positions on the slope of Cerro Providencia, did the line hold.

There was activity directly to Morales' front in the trenches as men in butternut uniforms scurried around. Seconds later, He saw them laying heavy boards across the trench. Moments after that, cavalry thundered across the planks.

Morales expected General Sesma's lancers to attack as soon as the Texian cavalry appeared, but Sesma waited to see what the enemy horsemen would do. By the time several hundred horsemen had crossed over the trenchworks, it was clear to even the inexperienced Morales the Texians intended to move toward the camp.

General Sesma must have come to the same conclusion. Piercing notes from a bugle rose above the din of combat. Morales watched the lancers surge across the open ground, intent to take the enemy cavalry in the flank.

"Captain Morales!" He turned and saw the Lt. Colonel in charge of the ad-hoc regiment of riflemen. "Get your men moving. We're to support General Sesma's counterattack."

With his rifle in one hand, Morales waved his other toward the backs of the lancers and urged his men from their hastily dug defensive positions.

The sun was setting. A rivulet cut across the narrow valley. One of his *Cazadores* dipped a canteen into the well churned, muddy water. His men had been without fresh water after they had retreated through the remains of their camp nearly ten hours before. Morales looked around him. When the day had been young, he commanded nearly thirty riflemen. He still commanded nearly thirty riflemen, but he couldn't find any joy in the thought. The regiment was under the command of a senior captain and had been consolidated into three remaining companies.

In his exhaustion, the young captain felt moisture building at the corner of his eye. The worst of the battle had not been when the regiment attacked the Texian cavalry's flank. No, that had slowed the attack, and had allowed nearly the entire brigade still in the trenches on the slope of the mountain to slip away, back toward the camp.

Nor had the worst come when his men had stepped over the dead *soldados* who had charged up the slope toward the guns the Texians had used to flank the army. The worst hadn't been seeing his men cut low when canister shot had crashed into them when they charged the howitzers.

Once the army had broken itself on the slope of the backside of the mountain, the only concern had been to save as much of it as possible. He had been sure his men were beaten as they retreated down the slope. Then General Almonte had ridden up to them.

Even now, hours later, the general's voice echoed in his head. "Men of Mexico! My valiant brothers in arms! Do not despair. The battle is not lost." He had paused, looking at the *Cazadores*, who had stopped streaming by and listened to their army's commander.

"We are victorious as long as our army yet lives. Today is only a setback, brothers! We will make the enemies of our homeland pay for every foot between here and Monterrey."

No longer running away, the men of the *Cazadores* regiment cheered their general. Morales wiped away the moisture at his eye as he replayed that image in his mind.

The worst had come afterwards. Much of the army was in headlong retreat and the *Cazadores* were ordered to hold a narrow point in the valley. More than two hundred riflemen had dug in between two ridges along the valley and waited for the Texians to arrive. They drove back the cavalry who had come first. Then they fought wave after wave of riflemen. That had been the worst of it.

Only half the men who fought with him escaped from there. They retreated beyond the other *Cazadores* regiment until they found another narrow space to defend between the ridgelines through which the valley ran.

Now, as the sun fled from the western sky, the two *Cazadores* regiments were ghosts of their former selves, but they had held back the onslaught of the Texian army. Tomorrow when the sun arose, the one thing Morales knew for sure was the fight would continue. If General Travis wanted Monterrey, he would have to pay for it with the blood of his men. Morales shuddered as he considered it would be his riflemen paying in blood to hold back the Texian advance.

Lanterns burned bright, reflecting light on the canvas hospital tent. Will stood at the entry. Doctor Smith was extracting a bullet from a soldier's shoulder. The tent was full of the wounded from the day's battle. Will felt no elation seeing that most of the men waiting for the doctor's attention wore the blue uniform of Mexico. All too many of his own men had passed through the doctor's tent or were buried in a nameless Mexican valley.

He stepped away from the tent and saw both Sidney Johnston and Ben McCulloch coming his way. McCulloch spoke first. "Hell's bells, Buck, Jack did us all proud. That flanking maneuver saved a lot of lives."

Still thinking about the row upon row of bodies waiting for the doctor's knife, Will held his peace as

Johnston nodded. "It could have been a lot worse. We took less than a hundred casualties before the Mexican line. The boys from the 7th Infantry took the worst when they went into the trenches. About half our casualties came from when they took the trenchworks."

Will couldn't help but acknowledge that portion had gone as planned. "That's true, Sid. Make sure that you pass along to your boys that they did a fantastic job. But damn it all. We needed to have bagged Almonte's army. And the sad truth is, we came up short."

McCulloch patted him on the back, "Buck, the army did a commendable job. Juan's cavalry was handling those lancers just fine until those damned *Cazadores* hit them in the flank. I think it's pretty clear Almonte was willing to sacrifice both his cavalry and his riflemen so that the rest of his army could escape."

Will cursed, "We should have bagged his army, Ben. There's no way that Almonte will allow himself to be brought to a pitched battle between here and Monterrey. Now we've got to clear his men out of the mountain passes and narrow valleys across the next sixty miles. Then we'll have to dig his army out of Monterrey."

Uppermost in Will's mind was a nagging worry that the war needed quick resolution. For that to happen, Texas had needed a large enough army to invade Mexico. He amended his thought, capture enough of Mexico to get Santa Anna's political allies to turn on him. He had convinced Crockett, when he had been president, and now Zavala, that a large army could quickly bring Mexico to the bargaining table. Texas was a land of no more than two-hundred thousand people and ten thousand of them were actively serving in the army. Another ten-thousand were in the militia. The cost to the treasury was more than the government could afford, especially if the war dragged on. In the world Will had left behind, the Republic of Texas had accepted annexation with the United States, and one of the reasons for it was because they had been unable to manage their own financial situation. If the war dragged on, did it increase the likelihood the economy would collapse? If so, would that strengthen the hand of hotheaded slaveholders like Robert Potter, who had been agitating for annexation since the revolution?

Johnston had been talking, and Will realized he had been woolgathering. "Why don't you get Hays' Rangers to see if there's a way around this route to Monterrey? We flanked Almonte once. Maybe we can do it again."

The idea of trying a flanking maneuver sounded good and Will said, "I'll write up the orders tonight. Tomorrow, we'll start on the road to Monterrey. With any luck, Jack will find a way around."

Chapter 15

27 April 1843

Shards of rock rained down on Jesse Running Creek's head as he ducked behind a boulder. He swore as he wiped his face and saw streaks of red on his hand. His face stung where the bits of rock had cut him. His teammate, Jethro Elkins crouched beside him. He wore a sardonic expression. "You still think we'll cut through the Mexican rear guard, Jess?"

Dabbing his face with a once-white handkerchief, the young Cherokee glowered at his fellow Ranger. "As I recall, I said that we'd make good time if Almonte's army hightails it back to Monterrey. This don't look anything like 'hightailing' it to me."

Elkins pulled on his luxuriant, brown mustache and chuckled quietly. "If that ain't an understatement, I don't know what is."

Jesse nodded. Six days had passed since the army had defeated the Mexicans at Candela. Six days and only thirty miles. Efforts to find a way around the Mexican line of retreat had, as of yet, gone nowhere. Major Hays had taken one of the other special Ranger companies and had yet to return from scouting a northern route.

He chanced a look around the boulder and saw a stone outcropping nearby. He checked his rifle and confirmed the percussion cap was still snugly set then he sprinted toward the outcropping's shelter.

A puff of wind breezed by his face and bullets zinged off the rocky ground as he ran. Despite furtive glances down the rock-lined gorge, he couldn't see where the shots were coming from. Seconds later, Elkins landed beside him. The other Ranger drew ragged breaths, matching his own labored breathing as they sheltered behind the stone outcropping.

He thrust his rifle around the ledge then jutted his head around in time to see a blue-jacketed *soldado* scampering across the stony ground. Jesse snugged the rifle butt against his shoulder and fired at the retreating figure. The bullet shattered against the gorge's rocky wall, bathing the Mexican in a shower of stone shards. As Jesse reloaded, he felt no satisfaction at paying back the enemy rifleman in kind.

A pat on his shoulder warned him that Elkins was moving past, running across the uneven ground. He made it to the place where the *soldado* had disappeared. No bullets tore at the ground around the Ranger. Jesse exhaled noisily. The cat and mouse hunting between the Texian vanguard and the Mexican rearguard was playing hell on his nerves.

He turned and called out, "Hey, Corporal! This vale is clear of Mexicans. Me and Ranger Elkins will move out and see if we can find the sons of bitches that have been shooting at us for the past hour."

Without waiting for confirmation, Jesse bolted after Elkins. As his boots pounded down the rocky path, he had to admit to himself the tactics the army used were saving lives, even if the process was slow. His team of four Rangers were part of five rifle-teams made up of half a company of Rangers. Of the four men in his team, one was back a few hundred yards, holding the reins of their horses. The corporal was following behind him and Elkins.

Over the past year's training, Jesse had come to admire the other men in his team. He knew if circumstances demand it, he'd readily risk his life for the other three men. He knew they'd do the same for him.

As he rounded the corner in the gorge, he heard the echoing shot from Elkins' rifle. Before the gorge curved again a few hundred feet further in, he saw a blue-clad rifleman. Jesse had learned to hate the *Cazadores* since the Battle on the Rio Grande what seemed a lifetime ago. While there was no contest between the Texians' breechloading rifles and the old Bakers rifles the *Cazadores* carried, the Mexican riflemen had been using similar tactics throughout the campaign across northern Mexico. It was as if they had read the Texian manual.

Elkins was reloading when Jesse arrived. "Any luck?"

The other Ranger spat a stream of tobacco juice, hitting a cactus leaf square in the center, "No. Scared them from where they were roosting, though."

He moved past his companion as Elkins reloaded. They would leapfrog the rest of the way down this gorge, until the next time they came under fire from the wily Mexican *Cazadores*.

Captain Javier Morales lowered the captured binoculars from his face. He had found them after his regiment had hit the Texian cavalry in the flank. The binoculars had been tied to the saddle of a horse. The rider was nowhere to be seen, and he was happy to purloin the fancy glasses. They were more compact than the spyglasses that other officers used. The fact that he could use both his eyes to sweep the rocky valley below, he thought, increased his field of vision.

Two rifle teams were pulling back from the advancing Texians. A ghost of a smile crossed his face as he watched a team of three cover the withdrawal of the others. Despite the near constant skirmishing between the Texian vanguard and the remnants of the two rifle-armed light infantry regiments, casualties had been relatively light. He was proud his men used the cover to their advantage.

The slight smile vanished as a couple of Texians, in their butternut uniforms came into focus. The taller one had a mustache. He crouched behind a boulder while the smaller one, with brownish features raced down the narrow trail until he slid up to another outcropping, where the sides of the valley were veritable cliffs. An irritated sigh escaped Morales' lips. If his men had suffered few casualties, as they slowed the Texian advance to a crawl, the Texians who pursued his men were equally cautious. From the dozens of daily reports his men provided him, Morales could verify his men had killed only a small handful of their pursuers.

2 May 1843

This was a good hill, he thought, as he stood atop the knoll north of Monterrey. No binoculars were needed for

Will to see down into the town. Just to the north of town was what his men had taken to calling the Black Fort. It was a partially constructed cathedral, with thick, adobe walls surrounding the structure. Each corner had a masonry bastion jutting out from the adobe-brick walls. Flying over the cathedral was a large green, white, and red flag. Will glared down at the fortification. Was Almonte there in the confines of the fort, or in town where most of the Mexican army had taken shelter?

It had taken nearly two weeks for his army to force the Mexican rear-guard back to Monterrey. That was two weeks he could ill afford. It had seemed like new correspondence arrived daily from the government in Austin, urging a quick victory. Will knew the government was hemorrhaging cotton-backs keeping his army in the field, but despite the cost, supply wagons kept rolling south from the Alamo almost daily, filled with the provisions his army needed to survive. Despite President Zavala's concern over the cost of the war, he twisted every arm in Congress to get every new spending bill through both houses.

To the south stood the former mountainside palace of the Bishop of Monterrey. One of Hays' Ranger companies confirmed that at least one regiment of Mexican infantry had fortified the position. Then there was the city itself. Monterrey was the densely packed home to more than ten thousand souls. From the outskirts, to the city center, barricades had been thrown up and rooftops had been fortified.

Were time of no consideration, Will would happily move his own battalions around the town, cutting it off from the south and wait until food ran short and Almonte had no other choice than to surrender. His latest letter from Austin killed any such dream. It was politely phrased, as were all the president's missives. But between the flowery prose, Will picked up on Zavala's desperation. The treasury department's latest bond auction had been poorly attended and they had been forced to sell the bonds at steep discounts. To make matters worse, the Commodities Bureau was printing cotton-backs in excess of available commodities. It was a shell game. If the war wasn't brought to a satisfactory conclusion sooner rather than later, the entire economy of the Republic could crash.

Will shook his head in frustration as his eyes watched a column of Mexican infantry snake down one of Monterrey's streets, marching toward the black fort. A long siege was out of the question. He needed a quick victory. Even before the transference into the body of William Barret Travis, Will had been no stranger to combat, having served a combat tour a few years earlier in Iraq, but the idea of throwing his army against the fortified positions around Monterrey gave him pause. So far, his army had taken relatively light casualties. Less than four hundred men had been killed or wounded during the first two battles, and Doctor Ashbel Smith and the other battalion surgeons had managed to keep the number of sick to a surprisingly small number. Nine out of every ten soldiers who had marched from the Alamo six weeks before were still with the army. To a soldier of the twenty-first century, the losses would seem staggeringly high, but to the men of the nineteenth, it was manageable.

He ground his teeth in frustration, his eyes scanning the town. The only question he needed answered was how long before he would be ready to attack. Hays' Rangers and one of Seguin's cavalry battalions were already here. Johnston's brigade would arrive on the morrow and

McCulloch's the day after. If he pushed his officers and men, in three or four days he could order the assault.

"On the other hand," he thought, *"if we bypass the black fort and focus on the city, there won't be any massed charges against heavily fortified positions. If we capture the town, the fort will have no choice but to surrender."*

He turned his back on the town and clambered down the hill, followed by several guards and orderlies. The thought of bypassing the fort buoyed his spirits as he mounted his horse and rode back toward his camp.

Latticed scaffolding rose along the inner walls of the half-built church that was the center of the black fort. General Juan Almonte perched atop the thick adobe walls. Dust clouds to the northwest announced the arrival of the lead elements of the Texian army. His *Cazadores* regiments had succeeded beyond his expectations. The fact that they had delayed the enemy for nearly two weeks was a minor miracle.

He had been able to fortify the Bishop's palace and bring from storage several old siege guns which had been part of the presidio's supplies. The old guns were serviceable and were mounted on the bastions of the fort. An entire brigade garrisoned the fort while another regiment had taken up residence in the former Bishop's Palace. The balance of the army, more than six thousand men, had displaced much of the civilian population of the town, many of whom had fled to Saltillo, sixty miles away.

A noise behind him caused him to turn. General Sesma stood behind him, gasping for air. "How, by the Blessed Virgin, do you manage to climb up here, General?" Sesma gasped.

His lips turned upward as he stepped over, offering a spot on the wall. "How are your men enjoying the charms of Monterrey?" Almonte asked.

The older cavalry officer carefully stepped onto the wall from the scaffolding. "I wonder if the only folks who didn't flee town were the prostitutes. I believe those are the only charms to be found, sir."

Almonte laughed. "Those are charms they should do without, but they are fighters, not priests. As you can see, General Travis has arrived with his army. I expect the whole of his force will be here within the next few days. If they try to encircle the town, do you think your lancers can break through?"

Sesma stared at the dust cloud to the north for more than a minute before he responded. "The answer you're looking for is yes. But the sad truth is that my boys took a serious beating holding back the enemy at Candela when you needed to extract the men who had been fortifying the mountain. I doubt I could scrounge up three hundred men on horseback. Against the Texians' rifles, we'd be torn to pieces."

Almonte hid his disappointment. In a moment of honesty, it was what he had expected. If Travis decided to besiege Monterrey, there was little he could do to stop him.

Chapter 16

11 May 1843

Dust rose behind the two youths racing their horses along the wide, hard-packed road next to the Rio Grande. Mountain runoff had long dissipated, returning the mighty river to its normal languorous state. Charlie Travis tore his eyes from the graded road before him and chanced a look behind. Victorio's mount was less than a horse-length behind as the young Apache warrior urged his mount to gallop faster.

The road snaked around a low rising hill and Charlie sawed on the reins, bringing his horse to a halt as the wide road ended. It was replaced by deep-rutted wagon tracks. The redheaded youth used his hat to wipe sweat from his brow as his friend drew up beside him. The last month had improved the young Apache's English. His grin was infectious as he said, "Charlie, what you do with the road?"

Charlie laughed and patted his pockets as though searching for something, "It twern't me, Victorio. I've no idea who stole the road."

The hard-packed surface's abrupt end was a mystery to the boys. Deep ruts, a half foot deep in places, gouged the trail where wagons had plowed through soupy muck, during a recent rainstorm.

In Spanish, a girl's voice called out, "Victorio, did Charlie beat you again?"

Charlie turned in his saddle and saw Lenna riding up to them. Behind her a squad of cavalry troopers approached.

The past month had cemented his friendship with Victorio. The young warrior was carefree. He enjoyed traveling along with the Texian column. Charlie would have enjoyed the friendship more, except for Lenna. When he tried to talk to her, his words became tangled. It was hard enough thinking of things to say to her, and when he tried to articulate them, they came out all wrong. Adding to the awkwardness was the way she looked at him. It had been bad enough when she would gaze at him with open curiosity. Lately though, the frank inquisitive gaze had been replaced by furtive glances and half-smiles that left Charlie awash in uncertainty. Sometimes, like now, when she made fun of her brother and smiled at him, his stomach knotted up.

When the mounted soldiers arrived, one with two black stripes on his sleeves said, "This is where the colonel told us to hold up for the day." He glanced at the three youths, "Why don't y'all ride on back to the column and let Colonel Crockett know we've reached the end of the military road."

Pushing thoughts of Lenna from his mind, the sudden end of the road made sense. The engineers had stopped constructing the military road north of Ysleta when his pa and the army had returned from Santa Fe. This must have been as far as they had come. A few minutes later they found the column. Nearly a thousand men were strung out over several hundred yards. Nearly nine hundred infantry were sandwiched between two troops of cavalry.

Later, after camp had been made and Charlie had finished his own chores, which largely included setting up his Uncle Davy's tent and helping to cook the officers' dinner, he pulled up a short log, set it near the campfire, and sat. He liked listening to his Uncle Davy's stories. Most evenings, the former president was gregarious, telling stories collected over close to half a century. Over the years, Charlie had heard nearly all them, but the old raconteur had a way of making even an old tale seem new.

This evening, though, the colonel was uncommonly reserved. The battalion's second-in-command, Major McCulloch, broke the silence. "Colonel, what's it going to be?"

Rather than responding, Crockett retrieved a pipe from a pocket and after lighting it, he puffed on the stem for what seemed an eternity to Charlie. Finally, he said, "Strange, for the past year events have been working towards this moment, Henry."

The young major held his peace as Crockett continued, "We told everyone that we needed to finish what Buck started last year and put the government firmly in control of Santa Fe. Lorenzo certainly talked it up to the newspapers across the Republic. Lordy, how they'll squeal like stuck pigs when they find out that we had bigger plans than just Santa Fe."

Charlie leaned in, listening to Uncle Davy. He hadn't heard this before. From the other side of the campfire, Henry McCulloch said, "It's your call, Colonel. We can keep marching north, come the morrow and in a week, we'll be in Santa Fe."

A log, mostly burned through, cracked in the center, sending embers spiraling into the night. Crockett's eyes reflected the flames, and to the boy, it appeared they burned brightly. "No, Henry. Too much has been invested in this venture. Tomorrow, I'll send Captain Benson, with three companies, north. He'll have enough to garrison the town. The rest of us, we're turning west tomorrow."

Charlie's eyebrows shot up in surprise. What was to the west, except more desert?

As though reading the boy's mind, Crockett continued, "In three weeks if we haven't captured Tucson, I'm not the Lion of the West." His eyes, still reflecting the campfire's flickering embers, burned. Long ago Charlie learned his Uncle Davy thought all the legends surrounding supposed exploits was nothing but hokum. But sometimes, Crockett was happy to use such hokum to his own advantage. "Another three weeks after that and we'll capture San Diego and Norte California."

Will turned to his orderly, "Make note of the time, Lieutenant."

The young officer squinted at the page in the notebook as he scribed the date and time, 13 April 1843, 6:30 a.m.

Was it a vanity, Will wondered, to make note of what he hoped to be the beginning of the final battle of the war with Mexico? He worried, was it vanity or wishful thinking? With two victories under his belt, Will was confident in his army's ability to defeat Almonte's larger army. But twice before, Almonte had escaped with his force intact. The enemy general's ability to sacrifice pieces of his army so the greater whole would escape to fight again grated against Will's hunger for a knock-out blow. Will was growing to appreciate that time was a greater enemy than the Mexican army.

Aware the orderly was staring at him, Will turned and said, "Send my compliments to Lt. Colonel Carey. He may open fire."

With a hurried salute, the young officer flung himself into the saddle and was cantering across the field north of Monterrey, toward Carey's grand battery.

In his mind, Will envisioned the orderly passing the orders to the artillery officer from Virginia. Carey's grand battery included all the army's artillery. The thirty-six guns were positioned in an arc, separated from the city and the Black Fort by an anemic creek, where a flow of water trickled toward the Rio Santa Catarina. The city's southern boundary was defined by the bank of the fast-flowing, narrow river.

Six guns faced southward, focused on the steep slope, atop of which sat the Bishop's palace. On the opposite end of the grand battery twelve guns faced the formidable walls of the Black Fort, including Captain Sherman's howitzers. The other eighteen guns angled to the southwest, facing the homes and businesses of Monterrey.

Will resisted the urge to look at his pocket watch. The glow in the east was still too dim to see the watch's hands. He didn't need to see it to know the orderly had arrived at the grand battery and was passing along the orders. In moments, shells would rain down on the buildings that ten thousand souls called home. Two days before, Will had sent an officer under flag of truce, demanding the town's surrender. He had sent it with no expectation that Almonte would acquiesce, but the sternly worded missive had warned Almonte that the full horrors of war would be visited upon the town if surrender wasn't forthcoming.

In a fiery crescendo, the Texian gunners opened fire. From north to south, each gun erupted, throwing shot and shell at their respective targets. The battle was joined. Will was mollified that many of the ten thousand *regiomontanos* had fled over the past forty-eight hours, but he couldn't help wondering how many had remained behind, convinced that Almonte's army would protect them. Will closed his eyes against the horror an exploding shell would wreak on the soft tissue of an innocent civilian. He offered a silent prayer that all civilians had fled the town as shells began detonating on the edge of Monterrey.

Coffee vibrated in the tin cup as a shell detonated in the distance. General Juan Almonte sent a fleeting glance at the mug, in which the liquid had long grown cold. The enemy's guns had been firing for more than an hour already, although none had landed within the walls of the citadel in the center of Monterrey. Semaphore signals from the Black Fort and the Bishop's Palace indicated the bombardment had been largely ineffectual.

He amended the thought. The enemy howitzers didn't need to breach the fort's thick walls, when they could lob their shells over the very walls designed to protect against this type of attack. Even so, apart from a few shells injuring men in the fort, the attack was largely sound and fury. The tin cup rattled again as another shell detonated nearby. For now, it was sound and fury. It wasn't likely to remain that way for long.

A little while later he climbed to the top of a bell tower, part of the citadel's chapel. He could see over the houses, most of which were only a single-story tall. The large green, white, and red national flag flew proudly over the incomplete cathedral which was the focal point of the Black Fort. Although he couldn't see them, he imagined hundreds of *soldados* crouching behind the solid adobe walls. Should the Texians attack the well-positioned fort, they would pay a terrible butcher's bill.

He swiveled his eyes to the west. The steep slope that led to the Bishop's palace was easy to see. The men who defended the residence were hard to spot, but he knew they ringed the entire plateau.

Between the fortified heights of the Bishop's palace and the walls of the Black Fort were several thousand homes and businesses tightly packed between the narrow crisscrossing streets of Monterrey. He feared this would be where the battle would be decided. Every building that could be fortified had been and barricades slashed across most of the streets. To Almonte's way of thinking, General Travis had one good option. Taking the city would cut off the other fortified positions. The only question was, how long before Travis would recognize it and attack?

The sun had been overhead for more than an hour when the question answered itself. The Texian artillery had reduced its fire to infrequent and sporadic bursts by the end of the morning. Whether it was because Travis found it to be ineffectual or because of supply issues with the Texians' ammunition, Almonte could only speculate.

Had the wind not blown from the north, Almonte wouldn't have heard the faint pounding of a drum. From the same direction a thin line of riflemen started across the valley. When they were only a few hundred yards shy of the city, they opened fire as they advanced. Behind the thin line came more men in ugly brown uniforms favored by the Texians. The battle was joined.

The air exploded from Jesse Running Creek's lungs when his body slammed against the house's adobe wall.

The ground behind him was pockmarked with .69 caliber musket balls. Private Elkins knelt beside him, aiming his rifle across the narrow street. Seconds before, a *soldado* had appeared on the roof, firing on another rifle team.

The mustachioed Elkins cursed under his breath, "Take the outer houses, they said. Clear a few roofs, they said. Give 'em one good kick and their defenses will crumble, they said."

Had their predicament not been so dire, Jesse might have found Elkins' editorializing humorous. As it was, the *soldados* were putting up a fierce defense. The Rangers had yet to clear the first line of houses. The men from the 3rd Infantry had followed the Rangers into the urban hell and now both commands were hopelessly mixed together.

The *soldado's* head reappeared on the opposite rooftop. Elkins fired, and the *soldado's* momentum carried him forward, until he pitched forward and fell to the road below with a heavy thud. How many more *soldados* were on top of that building? As Elkins pulled a percussion cap from his accoutrement box, Jesse said, "Cover me!"

The Cherokee Ranger sprinted across the street, and just before he rammed into the door, he turned, so his back slammed into it. For the second time in just a few minutes, his breath was knocked from his lungs.

Had the door been more sturdily constructed, he would have bounced off. Had that happened, he would have been lucky to have not drawn fire from the *soldados* on the other roofs, to say nothing of the ribbing he would have taken from Elkins and the other Rangers. Luck was with him, and the latch failed, and the door flew inward.

In a corner of the modest home a narrow staircase led to the roof. When he flipped the door open, he found the rooftop empty. The houses were built very close together, and in many cases were built side by side, sharing external walls. There was a narrow gap between this roof and the next. A thick, wooden board lay between the roofs.

The sound of the door to the roof opening startled a *soldado* on the next roof over, and he turned, swinging the barrel of his musket around. Jesse slammed his rifle into his shoulder and pointed it toward the enemy soldier. The *soldado's* barrel hadn't completed the arc when Jesse pulled the trigger. The .52 caliber ball struck the Mexican in the chest and he fell back, hitting the lip of the roof before tumbling to the street below.

Atop the nearby roofs, several *soldados* noticed Jesse standing exposed to their fire. Heavy lead balls turned the open trapdoor into kindling and splinters bit into his leg. Another shot passed inches over his head as Jesse fell flat on the roof. He was able to reload while lying prone. As he removed the fragments of the spent percussion cap, he was grateful to the gunsmiths of the Trinity Gun Works for their breechloader.

He raised up and saw a soldado standing up a few roofs over, reloading his musket. He aimed and fired. He ducked down as a bullet tore into the soft adobe brick on the wall below him. He became aware of something moving beside him and he turned and saw Elkins climbing through the trapdoor.

Between the two Rangers, in a few minutes they had cleared the other rooftops on this block of houses. The battle was far from over, but for Hays' special Rangers, they had captured the first housing block of Monterrey.

If the street had been narrower, a single overturned wagon would have been enough to block the way. Captain Morales sheltered behind the second wagon as the wood rattled with the impact of bullets. A fusillade of shots from the *soldados* on the rooftops behind him responded to the Texians' fire. He pulled the hammer back, flipped the frizzen up and checked the pan. There were enough granules of powder. He closed the frizzen and leaned over the side of the overturned wagon. A flutter of brown cloth at the other end of the street caught his attention and he aimed and fired.

He had no sooner ducked than the wooden frame of the wagon shook with more bullet impacts. The Texians had captured a line of houses on the edge of town earlier in the day once they had found their way onto the rooftops. Now they were using the same tactics against his men. Both sides had gunmen on the rooftops, taking shots at the other side.

Morales scanned the rooftop behind him and eyed several of his *Cazadores*. The truncated battalion of rifle-armed light infantry held a block of buildings a few hundred yards west of Monterrey's citadel. Texian riflemen had cut off the regiment holding the hilltop Bishop's Palace from the men in the citadel. In his hands he held orders from the Citadel, he was instructed to retake the city blocks between the divided forces, if practicable. More bullets thudded into the wooden boards he sheltered behind.

"If practicable," he growled. With the Texians holding the rooftops, any attempt to force their way down the streets was just suicidal.

As if to punctuate those thoughts, he heard a startled cry overhead and turned as a rifle clattered to the ground near his feet. The man, who seconds before had been aiming it, was dangling from the rooftop, blood dripping on the ground below, dead from a Texian marksman's bullet.

To no one in particular, Morales muttered, "it's not practicable." He grabbed a paper cartridge and began reloading.

15 April 1843

Will didn't think the thick, adobe walls of the Black Fort were impregnable. But two days' worth of bombardment had not damaged the outer walls as much as he had expected. He offered a silent prayer of thanks as the Mexican tricolor fluttered down. Cut off from the retreating army, the regiments trapped in the fort were surrendering.

Standing to his right was Sidney Johnston. "That would have been quite the butcher's bill, if they hadn't given up, Buck. I couldn't sleep a wink last night, thinking of leading my boys against those walls."

Will bobbed his head in agreement. What could he say, Johnston's brigade had more experienced men. Had it come down to it, Will would have sent his brigade forward. Hundreds of men would have been killed or wounded in such an attack. Both men breathed easier knowing it wouldn't happen now.

Taking the city of Monterrey and the central citadel in the heart of the town had come at a high enough price. More than a hundred men had died in the fighting, while hundreds more were wounded.

The Black Fort's drawbridge was lowered, and a few minutes passed by until the first of the Mexican *soldados* marched out. Having surrendered, they were parading from the fort without their weapons. Despite his army's best effort, Almonte had escaped with most of the men who had defended the town. Will's effort to cut off Almonte's army by sending Juan Seguin's cavalry across the river had been a failure.

The Mexican brigade marching out, played no music. Their musicians were stone-faced in defeat. Will's army brought no musicians to celebrate the victory. Will's thoughts returned to Almonte's escape. Seguin's cavalry had been tasked with cutting the lone bridge between the town and the road to Saltillo. But Almonte had positioned a regiment in an earthen fort which protected the bridge on the south side of the river. Dozens of men had fallen trying to seize the fort, but to no avail. At best guess, Almonte had escaped with close to five thousand men.

Will had read and reread Seguin's report of the battle, south of the river. Seguin maintained he had done everything within his power to take the objective. But with the escape of Almonte's force, part of Will couldn't help but wonder if Seguin had tried harder, or ordered another attack, if he would have succeeded.

When the last of the soldados left the fort, a company from Johnston's brigade paraded through the drawbridge and entered. Moments later, the lone star flag flew over the battlements. All of Monterrey was now under his army's control.

"General Sesma, if you can give me three days, I'll be able to get the remainder of the Army of the North to Saltillo."

General Juan Almonte's eyes pleaded with his cavalry commander. Sesma's horse was gaunt from the long marches the lancers had forced their horses to undergo. More than the scarecrow appearance of the brigade commander's horse was the haunted look Sesma gave Almonte.

His uniform grimy from days without being changed, General Sesma hesitated in his response. "Ah, General, I have scarcely three hundred men still mounted. If the Texians pursue, I can't promise my men can turn them back."

Almonte glowered at his subordinate. He had already endured a similar conversation from the senior captain who commanded the remnants of the *Cazadores* regiments. The army was spent, and Almonte knew it. The best he could hope for is to get to Saltillo. From there, he would decide his next steps. As it was, the army had been badly mauled in Monterrey. Three entire regiments, more than a thousand men had been stranded in the Black Fort. Part of him hoped they sold their lives dearly, bleeding the Texians of men they could ill afford to lose. But mostly, he hoped the men had surrendered. One thing he had come to appreciate, General Travis lacked Santa Anna's bloodthirsty refusal to take prisoners. Perhaps it would be for the best if the men in the Black Fort surrendered, he thought.

Some of the men who had fortified the Bishop's Palace atop the hill west of town had escaped after a harrowing running fight against Travis' riflemen. More than four hundred had defended the mountainous redoubt, but less than two hundred remained in the line of march now. More than a thousand men had failed to make good their escape from the rooftops and barricades in the town.

Almonte wore a stoic mask as he rode alongside one of his regiments. The Army of the North had started the campaign more than a month before with ten thousand men. Now, less than five thousand remained. Apart from a few hundred light infantry and lancers, he had lost the ability to screen his column. He knew it was a fool's errand, asking General Sesma to protect the army's rear against a serious effort on the part of Travis' Rangers.

In his marriage, his wife was the more devout of the two, but in that moment of hopelessness, Juan Almonte's fingers clenched the crucifix around his neck as he fervently prayed his army would break free of the Texians, and that somehow or another he would turn the army's fortunes around.

Chapter 17

17 April 1843

Wind whistled through Will's ginger hair as he stood on the balcony overlooking the central plaza within Monterrey's citadel. Warm rays of sunlight spilled over the mountains east of town. Steam eddied from the coffee mug which he had turned into a paperweight. Loose papers rustled beneath the ersatz weight.

Two days after the fall of the Black Fort, a semblance of normal was returning to the town. Despite evacuation orders, a few thousand *regiomontanos* of Monterrey had stayed, and when looting didn't materialize, store fronts began to open, and commerce started to flow again.

The top sheet of paper, Will thought, likely had more to do with the town not being looted than the goodwill of the average Texian solder. With a casual glance the lead sentence was easy to read, "Looters and Rapists Will be Hung!"

Despite the grim warning, two men were under guard in the citadel's stockade. Will's twenty-first century values had taken a drumming over the past seven years, but he had not batted an eye signing the court-martial's sentence of execution. While too many men had died taking the city away from Almonte's army, the two rapists were not, as far as Will was concerned, among that number.

He took a sip of the still-steaming coffee and thumbed through the various reports. Johnston's brigade had assaulted the town and had sustained the majority of the casualties. More than one-hundred-fifty dead and nearly three hundred wounded. More than fifteen percent casualties. The four battalions under Johnston now fielded less than two-thousand men. McCulloch's brigade fared somewhat better and still fielded nearly twenty-four hundred.

Seguin's cavalry, which included Hays' three special Ranger companies, was down to six hundred men. The artillery had come through the past couple of battles largely unscathed, apart from a few men who had become too ill to serve. Before meeting General Almonte's Army of the North on the Rio Grande more than a month before, Will had lead more than sixty-five hundred men. Now, after two pitched battles, a thousand men had been killed, wounded, or had become unfit for duty. The numbers were sobering.

Against that, he needed to weigh the government's goals. The army had been sent south to seek a peace treaty that would force Mexico to recognize Texas' independence and require the surrender of Santa Anna to Texas justice. Although it was the Zavala administration's official position, Will had fully supported both goals. But had he bitten off more than he could chew? He needed to pursue Almonte's army, but he also had to garrison Monterrey. Were he only concerned about the few thousand *Regiomontanos*, he could justify leaving a few companies from one of the reserve battalions behind. But the situation was more complicated than that. Between Laredo and Candela, he had been forced to leave a couple of companies to patrol the supply line. A few more were now patrolling between Candela and Monterrey. There were several cities and towns in northern Mexico capable of raising militia forces that could prey upon his army's supply line. Whether he wanted to or not, he would be forced to leave at least a battalion stationed in town.

A rapping on the balcony's glass paned door interrupted those thoughts. He turned and saw Sid Johnston looking through the window. Will forced a smile on his face and went back inside.

"Gentlemen, thank you for joining me. Before we can put Monterrey behind us, we have some tough decisions to make," Will said as General Johnston took a seat next to General McCulloch. General Juan Seguin took a chair on the opposite side of the table from the infantry officers.

Will collapsed into a high-backed wooden chair at the head of the table. "I've reviewed the casualty reports from each of the brigades, and it troubles me that we're down by a thousand men from a month ago."

Johnston grimaced at hearing the number before replying, "Sir, all our regiments have suffered more attrition than we expected. But most of those are men who are sick or wounded will return to their battalions, eventually."

Will inclined his head, "True, eventually. But we can't wait for them before we'll be forced to act. The first item I want to discuss is how large of a garrison should we leave here when we march on Saltillo."

Seguin leaned on the table, his elbows resting on the light mahogany. "More than half of the 2nd Cavalry are patrolling our supply lines between here and the Rio Grande, Buck. Add to that, a few companies of infantry have joined them. Even so, I think a single battalion would be more than enough to hold the town."

McCulloch chimed in. "Let's say that we leave one battalion holding the town, that would still give us about forty-five hundred men. We've destroyed at least half of Almonte's army. When we catch up to him, we'll be facing his army with even numbers. With our superior training and weapons, Almonte's going to have to surrender sooner or later. We should be on his tail, like stink on…"

Johnston made a cutting gesture with his hands, "Hold on, Ben. That's all well and good. But there's no guarantee, this far into Mexico, that we'll not be facing reinforcements from Mexico City. Would you want to go toe-to-toe with his army if it swells to twenty thousand?"

McCulloch swore, "I believe we could beat them in a fight."

Will cut through their talk. "I'll ask President Zavala to release another battalion or two to join us. It would be a mistake, I think, to presume Santa Anna won't reinforce Almonte. That request will go out today in the next mail packet to Austin. In the meantime, we need to get eyes on Almonte's army."

Seguin sighed, "Just when I thought my boys could have another few days of rest."

"No rest for the wicked, Juan," Will said with a tired laugh. "How many men does Major Hays still have?"

"Perhaps a hundred, maybe a few less."

Will nodded, "Tomorrow morning I want him moving toward Saltillo with one of his companies. We need to know what we'll face when we get there."

Will recognized the forced smile the Tejano brigadier general wore. He had worn the same smile on his face at the beginning of the meeting.

Scouting normally involved searching for clues about an enemy's trail, but as Major Jack Coffee Hays surveyed the road between Monterrey and Saltillo, he surmised even a blind man could follow the route of the retreating army. Broken gunstocks were scattered to either side of the road, along with bits and pieces of uniforms. Broken wagons were simply pushed to the side, empty of their contents if the Mexican soldados had found them of value.

He pursed his lips, an army in retreat was a strange beast. Serving in the Texian army over the past half dozen years, since his own arrival in Texas after the Treaty of Bexar, he had often wondered what would have become of him had the Texians lost the battles at the Rio Grande and the Nueces during the revolution. Images of Texians fleeing eastward toward Louisiana played in his mind.

His pursed lips lifted in a thin smile. He liked to think he played some small role in helping General Travis and President Crockett maintain an independent country. He treasured that moment from a few years before, when he had uncovered the Mexican effort to smuggle in counterfeit commodities certificates. There was no doubt in his mind he had played an important role then in propping up the Republic's struggling economy.

He was glad he had followed other Tennesseans west, like the former president or Ben McCulloch. He reached up and felt the shoulder boards on which golden oak leaves were embroidered. At twenty-six years of age, he knew Texas presented an opportunity for growth and advancement unlike anything available back east.

Of Hays' three special Ranger companies, this, his third, was the least battered. Of the company's original forty men, more than three-quarters of them rode with him. The other companies were back in Monterrey.

A horseman galloped toward him from the direction of Saltillo, one hand on the reins and the other clenching his hat. When he drew up before the major, Hays could see his horse was played out. The Ranger had ridden his mount hard to get back to the column. "Sir, Almonte's army, at least what's left of them, are in Saltillo. That ain't all. I seen a column of lancers riding this way."

Hays had hoped their defeat had demoralized the Mexican army, but if Almonte was sending troops back to keep an eye on the road to Monterrey, then obviously, they were not as defeated as he had hoped.

He wheeled his mount around and looked to the east. Nearly fifty miles separated him and his company from the rest of the army in Monterrey. How far would the Mexican lancers backtrack? With scarcely more than thirty men, did he really want a knock-down fight with their lancers? The rider was stroking his horse's neck as the animal continued to breath heavily. "Private, how many men do you reckon you saw?"

"Somewhere between one and two hundred."

One hundred lancers and he'd risk a battle. The revolvers and rifles his men carried gave him a disproportionate advantage over the lancers. But if there were two hundred, that was a seven to one numeric advantage. What was it that General Travis had said? Quantity has a quality all its own.

There had been a trail which veered from the road a mile or two back. It led to an adobe hacienda, nestled in the foot hills of the Sierra Madres. He was loath to retreat further until he knew the size of cavalry force moving his way. He thought it likely he and his company could shelter there until the lancers passed by. A few minutes later, the company galloped back the way they had come.

Less than an hour after that, Hays sized up the smallish hacienda. The two-story building faced the winding trail, which meandered through a dense field of mesquite trees and cactus plants. It backed up against a steep hill.

Pounding on the building's door brought nothing but an echoing boom. Hays figured the owner had fled to Saltillo when the retreating army came through a few days before. The hacienda was more than a mile away from the road between Monterrey and Saltillo and he hoped the cavalry patrol would pass them by.

If he was wrong though, he thought the hacienda had a certain appeal. It hadn't been so long ago the Comanches and Apaches raided this far south. The narrow windows would make excellent places from which riflemen could shoot. The building's second floor jutted out, creating a covered porch over the front of the building. Holes could easily be cut in the wooden floor, creating a kill zone against the front wall.

Yes, he thought. This would do for a defensive position in the unlikely event the lancers came this way.

It was the height of foolishness for Almonte to accompany the regiment of Lancers, at least according to his adjutant. As he rode by an abandoned wagon and the other detritus from the retreat earlier in the week, he wasn't sure he disagreed. He glanced over at General Sesma's horse and thought the animal was in even worse shape than at the beginning of the retreat from Monterrey. Now, though, instead of constantly moving away from Travis's army, his lancers were determined to scout the road and to alert the rest of the army to the Texians' approach.

But however decrepit his mount may appear; the normally dour cavalry general was in a buoyant mood. With half an ear, Almonte listened to the other officer. "I'm convinced Seguin's cavalry are in nearly as rough a shape as we are. Add to that, the men he has assigned to keep their supply lines open, that fool of a Tejano won't have more than a light cavalry screen with which to advance."

"If you say so, General Sesma." Almonte's response was devoid of emotion. After a campaign far worse than he had anticipated, he found Sesma's unfounded optimism troubling. Caution had allowed him to inflict hundreds of casualties against a better trained and equipped enemy. "Be mindful that you've got most of our eyes and ears here. We want to know where the Texians are, not to get into a fight that reduces our forces further."

Sesma smiled expansively as a troop of lancers trotted to the east. "Of course, General."

Later in the afternoon, the same troop raced back to where Almonte and Sesma were slowly riding down the center of the road. "General! There's signs of Texian cavalry nearby."

Almonte, curiosity piqued, allowed the excited men to lead them to where a trail intersected with the road. To him, it looked no different than the rest of the road, where an army of five thousand had trod only a few days before. But one of the lancers threaded his way down the side trail until he stopped and indicated that the rest of the men should join him. A small patch of brownish cloth had snagged on the thorns of a cactus plant.

While it was a thin reed to rely upon, Almonte found his pulse quickening. He held his peace as Sesma ordered several men forward to explore the trail. As the lancers disappeared down the path, he found himself making small talk with the cavalry commander. He was about to respond when a flurry of gunshots echoed up the trail.

The horses had been staked out behind the hacienda. A battered windmill, paint peeling from the wooden frame, fed an anemic stream of water into a series of troughs. With any luck, Hays thought, once the lancers had passed down the road, the company's mounts would be rested and watered.

He heard one of his men shouting his name and a few seconds later, several shots rang out. Hays raced through the back door and down the center hallway which divided the building in half. The front door was wide open. Several Rangers crowded around it, rifles pointing toward the dense brush beyond the front yard. A blue-jacketed lancer lay face down on the trail. His mount had moved back, where the horse had paused to nibble on a stray clump of grass. Beyond that, Hays watched two more horsemen disappear down the trail.

"Get out of the damned door," he growled. So much for avoiding detection. He swore as the men closed the door and dropped a heavy wooden bar across it, a legacy from the days when the owner's constant fear had been Indian raids.

Despite the worry he felt for placing his men in such an unforgiving position, his heart swelled with pride as those who needed to, retrieved their rifles from their saddle scabbards without any orders. In short order, every window facing the trail was manned with one or more riflemen.

The odds were against him, Hays knew. If one of his men could skirt the hills behind the hacienda, and get around the Mexican lancers, he could get word back to the army in Monterrey. His situation was dire, and he picked the company's youngest Ranger and hastily wrote a note to General Seguin.

His rider disappeared through the brambles and thorns of the heavy cover of mesquite trees that ran up the hillside. The hopes of Hays and his Rangers went with the young rider. If he was unable to beat back the lancers, at best, it would take Seguin three or four days to lift the siege.

The sun still hung low in the western sky when a dismounted lancer appeared on the trail, holding a white flag. With days to go until a relief column could arrive, Hays knew he needed to play for time. He allowed the lancer to approach the hacienda. Without a word, the lancer approached the door and delivered a sealed letter to Hays. He broke the wax seal and perused the letter. His command of written Spanish was far worse than the spoken word, and when he saw the letter was in English he sighed in relief.

In the letter, he and his men were promised safety if they surrendered. The letter also offered a broader truce with General Travis and offered a prisoner exchange between the two armies. Hays' eyebrows raised as he scanned the letter. When he saw that it was signed by none other than General Juan Almonte, he began to understand. Despite Santa Anna's history of ordering the execution of prisoners, rumors persisted that Almonte was opposed to such policies. But could Almonte arrange such an exchange? Hays was disinclined to doubt Almonte's intent but questioned whether he could deliver on such a promise.

The lancer remained on the trail, holding onto his white flag, near the tree line, waiting for Hays' response. He was torn with indecision. What would happen if the Mexicans attacked? Could he and his men hold them off long enough for the young Ranger to find General Seguin and bring a relief column? Hays couldn't say. The uncertainty weighed heavily on him.

Time passed, as the sun ebbed below the mountains to the west, and a twilight held sway around the hacienda. However much he wanted to trust Almonte, in the end, it was his overwhelming distrust of Almonte's president that decided Hays' fate. He and his men would fight.

A ragged volley of musket shots lashed out from the tree line after the messenger disappeared down the trail. The battle was on. "Find your target, boys!" Hays cried out as he passed through each of the hacienda's rooms. Despite the darkness, Rangers returned fire, aiming at the muzzle flashes. The lancers, fighting as dragoons with their shortened carbine muskets, traded shots with the Rangers throughout the night.

By the time the sky brightened, bullets had scarred and gouged the adobe walls around nearly every window in the hacienda. A bedroom facing the hillside behind the building served as a makeshift hospital and morgue. A few men had been hit during the back and forth shooting throughout the night. From one of the windows on the second floor, Hays looked out on the thicket of mesquite near the trail. There were plenty of tell-tale signs of the night's long battle. Bodies were sprinkled among the trees where they had fallen throughout the night. The dead were easy to see in their brilliant red and blue uniforms.

A bullet slammed into the adobe wall, inches away from where he stood, showering him in a fine, brown dust. Hays cursed as he involuntarily flinched.

"Their aim is shit, Major," a Ranger said as he scrounged through the cartridge box on his hip. "I don't suppose you'd mind me fetching some more rounds from my saddle bags, sir?"

The noisy, squealing windmill filled the troughs behind the building. Water wouldn't be an issue. But Hays began to wonder how long the company's limited amount of ammunition would hold out. Each ranger had several dozen reloads of .44 caliber ammunition for their pistols and a hundred cartridges of .52 caliber rounds for their rifles, most of which had been stashed in their saddlebags.

"No need. I'll send a few of the boys downstairs to fetch it. I'll see to it that they bring up some for y'all." Hays retreated downstairs where he ordered several men to bring anything of value from the packs on the horses.

The sun was high overhead. Hays crumbled some cornbread into a mash of grits and salt pork before wolfing the gruel-like substance down. Food supplies wouldn't last another day. But as long as the rider returned with a relief force, he and his Rangers could survive a few days without food. It was the ammunition that worried him. Based upon the number of flashes from musket fire, there must have been several hundred men surrounding the hacienda. Once the Rangers' ammunition was gone, he had little doubt the dragooned lancers would charge. What would happen then?

He worked his way through the building, encouraging the men in each room. His doubts he kept to himself. Even so, he saw the uncertainty in each of his Rangers' eyes. Sure, it was mixed with bravado and hubris. After all, these men were the best of the Texian army. But below the surface, there was a growing sense of hopelessness in their eyes.

A white flag fluttered above a fallen tree trunk. The sporadic gunfire from the tree line fell away to an eerie stillness, emphasizing the sound of the flapping flag. The Rangers held their fire as Hays rushed to the front door. An officer in blue and red held the flag and slowly approached the door. Hays expected him to use a knife to stick a letter to the door. Instead, he raised his fist and knocked.

The sturdy door was pitted and damaged by hundreds of bullets, but it had been made to withstand a siege from rampaging Comanche warriors. The bar was taken down and the door groaned as Hays pulled it open. Hays eyes widened. He had expected a young under-officer. Instead, a middle-aged man with greying hair stood before him. Golden epaulets proclaimed his exalted rank.

Hays' voice failed him. Into the silence, the other officer spoke, "Major John Hays, if I'm not mistaken."

Of all the scenarios Hays had expected, this wasn't one of them. He nodded and to his own surprise, he offered his hand.

The Mexican officer shook it, "General Juan Almonte, at your service."

Hays glanced out the door, toward the tree line. Glimpses of uniforms flickered as lancers shifted in their spots where they sheltered behind cover. "You have me at a disadvantage, General Almonte. I wasn't expecting company this afternoon."

Despite a twinkle in his dark eyes, Almonte's face remained grave. "Yesterday, you chose to fight when I gave you an option of honorable surrender. I do not want to see any more of your men or mine die fighting over this worthless pile of bricks, Major. I hope by coming and speaking directly to you, you will see the wisdom of surrendering. You spoke the truth a moment ago, I have you at a disadvantage. My men outnumber you ten to one. If you surrender, you have my word that you and your men will be treated as prisoners of war. Further, I will endeavor to seek a truce with General Travis to arrange a prisoner exchange."

Hays eyed the commander of the Army of the North. In as much as he could be sure of anything, he felt that Almonte was an honorable enemy. But as much as he wanted to believe Almonte, he couldn't. Any order given by the general could be undone by Santa Anna. "A similar promise was made to Texian soldiers last year by your fellow officer, General Woll. Sixty of our number were marched into the wilderness and executed by your army. How can I possibly trust you when, ultimately, you must answer to your own president? Santa Anna has made clear his policy, sir."

The pain in Almonte's eyes was clear to see. "I'm sorry for you, Major Hays. This fight here will only have one outcome. Of that I can promise. I have done my duty as my Catholic faith demands of me. The blood of your men will be on your head."

Hays stood, framed in the doorway. While the words were not unexpected, the melancholy tone caught him off guard. The Mexican general, passing a sentence of death on Hays and his men couldn't have sounded more miserable.

Almonte disappeared down the trail and when the white flag disappeared the Mexicans opened fire. Bullets tore into the wooden door and gouged chunks of adobe from the wall. Hays leapt back and slammed the door closed.

Throughout the night, the Mexican lancers relentlessly fired at the building. Rifle ammunition had long ago run out. Most of the men had sustained injuries and ten bodies crowded the floor of the back room where they had been laid.

Two days had passed since the siege began. Even if his rider had managed to escape and get to the army at Monterrey, they would arrive too late. Instead of the deep silence that was common in the dark before dawn, the noise coming from beyond the tree line indicated that Almonte's lancers had grown tired of the siege. Hays expected them to rush the battered hacienda with the rising of the sun, which was now only minutes away.

Their rifles were only expensive clubs now, but each Ranger still had their revolver. The range between the hacienda and the tree line had made the pistols a poor choice. But that would change, Hays thought, with the coming of the dawn.

The thought had crystalized in his mind at the very moment fiery red tendrils of light peeked over the eastern mountains. A clattering of boots over rocky ground indicated the Mexicans had been just as alert as he was. A wall of men in their blue and red lancer uniforms materialized from the tree line. For the most part they carried short cavalry carbines, although, here and there, he saw men carrying long spears the lancers normally carried into battle.

A smattering of gunshots whipped from the Mexican line and, as though without orders, they charged across the open ground, less than two hundred feet separating them from their goal.

Hays cursed as he pulled his Trinity Arms pistol from its holster. This wasn't how he had imagined things would end. His voice thundered throughout the building, "Give them hell at fifty feet!"

These men he had trained for more than a year were the best shots in the Texian army. At fifty feet they were as lethal with their revolvers as they had been with their rifles at longer ranges. When the charging line came within the final kill zone, every Ranger aimed their pistol and unloaded six rounds into the line.

The charging mass of dismounted lancers had run into a wall of lead. Several hundred bullets crashed into the line over the span of ten seconds. Scores of men fell, dead and wounded. The wounded cried out, rending the morning dawn with shrieks of pain.

Scores more slammed into the adobe walls. A heavy wooden beam had been constructed well away from the hacienda during the siege and now was brought to bear against the hacienda's ventilated door. Muskets were poked into the downstairs windows and triggers were pulled. A thick haze of smoke swirled about the building.

Less than a dozen strokes from the wooden beam stove in the door. It had withstood more than a few brazen raids by both the Comanche and the Apache, but the concerted effort of scores of lancers overcame the sturdy door. The entry breached, lancers flooded into the building, overwhelming the remaining Rangers. Those who had them, ejected spent cylinders and inserted fresh ones and fired even as they were swarmed over.

Silence had barely descended upon the hacienda when General Almonte ignored the pleading of his adjutant and moved back toward the remains of the adobe building. He broke through the tree line and stopped in shock. From the edge of the building to less than twenty paces from it, the ground was carpeted with scores of his men. The Texians, no doubt, had used their revolvers to good effect. But seeing the carnage, it was hard to accept.

Through the broken door, he watched the survivors of the attack pulling the bodies of wounded and dead men from the adobe building. It was an even mix of tan-uniformed Texians and his own lancers. As he dismounted, a young officer raced over, "Sir, one of the Texians is still alive."

Almonte was amazed his lancers, whose blood was up, had allowed any of the enemy to surrender. But when he entered the building, he saw it was not so. Lying in the hallway, he found the young Texian major unconscious, but still breathing. His left arm was badly mangled, where a heavy musket ball had likely shattered the bone. Blood seeped through his jacket where a bullet had hit him in the shoulder. His leg bled from where the tip of a lance had pierced his skin.

Almonte called, "Get this man a stretcher, and fetch a doctor!"

He had no idea how the Texian major still breathed. Any of the injuries could turn out to be fatal, but as he watched the other man's chest rise and fall, he decided that if the brave young officer could be saved, Almonte would see to it.

Chapter 18

28 May 1843

The cane rhythmically tapped on the red brick walkway as Lorenzo de Zavala hurried from the presidential mansion. The domed Capitol building stood just across the street, but dark clouds threatened to unleash a torrent of rain. His wife, Emily, harped on him to stay out of the rain. She was too kind to mention it, but the president was susceptible to chills and became sick more easily than she liked. More sickly than he liked, if he were honest with himself.

The Capitol building stood on top of a hill overlooking Congress Avenue, where most of the government buildings had been constructed over the past few years. Zavala crossed over the dirt road. Here and there, heavy drops of rain kicked up tiny puffs of dust when they hit the ground. Despite the damage done to the dignity of his exalted office, he picked up his pace and jogged across the road. He followed a red bricked path winding up the hill and ran up the flight of stairs to the building, ignoring the pain in his fifty-four-year-old knees.

He passed between two of the Corinthian columns which fronted the building. The doors swung out and as soon as he crossed the threshold, the skies opened, and the rain fell in torrents. A guard stood inside the doors and came to attention as he passed by. A black doorman pulled the door closed as the wind added its strength to the pattering rain. Zavala climbed the stairs to the top floor to his corner office.

He unlocked the door and had just sat to catch his breath when the door rattled with a persistent knock. "Come in!"

Another of the Capitol guards stood next to a young man who wore a jacket proclaiming he was a courier for the All-Texas Telegraph office. The local office opened a few months earlier, after a telegraph line had been completed between San Antonio and Austin. With the war playing hell on the economy, the president was uncertain when the telegraph lines in East Texas would connect to the nation's capital. The courier pulled a folded sheet of paper from an oilcloth bag. With a nod from Zavala the young man disappeared down the hall. Alone again, Zavala unfolded the telegraph message and read.

His eyebrows raised as he saw the length of the missive. Messages tended to be short and to the point. But apparently someone in San Antonio decided to send the entire letter from General Travis by telegraph when it arrived earlier at the Alamo.

17 May 1843

To Pres. Zavala

We have secured the city of Monterrey, defeating the Mexican Army of the North after a short siege. We have been victorious in every battle and have destroyed half of the enemy's force. Victory has not come without loss. Our army has been reduced by a thousand men due to attrition and battle casualties. To secure our supply line and to hold the city of Monterrey, circumstances require that I leave an adequate garrison behind. If Santa Anna reinforces the Army of the North, our current deployment may not be adequate to defeat the enemy. I request additional forces be rushed to Monterrey in order to carry the war goals to successful completion.

Your obedient servant,
W.B. Travis, Gn'l commd.

Zavala set the letter down with a loud sigh. Why couldn't fortune favor this endeavor with greater success? When he, David, and "Buck" Travis had developed the plans for the current war, he had thought a quick victory at the Rio Grande and a forced march to Monterrey would result in the enemy's surrender. He had always been skeptical of the second goal, of forcing the Mexicans to surrender Santa Anna to them, but forcing them to recognize the borders had seemed an easy goal at the beginning of the campaign.

It appeared Almonte was still in command of what remained of the Army of the North. Implicit in the letter was that he was retreating deeper into Mexico. The war's active campaigning had entered its third month, but in reality, Texas had spent the better part of a year gearing up to fight Mexico on what Travis had considered even terms. So much time had elapsed since many of the men in the army had left their families, farms, or businesses. The latest report from his Treasury secretary indicated the national economy was shrinking. Tax revenue had fallen precipitously and, until the war was concluded, Zavala knew the situation would only change for the worse.

Before a decision could be made, he needed to consult with his cabinet.

Rain still spattered against the window panes when Erasmo Seguin arrived in the president's crowded office. Zavala nodded to him as he waited for the director of the Commodities Bureau to take his seat. Next to Seguin sat Michel Menard, the Republic's Treasurer. Representing the military was the commander of the militia, General Tom Rusk.

Ignoring the chair behind his desk, Zavala stood between the other men and the window. Everyone had read General Travis' letter. Zavala asked, "Can we afford to acquiesce to General Travis' request for more men?"

Menard responded, "We need our troops returned as soon as possible, Mr. President. Every day the war drags on, the worse our financial house becomes." Despite his lengthy residence in the Republic, second only to Erasmo Seguin, his accent still betrayed his Quebecois origin. "Our recent bond auction was poorly received, and we were forced to sell the bonds below their face value. Our creditors may come to doubt our ability to repay our debts, and when that happens, we may find no buyers for our bonds."

Zavala nodded. The bonds brought in the gold and silver the nation needed to buy war supplies, most of which were purchased from merchants in the United States. "Without specie," Menard mentioned, "Our suppliers would be scarcer than whiskey at a camp revival."

Erasmo Seguin chuckled. "You're just attending the wrong camp revival." He turned serious, "A war ending in a muddle of no clear victor only sets the stage for the next war, Michel. We must give the army the tools necessary to win, even if it depletes our fiscal cupboard."

"We're not talking about a depleted cupboard, Erasmo. The state of the Treasury is that we're as poor as Job's turkey. We're engaging in cheap parlor tricks to pay our own soldiers."

Seguin frowned at that. "That's not fair. The Commodities Bureau will print enough currency to cover those obligations. So long as we don't go overboard, we'll hold inflation in check."

Menard fired back, "That's not the way we set things up to run. Your bureau wasn't to print any more certificates than the commodities they backed. For the better part of the year, that hasn't been the case. Eventually, someone's going to figure out we have far more cotton-backs in circulation than the commodities they cover. What's going to happen then?"

As the two financially minded members of the group became angry, Thomas Rusk interjected, "I don't care a tinker's damn if the Republic ain't got a pot to piss in, we sent Travis and the army down there to whip Santa Anna, and we best figure out a way to skin that cat."

Zavala eyed Rusk with surprise. A key ally to the pro-annexation party in Congress, Rusk was a close friend to Robert Potter. Before his predecessor had tapped Ben McCulloch to form a reserve army, Rusk had poorly performed his duties as General of Militia. It was the invasion that resulted in Rusk's own increased military role. In the horse trading that went on between Zavala and congress, the president had been forced to put Rusk back in command of the militia to get support from Potter's faction. Sometimes even a bad deal pays off. Since Woll's invasion the previous year, Rusk had taken a more proactive role in making sure all eligible men were enrolled in the militia and that each militia company drilled frequently. He had also performed conscientiously, funneling supplies to the reserve battalions that had not been included in Travis' invasion plans.

In a show of approval, Zavala placed his hand lightly on Rusk's arm, "General Rusk is right, Michel. We can ill afford another war with Mexico. The surest path forward, no matter the financial cost, is victory. Rather than belabor how much this is going to cost the treasury, why don't we focus on how much additional support will be sent?"

Rusk said, "We already have the 6th Infantry at the Alamo. Give me the word and they'll be on the march within two or three days. The only problem with the 6th, is that it is undersized. There's only six companies, maybe four hundred fifty men. I'd also recommend we send the 12th Infantry. It's spread out between here and Laredo, but they're the only other battalion that can be assembled and put on the road within a few days."

Still out of sorts, Menard said, "But that will leave everything from the Rio Grande to the capital unprotected. We saw how well that turned out last year."

Rusk waved the comment away, "Only for a few days, Michel. There are ten battalions of militia that haven't been mobilized."

Menard shot to his feet, "For good reason, Tom. Those men are needed to run their farms and keep what enterprises that are still turning a profit, operating."

"Cool your heels. We can mobilize the 14th. They've been partially mobilized already, overseeing construction on the railroad from West Liberty to Houston. It'll take a bit of time, but they can fill in the gap."

Zavala quickly agreed, which ended Menard's objections. The president told Rusk to prepare the orders. It would take time, but he was determined to provide General Travis and the army every necessary tool.

1 June 1843

Sand and gravel crunched under his boots as Charlie Travis hurried along between the two rows of faded white canvas tents. He tugged at the ill-fitting tunic his Uncle Davy had found for him after he added the fourteen-year-old to the 9th Infantry's roster. The youth felt ill used as he hurried around a campfire. He had run the entire length of the camp, delivering a message to Major Henry McCulloch, Crockett's second-in-command.

He recalled how Crockett had made a big deal when Charlie's name was added to the roster. "There you go, Charlie. Now you get paid for running away from home." After the laughter had subsided, his Uncle Davy had told him, "You're Ensign Travis now, Charlie. Think of it as being a junior officer."

The thought left him swearing below his ragged breath. *"Ensign, my ass,"* the boy thought. *"More like gopher. Charlie, go fer this and go fer that. That's all Uncle Davy has me doing is fetching things for him."*

What made it worse was that the Sonoran Desert was blistering hot only an hour after sunrise, and Crockett had him running errands since before breakfast. A tarp had been set up in front of Crockett's A-frame wall tent. In front of the tarp, a small campfire burned. The smell of mesquite and burning cactus filled the air and made his eyes water. His friend, Victorio sat cross-legged in front of the fire roasting some small animal he had caught. Lenna, his sister, sat beside him. For a moment, Charlie forgot to be mad at his Uncle Davy as his breath caught in his throat when he saw Lenna.

Her thick, black hair was tied in a single braid down her back and she was wearing a blue calico print blouse. When she looked up and saw Charlie, her lips turned up at the corners a bit and she turned and began talking with her brother. Talking with her had never been easy, but lately, every time he tried talking with her, Charlie found it hard to think of what to say. And the problem was, he really wanted to talk with her and spend time around her.

He was about to sit when the flap to Crockett's tent opened, "Charlie, what took you so long? It's time. Chief Alejandro and his folks will be here directly."

With a sign that brought smiles to both the young Apaches, Charlie turned away from the fire, kicked a pebble with his toe and waited under the tarp.

It was a short wait. Apart from the embroidered shoulder boards with the golden eagles, Crockett wore the same uniform as any of his men. The only exception was a pair of riding boots. Normally they were scuffed and dull from heavy use, but Charlie had stayed up late the previous night polishing them to a shine.

Next to the camp a small crowd of men waited. Charlie thought they looked Mexican in appearance, but as he and the officers headed toward them, Crockett leaned over, "Don't let that look fool you, son. They ain't no more Mexican than you or me. They've been living under the boot heel of Spanish for the better part of two hundred years. Now the Mexicans have made a worse mess of things, and Chief Alejandro there is interested in kicking them out."

While not fluent, Charlie understood enough Spanish to follow along as the tribal leader talked with Crockett through a translator. Chief Alejandro told Crockett that he had grown up in the presidio in the valley below, only fleeing into the mountains north of town when the Mexican governor to the south had tried to force high taxes onto the Yaquis people and an end to tribal ownership of land.

From what Charlie could piece together, he thought Alejandro had convinced himself the Texians were a better bet than the Mexicans in the Presidio San Agustín del Tucson, despite being an unknown force. When Crockett pointed this out to the Yaquis elder, the response brought laughter all around, "Better the devil I don't know than the devil that I do."

Alejandro explained that the Mexican governor in Hermosillo had tried repeatedly to compel the Yacquis to pay heavy taxes to the Mexican state of Sonora, as well as enacting legislation to strip the Yaquis of their tribal lands.

Charlie wondered what Crockett's thoughts were. His curiosity was rewarded when the Texian officers withdrew a short ways to discuss their options.

Major McCulloch said, "We can take the presidio without them, Colonel. But having friendly folks behind us is a sight better than having enemies to our rear."

Crockett agreed. "I doubt the Mexican officer in command of Tucson has any interest in fighting us. And turning the presidio over to Alejandro and his people would improve things in the short run. But let's think about what this will mean later. As I understand it, the Sonoran state government treats these Yaquis not much better than we treat our Negros. But Alejandro wants independence of sorts, and that's the question we need to consider."

McCulloch grunted like he had been kicked in the stomach, "Do you reckon that dog's going to hunt with the government back in Austin?"

Crockett shrugged, "If Lorenzo knows what's good for him, he'll figure out a way to accommodate these folks. We've got a pretty good thing going with the Cherokee. Charlie's Pa calls it a win-win situation. I'd like to think we could arrange something as beneficial here. But before we start putting the cart before the horse, this is just a way-point for us. It ain't going to matter a tinker's damn unless we succeed with the rest of our plans."

An agreement for cooperation was quickly negotiated and Charlie, once again, found himself rushing from one end of the camp to the other with orders as Crockett directed his men to break camp. The small army snaked down the mountainous trail until they were less than a half mile away from the presidio of Tucson. Such as there was of it. He had been told that the town had once been thriving in the years before the Mexican War for Independence. But since then, the presidio had withered under Mexican neglect and the blistering Sonoran sun.

That same sun was halfway across the sky when Charlie watched two companies of infantry deploy along with one of the cavalry companies which anchored the riflemen's flanks. According to the Yaquis, the Mexican garrison had been allowed to atrophy to as few as a dozen men. Despite the solid look of the adobe walls, twelve men couldn't hope to defend them.

The men barely started their advance across the arid ground when a smile lit Charlie's face. The Mexican tricolor floated down the flagpole flying over the fortified walls. The tiny garrison had surrendered.

Charlie sat astride his mount behind Crockett as the three companies advanced through the presidio's gates. Seeing the Texian flag raise over the adobe fortifications, Charlie said, "If they would have put up a fight, we'd have whipped them good, right?"

His Uncle Davy frowned in response. "Why'd you want to fight them, son, if it weren't necessary? I'll always take a bloodless victory over one that costs us even one soldier," he paused before slowly wheeling around, looking at the rest of the battalion, where the men were setting up camp outside the presidio's walls. "Son, if there is one lesson this running away business can teach you, it's this: we owe it to our men to spend their lives with care. Just because they have read a dime novel or two, they think I'm this great Lion of the West. More than a few of them would follow me into hell if I asked them to."

Crockett's eyes bored into Charlies. "To hell with that. My goal is to get as many of them as possible to California then back again to Texas. Everyone that I bury along the way is a personal failure."

Chapter 19

3 June 1843

Lorenzo de Zavala's stomach was still upset from the previous day's coach ride. The durable leather straps suspending the coach supposedly made for a less bouncy ride, but the president was unsold on that bit of marketing as he wondered how long it would take for his stomach to return to something he considered normal.

He would rather have been somewhere else, but as he watched the two battalions gathered in the Alamo's large plaza, duty demanded he make an appearance and say a few words. Zavala lacked the story telling chops of his predecessor, but he was considered a gifted orator in his own right. His lips twitched at the thought. *"Unlike David, I prefer to stick to the facts."*

He stood on a makeshift stage and told the thousand assembled men of their duty to their fellow soldiers, their wives and families, and to Texas. It was short and to the point. While it may have lacked Crockett's flare for the theatrics, it was also significantly shorter.

He allowed an expansive smile to split his face as martial music filled the air, and the 6th and 12th Infantry battalions smoothly transitioned from standing at attention in their long lines to the columns of four men abreast. They paraded through the fort's gatehouse; a thousand pair of feet kicked up clouds of dust.

Ten minutes after the first men filed out of the Alamo's gate, silence descended again on the plaza. The only sound was that made by the company of soldiers still assigned to the post, as well as several dozen men who were under the care of the fort's doctor, who was contracted from San Antonio.

The coach would swing by the Alamo on the way back to Austin the next day. This evening, the president would stay in an empty room in the officer's quarters. He descended the stage and now that he was alone, allowed the doubts to eat away at him. How many acres would lay fallow because of his decision to send more men south? Would children go hungry this fall, or would they and their mothers manage to plant and harvest enough to stave off hunger? Not knowing the answers, he climbed the stairs to the officers' quarters, where he hoped a brief nap would restore his mood and appetite.

The next day, 900 miles to the west, Zavala's predecessor watched his little army of seven hundred follow wagon tracks westward. He had been assured by the Yaquis chieftain, Alejandro, the road ended at the western sea, which Crockett understood to be the Pacific Ocean. With a little luck, he had told Charlie, he expected the command to reach the Mexican town of San Diego within three weeks.

Charlie shifted in his saddle and watched the presidio of Tucson disappear as the battalion snaked along the trail. He swiped a bandana from his pocket and wiped the sweat from his face. It was too early to be sweating this much, he thought. At least he wasn't marching, like most of the men in Crockett's command. At the moment, the only dirt he was eating was that which was kicked up by Crockett's horse. The men at the back of the column were forced to eat a lot more dust.

As his horse kicked up dust, the youth's thoughts went back to the past few days. The presidio had fallen with nary a gunshot, but he knew his Uncle Davy worried about keeping the peace. They had left the Yaquis chieftain, Alejandro, in charge of the presidio. It only made sense. After all, well over half the population of the people living in and around the town were Yaquis.

He recalled talking with Crockett the previous evening after he had completed his chores. "Charlie, Alejandro's people are betwixt and between. They're not uncivilized like the Apache or the Comanche. First, they lived under the Spanish and now, for a generation, under the Mexicans. They've adopted a lot of the ways of the peoples that have tried to control them. That's why I'm optimistic that we can work with them should we hold this territory once we have a peace treaty with Mexico."

Charlie's thoughts returned to the present moment as his horse stepped over a large rock in the road. For the life of him, he couldn't understand why anyone would want to fight over this stretch of desert.

5 June 1843

North of the town of San Luis Potosi the ground next to the Rio Paisanos was carpeted by a temporary city of white canvas. Thousands of tents proclaimed to the citizens of San Luis that Santa Anna had arrived with the army. Adrian Woll, adjutant general of the Mexican army, felt a sense of déjà vu as he stared at the encampment. It dwarfed the camp he had established in Texas the previous year when he had captured San Antonio and nearly captured the Alamo.

Since learning of General Almonte's failure to advance into Texas, his Excellency had ordered Woll to assemble every available regiment and march them north, where they would assemble here at San Luis Potosi. His career in Mexico hadn't fallen as far as it could have. He went from shuffling papers for a couple of months to overseeing the training camps around the capital where he had served since late last year.

Woll's familiarity with the officers and men in the new army led Santa Anna to grab him on the dictator's way out of Mexico City. Santa Anna would show Adrian how to destroy the *Yankee* pirates.

His Excellency had taken over the alcalde's house near the central plaza. The comfortable ranch-style home now overflowed with various staff members. Woll drew his horse up in front of the gate. The courtyard was filled with horses, and Woll thought better of going inside yet. He left his mount in the care of the alcalde's stable hands and walked a short distance to the plaza.

Even though most of the army was already assembled, he watched troops from the south march through the plaza on their way to the encampment north of town. The contrast in men perplexed him. Unlike the men he led north the previous year, most of the men who paraded before him wore rope sandals. Woll had seen correspondence and knew the army had outgrown the nation's ability to supply it in the short term.

Instead of the navy-blue jackets cut in the Napoleonic style of the previous generation, these men wore white, beige, and gray tunics, the products of whatever the supply depot from which they were equipped had been able to obtain. But one thing Mexico had aplenty were the ubiquitous Brown Bess muskets purchased from Britain fifteen years earlier. Instead of leather cartridge boxes, though, the men carried haversacks, where they stored their paper cartridges.

Woll shook his head after the men had paraded by. Some of the regiments Santa Anna was assembling were quality units, like he had led, but many were militia conscripts who had been hastily assembled and sent north. Woll had faced the Texians and knew the kind of army General Travis led. Against that, there would be nearly thirty regiments, almost fifteen thousand men, plus however much of the Army of the North remained. As he returned to the alcalde's residence, he couldn't help but wonder, "*Will it be enough?*"

9 June 1843

He adjusted his hat once his feet hit the ground. He tied the reins to the hitching post outside of the house His Excellency used as his headquarters in San Luis Potosi. A glance at the sky convinced him he was on time. In a moment of honesty, General Juan Almonte wanted nothing more than to delay his meeting with Santa Anna.

He had arrived the previous evening with what remained of his army. His men were still setting up camp when instructions arrived to present himself before His Excellency at ten in the morning, sharp. He stepped over to a wooden water trough and looked down at the still water and saw his reflection.

Never the most robust of men, Almonte's cheeks were gaunt from too many days on the march. While his navy-blue jacket was cleaned and pressed, it was faded from too many days under the harsh sun. His white pants had been washed plenty of times and had faded to grayish-brown. While his Excellency liked his officers to dress well, as befitted their stations, the battered look to his uniform, Almonte knew, was the least of his worries.

When he decided to defend the Rio Bravo del Norte instead of invading, he had done so using a liberal interpretation of His Excellency's orders. That General Travis had met him at the Rio Bravo with an army nearly as large as his own, proved his strategy superior to a more aggressive interpretation favored by the late General Raphael Vasquez. Now, he was summoned to appear before His Excellency to answer for his interpretation.

He turned away from his reflection and wound his way through orderlies and couriers who clogged the building's courtyard. He couldn't help but thinking, he had done the right thing, given the circumstances. The breechloading rifles the Texians used were a game changer, and Almonte strongly suspected no army from Mexico with surplus British muskets would prevail. It was, he felt, a minor miracle he had arrived here with half his army still intact.

He was ushered into the cool adobe building. A young officer in a crisply starched uniform left him in a small library. Books lined the shelves. A small, sturdy desk backed up to a bookshelf and a high-backed wooden chair faced the desk.

He gave up trying to focus on any of the books when the door opened, and His Excellency entered. Forgetting the books, Almonte drew up next to the wooden chair and came to attention. He eyed his commander-in-chief as Santa Anna strode around the desk and leaned in, glaring at Almonte.

After a pause that lasted far too long for Almonte's comfort, Santa Anna said, "I'd be lying if I said I was glad to see you, Juan."

That His Excellency dispensed with any honorific and referred to him by his first name was hopefully a good sign.

Almonte shrugged, "I wish it were under better circumstances, too, Your Excellency."

Santa Anna frowned as he took his seat. He then waved for Almonte to sit, as well. "You've put me in an awkward position. I had ordered General Vasquez to capture San Antonio and hold it this time. I gave him an army large enough to do the job."

Almonte sat upright in the chair, wondering where His Excellency was going.

"The poor fool had to die in a fall from his horse. Of all the damnable luck. But Juan, you knew my orders and you disregarded them."

Silence descended upon the room. Santa Anna cocked his head as though listening for something. It was Almonte's turn. "Ah, Excellency, the facts on the ground had changed by the time I took command. Spies in Texas reported that General Travis was marching south with a much larger army than we had expected. We have all read the reports from Woll's expedition of the breechloading rifles the Texians now carry. An attack against fixed positions would have destroyed our army. I thought it better to turn the tables on the Texians and force them to attack our fixed position."

Santa Anna leapt to his feet, "And you lost, Juan. Not once, not twice, but three times!"

Almonte wanted to defend himself. He had faced an army with new and better weapons and better training that made effective use of the new weapons. But the crux of His Excellency's argument was true. In three engagements with Travis' Texians, Almonte's Army of the North had lost each battle and half its strength. If he hadn't been present, Almonte wasn't sure he would believe his own defense.

"But, Excellency, we inflicted heavy casualties against the enemy."

Santa Anna sat back down, "But not enough. No doubt the *norteamericano* pirates will be arriving at Saltillo any day now. I will take all the army north and do what you failed to do. I will destroy Travis' army and kill him like the cur he is. There will be a trail of bodies all the way back to San Antonio and when I get there, I'll hang that traitor Zavala from gallows built atop the bones of his followers. Then I'll drive the Yankee interlopers back to the Sabine River and end the *norteamericano* threat once and for all."

"*Is my jaw hanging open?*" Almonte wondered as he listened to His Excellency pontificate.

"Had you not failed me, you would be at my side, Juan. But that's not possible now. There are some in the army that believe an example should be made of you."

Almonte tensed as Santa Anna continued, "I would sign the order of execution were it not for the friendship I still hold dear, Juan. I understand you disobeyed my orders not because you are disloyal, but because you wanted to preserve the army. Had you won even one decisive victory, that would have wiped out the stain of disobedience. An army, even this one, will forgive much when victory is achieved."

In a small voice, as he thought of his wife and wondered if he would ever see her again, he asked, "What will you do, Excellency?"

"For the time being, you must leave Mexico, Juan. You've been a friend to me longer than most and even though you have failed me, I owe you that much."

Exile, then, Almonte thought. It could be worse, much worse.

It was clear Santa Anna was finished. When he reached the door, Almonte was turning the knob when His Excellency said, "Before you leave, turn over any prisoners in your possession. I will send a message to Travis of what to expect when we defeat him."

Mid-June 1843

A trickle of black smoke curled up from the locomotive's smokestack. One of the men who climbed down from the car, dressed as a common laborer, crossed the tracks in front of the train and hurried into the nearby woods.

Mark Stewart scratched at his neck. The grimy shirt he wore itched wherever it touched his skin. When he had left the British consulate in Galveston early that morning, it had seemed best to wear the clothes of a day laborer. But as he raised his hand to his neck and scratched, he wondered about the hygiene of the man whose clothes he had stolen.

The Irish laborer had seemed a likely target. Mark was able to affect the lilting brogue common among the working poor from the Emerald Isle who worked the docks of Galveston. But he regretted not washing the clothing after he had purloined it.

The grove of trees ended a few hundred feet from the edge of West Liberty. But Mark had no interest in the town this afternoon. Perhaps another time it would be worth exploring. Without the Gulf Farms Corporation, the town would likely not exist, he thought. And certainly, the lone railroad in Texas wouldn't connect it to Galveston Bay were it not for the farming conglomerate. Any other time, Mark would have been fascinated to study how the owners of Gulf Farms competed with the slave labor of the plantations.

As he stepped over a fallen branch, Mark shrugged at the thought. Perhaps now wasn't a good time to compare. He had overheard one of the men on the train complaining that a majority of the farmers employed at Gulf Farms had been called up into the military. No doubt the current war with Mexico was putting heavy financial stress on the corporation.

No, he thought, his real interest lay ahead, through the thick grove of trees. He had walked through the woods for more than an hour when the tree line ended. He stopped under the shade of a towering live oak and stared.

For the past year, the republic's militia and reserve battalions had used the fallow fields and pastures east of West Liberty as a place to drill and train for war. The Republic's military leadership had picked it because of its proximity to the railroad connecting the town to Anahuac and Galveston Bay.

At its peak, the Texian army had drilled a half-dozen battalions in the fields in front of Mark. At least that's what the newspapers in Galveston had reported. Now, most of the reserve battalions had marched south with the Texian army and most of the men in the remaining militia battalions had returned to their farms.

Despite that, Mark watched a few companies drill. It was late in the afternoon. He was sure they would dismiss the men back to their camp shortly. And that's what he was waiting for.

He settled against a tree, eying the sun. For what he had planned it was best to wait until after sunset. He had read in the *Telegraph and Texas Register* that of the nearly one hundred militia companies, organized in eight battalions, Thomas Rusk, general of the militia, rotated a few companies through the camp at West Liberty each week. Ostensibly, it was to prepare the men serving in the militia to mobilize if they were called into service. Mark suspected the Texians wanted to have a few hundred men under arms in the eastern part of the Republic, in the unlikely event Mexico should try to invade by sea.

On the other side of the field, the men dispersed back to their camp. The sun would set within the hour. He chuckled at the thought of Mexico invading Texas by sea. The young republic owned four purpose-built warships. The largest, the *Fannin*, was a screw-propelled steam frigate. The other three were steam-powered sloops-of-war. Mark shook his head as he recalled seeing the two warships British merchants had sold to the Mexican navy riding at anchor in Galveston Bay. After the battle of Campeche between Texas and Mexico last year, the Mexican navy, as the Texians were fond of saying, didn't have a pot to piss in, anymore. The western Gulf of Mexico was, for the time being, a Texas lake.

And that was why Mark was leaning against a tree, waiting for the last vestiges of light to flee the western sky. His employers favored an independent Texas. Anything with the potential to act as a counterweight against the growing power of the United States was worth supporting. But Texas, Mark thought, was a poor mistress for Britain to cozy up to. Much of the eastern portion of the Republic was given over to a plantation economy, built upon the backs of black slavery. That made his employers nervous.

The sun slipped below the horizon and Mark left the tree cover and casually crossed the field toward the militia camp. When he was within a hundred feet of the edge of the camp, he squatted down and watched. The tents were lined up on each side of the company's street. Cooking fires lined the center of the camp. At the front of the street, the company had stacked their arms, interlocking the bayoneted rifles stacked together.

Mark waited. As the men of the militia company ate, there were no guards posted around the camp. But he needed to be patient. His goals would be for naught if anyone saw him approaching. It took several hours before the men settled down. Fires eventually died down, becoming beds of glowing coals. Normal nighttime noises replaced the sound of men moving about. Unfortunately, before retiring to bed, the militia company's captain posted a guard on the camp, forcing Mark to crawl further into the field to avoid detection.

"A small price to pay," he thought. It was but a single man, circling the camp. The rest, the Englishman thought, was easy enough. The guard was behind the camp when he made his move. Mark ignored the stiffness in his knees

and raced toward the nearest stack of standing rifles. The sound of the guard, marching along the back of the camp, was faint and he unlocked the stack. He pulled a rifle out and set it on the ground then locked the stack back in a triangle. Taking the time to relock the stack was a calculated risk. If the guard discovered the stack was missing a rifle, then he had sacrificed precious seconds. But if it went unnoticed, he smiled as his hurried back across the field, *"then I've made good my escape with a rifle my employers will be happy to study."*

Chapter 20

The ride back to the encampment north of town was long, made all the longer as Juan Almonte contemplated exile. It was hardly the worst fate His Excellency could have doled out, but the sense of abandonment and betrayal whistled through his soul like a blue norther. If faced with exile, Almonte knew he could live with it. But his wife, Maria, how would she adjust to the loss of her home, friends, and country? As he guided his mount along the well-travelled road, he couldn't predict her response. She was in the capital city and somehow, he felt Santa Anna would order him directly to Vera Cruz or Tampico. Despite all that Maria would give up in exile, there was a certitude in Almonte's heart that she would come as soon as he sent for her.

Thoughts of his wife faded from his mind as he reached camp. It was replaced with thoughts of Major John Coffee Hays. The lone Texian survivor of the hacienda fight, Hays was still recovering from his injuries. Almonte's surgeon had been forced to remove the major's left arm above the elbow. A .69 caliber musket ball had shattered the bone. Almonte knew the Texian was fortunate to have survived. His shoulder injury could have been much worse, he was lucky the ball had exited the back, hitting no bones or vital organs. His leg was healing nicely where a lance had pierced his calf muscle. But he still needed a crutch to walk, although Almonte only permitted it when Hays was under guard.

Now though, His Excellency's order to turn over any prisoners bode ill for the young Texian major. Almonte's long service with Santa Anna left no doubt in his mind what His Excellency intended. As if thinking of someone conjured an appearance, Almonte saw Hays hobbling around outside his tent. A young officer from the remains of his *Cazadores* regiments sat nearby as another rifle-armed *Cazadore* guarded the injured Texian.

Almonte forced a smile onto his face, "Captain Morales, how are you and your charge doing this fine morning?"

Almonte recalled the first time he had met the captain. He had been a courier from the capital reassigned to the Army of the North. Almonte had had no need of more couriers but he was short of officers for the newly formed *Cazadores* regiments. It seemed a lifetime ago, although it had only been a few months. Then, the freshly minted platoon commander had been a fresh-faced officer with a hint of the *Colegio Militar* of Chapultepec about him. Now, he commanded the remnants of several companies of riflemen and his eyes were sunken and framed by dark circles. His face was lined with a week's worth of stubble and his once navy-blue jacket was faded to a washed-out purple.

As he swung out of the saddle, Almonte dreaded giving the order that would turn the Texian over to Santa Anna. He strode by the three men and pulled the tent flap closed behind him. After unbuckling his sword, he collapsed on his cot. He squeezed his eyes shut. It would have been better for his men to have killed Hays instead of capturing him, he thought. Far better than being lined up against a wall and executed like a common criminal.

He shook his head. Seven years before, Almonte conceded, His Excellency's argument to treat the Texians as rebels might have made sense. But even though Santa Anna had been forced into a treaty he had not wanted, and in truth, had repudiated it as soon as he had set foot on Mexican soil, the Texians had done their best to build their own nation north of the Rio Bravo. Executing a captured soldier from Mexico's northern neighbor struck Almonte as a vindictive act of petulance. When part of Woll's army had been captured the prior year by General Johnston, the Texian general had treated those soldados as prisoners of war. Despite Santa Anna ordering the execution of prisoners, Johnston had not retaliated, even though no nation would have looked askance had Johnston done so.

Almonte looked back at the tent flap. To kill Hays made no sense. *"I've lost my command and I've been cast aside as a useless tool,"* he thought, *"But I still have my integrity. I won't be party to any more petty vengeance."*

Realization settled on Almonte, he was free of Santa Anna's command for the first time in years. He could leave without a backwards glance. He swung out of the cot and grabbed his trunk. It was still loaded. He eyed it. It was heavy. If he intended to ride away and leave this all behind, he needed to pack lighter. He flung the lid open and rummaged through clothes until he drew out a carpet bag. He had bought it while serving as minister to the United States. The irony of the situation wasn't lost upon him. Exile likely meant returning to the United States.

He hefted the bag after throwing clothes into it. It was light enough and could be tied to the back of his saddle. He strode from the tent and crossed in front of the prisoner and his guards and secured the bag behind the saddle.

After checking his mount and the saddle straps, he became aware of the eyes on him. He turned and saw the Texian major standing next to Captain Morales. The enlisted guard had set the rifle butt on the ground and leaned against the barrel, watching.

Almonte did the only thing that made sense. He shrugged. "His Excellency has seen fit to remove me from command of the Army of the North. I have been ordered to vacate Mexico. So, you see, I may not tarry any longer."

Both Hays and Morales stared with mouths agape at the news. Hays recovered first, "What does that mean for me, General Almonte?"

Almonte spread his hands wide, "I cannot say, Major. I'm sorry."

Hays' eyes went wide, "The hell you say. If you ride out of here, General, I'm a dead man."

Almonte started to push past Hays to remove anything else from his tent, when he saw Morales' hard stare. "What, not you too, Captain?"

Morales stepped back and pulled Hays out of Almonte's way. "I have watched you keep our army alive, General, when by all rights, it should have broken apart. As a rifleman, I am not blind to the advantages the Texians have over our men when it comes to both their tactics and weapons. Anybody other than you would have been swept aside at the Rio Bravo, sir."

Almonte stopped in his tracks, halfway between his horse and his tent. "I'm afraid that His Excellency doesn't agree with you, Captain."

"Then Santa Anna is a fool." The words were hardly out of his mouth when Morales cast a furtive look around. Even the enlisted guard nodded along to his words. Emboldened by his own audacity, the captain continued, "I'd rather follow you away from here, General, than be led to certain defeat by some new commander. Also, even though I wasn't there when General Sesma's lancers captured Major Hays, I can say, having faced his men in combat on several occasions that he is an honorable enemy. If we allow his execution, if this large army loses to the Texians I fear for the lives of all the men who have fought from the Rio Bravo all the way to Monterrey with you."

Even though the conversation was in Spanish, Hays appeared to have understood it, "You should listen to the captain, General Almonte. If you're not going to be staying here, I'd happily join you in getting the hell away from Santa Anna."

Hays' comment was absurd, but Almonte was convinced Santa Anna's judgement against prisoners was equally absurd and would certainly bring about a worse set of circumstances should the Texians triumph. He shook his head at how surreal his circumstances had become. The fog of uncertainty in Almonte's mind burned away as he suddenly knew his next step. "I am heading into exile, I will go north, by way of Saltillo. Now, Major, if you would like to join me, I would be honored with your company."

Hays said, "Hell, yes."

"Captain, can I implore upon you a bit of time before letting anyone else know that we have left?" Almonte asked of Morales.

Morales said. "If you're not going to command us, me and a few of my men will go with you at least part of the way. A few more deserters won't be noticed."

The comment laid bare a problem that even Almonte had not been able to solve. Since the defeat at Monterrey, a steady trickle of men had stolen away nightly. Although, since arriving at San Luis Potasi it appeared to have stopped. "Captain, I can't allow that. If you are caught, Santa Anna will make an example of you and your men. I won't have anyone executed over this."

Morales' laugh rang with bitterness. "Death by firing squad is no more likely than death in the next battle." Almonte was about to issue a command when the captain continued, "And, as you said, you're not in command anymore."

The sun was still in the sky when Almonte rode north with Hays, the *Cazadores* Captain and a dozen riflemen who, like their captain, decided their war was over.

Slipping out of the camp proved easier than any of them had anticipated. Both Almonte and Hays had donned uniforms purloined from a laundry line in the *Cazadores* camp, and when they arrived at a picket line, they found it guarded by riflemen, who took Captain Morales at his word that he and his patrol were scouting to the north.

When they were well away from the camp, Hays said, "Hot damn, General. I thought that guard would have asked for papers or something more than just the captain's word."

Like a gambler whose mask has slipped, Almonte's eyes slid over to Morales and with a slight smile said, "We had that covered, too."

Morales produced a letter from a pocket, "Orders signed by none other than General Almonte this morning. The odds of one of our guards learning of the General's fall from favor before we escaped was a calculated risk, Major, but one that paid off"

18 June 1843

Despite a love of Texas history, Will was frustrated by his lack of knowledge about the United States' war with Mexico from his own memories. While he knew the United States had goaded the Mexican army into attacking by sending an army into the disputed territory of South Texas, and that the United States had later invaded by sea at Vera Cruz and marched across central Mexico to capture Mexico City, that was the extent of his knowledge.

He was sure the US had captured Monterrey which now lay more than sixty miles behind him. Had the United States army reached Saltillo? He didn't know. But had they, they would have found what he saw. Saltillo was the center of commerce in Coahuila, and according to the alcalde, the city and surrounding farms, ranches, and villages numbered ten thousand souls. More than that though, just south of town the road to San Luis Potosi ran through a rugged, narrow valley, a little more than three miles across from one side to the other.

The memory of what it cost in time and men to dislodge Almonte's army from their fixed positions at Candela nearly two months before left a sour taste in his mouth. For the time being, though, his men were digging defenses across the narrow valley. He shook his head as he considered the vagaries of war. When he and the 1st brigade had arrived ten days earlier, he had expected to find Almonte's army entrenched in the town, but to his surprise, it lay undefended. The town's alcalde had informed him the Mexican Army of the North had started to build fortifications around the city but stopped after a few days when word came from the south ordering the army to join a larger force assembling at San Luis Potosi, two weeks' march away.

As he watched men from the 1st Infantry shoveling dirt, constructing an earthen redoubt in the center of the valley, he thought back to the meeting he had held with his officers after arriving at Saltillo a couple of weeks' prior.

Early June was getting hot in the arid mountains of northern Mexico, but the shade from the pavilion cut the worst of the heat. His camp desk was in the center of the pavilion and he, Sid Johnston, Ben McCulloch, Juan Seguin, and Lt. Colonel Carey of the artillery had crowded around the desk.

"We're in a bit of a pickle, gentlemen," Will had opened the meeting, "According to the local mayor, Almonte is rendezvousing with Santa Anna south of here. While I have received word that President Zavala has authorized two more battalions for service, they won't do us much good as they will be used to shore up our supply lines and garrison Monterrey."

Johnston leaned forward in his chair, "I don't think our situation is particularly grim, as of right now, we've got all the 1st brigade hereabouts as well as Lt. Colonel West's Marine battalion. That's twenty-two hundred men, not counting our cavalry or artillery."

Seguin added, "Those not currently tied to securing our supply line or Monterrey are making their way to Saltillo over the next week or so."

McCulloch was looking at a small notebook when he said, "According to the latest reports from the north, the relief column left the Alamo two weeks ago. Assuming they don't run into any problems, we can expect their arrival at Monterrey any day now. Once they arrive, we can pull the rest of our soldiers from Monterrey and bring them here."

Will was drumming his fingers on the desk, "We're damned lucky the president agreed to release more soldiers to shore up our supply line, but let's not kid ourselves. At best, we have one more chance to win this war before our ability to wage war is done. I've received a steady stream of letters from the president and various congressmen wanting to know when the reserve battalions can be demobilized. Too many farms are fallow, and storefronts are being run by wives and children."

It was a sobering reminder the army was reaching its limit. He continued, "If we assemble our army and march it south, are we certain we can so thoroughly defeat Santa Anna's new command as to force him to peace?"

Juan Seguin shook his head, "The land around San Luis Potosi plays to the dictator's strengths. The valleys are wide, and his army will have plenty of room to maneuver. While I think we can defeat his army anywhere we choose to fight, the land directly south of Saltillo is some of the most defensible land we're likely to find. Better yet, we're the ones sitting on it, not the Mexicans. According to the Alcalde, Santa Anna is marching north. He's not going to play the defensive war that Almonte favored. Buck, if you want a victory that will knock Santa Anna out, our best chance is here."

Both Johnston and McCulloch nodded. Seguin had earned a reputation for impulsive attacks. That he was urging caution wasn't lost on the other men. "I've sent a few patrols to our south over the past few days. We'll know within a day or two of Santa Anna's army's arrival. But as God is my witness, I wish I had Jack Hays back. Losing one of our best Ranger companies and their commander has been a disaster without equal."

The thought of Jack Hays' death brought Will back to the present. His battalion of special Rangers were down to less than seventy men, and while they were under the command of their senior captain, Will missed the young and reckless major. Although his messenger had arrived back in Monterrey in less than two days, by the time Seguin had managed to race his battalion of regular cavalry to the hacienda, it had been too late. Hays' was the only body not recovered from the bloody battle waged between the Rangers and Almonte's lancers. His absence gave Will a hope, however faint, he still lived. But with each passing day, Hays' survival seemed more remote.

A commotion erupted near the road, where riflemen were deepening a trench in front of the redoubt. Will retrieved his Italian-made binoculars and raised them to his eyes and focused on the road south. A cavalry detachment in squad strength was galloping across the planks laid over the trench where it cut across the road. Will scanned the road and saw, tiny as ants, three mounted figures riding from the south. Despite the strong magnification, it took several minutes to see that two of the men were dressed in blue uniforms, common among their rifle-armed light infantry while the third was dressed in a butternut jacket. He thought he recognized the rider.

He put the binoculars away and raced his horse down the road, until he found the three men surrounded by a dozen Texian cavalry troopers. Sure enough, through the bramble of facial hair, Will recognized the gaunt face of Jack Hays. He was alive.

Later, Will was joined by Juan Seguin who greeted the young major like the father welcoming the prodigal home. "We thought you were dead when we found where your company had been attacked, Jack. How did you survive?"

Sitting under the canvas pavilion, around Will's camp table, Hays gestured to the two men wearing *Cazadores* uniforms. "They found me alive and saved my life." He then nodded to the empty left sleeve of his jacket. "My arm was too badly damaged to save, but the rest of me was nursed back to health."

Will resisted the urge to tousle Hays' hair, like he would have with Charlie before asking, "How did you escape?"

Hays said, "I expect you've heard Santa Anna's coming this way with the biggest damned army he's managed to collect. The old boy still has this thing about killing prisoners."

Will swore and shook his head in disbelief. "You see, Juan, this is the reason we're stuck hip-deep in Mexico. We're not going to stop until we've put that that jumped up pissant of dictator against a wall and shoot him.

"Were it not for these fine gentlemen, I'm afraid Santa Anna would have been the one to put me up against a wall."

The two Mexicans had been silent until then. The shorter of the two stepped forward and bowed toward

Will. "General Travis, I am Juan Nepomuceno Almonte, formerly of the Mexican army. I and my traveling companion, Javier Morales seek political asylum."

Chapter 21

Will was speechless. Standing before him in a simple uniform of a Mexican rifleman was the man who had ably blocked his army from a quick victory since the beginning of the campaign. What turn of fortune had caused his enemy to show up on his proverbial doorstep? Almonte was an opponent, but he had conducted his campaign against Will's army with skill, determination, and, unlike Santa Anna, a code of honor that respected the lives of prisoners. Almonte was an honorable enemy. If Santa Anna had chased him off, then the rules of engagement could be ugly when next the two armies clashed.

Finding his voice, he said, "Asylum? General Almonte, you have made my life very difficult, and from where I am standing, the way you conducted your defense, you have unnecessarily drawn out this war. Why should I grant you asylum?"

Almonte pulled the tall shako from his head, revealing black hair slowly losing ground to gray at the temples. He pulled out a dirty handkerchief and wiped his brow before he responded. "Duty is a jealous wife, General Travis, would you not agree?"

Will acknowledged the words with a single nod before Almonte continued, "My duty has always been to the people and institutions of Mexico. When I opposed you on the Rio Bravo del Norte, it was clear that the balance of power was in your favor, given your new rifles and tactics. Unlike Adrian Woll, I saw no good reason to fertilize Texas soil with Mexican blood. From where I stood, it was better for your soldiers to assault our trenches rather than the other way around."

Will frowned at Almonte. Well over a thousand men had been killed, wounded or taken ill over the previous months. Those were men that Texas could ill afford to lose.

Almonte continued, "You see, General, before taking responsibility for the army of the North, I had served my country as Minister Plenipotentiary to the United States. During that time, naturally I learned everything I could about the changes you were making in Texas. Copies of your training manual are available for a price there and I had some idea of the kind of army you were building. But your army is a hungry beast, and Texas is too fragile a host to sustain it. Aside from a miracle from the blessed Virgin, it was unlikely my army would defeat yours in battle, but time favors Mexico. Before long, your nation's economy will collapse under the weight of your army."

Will was stunned to hear Almonte give voice to his own nightmares. The steady stream of letters from the government in Austin counseled a quick victory because of those very issues. That Almonte surmised the truth shocked Will.

Almonte gazed across the small camp table at Will, "For reasons of his own, His Excellency, Santa Anna, chose to rid the army of my services and in doing so, revoked my orders regarding the treatment of prisoners."

Despite the oppressive summer heat, a chill wind cut through Will's heart. Even before the revolution, Santa Anna had ignored the rule of law when it came to his treatment of prisoners. When he had crushed other revolts in the mid-1830s, he had dealt harshly with those captured. Sometimes lots were drawn and a portion of those found in rebellion were killed and other times, all captive rebels were executed. Even though Will and the revolutionary government of Texas had forced upon him a treaty in 1836, Santa Anna had repudiated it.

No government which had taken power in Mexico City over the past seven years, and there had been many, recognized Texas' independence, but Santa Anna took it to an extreme. He had no sooner returned to power than he confirmed the Tornel Decree was still in effect. The decree condemned to death any foreign-born person on Mexican soil captured under arms.

"The state of our economy and our army are not related, General Almonte," Will said. It was a weak lie, but one the Mexican general, standing before him, requesting asylum, was in a poor position to question. "Unlike Santa Anna and his bloodthirsty vendetta, there is only one Mexican that I will bring to justice. If he is coming here, then we'll greet *his excellency* with a very warm welcome."

27 June 1843

The ridgeline ended abruptly, and he pulled the reins, stopping his mount a few feet from where the ground fell away sharply into the valley below. David Crockett gazed westward. At the end of the valley he saw the walls of the presidio gleaming gold in the setting sun.

A wry smile played at his lips. It was a fool's gold. He knew from scouting reports the walls of the presidio were the same adobe that constituted dozens of other small Spanish outposts across northern Mexico. Crowding around the presidio walls were scores of small houses. The same scouts informed him a few hundred souls populated the area surrounding the presidio. The population was a mixture of mestizos, creoles, and Kumeyaay Indians, who had lived in the area since time immemorable.

Crockett wasn't worried about the populace. *"Hell, I'm not even worried about the soldados,"* he thought. The presidio was garrisoned by less than a dozen men. So said the intelligence he had received. He turned to the source of his intelligence, Juan Bandini. Despite being more than a dozen years younger than Crockett, his salt-and-pepper hair was more salt than pepper.

Bandini had appeared the previous day along with a few riders, men who worked his land grant. He was Peruvian born, but of Spanish parents. It hadn't taken long for Crockett to discern Bandini's motives were largely financial. Under the Mexican government, the town and presidio of San Diego was dying on the vine. The provincial capital in Monterey was more than four hundred miles to the north. As if to confirm Crockett's thoughts, Bandini said, "I have your promise the Texas government will respect Spanish and Mexican land grants, Colonel?"

"I gave my word once, Señor Bandini. Giving it again ain't gonna change the answer. There ain't no doubt I can lay claim to Alta California for Texas with this here army. Whether we keep it once a treaty is written is another thing. If President Zavala don't give it back to Santa Anna, then we'll respect your property rights."

Crockett eyed the Spaniard as the other man gave a perfunctory nod. He had been a public official for most of his life and had learned to read other men. Bandini was a big fish in the small pond that was San Diego. Co-opting him went a long way toward securing this part of California. Unconsciously, he looked back the way he and his tiny army had come and swallowed hard. Bandini didn't need to know how badly Crockett needed to secure San Diego. Even though he held Tucson, supplies from the east remained nonexistent. His army needed the provisions available in the countryside surrounding San Diego.

A few days later, Crockett smiled as his stepgrandson, Charlie Travis, escorted Bandini and a grayhaired Mexican officer into the alcalde's office in the presidio. He grinned at the two men. Things had gone well. The garrison had surrendered without a fight. There had been an even score of soldados garrisoning the citadel. He had found the twenty men to be ill-equipped. Apparently, the aging lieutenant had agreed. After Crockett had paraded the men of the 9th Infantry in the valley before the presidio, the town had surrendered, without firing a shot.

Now, as he watched the two men settle into their chairs across the desk from him, he waved Charlie to one side of the room.

The lieutenant spoke first, in Spanish, which Bandini translated. "Colonel Crockett, on behalf of my men, thank you for paroling them. I doubt were the situation reversed I would be given such latitude."

Crockett leaned back in the high-back chair, listening to the legs creak beneath his weight. "That's the difference between me and Santa Anna, Lieutenant. He wants to govern you through fear. Me, I'd rather be your friend. Friends get more done than peons, wouldn't you say?"

While the Mexican constitution banned racial slavery, Crockett had seen there were many shades of citizenship under the government in Mexico City. In San Diego the impoverished Kumeyaay Indians labored under the weight of wage peonage, scarcely a step above chattel slavery.

Crockett glanced at Charlie as he thought of the boy's father. Buck had strong views about slavery, views which were growing on Crockett. But his own concern was more practical. He needed a secure supply line, and if he was to have it, he had to build it in San Diego. Bandini said, "About our property, Colonel..."

Crockett wondered if the Spaniard held any of the Kumeyaay in debt peonage. He forced a smile onto his face before interrupting. "All done, Señor Bandini. Your rights are secure. But I need something from you and yours," he paused only a moment before continuing. "I need wagons and supplies from this region."

The color faded from Bandini's face. "But we're poor, Colonel. Would you have us starve our children?"

Crockett allowed his eyes to grow hard. "Not so poor as you make yourself out to be, Señor Bandini. But I'm not a hard man. How many Kumeyaay make their homes nearby?"

The question caught Bandini by surprise. He said, "Around the presidio, maybe a couple of hundred."

"How many in the surrounding countryside?"

"Maybe as many as three thousand."

Crockett nodded. "I know they're a poor lot, but they're all the poorer because the Mexican government has taken their land away from them. We can hammer out the specifics later, but I want you and the alcalde to parcel off some land nearby for the tribe. We've worked out arrangements with both the Cherokee and the Apache that is proving mutually beneficial. I believe that with your help, we can do something similar with the local Indians."

Bandini wore an incredulous look. "what does that have to do with supplies?"

Crockett laughed, "By God, man, don't you get it? I'm willing to move heaven and earth to recognize your property rights. If I scratch your back, I expect you'll scratch mine. Why would the Kumeyaay be any different? If I recognize they have property rights, too, they'll look to Texas to respect their rights. I'd think you'd see that between the townsfolk in San Diego and the Kumeyaay working the outlying farms, that supplying my army is in your best interests, Señor Bandini."

Bandini looked thoughtful, weighing Crockett's words. Finally, the Texian colonel reached into his vest pocket and lay a stack of Texian commodities certificates on the table. "Did I forget to mention we're willing to pay?"

June 1843

The chair scraped the wooden floor as Gail Borden returned to his seat. The journal was open to where he had left off writing. Dipping the ink into the well, he wrote,

By washing the gun-cotton in a water-based solution for several days and allowing it to dry in the shade of my laboratory, I have found it far less likely to self-combust. A discovery I am very happy to have

made. Now, I can only hope my eyebrows grow back soon.

This is a major improvement in the process for creating the gun-cotton, I believe. It does not solve the problem brought to me by Andy Berry, who continues to insist the powder is much too powerful for any gun that the gun works can produce. Having seen the parts of the rifles blown up by the granulated gun cotton, I cannot disagree with his assessment.

Borden's pen was poised to continue putting his thoughts on paper when the ground shook. A moment later he heard an explosion in the distance. He dropped the pen and stepped over to the door and looked out. Above the tree line to the south, he saw a plume of smoke. It was in the direction of West Liberty.

Several men ran out from the gun works. They pointed toward the rising cloud of smoke. Several hurried down the wagon road and Borden joined them. If something had exploded in town, perhaps he could help.

Long before he and the workers from the gun works would have reached the town, the road broke through the trees and passed through a field. In the middle of the field a tree burned, sending tendrils of black smoke curling into the air. In front of the burning tree Borden saw someone hopping around. He and the workers ran across the field towards the figure. As they neared, Bordon recognized the figure as Andy Berry. The younger son of John Berry wore a large grin on a face blackened with soot. As the men approached he yelled, "Eureka!"

The tree behind Berry crackled, fire consumed it as Bordon reached the young man. "Alright, *Archimedes*, what have you discovered?"

In front of the tree, Berry pointed to a jagged hole in the ground. Translucent wisps of white vapor rose from it. "I might have found a dozen ways to break a rifle using your dashed gun-cotton, Mr. Borden, but by God, on my first try, I used it to take out a huge stump of a tree."

Borden stepped over to the hole. It was true, he could see bits of the root system sticking out from the dirt. Berry came up beside him and looked down. The explosion had gouged a hole deeper than a man was tall. The young man, still grinning, said, "Even if we can't tame the gun-cotton to fire from one of our rifles, Mr. Borden, imagine using this to clear fields of roots or to blast out a mine."

Bordon nodded absent-mindedly as Berry talked. In his mind, he saw its use on the battlefield, blowing up soldiers with a power gunpowder simply couldn't provide.

As he walked back to the gun works with the younger Berry, Borden wondered what he had created.

Chapter 22

1 July 1843

The dust cloud leapt into view as Will fumbled with the focusing knob on the binoculars. He shook his head. It *was* a big dust cloud. Almonte's information on Santa Anna's army appeared to be correct. Although still too far away, he imagined the long columns of men it took to create such a cloud. *"Twenty thousand men kick up an ungodly amount of dust,"* he thought.

He turned away from the sight and let his eyes sweep over the narrow valley in which his army would make a stand. It was three miles at its narrowest. With less than five thousand men in the ranks, Will knew he didn't have enough men to fortify the entire width of the valley. Instead, he and Sidney Johnston had created four redoubts positioned across the valley.

Since arriving at Saltillo three weeks earlier, it had been clear this was the place to stop Santa Anna. Each redoubt was five sided and had trenches surrounding the earthen ramparts. Guns poked through wooden-framed embrasures.

Will's attention was diverted by the noise of boots kicking the ground behind him. He turned and saw Major Jack Hays, whose jacket hung from his shoulders. One glance confirmed the young man was still adjusting to the loss of his left arm. His linen shirt sleeve was pinned up at the elbow. He scowled as he saw the distant cloud.

"I'm ready to return to duty, sir. We've got one hell of a fight coming our way and I can't do damn all here."

Will returned the scowl. "The hell you say. I talked with Doc Smith earlier today and you're lucky I'm letting you stay in the redoubt here. By all rights, you should be resting back in Saltillo."

With his good hand, Hays gestured southward. "And miss this shindig?"

Will saw his gaze slip. Hays knew the army was facing its greatest challenge since the revolution. The young officer leaned against the rampart, "We're taking a mighty big risk, General. We're depending on four redoubts to stop Santa Anna, and they're spread across the valley."

"You're preaching to the converted, Jack," Will said. "There's around twelve hundred yards between each of the redoubts. How far out can your best rifleman shoot? Four, five hundred yards? That leaves a few hundred yards between each position covered only by our artillery. That's why the two middle redoubts have two batteries each. With a bit of luck and a lot of canister and grapeshot, we'll turn the ground between the redoubts into a no-man's land."

Hays nodded, "You know, my Rangers are just a couple of hundred yards away, I could go and conduct a brief inspection, get back here in three shakes of a lamb's tail."

Will laughed. "Don't even think of it." He had set up his headquarters in the left-most redoubt. The 4th and 7th Infantry battalions were stationed there along with a battery of artillery. Patrolling between the redoubt and the rocky crags of the nine-thousand-foot-high mountain to the valley's east were the Rangers. The terrain they patrolled was ill-suited for anything other than light infantry. In addition to Hay's two remaining companies of specialized Rangers, six more companies from the frontier battalion were acting as dragoons, taking a defensive position in the naturally occurring ravines.

Faint music wafted on the breeze. Will and Hays turned to the south. To the naked eye, smaller than ants, the lead elements of Santa Anna's army appeared.

It was time. Will called over an orderly and moments later, a signal flag rose above the ramparts. Over the past few weeks, the Texian army had camped in the valley between the redoubts and Saltillo. At the flag's signal, the soldiers broke camp and streamed into the fortifications' rear-facing sally ports. Before long the battle would be joined.

Captain Bill Sherman set his pen down. His letter to Ellen would have to wait. He closed the leather-bound writing journal and placed it in the folding table he used for paperwork. He saw the signal flag rising above the redoubt. It was time. The earthen fort was pentagonal in shape. The rear was a wide wall with a narrow gate. He heard the drawbridge slamming in an upright position against its frame. The men in the redoubt were cut off from the rest of the army. The trench around the walls was eight to ten feet deep. Anyone trying to assault the position, first had to cross through the dry ditch before scaling the embankment's steep slope, which rose nearly twenty feet from the bottom of the ditch.

The five-sided structure came to a narrow point, facing south. His battery was responsible for two sides, while another battery was positioned along the other two forward-facing sides. The fifth side faced the rear. No guns faced that direction although a few embrasures had been constructed, so if the need arose, guns could be wheeled from their current positions.

Sherman hurried to his number one gun facing directly south, toward the Mexican army. Even without his orders, his men were already loading the gun. Confident his men knew their duty, he looked down into the redoubt's small plaza and saw General Johnston climb down from his saddle. He would directly command more than a thousand men of the 1st and 3rd Infantry battalions, as well as the two batteries of artillery in the redoubt.

Sherman knew General McCulloch oversaw a similar setup in the next redoubt over, where the 5th Infantry and Lt. Colonel West's Marine battalion were situated. The last redoubt was garrisoned by the 2nd Infantry and the 8th Infantry. Sherman glanced to the west, imagining the men of the Cherokee Rifles taking up position in the last redoubt. He found it impossible to not appreciate the ability of the riflemen from the civilized tribe after watching them fight their way through Monterrey the previous month.

A team of men raced by, carrying shells and bags of gunpowder, forcing Sherman against the earthen wall. He turned towards the first redoubt, where General Travis was headquartered. Beyond it were the Rangers. Sherman offered up a prayer that if the Mexicans tried to turn the army's flank, the two hundred men hunkered down in gullies worn in the mountainside would be able to turn the enemy back.

Thoughts of what was happening beyond the walls of his own redoubt fled when Sherman became aware of a voice calling from below. General Johnston was looking at him, "Captain, what's the range on the Mexican advance?"

Lifting his binoculars to his eyes, Sherman quickly focused on the lancers who were in the vanguard. They were still well beyond the range of his howitzers. "Looks like they're still more than a mile away, sir!"

Moments later, Johnston ran up the ramp from the parade ground. "God in heaven, Captain. That's an army!"

Sherman could only agree. Filling the entire width of the valley's entrance, the Mexican army spread out like a blue and red blanket, carpeting the valley.

"Do you think they'll make an attempt today, sir?"

Johnston tore his eyes away from the sight. "They've got at least eight more hours of light, Captain. If I were Santa Anna, I'd be doing whatever was necessary to turn our flanks. Let's hope he prefers a more direct approach."

Sherman found the general's words prophetic. The sun was still high in the sky when several regiments surged from the Mexican position, marching toward the middle of the valley. A quick look with the binoculars revealed at least a brigade was marching directly toward his own redoubt. The green, white, and red Mexican flags flew above the advancing line.

Sherman failed to suppress a grin when the longer-ranged six-pounders opened fire. Unlike his howitzers, they had a range of nearly a mile. The valley floor was sunbaked and dry. The first guns to fire hurled solid shot.

When the heavy, round balls landed, they skipped across the packed earth, and plowed into the densely packed line of *soldados*, knocking them over like a petulant child angrily scattering his toy soldiers. Only these soldiers bled and died. At fifteen hundred yards, Sherman could only imagine the cries and screams as bodies were torn apart.

But the line of soldados never wavered. The officers and NCOs closed the ranks and pressed forward.

When the advancing line was within eight hundred yards, Sherman turned to the nearest gunner, leaned forward, and said, "Open fire."

The round screamed down range. Unlike the guns which fired solid shot earlier, this shell flew over the advancing Mexican line and detonated overhead, sending fragments of iron raining down on the unprotected heads of the advancing soldados.

Still the line didn't waver. The tattoo of drummers reached the walls of the redoubt and Sherman could hear them beating out a quick march. Whisked along by a light breeze, the acrid-smelling smoke dissipated before the men had reloaded their guns. At six hundred yards, he didn't need the binoculars to see the men advancing across the valley. The forward-moving regimental lines were not quite as well ordered as they had been. Scores of men had fallen from the incessant artillery barrage.

Despite the steady booming of the guns, Sherman became aware of the rising din of rifle fire. The front two angles of the redoubt extended no more than four hundred feet. Six artillery pieces were comfortably arranged along those two sides. Filling every spare foot of space between the guns, hundreds of the fortification's defenders lined the walls. When the range fell below four hundred yards, they opened fire.

"Switch to cannister!" Sherman cried out. The Mexican line had shifted just enough so that there was no doubt where they intended to come straight at his redoubt, and Sherman was going to kill as many of them as possible before they closed the distance.

The advancing line focused on one redoubt, preventing the riflemen in any of the others from helping. But, nearly half of the Texian artillery was able to direct their fire at the advancing line of infantry and shot and shell tore gaping holes in the advancing ranks.

At two hundred yards, the Mexican line, with gaping holes in it, surged forward in a mad dash toward the redoubt.

The gun next to Sherman recoiled as flames shot from the barrel. He watched as dozens of men were knocked from their feet as scores of metal balls struck them. Still, the blue-jacketed soldados raced across the ground, eager to reach the redoubt.

"Gunners! Cease fire!" Sherman called out. The attack had carried the enemy under the guns.

Hundreds of men leapt into the dry moat. Sherman involuntarily ducked as he felt a bullet buzz by his head. He shook his head in wry amusement. *"You don't hear the one that gets you*," he thought.

Men who fell were dragged away from the firing line atop the redoubt's wall. When one fell away, another rushed forward, replacing him.

Despite the steep slope, soldados dug their fists into the dirt and climbed. With the howitzers unable to fire into their midst, Sherman drew his revolver and joined the crowded firing line. The ground below was covered with the fallen even as men surged up the steep incline. He snapped off round after round until the hammer landed on an empty chamber.

Twenty feet might as well have been two hundred. None of the soldados reached the top of the embankment. Those still on their feet fell back, still under fire. Sherman's guns remained silent, cooling as the sun dipped below the western mountains. Where had the day gone? To Sherman, it felt as though only a couple of hours had passed. But twilight would soon fall, ending any further attempt for another attack until the next day.

Slowly, he became aware of the weak cries coming from the injured in the ditch below. From where he stood, it looked as though a hundred men, dead and badly wounded, clogged the trench. He and the other men in the redoubt had shattered one of Santa Anna's brigades. Even so, Sherman looked south; Santa Anna had more brigades, a lot more.

As he took a swig from his canteen, he heard one of his men talking to another, "What do you mean that was half our ammunition?"

First Sergeant Julio Mejia was jostled awake. "Sergeant! There's movement to our front!"

His eyes slammed open as he reached for his rifle, thoughts of sleep swept aside. Apart from a few lanterns burning in the redoubt's parade ground, it was still dark. His hands fumbled in his vest pocket until he withdrew a small pocket watch. Since his promotion to first sergeant the previous year, his responsibilities had grown exponentially. Knowing the time came in handy, he thought, and investing some of his increased pay in a watch had already paid off more times than he could count. Enough lantern light illuminated the watch's face to see the time. Dawn was near.

He followed the sentry up the dirt ramp. Another rifleman, standing guard with his weapon pointing into the inky darkness, waited for his companion's return. Sure enough, in the distance, he heard feet scuffling and leather creaking. "Sounds like all of Santa Anna's army is moving about," one of the guards said. In the darkness of predawn the moon had already set, and visibility was, at most, a couple of hundred feet. Mejia feared the soldier was right.

Moments later, Lieutenant Hiram Oats jogged up the ramp and joined them along the ramparts. Oats commanded the company since Captain Edwards' injury at the Battle of the Rio Grande.

The lieutenant said, "Sergeant Mejia, let's not make a ruckus of it, but roust the boys. I want the entire company on the wall, now."

On his way across the courtyard, Mejia saw General Travis come from his tent. While he was loath to deviate from his orders, it would only take a moment. When he reached the general, Travis was taking a tin cup full of coffee from an orderly. "Sorry to bother you, sir. But there's movement coming from the Mexican camp. A lot of it by the ruckus they're making."

He watched the army's commander take a sip of the coffee before grimacing and handing the cup back to his orderly. Mejia saluted and hurried away. When Mejia arrived back on the wall, riflemen were packed between the artillery pieces.

From behind, Mejia heard a loud pop. He turned and watched a trail of smoke leave the ground and arc into the sky, trailing sparks and flames. Hundreds of yards away, high in the predawn sky, an explosion briefly turned night to day.

Mejia's eyes followed the flare as it arced toward the ground. His eyes grew wide as he saw, standing barely a thousand feet away the Mexican army. *"Madre de Dios,"* he whispered.

The flare, as it fell to the ground, faded. The light hadn't disappeared across the valley when Mejia heard another loud pop from behind, and seconds later, another flare exploded over the Mexican army. Lieutenant Oats cried out, "Open fire!"

More lights flickered above the valley as the other redoubts launched flares into the sky, and Mejia watched as the Mexican army began marching across the valley. From his vantage, Mejia swore again. In addition to the line advancing toward his own redoubt, he could see dense formations advancing on the redoubts to either side of his own. Evidently, Santa Anna was determined to push through the Texians' fortified positions.

The largest part of him wanted to force his way to the firing line and kill the enemy who were surging across the artificially lit battlefield. As first sergeant, he clamped down on the desire. His job was to monitor the riflemen standing in front of him on the parapet.

The ground shook under his feet when the nearest 6-pounder fired. Mejia coughed as he tasted the bitterness of burnt gunpowder. Smoke hung in the air, obscuring their view of the advancing Mexican army. Despite the smoke, the rate of fire from his riflemen didn't fall off.

Before the gun fired again, Mejia saw scores of men carrying ladders as part of the assault. The steep embankment made climbing by hand difficult. If the Mexicans could throw the ladders against the embankment, scaling it would be much easier. "Kill the men carrying the ladders!" he called out.

Despite the incessant, punishing rifle fire, punctuated by the steady booming of the guns, the flares overhead revealed the soldados were nearing the trench surrounding the redoubt. Mejia was an experienced soldier. But seeing the mass of *soldados* streaming into the ditch sent a cold shiver up his spine. "*I've been in tighter spots than this*," he thought. The heavy odor of gunpowder in the air reminded him of a road outside of Reynosa where he had barely escaped a massacre with his life.

"*Mierda*," he swore as the first ladder was thrown against the earthen wall.

Jesse Running Creek yelled, "More cartridges!" He levered the rifle's breech closed and found another percussion cap in the box at his waist.

The sun had climbed over the eastern peaks, bathing the valley in golden light. It made killing the dismounted lancers easier, Jesse thought as he raised his rifle to his shoulder. A moment later, it kicked, and he saw a blue and red uniformed man tumble to the ground.

Out of ammunition, Jesse drew his bowie knife from its scabbard. The brass hilt had been modified, a ring had been inserted, allowing it to fit over the end of the rifle barrel. He locked it in place and edged over to one of his teammates. "You have any more cartridges?"

The Ranger nodded toward the rifle team's corporal, who lay at the bottom of the ravine. His face was gone. Jesse looked away. It looked like a shotgun blast had ended his fight. More than a few lancers, forced to fight on foot, had fallen back on short carbines. Some used musket balls, others used small scraps of metal. The corporal apparently had been hit with the latter.

Trying not to stare at the face, Jesse scampered over to the dead man and flipped open his cartridge box. There was a tin of cartridges. He grabbed them, then unslung the haversack. In it, he discovered two more packets of cartridges.

He tossed one of the packets to his teammate and reloaded his rifle. Edging up to the lip of the ravine, he saw a few lancers retreating.

"Lord have mercy," the other Ranger said. The slope in front of their ravine was sprinkled with dead lancers. A sob escaped his lips. Jesse knew how he felt. The dismounted lancers had arrived with the dawn, shortly after Santa Anna had sent his infantry against the redoubts in the valley below.

Thinking of the redoubts, he looked down in the valley. It was covered in a haze of smoke. But the deep booms from the artillery still echoed against the craggy heights and the steady staccato of gunfire confirmed that the battle still raged. From his vantage point, it appeared the redoubts were holding.

The right flank, three miles away, was defended by the rest of the cavalry, fighting dismounted, under General Seguin. Under normal circumstances, Jesse would have been able to see the slope they were defending, but not this morning. Hazy smoke blanketed the valley. Had more enemy lancers succeeding in turning that flank?

Rocks tumbled down the hill behind him, and Jesse spun around, keeping his rifle at the ready. An ordinance sergeant growled, "Point that damned thing somewhere else. You ought to be happy. I'm the man bringing you some more ammunition."

Jesse lowered his rifle in time to catch several paper-wrapped arsenal packs, which contained ten rounds per pack. They also held a tiny tube of percussion caps. He divvied them up between himself and his teammate as the ordinance sergeant hoisted a box onto his shoulder and moved further up the ravine toward the next rifle team.

"Jesse, look sharp, there's more a-coming." Turning, he saw a thin line of soldados moving up the hill in skirmish formation. He broke open one of the packs and took a thin tube of percussion caps and dropped them into his cap box. He capped his rifle, aimed, and fired.

Chapter 23

Will, leaned against the earthen wall, coughing, as he tried to clear his mouth of the choking taste of gunpowder. Part of him was amazed he was still alive. For a little while it had been a close fought battle. The sun had already crested the eastern mountains when the Mexican regiments facing his redoubt attacked with everything they had. Dozens of ladders had been placed against the redoubt's earthen walls, and soldados had swarmed up and onto the ramparts.

When it appeared to him the battle was hanging in the balance, he had led his own orderlies up the ramp and into the thick of battle. Only now did he look down and see his revolver in his left hand and his sword in his right. The sword was caked with drying gore. As he thought back over the past hour, he remembered parrying and thrusting. He was at a loss recalling how he had come through unscathed. There were dozens of men, sitting and leaning against the wall, whose injuries were not severe enough to drive them from their position. But when Will looked at the small parade ground within the redoubt's walls, the ground was covered with the dead and dying of the two battalions.

He shook his head. His voice cracked, "Dear God in Heaven, another victory like this and we're ruined."

"Sir, what are your orders?" He turned and found an orderly waiting. The young man, barely twenty, had his head wrapped in a bandage, and a dried rivulet of blood ran down the side of his face. Will vaguely recalled his orderlies joining him during the earlier defense.

The two battalions who had defended the left most redoubt had been battered. But what of the Mexican army? Will scanned the valley beyond the redoubt's walls. In the dry moat around his position, the ground was carpeted with dead and dying soldados. Beyond the ditch, perhaps another couple of hundred had fallen, and the ground was covered with the detritus of a defeated army. Muskets had been cast away, jackets and packs were scattered where they had been dropped.

But he could see, beyond extreme rifle range, companies here and there, still holding their formations. And beyond those companies, larger formations of regiments. They may have been shadows of their former size, but if even if a third of Santa Anna's army had been shattered, there were still more than ten thousand men whom Santa Anna could rally, if given a chance.

With a heavy sigh, Will said, "Signal the other redoubts, I want ten companies from each to assemble and destroy the enemy formations. Also, signal the cavalry and Rangers on our flanks. They're to mount up and support the infantry, and if possible, cut off the enemy's retreat."

As the signal flags were raised, Will found the battalion commanders and instructed each of them to assemble their five largest companies in the valley behind the redoubt. The colonel commanding the 4th battalion quickly assembled five of his ten companies. At full strength, each fielded three officers and seventy-two riflemen and NCOs. The war had taken a heavy toll. None of the companies fielded more than forty-five riflemen. Men were pulled from the rest of the battalion, so the five companies would field three hundred men. Together, the two battalions deployed six hundred.

Will choked back a sob. Even before the transference so many years before, he had considered himself a veteran, but nothing he had faced in Iraq prepared him for the loss of life his army had endured since this war began the previous year. He couldn't help but wonder what these losses would mean for the republic. How many wives were widowed? How many children orphaned? And for what? So that Texas could lay claim to land disputed since the revolution?

"Enough," Will muttered. If he could end the war here in the valley south of Saltillo, then those pressing issues could be more closely examined later.

"Ah-hem."

Will spun around, surprised at the noise. Jack Hays wore a wry grin as though listening in on Will's private thoughts. "Sorry, sir. Didn't mean to come up on you unawares."

Will gave a curt nod as his nerves relaxed. Hays wore his jacket pinned at the elbow. At his belt he wore his pistol and bowie knife. The grin faded from his face as he said, "Let me join my boys, sir. I'm useless here. Me and my Rangers can fix Santa Anna's flint, with your leave."

Will's eyes drifted toward the gate, where riflemen were pouring through, leaving the fortified position. Given the heavy losses the army had sustained throughout the battle, he wanted to protect Hays from further harm. The young major had nearly died during the push from Monterrey to Saltillo, and yet, he asked nothing more than to rejoin his men.

He wanted to refuse the request. Instead, he said, "Granted, Major." Having ordered several thousand men out of the relative security of the redoubts, keeping Hays back seemed a coward's way of keeping one man safe. He simply couldn't do that.

As Hays galloped out the gate, Will said a silent prayer for his safety. Then, as he turned around, scanning the parade ground, he saw the broken and dying and added to the prayer. *"Forgive me for all the men who have died following me."*

Jesse Running Creek fished a few loaded cylinders from the haversack of a dead Ranger and shoved them into his own pockets. When he looked up, he saw the soldados running away. Some, though, were assembling outside of rifle range as they tried to maintain unit cohesion. Jesse understood its importance. Major Hays had told them repeatedly, a man on his own is much easier to overcome than a group. The greater order among the men, the harder it would be to destroy their ability to fight.

He glanced over at his teammate, Jethro Elkins. He and Elkins were the only remaining men in their rifle team. The whole company was in bad shape. Hays' special Ranger battalion had begun the campaign with one hundred twenty men. One company had been wiped out at a hacienda between Monterrey and Saltillo and the other two companies had fifty men between them. Fortunately, their flank had also been defended by six regular Ranger companies, although they were scarcely in any better shape.

What had Major Hays called his Rangers? *"The tip of the spear,"* Jesse recalled. He was amazed he had survived when so many had not. Others' bodies had been torn and disfigured. The survivors would return to their farms, stores, and mills broken men. He was sick of being the army's tip of the spear. At that moment as he watched the Mexican army retreat, he wanted nothing more than to be back home. If all he did the rest of his life was keep the books for his father's mercantile interests, he would be fine with that.

His melancholy was broken when a horseman rode up the slope. He heard others calling out, "Major! The Major's back."

He climbed out of the ravine and saw Major Hays riding by. "Up, boys! Up! One more push and the war will be won!"

"Would it?" Jesse wondered. Despite the doubt, he and Elkins joined the others as they headed down the hill, toward their horses.

Sidney Johnston nudged his horse forward as he followed behind the five hundred odd men who advanced across the valley floor. The men from the 1st and 3rd Infantry battalions were cautious as they moved beyond the battlefield. From behind, he heard the steady tramping of feet. Turning, he saw the men of the 11th Infantry coming up fast. They had been held as a reserve regiment in Saltillo throughout the battle. Now, General Travis had ordered them up to support the advance.

The 11th deployed into skirmish line and, with them, he now led a thousand men as he pushed hard after the Mexican army. Johnston watched his men checking soldados for weapons as they collected them when they surrendered. Once his men had rounded up around a hundred prisoners, he detailed a few men to escort them back toward the redoubts. He had no idea how the Texian army would manage the prisoners they were collecting, but one thing at a time. Every soldado taken prisoner was one less available to Santa Anna.

At the valley's opening, he saw a wall of men standing under several green, white, and red flags. At first glance, it was a formidable wall, totaling several thousand men. Johnston dug his binoculars from a saddlebag and stared at the enemy.

What had first appeared a solid wall of men were several distinct clumps, standing behind their battle colors. Some groups numbered several hundred, while others were no more than a handful of men. Their uniforms were torn, and many of them were walking wounded. Almost half of them were unarmed.

He lowered the binoculars and sent orders to his battalion commanders, to hold the line a few hundred yards from the Mexican formation.

When Johnston's men reached the imagined line, they halted. Tactical training took over and riflemen took advantage of whatever shelter was available as they waited for the next command.

Johnston had ridden behind the line until he found himself beside the Texas battle standard for the 10th Infantry. The only man on horseback, other than him, was the battalion's commander. Johnston said, "Colonel, let's see if we can end this without any bloodshed. Take a white flag and let them know what will happen if they fight."

The officer pulled a linen shirt from a saddlebag and tied it to his sword. Saluting him, the colonel trotted across the field. Johnston watched intently as the battalion commander came close to the Mexican line. An officer stepped out and approached the Texian colonel. The two men talked. As time passed, Johnston wondered what they were saying. If it came to a fight, he would order his men to keep their distance and use their superior range to decimate the Mexican line, such as it was.

After a few minutes, Johnston watched the Mexican officer turn away and return to the line. Moments later, he saw the Mexican flags dip. Men who had given their all earlier in the morning, storming the Texian fortifications, now let muskets fall to the ground as they cried. Others just stood there, shocked into silence.

Johnston allowed a smile to play across his face. Even though there were still thousands more men to secure, lest Santa Anna reform the remains of his army, a sizable force was no longer a threat.

Jack Hays held the reins with his remaining hand as he galloped at the head of his Rangers. He and his men had parted ways with the Rangers of the frontier battalion earlier. They had run into the men from the 4th infantry engaged in a running battle with a column of soldados who were trying to withdraw. The Rangers from the frontier battalion swept around, intent on cutting the column off from the south.

Hays and his men left the battle to the others. He wanted to get ahead of the retreat. Somewhere up ahead, the only Mexican soldados would be those behind him, and that's where he wanted to be.

The sun was overhead, and his stomach rumbled, letting him know it was past noon. The road between Saltillo and San Luis Potosi was empty, save for Hays and his men. Since arriving at their present spot an hour before, they had not seen anyone. But that changed as a small clump of men in blue jackets with red trim came along. A squad of Rangers surrounded the clump and in short order, they started collecting prisoners who straggled up the road.

After a bit, Hays thought he saw something, or someone, moving through the brush well away from the road. He turned, looking for one of his men to send and investigate. But the nearest was corralling a few prisoners toward a natural bowl where the Rangers were collecting them.

"I've got it," he thought, and he nudged his horse in the direction of the brush.

He guided his mount around a fallen log and saw a scrap of blue cloth hanging on a long thorn on a cactus bush. Was his imagination playing tricks on him? He felt like something or someone was watching. Hays climbed from his horse and tied the reins to the fallen log and drew his revolver.

Away from the cactus, Hays' eyes were drawn to a giant yucca plant. Several of its sword-shaped leaves were quivering. Had they just stopped moving? With his pistol in front of him, Hays slowly approached. Was it his imagination, or did he hear rustling? Unsure, he cocked the pistol and continued forward.

When he was only a few feet away and about to edge around one side, he saw a man in a worn and faded blue jacket run from the other side. He was racing toward Hays' horse.

"Stop!" The man didn't miss a beat. Hays aimed and snapped off a shot. It kicked up dirt between the fleeing soldado's feet.

"Stop, or the next one will be in your back." Hays had no idea if the soldado understood him, but he stopped, and hung his head low.

Using his pistol as a prod, Hays poked his prisoner in the back, "Move it, *hombre*."

He untied the reins and led his horse as he walked behind his crestfallen prisoner. Holding the reins while also keeping his pistol pointed on the man proved difficult. But the soldado seldom looked back as Hays guided him toward the bowl where they corralled prisoners.

Despite the threadbare jacket and grimy white pants, Hays wondered if his prisoner was truly a common soldier as he was dressed. Although mussed from slinking through the brush, his hair was neatly cut. His features were whiter than the average Mestizo soldado. Perhaps he had found himself an officer.

When they arrived at the bowl, more than a hundred prisoners were settled in, waiting to be taken back toward the redoubts. "Get yourself on in there," Hays said as he pushed the soldado forward with the barrel of his pistol.

He climbed back into the saddle, which proved no easy task with just one arm and watched his prisoner slink down on his haunches on the edge of the circle of disarmed soldados. Several of the men closest to him started whispering among themselves. Hays smirked. Apparently, he had found some muckety-muck.

Three prisoners came to their feet and swept their hats from their heads and saluted. As word spread through the *soldados* that the newcomer was someone special, Hays thought he heard what they were saying, "*Excellencia*," said one. Another exclaimed, "*Presidente*."

Hays swore, "Sonofabitch!" He had done more than capture some high-ranking muckety-muck. He had captured, Antonio Lopez, by God, Santa Anna. His Rangers, those nearby, noticed their prisoners' excitement and they approached the bowl.

"Boys, we may have just ended the war," Hays said, "That dirty older fellow is none other than Santa Anna, hisself."

General Travis needed to know. He scanned the nearby Rangers and settled on the lone Cherokee in his command. "Running Creek, get yourself on a horse and ride like hell for General Travis. Tell him who we've got here. Be quick. If I find a tree, I may do both countries a favor and string his bastardness up."

The day following the battle, Will called for a staff meeting. His army was stretched beyond capacity in managing the flood of prisoners, and he needed a solution. He grumbled, "I guess there is too much of a good thing."

He leaned on the makeshift table and scanned the faces of the men in attendance. They were a haggard group. If they were like him, they hadn't slept much over the past couple of days, and the lack of sleep was catching up with them.

Sidney Johnston sat on a barrel of salted pork resting his hand on the rough wood. It was bandaged. To hear him talk of it, it was nothing. He had cut his hand on his own blade. "Clumsy of me, if you must know."

Will had learned from men who had been present during the battle that Johnston had been in the thick of things when the artillery had run out of ammunition. He had been attacked by an officer, and in the ensuing scuffle, his hand had been sliced open.

General Juan Seguin waved away Johnston's comment. "At least Dr. Smith says you shouldn't lose the use of it. For that, Sid, you should count your blessing. I'll light a candle for you."

Will cleared his throat, "Light one for us all, Juan. If we handle the situation we find ourselves in the right way, this nightmare of a war may be over." He glanced at a lengthy list secured under a rock he used as a paperweight. "We've got more than ten thousand prisoners, and we're going to be hard-pressed to feed them by the end of the week. We need a solutions."

Ben McCulloch, from his position at the other end of the table, said, "Parole the privates, sir. Power in this country is found in the officer corps. Most of the men who have worn the crown of the presidency had risen from it."

He gingerly sat on a stack of ammunition crates. Will noticed he winced as he sat. McCulloch wore only a cotton shirt. The previous day, he had barely managed to avoid being cut in two by a sword. Instead, he had received a long gash along his ribs.

Will knew paroling one's enemies was a time-honored tradition in the nineteenth century but was unsure if it would simply feed the parolees back into a Mexican army. He didn't want to endanger the victory that was nearly within Texas' grasp. "What do you think, Juan?"

"We've captured every significant general not in Mexico City, Buck. If we parole most of the enlisted men, very few of them will go anywhere but back to the farms from which they were conscripted. I think it's a low-risk way to reduce the number of mouths we need to feed."

Will went around the table and found all his generals in agreement. "Alright. We'll work out the specifics, but let's parole these soldados back to their farms."

"What about Santa Anna, Buck? Jack has been on me since his men brought the dictator in yesterday. That boy can hold a grudge," Seguin said.

Will softly chuckled. "It's probably a good thing there aren't a lot of trees in this part of the country. I'd be inclined to hang him from the tallest one I could find, too. But that's not our job. We captured him and it's going to fall on President Zavala to decide what kind of peace we'll get out of this victory."

Johnston asked, "When will you send word north and let him know?"

"The letter is already written, but I've got my orderlies pulling together the reports," Will said, "We lost so many men here that getting those reports ready to go has taken longer than anticipated."

He took his hat off, placing it on the table. "We suffered nearly a thousand casualties yesterday. More than two hundred of them have already been buried. When I spoke with Dr. Smith earlier, he expects we'll lose another hundred before his doctors have finished patching up the rest."

McCulloch said, "Juan, if you're going to light any candles, don't burn down the church. As God is my witness, the only thing worse than a battle won is a battle lost. The 2nd suffered a hundred thirty men killed or wounded, and that was just one of my five battalions."

Seguin said, "Come with me, Ben, after all the death we've seen we could all stand to kneel at the alter and say a prayer or two." He shifted his gaze to Will, "Prayers aside, Buck, what do we do now?"

Will let his eyes drift to the north. "We wait for President Zavala's instructions."

Chapter 24

7 July 1843

Each time the horse's hoofs struck the rocky ground Charlie felt the animal's power jolt up his body. He gripped the beast with his knees a little tighter and leaned forward even more. The drumming of hoofbeats to either side confirmed his lead was shrinking. He dared a glance to his right. Lenna was leaning against her mount's neck, urging it to run faster. Seeing Charlie's glance, she smiled at him.

The butterflies he had felt when they first met had faded with time, although he still got flustered on those rare moments they were alone together. "Dammit," he cursed under his breath. Lenna was pulling even. He refocused, ignoring Victorio's horse as he came up on Charlie's other side.

The road they raced down was approaching a crest, and as the three youths flew over the top of the low rise, the town of Los Angeles appeared before them, nestled alongside the Pacific Ocean. Charlie and the two Apache youths pulled hard on their reins. Less than a hundred yards after they crested the hill, they saw a squad of cavalry from their little army. These men, like most under Crockett's command, had been civilians less than a year before.

One with sergeant stripes on his sleeve waved at the three youths who drew up before the squad. "What in the name of Sam Hill are you kids doing out this far? You're supposed to be with the main column."

Charlie stood in the saddle, retrieving his hat from where he had sat on it while racing his friends. He ran his fingers through his sweat-drenched hair before returning the hat to its rightful place. "Howdy, Sergeant, ah, Jones," Charlie began as he belatedly recalled the NCO's name. "We were just riding forward to find you."

"The Hell you say. And you're probably going to tell me that Colonel Crockett dispatched you with a note to pass back any news?" the Sergeant glowered at him.

That was exactly what Charlie had been about to say. He mustered up a half-hearted smile and said, "Sounds about right. What should I tell him?"

The sergeant's laughter sounded like a barking dog to Charlie. "Hell, you and your friends, get yourself back to the column, and if you're of a mind to do so, let the colonel know the town is garrisoned by a few hundred provincial troops. It ain't going to be as easy a nut to crack as Tucson or San Diego."

With a final wave from the sergeant, Charlie pulled on his horse's reins and turned about. He didn't need to see them to know Victorio and Lenna were right behind him. The column was a couple of miles behind the advanced scouts, and when the three youths arrived, Charlie pulled up next to Crockett, "Uncle Davy, Los Angeles is only a few miles away. Sergeant Jones says there's actually more than a few hundred soldados defending the town."

"Tarnation, Ensign Travis, have a little respect for the position. That's Colonel Crockett," the former president said with a frown.

Charlie was unable to repress his grin. Over the past couple of months, this had become a bit of a tradition between the two of them. Crockett, never one for pomp and ceremony, had run an informal command structure, and no amount of urging from Major McCulloch would change that. With few exceptions, David Crockett hated the nickname bestowed upon him by dime novelists, and normally despised its use. But for Charlie he made an exception. The Colonel had been "Uncle Davy" long before his pa had married Becky Crockett, and even though Colonel Crockett was his grandfather by marriage, he would always be "Uncle Davy" to Charlie.

But he never failed to rail against it when Charlie used the familiar nickname in public, which made it so much fun when the teenager used it.

While his friends matched their horse's gait to that of the marching infantry, and fell in beside the column, Charlie rode beside Crockett. Having returned to the column, he was resigned to his role of courier. He listened to Crockett and McCulloch talking.

"Let's see if our scouts can corroborate what Juan Bandini had to say," Crockett said to Major McCulloch.

The young major shrugged, saying, "Bandini is looking out for Bandini first, middle, and last, sir."

"I ain't met too many politicians that I couldn't say that about, Hank." Crockett may not have been fond of his own nickname, but that didn't keep him from using others. "He knows we're likely to outnumber any force the

Mexicans in Los Angeles could put together. I don't think he's going to play us false, at least, not here."

The two officers rode in silence while Charlie wondered if there would be a battle. Part of him wondered if he would feel the same sort of terror he had faced when he had been part of the final defense in the Alamo chapel the previous year. He turned in his saddle and saw Lenna, riding next to her brother. When he locked eyes with her and she smiled at him, he hoped he would be brave.

David Crockett eyed the mountain of papers on the desk with apprehension. Some, he knew, predated the capture of Los Angeles a few days before, but most had accumulated since the town had surrendered. He had felt less dread when he had led his boys against the presidio earlier in the week.

He leaned back, procrastinating, as he recalled the shock and horror on Henry McCulloch's face when he had led his boys toward the presidio's walls. And, if he were honest, he had nearly wet himself when he felt the hot breath of musket balls flying so near his head as he heard them buzz by.

Once the men of the 9th had cleared the houses near the presidio, they had forced the defenders to keep their heads down, and it had become a matter of time before the Mexican officer in command of the garrison lowered the flag and surrendered.

Now, he reflected, he had traded his military hat for that of military governor. With the fall of Los Angeles, it would be hard to argue that Texas hadn't captured Alta

California. Other towns further north, like Monterey, had yet to surrender, but that was likely just a matter of time.

His first act as military governor was to notify President Zavala of California's change of allegiance. He pushed the stack of papers to one side and stared at the blank page lying before him. In all his fifty-seven years, the minutia of administration had been the one thing he hated. He inked the quill and began writing.

Tattered curtains fluttered in the open window. The breeze from the Pacific Ocean kept the room comfortable. Small stones weighted down the parchment as Obadiah Jenkins leaned over the table, pen in hand. His shirtsleeves were rolled up, exposing a lower arm red with grotesque scar tissue. He scratched at it absentmindedly before adding a detail to the parchment. With a flourish, he straightened up and moved the paperweights away from the document. He took a shaker and scattered sand across the parchment. "Once this dries, not even the Spanish Viceroy could tell this isn't his signature."

Elizondo Jackson, his long-time business associate, set a book aside and stood and walked across the adobe-walled room until he stared down at the unnaturally aged document. The Viceroyalty seal of New Spain was prominently displayed at the top of the document. "That would be quite something. Nice touch, using a date before Mexico claimed independence. Some of your better work, I believe, Obadiah. I wonder, though, if our new overlords will make things too difficult for us."

Jenkins set the parchment down and secured the corners with the small stones, to let it dry. "I can't say I feel good about this, although watching that column of

Texian infantry parade through the pueblo was something to behold. But damn it all, why in the blazes did Davy Crockett have to be leading the pack? I thought we were rid of him and his high-handedness when we left Texas for greener pastures."

His fingers traced along the splotched scars on his right arm. He had lost track of the times he'd woken up in a cold sweat, reliving the moment when he had been forced to flee for his life. All thanks to David Crockett. At first Texas had been a dream come true to Jenkins and his partners. In the years before the revolution, a man could swing a stick and hit someone who needed a title to the land they were on. He had provided a valuable service to many of those who came into Texas after Mexico had officially ended American immigration in 1830. But after the revolution, Crockett's government made it difficult to stay in business.

He stepped over to the open window and looked across the pueblo, in the distance he could see the lone star flag flying proudly over the presidio's walls. At that moment, he was back in Harrisburg. He had been in bed with Nancy. Her lot had been far worse than his. She and her husband had come to Texas a few years before. He had died in a cholera epidemic the previous year. Childless, and unable to return to family in eastern Tennessee, Nancy had found whatever work as was available. She had worked as a laundress and also in one of Harrisburg's bars, but what kept her fed was her work in the oldest profession. That hadn't bothered Obadiah Jenkins in the least. Over the year he operated out of Harrisburg, he and Nancy had fallen into a comfortable pattern. She came to his bed often. She had convinced him to take her with him when it came time to move on. And he had intended to keep that promise.

The flag in the distance blurred in his eye as the memory played on. It was late, a candle burned on the stand next to his bed. She had just finished satisfying him when the door to the small rent house was stove in. Framed in the open door was a tall, bearded man, "John Peirce? You're under arrest." It was the name he was using at that time. He had leapt from the bed, grabbing the sheet to cover his nakedness. Now, more than ever, he regretted that act. He had left Nancy exposed, lying in bed, open to the leering eyes of Crockett's uniformed customs officer.

But at that moment, the officer was distracted, and Jenkins used it to rush him. He collided with the officer right as the pistol discharged. The shot went wild, missing Jenkins. Instead, it hit the candle holder, which spun from the night table, and hit the curtains. The tiny fire on the candle's wick spread up and down the curtain until the window was awash in flames.

"Nan, get the hell out of here!" Jenkins had cried out as he wrestled the pistol away from the officer. The heavy, flintlock dragoon pistol was useless as a firearm at that moment, but as his fingers closed around the barrel, Jenkins intended to rip it out of the officer's hand and beat him down with it.

His thoughts were ripped back to the present when Jackson stepped over to the window and said, "Business has been good these past few years. I'm still amazed at the number of people stepping off the boat who are in the market for one of our 'Spanish land grants.'" His voice still held a trace of his upbringing in Spanish Florida.

The two had had known each other since Jenkins had moved to Florida shortly after the United States annexed the Spanish territory. They had peddled forged Spanish property titles to unsuspecting newcomers who had been eager to buy land in the new territory. More than twenty years later, they had worked their way across the continent, coming to California after Crockett and his government had driven them from Texas six year earlier.

Jenkins felt all of his nearly fifty years. He let a sigh escape his lips. "Yeah, it's been a good run, I'll allow. But damned Davy Crockett! If there's another man who has cost me as much I don't know his name."

He closed his eyes, willing the image of Nancy away. But the image was too strong. He couldn't shake it. She had climbed out of the bed as he wrestled with the officer. She had picked up the sheet and wrapped it around her. The back door should have opened to her touch when she lifted the latch, but something had barred the door closed from the outside. Had that not happened, how much different his life might have been. Instead, sparks were swirling about the room as the wall next to the bed was covered with fire. Some of those sparks landed on the sheet and, in seconds, Nancy was screaming as flames licked the dry cotton in which she was swaddled.

In all his years, Jenkins had killed only one man. When he wrestled the gun away from the officer, he swung it at his head with all his might as Nancy's screams pierced his ears. He had stepped over the body, but it was too late. The flames consumed the wrapping and she had collapsed. He had raced toward her, and grabbed at her exposed skin, determined to get her out of the growing inferno. Flaming strands of the sheet had landed on his arm when he heard a loud thud then a voice, "Boss, get out of there!"

His hopeless thoughts were broken by the same voice, which came from the back of the adobe hut. "What about going straight."

Jenkins turned and saw Bill Zebulon climb down from one of the bunks against the back wall. He forced a smile onto his face. Bill had saved his life that night, when he pulled him from the burning cabin. Zebulon's large size had always been an asset when someone needed to be incentivized. In fact, Jenkins would have been captured or killed that night had Zebulon not knocked out the officer's partner outside the cabin. The two men had been boys when they had started working scams in South Carolina more than a quarter century before.

"Morning, Bill. The thought has crossed my mind a time or two. Before I saw that bastard, Davy Crockett, riding into town I would have considered using one of our land grants, maybe buy the debts of a few of these Indian peons hereabouts and become bonified Spanish Dons."

Jackson chuckled, "Obadiah, you'd go straight sometime after Gabriel blows his horn."

Jenkins snorted, "You mean a few days before you?"

"Sounds about right."

Jenkins heard a creaking sound from behind as Zebulon sat at the table. "That's some good work you done, Ob. Damned if not some of the best I've seen. Shame about Crockett coming out here. I thought we were well and done with Texas."

A fourth voice came from the doorway, "It *is* a goddamned shame, is what it is."

Still shaking off the effects of the powerful memories, Jenkins managed to avoid appearing startled as Hiram

Williams came through the door. His black hair was disheveled, and he had dark circles under his eyes. He couldn't help quipping, "Long night, Hiram?"

Williams was the shortest of the four. He wore the clothes of a Spanish dandy, although they were grimy and soiled. No doubt won in a game of chance that Williams was so fond of. "You could say, but the *puta*, she had such stamina."

Jenkins bit back a groan. Williams was prone to bragging of his sexual conquests, but this morning, he was in no mood to listen to that. Instead, Williams said, "I hate to see a good thing come to an end, and God knows, business has been very good to us." He was referring to his own scam. As a gambler, he had on many an occasion, used one of Jenkin's forgeries as collateral. When he lost, the other three men would dress up as Mexican officials and pay the new owner of a "fine tract of prime California farm land" a visit and inform the new owner that the previous holder was delinquent on taxes, and if he didn't want to lose the newly acquired title, he would need to make good the back taxes.

Williams continued, "But as I see it, we've got us a few options. We can help *Colonel* Crockett meet his maker."

Jenkins eyes grew wide. In all their years of petty larceny and theft, apart from the customs officer, the only other time anyone had died was when Zebulon had accidentally beaten one of their marks to death. Killing men had a way of bringing the law down on them like nothing else could.

"Seems a bit drastic, don't it?" Jackson said.

Williams shrugged. "Just offering a solution, Eli."

Jenkins didn't want to admit it to the others, but Williams' idea had a certain appeal. In all the years since Crockett's officers had stolen Nancy from him, he had never dreamed an opportunity for revenge would present itself.

Jenkins shook off the thought. Unless they could find a surefire way of making good an escape, killing Crockett sounded like a good way to get them all killed. "Alright. Before we go about trying anything that final," Jenkins said as he grabbed his hat from one of the bunkbeds, "I'm sure Crockett and his army have a soft underbelly. We just need to find it. I'll take Bill. Eli, why don't you take Hiram. Maybe we can find a way to turn this setback around."

Jenkins set the clay-fired shot glass down, his lips tingled at the taste of the fiery tequila. Near the edge of the pueblo, the cantina catered to several ranchos and haciendas north of town as well as the locals. A few mestizos and Tongva Indians occupied a couple of tables. He and Zebulon sat at a table in the corner. They were still waiting for Jackson and Williams to arrive.

Zebulon spat a stream of tobacco juice into another clay cup.

"Where'd you get the tobacco, Bill?"

"Captain Palmer's in town. I bought it from his first mate."

Jenkins licked his lips. It had been a long time since he had smoked a cigar. The main port in California was Monterey. It was the provincial capital, and ships were expected to transport any goods coming into Alta California through it. After all, the tariffs collected there were the lion's share of Alta California's revenue.

Jenkins knew Captain Palmer of the schooner *Orion*. He was one of several ships' captains who smuggled goods into Los Angeles. A little coin in the alcalde's palm and the pueblo's civil government turned a blind eye. It was good for business, both legitimate and the other kind. Jenkins preferred his tobacco untaxed. The import duties on tobacco more than doubled the cost of what one would expect to pay for the fragrant leaf.

Another of Palmer's redeeming qualities, as far as Jenkins was concerned, was the captain was known to be morally flexible. On those occasions Jenkins and his associates had branched out from forgeries, the wily captain had been willing to bring in or take out their goods for a price.

He ran his finger along the inside of the glass and watched the tequila swirl around. Throughout the day, he kept coming back to Williams' idea. He had vowed, years earlier, to avenge Nancy if the chance presented itself. But, he was no martyr. He had no interest in killing Crockett if it meant Texian soldiers would turn him into a pin cushion moments later. The only other option was getting out of Texas-held territory. He wondered if the captain would be willing to take them up the coast to Monterey. When he mentioned the idea to Zebulon, the big man surprised him with his answer.

"Crockett and his men will probably head for Monterey next, boss. Maybe we can go deeper into Mexico?"

The door opened, and Jenkins looked up and saw Jackson and Williams. As they settled into the other chairs around the table, the bartender sauntered over and set down a couple more glasses and left a bottle of tequila.

Jackson poured a drink. He looked frazzled and tired. He downed the strong drink before he said, "Crockett's saying that not much will be changing around here now that he's arrived, but when I paid a visit to the Alcalde, I saw one of Crockett's officers following the fat little greaser around like a puppy."

Jenkins' frown couldn't have grown much deeper at the news. On those rare occasions the alcalde's eyes fell on their enterprise, a bag of pesos was enough to let things return to normal. If the Texians planned on keeping a close eye on things, then it was a sure thing their pickings had dried up.

Morose at the news, Jenkins picked up the clay shot glass and drank the contents in a single gulp. As the fiery liquor warmed his insides, he said, "What about Crockett?"

Jackson said, "Forget him, Ob. It ain't worth it."

He wanted to say more but held his peace when he saw the stormy look Jackson gave Williams.

"Hold on just one damn minute." Hiram Williams grabbed the tequila bottle and pour four generous shots as the others waited for him to continue.

"Ain't it funny how two men can look at the same situation and one sees nothing but problems while the other sees opportunities," Williams said, eying Franklin with disapproval.

Jackson ignored the drink in front of him. "Where you see opportunity, I see a short walk to the gallows."

Williams' haunch came out of his seat as he leaned toward Jackson. Jenkins had seen this too many times before. "Enough, you two. Let's hear what Hiram's got to say, I'll be the judge of what's too dangerous."

Williams sat back down and took a sip before saying, "Ob, you're always saying that we need one big score then we'd be set. Right?"

Jenkins' tilted his head. Since leaving South Carolina more than half a lifetime ago, he had been looking for the *one*. The night Nancy had died, he had been telling her of his latest plans. He had told her he needed the right job and he would marry her and they would return to South Carolina with gold pouring from their pockets. He had told her they could sip sweet drinks under a veranda, while watching his darkies work in the fields. So many of his dreams had died the night Nancy died, but the dream of one final job lingered.

Williams continued, "I found a job that will set us up for life."

Jackson leaned back, content to let the other man dig his own hole. "Colonel Crockett brought his grandson with him."

It wasn't what he had expected. "So what, Hiram? I might not pass up the chance to stick a knife in Crockett's ribs under the right circumstances, but I'll be damned if I'll harm some kid."

Williams shook his head, "No, Ob, you've got it wrong. Who's David Crockett's son-in-law?"

Jenkins shook his head. He had no idea.

"Crockett's daughter is married to none other than William Barret Travis!"

Jenkins' eyebrows rose. He knew of Travis. Defeating Santa Anna had made the young officer the hero of the republic. But all four men had heard rumors the general had done incredibly well for himself. He owned large tracts of land along the Trinity River. Also, there was a persistent rumor that when Santa Anna had invaded Texas, the dictator had brought a box full of gold with him. Supposedly it was to be used to pay his army. According to Crockett's government, the gold had never turned up, and Jenkins had long suspected Travis had used the money to invest in several businesses.

But what did that have to do with the kid? Jenkins asked, "So, what? Crockett brings the boy with him, and what's that to us? Another possible witness?"

Williams leaned forward. Jenkins could smell the tequila on his breath. "Ain't it obvious? We kidnap the brat. Papa Travis will pay a huge ransom to get his kid back."

Jenkins blinked in surprise. The idea of kidnapping wasn't entirely foreign to him. God alone knew how many stories he had heard about the Comanche kidnapping folks along the frontier while he had lived in Texas. But the idea of civilized men kidnapping a boy for ransom was something he had never considered.

Jackson said, "Hiram, if we do that, we'll be wanted from one end of the continent to the other. How long before we swing for such a thing?"

Williams snorted at the other man, "I'd thought you'd be used to living life on a knife's edge, Eli. What you seem to have forgotten is that in addition to having that gold he stole from Santa Anna, he's also a true believing abolitionist. I can think of several holes we could crawl down where a nigger lover like Travis won't ever find us."

Sure, he had heard the rumors General Travis was a dyed-in-the-wool abolitionist. Williams was likely right, there was places back in South Carolina where they could disappear that an abolitionist like Travis would never find them. But kidnapping the boy for ransom was simply unheard of.

He shook his head, "Kidnapping some kid would make us no better than a pack of uncivilized savage Indians, Hiram. Why do that?"

Williams took another drink, before chortling. "Shit, I don't care a damn if all Texas thinks I'm worse than a savage Indian. What I care about is a job that can put us over the top. Did I mention, Crockett positively dotes on the boy, Ob. Take the boy and Crockett will suffer a thousand deaths. You really want to make the bastard pay for what he did to Nancy?"

Jasper's thirst for revenge overcame his reluctance, and he found himself nodding.

Williams leaned in, "This is what we need to do…"

Chapter 25

15 July 1843

José Joaquín de Herrera closed the door behind him. He should feel something more. "What man, having ascended to the office of the presidency, wouldn't feel a sense of accomplishment?" he muttered. Several men, dressed in somber black coats, sat around the office's conference table. If any of them heard him, they ignored the remark. Herrera was certain more than one of them had breathed a sigh of relief that Herrera had won the vote.

He tried to keep any hesitancy from his steps as he came over to the table and took his seat. "*Madre de Dios*. What I would give to have Santa Anna sitting here instead of me?"

The other men smiled, knowingly. Valentin Canalizo said, "Come now, Jose, your chair is certainly more comfortable than the one in Santa Anna's cell."

Herrera frowned as he eyed the other man. On one hand, the office of the presidency demanded his deference even if Herrera didn't. One the other hand, Canalizo spoke nothing but the truth. Word had reached the capital just the day before of Santa Anna's capture and the destruction of his army.

Herrera's eyes moved, settling on the man sitting next to Canalizo. "Don Valentin, what are your thoughts?"

In his sixties, Valantin Gomez-Farias was the eldest man in the room, and like Canalizo, a former president of the Mexican Republic. He bit his lip before saying, "It's hard to imagine a worse situation, Presidente. Since the start of the campaign earlier this year, we have managed to lose upwards of thirty thousand men. Given time, I'm sure we can build another army. But there is every chance that such a command would have to be used to put down revolts rather than drive the Texians back, if that is even possible. It galls me to say it, but you are going to need to seek terms from the Texians."

Herrera blanched at that. "They will insist we honor the Faustian bargain they call the treaty of Bexar. Nuevo Mexico east of the Rio Grande will be taken from us. That includes Santa Fe and Albuquerque."

Gomez-Farias nodded. "Indeed. Also, they will not release Santa Anna to us. We should steel our hearts to watching a spectacle play out in Texas where they are sure to put him on trial."

Herrera hadn't considered that. "Why? It is customary to release high-ranking officers once a truce is brokered."

"Normally, yes. But don't forget Santa Anna ordered General Woll to put the garrison of the Alamo to the sword."

"But, Santa Anna was acting under the authority granted by the Tornel Decree. Even though it was enacted prior to our misfortune during the Texas rebellion, it remains the policy of our government even now," said Herrera as he scratched his head in confusion.

Gomez-Farias pursed his lips before saying, "It was one thing to enact such a decree at the beginning of the rebellion in the north, but another once they had de facto independence. When Santa Anna ordered General Woll to go north and invade, who among us here really thought there was any chance that we could expel all of nearly two hundred thousand Yankees and Europeans living in Texas?"

Silence greeted him. Finally, Canalizo said, "It was our right to execute those rebels, Don Valentin. By our rights, Texas is a province in rebellion. Nothing will change that."

Gomez-Farias shook his head. "Will it not? I wonder. We may view the Texians as rebels, but even Great Britain, our closest trading partner, has extended recognition to the Texians. For us to continue viewing them as rebels is a fiction which has blinded us to sensible action."

From his chair at the head of the table, Herrera raised his eyebrows, "What is sensible? On many positions I have disagreed with Santa Anna, but on the territorial integrity of our country, he and I see eye to eye. Agreeing to give up our territory north of the Rio Grande won't endear us to our fellow countrymen and it sets a dangerous precedent. Don't forget, Texas shares a border with the United States. Texas' success could encourage the Yankees to try wrestling Alto California from us."

"That is a legitimate fear," Gomez-Farias conceded. "But an equally legitimate fear is that Texas can continue the war. I would rather not see San Luis Potosi turned into a battlefield. Should we risk the loss of another ten thousand?"

Herrera said, "I value everyone's input, but it will fall to me to make a truce with General Travis. I would trade away ten Santa Annas before I agree to trade away any of our territory."

Gomez-Farias gave a half bow from his place at the table, "You are the president."

Herrera allowed a cloud to cross his face. In truth, he wanted the office like he wanted cholera. But having been elected, it seemed he had few choices available to him. The first was to find a way to end the war without giving away the keys to the kingdom.

16 July 1843

The corn tortilla tasted bland. The idea of returning to South Carolina was growing on Jenkins the longer he thought about it. It was only a memory, but his mouth watered, longing for grits and bacon. He pushed away the memory and swallowed. The cantina did a brisk business, serving breakfast to a steady stream of customers. But he sat with Elizondo Jackson, while Williams and Zebulon were scouting around town. How difficult could it be to find a white teenage boy in a town full of Mestizos and Indians?

Jackson used a bit of tortilla to clean the last bit of beans from a bowl and plopped it in his mouth. He took a drink of water and said, "We're not really going to go through with this, are we?"

Jenkins' mouth tightened. The half-breed Spaniard from Florida had urged caution after Williams had explained his scheme. "I thought you had worked this out of your system already, Eli. Did you talk with Captain Palmer?"

The chair creaked under his weight as Jackson leaned back, "Of course. I had to promise every peso we've got, but he's willing to take us and our cargo. There's a couple of stops to make between here and there, but he's willing to take us to Panama City."

Silence descended until he added, "Ob, is this really what you want to do? We do this and there ain't no going back from it. In the past, if the game was up and we had to leave, we'd just move somewhere else and start a new job. We fail at this, and Crockett and Travis will hunt us down and kill us. Hell, even if we succeed, and they pay a ransom, they'll likely still hunt us down."

Jenkins admonished him, "You worry too much, Eli. You're not telling me anything I haven't already considered. I aim to use Travis' abolitionist views against him. His views make him a pariah to most people in the South. I've got some ideas about who we can work with once we return to South Carolina. From there, it's a simple matter of letting Travis know the price. He'll pay. If he doesn't he'll never see the boy again."

Jenkins' eyes burned with intensity as he spoke. Jackson exhaled sharply, "Why, Ob?"

The cantina's door opened, and Williams and Zebulon strode in. Jenkins replied, "Revenge."

Williams reeked of nervous energy, "You ain't gonna believe this, Ob, but we've got us a two-fer."

Jenkins rose, pushing his chair away from the table. He cocked an eyebrow in anticipation.

The shorter man lowered his voice and leaned over the table. "Travis' brat is eating breakfast with none other than Crockett."

Jenkins tossed enough money on the table to cover the meal and said, "Let's do it. We may not get another chance like this."

The hotel's common room was empty except for Colonel David Crockett and Charlie Travis. After the challenges of governing the greatest portion of Alta California over the past week, Crockett enjoyed a quiet breakfast with his grandson.

He watched the teenager using his fork to move the remains of his breakfast around the plate. The boy had something on his mind.

"Cat got your tongue, Charlie?"

The youth set his fork down and said, "Uncle Davy, why did Victorio and Lenna leave? I thought they would stay around for a bit."

"Given the way you've been ogling his little sister, I imagine Victorio figured her virtue and honor were at stake," Crockett said, his eyes sparkled as he watched Charlie's expression.

The boy's face turned red as his mouth tried to make a sound. Finally, he squeaked, "I didn't think anyone noticed that I liked Lenna. I never even held her hand. How'd Victorio find out?"

Crockett chuckled. He remembered being the boy's age, many years before, and still recalled the discomfiture of first love. "I was just funning you, Charlie. I believe Victorio and Lenna left because they had seen and done what they wanted. They were the first of their band to see the Pacific Ocean. They were ready to go back to Texas," he paused, thinking about the various tribes with whom Texas was trying to keep the peace. "I suspect they are eager to see how their people are adjusting to the land in West Texas that they've acquired."

He hid a smile when Charlie said, "So, you don't think that Lenna knew I liked her?"

Crockett patted him on the back, "No, son, not unless she was deaf, dumb and blind. If an old man like me could see it from a mile away, I'm pretty sure she knew how you felt."

Crockett didn't think the boy's face could grow any redder as the boy muttered, "Oh, hell."

Crockett eyed the towel covering a few corn tortillas, trying to decide if he could eat another one, when the door to the small dining room smashed open. A smallish man with a week's worth of beard on his face stepped through the door. He was well-dressed, although the clothes were unkempt and dirty. A glance was enough for Crockett to recognize the pistol in the ruffian's hand as one of the Colt Paterson revolvers.

The man stepped into the center of the room, pushing aside empty tables. Several more men followed him through the door and spread out. Although it was nearly imperceptible, Crockett saw the man's gun hand shaking.

"Keep your asses in your chairs and ain't nobody getting hurt."

Crockett's right hand had been in his lap when the men had burst through the door. He moved it until it rested on the butt of his revolver. How he managed to slip it from the holster with the nervous little man waving his pistol between him and Charlie was more than he could say.

Next to the door, the oldest of the intruders spoke, "Bill, tie up Mr. Crockett. Hiram, grab the boy."

The small, weaselly man took one step toward Charlie when all hell broke loose. Shooting from the hip, Crockett fired, hitting the dirty little man. The pistol spun from his hand as his body twisted. The bullet had struck him in the shoulder. He fell to his knees as a bull of a man charged by him.

As the large man raced by Charlie, a fist lashed out, knocking the teenager from his chair. Then the beast was in Crockett's face. As he struggled to stand, Crockett fired his revolver again, but the round went wide, missing his assailant.

Stars danced before his eyes when the beefy man struck him in the face, knocking him back into the chair. His head slammed into the wall behind him and the room spun around. The fist lashed out again, and Crockett felt himself being propelled from his chair. He landed with a thud, and the air was knocked from his lungs.

He hadn't been hit like this since his brawling days when he was a young man hauling freight on the Mississippi. He struggled to focus his eyes, to see where Charlie had landed. Through a blur, he saw the boy being hauled to his feet by a man with a swarthy complexion.

"No!"

A boot slammed into his ribs, and Crockett's body involuntarily curled up. He clung to consciousness as he tried sucking in a lungful of air. He heard a hard slap and as though he were at the bottom of a well, a faint voice was saying, "Tie the boy up and put this sack over his head. Be quick, those shots are sure to bring soldiers."

His entire world was pain. The taste of iron filled his mouth. He struggled to move his legs, and his body protested, as lances of agony shot through him.

The older man, the one Crockett gaged was in charge, placed his foot on his back and forced him prone. "Lay there like that, Mister President Crockett, and we'll leave you be in a moment."

Crockett spat blood onto the floor, clearing his mouth, "Why?" he croaked.

The man leaned over, "You took from me, and now I'm taking from you. You want the boy back, so tell General Travis we'll be in touch."

Crockett's life had been one of epic swings. He had started businesses only to watch them crumble into dust. Then he had ridden a wave of public support to the halls of the United States Congress, only to lose an election two years later. But he had come roaring back two years after that to win again, only to have Andy Jackson's surrogates trounce him a final time. Texas had been a new beginning, and with the help of Buck Travis, he had reached heights he had only dreamed of. Despite that, he had lived in the shadow of his own myth. Now, as his assailants hustled Charlie from the ruined dining room, all that had been swept away. His groan wasn't the agony of a man beaten into submission, but of abject failure. California was supposed to be his swan song, something to rival the legend he had crafted around his image.

Three of the men had hustled the boy out the door. Crockett didn't see the one he had injured climb to his feet and stumble over and retrieve his pistol. He didn't hear the little weasel of a man approach. Nor did he hear the cock of the hammer.

At that moment, he realized chasing after the legend had been folly. What mattered most was his family. How would he be able to face his daughter and son-in-law? He didn't hear the final shot.

Working with Jackson to lift the boy into the bed of the wagon, Jenkins jerked his head around when he heard the shot from within the hotel's common room.

"What the hell?" he muttered. He looked around and saw that Williams was missing. He jumped from the wagon and raced back into the building. Hiram was standing over Crockett, smoke curling from the barrel of the pistol in his hand. Blood pooled beneath the body.

"What have you done, you fool!"

Williams looked up and Jenkins saw madness lurking in the other man's eyes. "He shot me. I killed him."

A deep red splotch was spreading from the hole in Williams' shoulder. Jenkins wanted to rip the gun from the homicidal maniac's fingers. The look in Williams' eyes dissuaded him. Instead, he said, "Get beside Bill on the wagon. We need to get over to the harbor."

As the wiry man swayed by, he added, "And put something over that. You'll bleed out."

Left alone in the room with the body, he wondered if that might be best. Williams had made a hash of things. He stood over the body. He had wanted nothing more than to make Crockett suffer like he had all these years. In a single fit of rage, Williams had ripped that from him.

He realized only a couple of minutes had elapsed since he and his partners had broken through the door. It wouldn't be long before soldiers came rushing over to check on the commotion. Despite the void he felt seeing Crockett's body, he knew things would only go from bad to worse if he stayed there.

He raced from the room and climbed into the wagon bed next to the boy. Jackson snapped the reins and the wagon lurched forward, rolling toward the waterfront.

To President Lorenzo de Zavala
Austin, Republic of Texas
18 July 1843

Sir, I have the duty to inform you that yesterday morning, former president David S. Crockett was found shot to death in one of the hostels of Los Angeles. I have been able to ascertain a party of four men assaulted him while he was breaking his fast. It is possible one of his attackers was wounded during the assault. I ordered our men to scour the land around the town of Los Angeles, and by way of information received, learned of an American flagged ship, the Orion, that sailed out of the harbor shortly thereafter. Reputable witnesses confirmed a boat slipped away from the wharves with four men who were reported coming from the direction of the ambush.

As though the news I bear is not grievous enough, I must ask that you pass along to General Travis that his son, Charles E. Travis, was breaking fast with Colonel Crockett when the assault happened. Said witnesses confirmed a fifth person was forced onto the boat, albeit bound and covered. It can only be presumed the boy was captured.

Until I receive orders to the contrary, I will execute Colonel Crockett's directives. Half our command has been dispatched north and will bring Monterey and its environs under the Texas banner.

I remain your obedient servant,
Henry McCulloch, Major commanding

Los Angeles, Alta California

23 July 1843

The stagecoach was parked at the foot of the Capitol lawn on Congress Avenue. President Lorenzo de Zavala watched his wife, Emily, move the curtains aside and look out across the street. "Oh, I hate saying goodbye, my love." She let the curtains fall back in place as she threw her arms around his neck. He felt her hot tears against his collar.

"Em, it's all right, my dearest. If there's any hope of ending this war on a favorable footing, I must go. The surest way to obtain a lasting treaty is for me to negotiate it."

The pout she wore he had seen on many occasions. He seldom refused her petulant expression. He had learned a long time before that while he may preside over the republic, within the walls of the presidential mansion, he was but a servant to her desires. But this was no ordinary mission. The fate of the nation would travel with him as he headed south.

He untangled her hands and kissed her with all his passion, until interrupted by a knock at the front door. Zavala waved away Emily's black servant, "I've got it."

Breaking the embrace, he opened the door. The head of the Commodities Bureau stood before him. "Señor Seguin, what a singular honor."

Erasmo Seguin shook his hand, "Mr. President, we don't want you to be late. If we can get you on the stage in the next few minutes, you should get to San Antonio before sunset."

Zavala leaned over his wife and gave her a final peck on the lips, "I am but a slave to my office. I shall write to you, my love." With that, he took his carpetbag from the servant and stepped through the door and, with a final wave at his wife, walked down the sidewalk with Seguin by his side.

"Even after almost forty years, I find it hard to leave my Maria." Seguin offered as they started across the wide street.

Zavala nodded, "After sixteen years, I hate leaving Emily even more than when we first wed. But what's a president to do?"

Seguin laughed. "That's easy. Bring home a favorable peace."

Zavala sobered at the comment. "Light a candle for peace, Erasmo. You're closer to the financial situation. How much longer can we continue the war before we destroy our economy?"

Seguin's face lost its humor, "We are fast approaching that point. If you saw the most recent *Telegraph and Texas Register*, we have been forced to rebalance the basket of commodities to reflect the fact that there are more cotton backs in circulation than there should be. We're scraping by now, but come harvest time this fall, even if we managed to plant enough to feed everyone, there's no guarantee we'll have enough folks to harvest it. If that happens, then we may be the beggar with hat in hand, coming to the United States and other nations, pleading for food to feed our people."

Zavala stopped as they neared the stagecoach, "Please tell me that a nation of farmers isn't facing starvation."

Seguin forced a sad smile onto his face, "My friend, you don't pay me to give you only the good news, but the bad with it. While I may be more pessimistic than I should, the surest cure is a peace treaty with Mexico that gives us security and allows us to demobilize our reserves."

A small troop of mounted militia were already waiting behind the stagecoach, the president's escort to San Antonio. "I shall do my best," Zavala said as he climbed into the coach.

He settled back in the worn, cloth-padded seat as the coach got under way, pulling away from the Capitol building. More than any other time since rising to the office of the presidency, Zavala felt the heavy weight of the office. The success or failure of the nation rode heavy on his shoulders.

Chapter 26

5 August 1843

Jose Joaquin de Herrera groaned as he stepped down from the enclosed carriage. After two weeks in the carriage he would be happy to never step foot in it again. The town of Saltillo looked like most towns and cities of northern Mexico, with its central plaza the focal point of the town. On one side of the plaza was the town's main church and on the other, the town's governmental offices. But in the ways Saltillo differed from other Mexican towns, it was like a strike in the face.

Over the governmental buildings flew the red, white, and blue lone star flag. Soldiers in their muddy brown uniforms were everywhere. Herrera wasn't sure if he could have steeled his courage to ride into this stronghold of Mexico's enemy were it not for the company of lancers who stoically remained on horseback, behind the carriage.

From a nearby governmental building a man wearing the same uniform as the soldiers, but with shoulder boards favored by the *norteamericanos* denoting his high rank, approached. His face yet unlined by age, and his red hair, uncovered, Herrera recognized General Travis. His two weeks of travel had not been wasted. He had read everything he could about Mexico's breakaway province and its political and military leadership.

The enemy general wore a warm smile, and Herrera couldn't fault him for it. He had won every battle the two nations had fought since the revolution in Texas seven years earlier. He came to attention, then saluted the Mexican president. *"The forms must be observed,"* Herrera thought as he offered his hand to Travis.

In strongly accented Spanish, Travis said, "Welcome to Saltillo, President Herrera. Like you, I trust, I look forward to putting this disagreement between our two nations behind us."

As he walked beside Travis, heading toward the governmental building, Herrera said, "I'm familiar with Saltillo, General Travis, it is, after all, the capital of one of our districts."

A soldier, with one of the new model rifles the Texians favored slung on his shoulder, opened the door and saluted as they approached. "I assure you, sir, you will not find anyone more interested in returning it to you than I. That's one reason I'm grateful you have arrived."

Even Herrera heard the bitterness in his own laughter, "Nothing is preventing you from assembling your army and returning to the north, General."

Travis escorted him into the civil building's library. A conference table stood in the center of the room, and comfortable chairs were placed close to the bookshelves. Travis took one and offered another to him. With a slight smile, he said, "Touché. I could, but how long before our two nations once again are at each other's throat? Texas wants a peace that secures our border and provides us with guarantees against future aggression."

"You have a strange way of showing it. It was your army that invaded Mexico, twice in the past year. You seem a nice sort, General, but you have a strange way of showing your interest in peace."

After waiting for a serving girl, who chose that moment to enter the room to serve refreshments, Travis said, "I suppose Adrian Woll was simply lost and looking for directions last year?"

Travis' response was a reminder the general was quick witted, and verbal reposts were part of his arsenal of weapons.

Holding his hands up, in mock surrender, Herrera said, "That was the policy of my predecessor, Santa Anna. As you no doubt are aware, the Congress in Mexico City removed him from office upon learning of his capture. Speaking of which, how is Antonio?"

"He is enjoying the hospitality of my army at the moment."

"Somehow, I imagine any enjoyment he may be showing is feigned. On that note, the people of Mexico would like to see him restored to us so that he can be properly reprimanded for his failures."

Travis tilted his head and paused before responding, "I will advise President Zavala of that. I have received word that he will be arriving within a week." Herrera could tell Travis was weighing saying more. "Texas and Mexico, we are both republics, yes?"

Once Herrera nodded in response, Travis continued, "As an officer in my nation's military, I answer to the president. I have no authority not granted to me by my country's government. So, I will stand aside while you and President Zavala work to end this conflict."

For once, Travis said something with which Herrera was in complete agreement. He had despised the loose alignment between the office of the president and the military. It seemed every time the nation was at war with itself, the first thing previous presidents did was invite Santa Anna back to power. Except in regard to Texas and the Yucatan peninsula, Santa Anna had crushed every revolt, but it always came with the loss of civil control. At his heart, Santa Anna was a dictator.

Travis was right. The military should always be subject to the civil government's control, not the other way around. As he sipped his drink, Herrera's thoughts wandered to Santa Anna. He was in a quandary. The dictator had popular support in the area around the capital and it included the poorest peons to some of Mexico's wealthiest landholders. Herrera took another sip and worried about the future.

Austin's Stagecoach Inn was not highly regarded for its kitchen's table, but its proximity to the Capitol building, and other governmental offices, made it a popular lunch spot for civil employees. Erasmo used his fork to pull the meat from a chicken quarter as he watched his companion cutting into a beefsteak. While not a nonentity, Vice-President Richard Ellis was an outsider in the Zavala administration. A Southerner, originally from Virginia, Ellis had arrived in Texas a decade before by way of Alabama. A plantation owner as well, the glue that brought Zavala and Ellis together had been their determination for Texas to remain independent. It was an unpopular view among the most diehard Southerners, especially those with slaves.

But Ellis' alliance with Zavala had split just enough of the southern vote in the last election to deny Sam Houston the office of the presidency.

Ellis ate the last of the steak before saying, "What's the latest from Saltillo? Have you heard anything from your son or General Travis?"

Seguin gave up working the last bit of meat from the bone. The bird was dry and tough, he thought, rather like the hot August day. "If the president keeps to his schedule, he'll arrive in Saltillo in the next couple of days."

"How eager do you think the Mexican government will be to negotiate peace, Juan?"

Seguin shrugged, "I've no better an idea than you. But according to a report from General Travis, Mexico has lost upwards of thirty thousand men since this war began."

Ellis' jaw was slack, "That many men? How?"

"Perhaps a couple of thousand of them were killed in battle. Another fifteen thousand were captured at the battle of Saltillo alone. Nearly all the enlisted men, as I understand it, have been paroled. I imagine the total includes a sizable number of deserters, too," said Seguin.

The door swung open, banging against the wall, startling the two men. One of the Capitol building's guards stood framed in the door. Without pausing to catch his breath, he shouted, "Crockett's done it, he's captured California!"

Seguin leaned in, and said in a low voice, "The president needs this information. With this, it will put us in an even stronger negotiating position."

Ellis agreed. "Let's see how well this new telegraph system we have works." With that, the two men paid their bill and hurried to the telegraph office.

Over the past few years, the electric telegraph had undergone several upgrades as its inventor, Samuel Morse, had worked with the military at the Alamo as well as with an investment group responsible for running lines between West Liberty and Houston and most recently between San Antonio and Austin.

The message, once sent, would get to San Antonio almost instantly, saving a full day or more travel. Once received by the fort's commander, he would send it by relay rider to the south. Even so, it would take nearly two weeks for the message to reach the president.

Seguin fell into step beside Vice-President Ellis on their way back to the Capitol building. Ellis confided, "I just hope the message gets there in time to be of use to us."

10 August 1843

Lorenzo de Zavala stood from his seat at the conference table, glaring at Jose Joaquin de Herrera. His back was aching, having been mercilessly jostled in the two-week ride from Austin. The single day before the peace negotiations hadn't been enough for his back to return to something approaching normal. But his back wasn't the reason for his scowl.

As a courtesy to his Mexican counterpart, he had agreed to hear Mexico's peace terms.

Herrera had just finished telling him that Mexico would agree to acknowledge Texas' independence and recognize the border between the two nations as the Nueces River. Herrera had also insisted Texas free all the officers still held following the recent battle, including Santa Anna.

Standing behind his chair, Zavala stretched his back, wishing it would quit hurting. He took a deep breath, reminding himself his counterpart was simply laying out Mexico's starting position in the negotiations. "A lot of water has flowed down the Rio Grande since Mexico cobbled together Coahuila and Texas into a single province. Any treaty between our two countries must recognize the Treaty of Bexar. This naturally includes the towns of Ysleta, Santa Fe, and Albuquerque."

He saw Herrera's eyes grow hard as he stared across the table. "Further, your predecessor's casual disregard for the rules of war has created intense enmity between our countries. Wantonly killing prisoners, especially those who surrender honorably, is a crime. These needless executions caused families to lose their sole provider. We insist that any agreement provide restitution to the families killed by Santa Anna's brutal actions. Further, the blood of the innocents demands justice. Santa Anna will return to Texas, where he will face a tribunal."

Herrera was quivering with anger, barely remaining in his seat. "You don't ask for much, do you?"

Zavala took a deep breath and bit back an angry retort. "I'm not finished. Mexico is to reduce its fleet in the Gulf of Mexico and will not attempt to buy ships from European shipbuilders. Additionally, a treaty of friendship exists between our nation and the people of the Republic of the Yucatan. We require that your government come to terms with the Yucatecan government and end your attempt to conquer them."

This time Herrera leapt to his feet, "How dare you presume to tell me how to deal with our internal affairs. The status of the Yucatan is not open for debate."

Zavala resisted the urge to smile. Left unsaid, everything else, to one degree or another, was negotiable. "Please, President Herrera, this is but our first day. It is important that we establish our goals. I was quiet while you told me that Texas needed to give up more than half our territory, the least you can do is extend to me the same courtesy."

Returning to his seat, Herrera bent his head in acknowledgement. "My apologies, President Zavala. I simply do not want you beating a dead mule on an issue where there can be no compromise."

Before Zavala took his seat, he said, "From where I stand, you're not in a position of strength. We hold the capital cities of two of your states. If you choose to resume the war, you will be hard-pressed to build an army as large as the one Santa Anna did. And if you did so, and marched them north, there will be someone standing behind you with a knife. In a little more than twenty years since Mexico's independence, the office you hold has changed hands more than twenty times. A peace treaty, even one that takes from Mexico, is better than the alternative."

That evening, Herrera was resting in the home of Saltillo's alcalde. The town's administrator was staying with family, allowing the president and his staff the privacy required for the hard battle ahead, saving what was left of Mexico's honor.

He was sitting in the kitchen with several men, when his secretary, Ignacio Comonfort, asked, "Don't the

Texians realize we hold an insurmountable advantage over them?"

The president said, "In what way, Ignacio? We have more people and land, but the Texians have better equipment and their soldiers are well trained. I might be inclined to believe our advantages meant something, had we achieved any meaningful victory."

His secretary asked, "What does that mean for these negotiations?"

Herrera sagged in his chair, admitting, "Nothing good. I will bluster and posture until I fall over dead, but I doubt Zavala is going to relent on the border. That fool Santa Anna has caused us irreparable damage. That ruinous Treaty of Bexar in 1836 is not something Zavala has any intention of letting go."

The secretary said, "What of their other positions? Forcing us to a treaty with our Yucatecan rebels seems outlandish."

Herrera scowled. "Zavala threw that out there to see how far he can push me. The only reason Texas gives aid to the rebels is that a destabilized Yucatan peninsula forces us to focus our energies closer to home. I fear the two issues on which Zavala will be intractable is regarding the borders and Santa Anna."

Lorenzo sat on the porch in front of the city government building, in a rocking chair. There was something about watching the sun sink below the low mesas to the west that soothed him. On a bench, next to the rocking chair sat General Travis.

The two had been talking for a bit about the earlier meeting with Herrera. "There you have it, Buck. We're about as far apart as one can be and still be in the same room. If we can't settle with Herrera, do you think you can capture San Luis Potosi? Surely if we started capturing cities in central Mexico that would force them to the table."

Travis said, "God, I'd hope it doesn't come to that. There are so many variables to include that any answer becomes meaningless. If we mobilized more militia battalions, we could use them to make our supply line more secure, and that would allow us to push on to San Luis Potosi. But that would destabilize our economy, right?"

Zavala shuddered, "More soldiers means fewer farmers, and we have few enough as it is. I'd really like to get our boys home before harvest time this autumn. Every time Michel Menard wants to meet with me, he keeps saying that if we think of our economy as a wagon, the wheels are about to come off. Already, imports, like tea and coffee, have doubled in price since the war began. Erasmo Seguin is playing some commodities against others in an effort to keep the domestic price of grain reasonable, but if we can't get a decent crop harvested then Seguin's efforts won't matter a damn."

As the sun slipped below the western mesas, Travis' features became shadows. "I wish to hell we had new information from David. What's the latest?"

Zavala said, "The three companies assigned to the Santa Fe region have reestablished our rule along the northern stretches of the Rio Grande. But that aside, there's been no other news. Have you received anything else from Charlie?"

"I'd wear his hide out, if I thought I could get away with it, Lorenzo. I nearly died inside when I got his letter. I still don't understand what got into that boy to pull a stunt like this. When they get back home, I'm sure Becky will have a few choice words for both of them. If he had run off with anyone other than David, I don't know what I would do. How I wish he hadn't filled my son's head with all his stories. I know he ran away from home when he was just thirteen, but, dammit, had I realized my son would do the same thing, I would might have chained the boy to his bed."

Zavala replied, "Emily says a prayer for his safe return every night. Me, I pray that we receive word soon. If David was successful in wrestling California away, it will completely change the negotiations."

Chapter 27

24 August 1843

Will rose from the conference table and stepped over to a credenza where refreshments were available. As he poured himself a glass of lemonade, he wondered what had possessed Lorenzo to include him as a member of his delegation. To Will's twenty-first century mind, there were good reasons to separate the military and civilian duties within the government.

Nearly two weeks had passed, and it appeared the only accomplishment was for the two sides to find creative ways to restate their starting points. He would rather be anywhere than in the room with the diplomats. Lorenzo had probably added him to the diplomatic team because Herrera had included one of his generals in the Mexican delegation. Will had heard of General Jose Urrea, both from the history he recalled from his own past, in a world gone forever, and as one of the generals who had served under Adrian Woll the previous year. Urrea wore his black hair slicked back. He carried himself with a confidence that Will thought bordered on outright arrogance.

Will had to remind himself on more than one occasion this version of Urrea wasn't the same as the one from his own past who had carried out the Goliad massacre. There had been several receptions over the past week, hosted in the hope that the two delegations mingling in a relaxed setting would hasten a treaty, and he had spoken at length with the Mexican general. While he hadn't found Urrea to be as warm as General Almonte, there was still a sharp mind behind the arrogant eyes.

His thoughts were broken by the man sitting to Zavala's right. John Wharton, who was Texas' chief diplomat, said, "President Herrera, your intransigence is unsettling. Your armies are decimated and scattered. You've got rebellion brewing outside of places like the Yucatan, and yet you persist in refusing to negotiate. Tell me why President Zavala and I shouldn't return to Texas and let General Travis complete the job he has started."

Will saw the storm clouds gathering around Herrera, but Wharton ignored it, "Tell me, do you honestly believe even as brave an officer as General Urrea could stop our army from capturing San Luis Potosi?"

Urrea bristled, but it was Herrera who spoke, "Secretary Wharton, Mexico is not defeated. We sought a treaty to end the war, not because you have conquered us, but to save lives. But you bring your demands that would strip us of our land and of our principals. The treaty you propose would never receive enough votes in our Congress to be ratified."

Zavala placed a hand on Wharton's arm, silencing a retort. He removed his glasses and took out a handkerchief and methodically cleaned the lenses before saying. "We really need to spend some time focusing on what is achievable. President Herrera, the treaty you propose would, as my predecessor would say, stink like a polecat in Austin. Were I to bring it to our congress, they would tar and feather me and run me out of town on a rail."

Will hid his smile behind the glass of lemonade. It was something he would expect to hear from Crockett, but coming from Zavala, the comment struck him as funny. But also, very true. Too many men had died defending the Alamo the previous year and storming the Mexican positions at the Rio Grande and again at Monterrey, for Texas to take anything less than the boundaries defined in the Treaty of Bexar. And Santa Anna. It would be a cold day in Hell before Will would allow Santa Anna's release back to the Mexican government. The former dictator had much to answer for.

A rumble in his stomach was validated by a comment from Herrera's secretary. "Let's take a break for lunch. Perhaps we can approach our problems with a fresh perspective on a full stomach."

There were no objections, and a few minutes later he stood under the building's veranda. "Mr. President, if we don't get a breakthrough pretty damn quick, we're going to need to start marching on San Luis Potosi. Herrera has damn all between us and central Mexico. But if we go that route, we'll have no choice but to mobilize another two or three thousand men."

Zavala stifled a groan. "Such a campaign would eat into the autumn, and if we mobilized three or four more battalions, that might make the difference between getting enough of our harvest in and starvation."

Will cursed. Then thinking about Texas' terms, he asked, "Which of our demands is most negotiable?"

Without hesitation, Zavala said, "Obviously, the Yucatan gambit is worthless, but it was worth a try. But, as much as I want to see to the welfare of our widows and orphans, I would sacrifice the indemnities, too. I would even consider giving them back Santa Anna before I would budge an inch on our borders."

"Too many men have died, Mr. President, defending the treaty boundary for us to negotiate that away. Have we considered offering any kind of financial arrangement for the settlement of the boundary dispute?"

"With what, General?" Zavala countered. "This war has played hell on our budget."

A rider came galloping into town's central plaza from the east, from the direction of Monterrey. His butternut uniform was caked with gray dust, and as he slowed his mount to a canter, Will saw the rider looking around the plaza. When Will met the rider's eyes, the horseman veered toward him. He drew up and cast a quick salute, "General, Colonel Crockett has done it, he has captured California!"

30 August 1843

Were Lorenzo de Zavala a cat, his whiskers would have drooped heavy with cream. But he was only a man, albeit a happy one. The conference had gone to hell when the Mexican president and his delegation had learned of Crockett's conquest.

Herrera had stormed from the library and threatened to leave Saltillo. It was his own general, Urrea, who had taken him aside and reminded him the only choices were between bad and worse. Santa Anna had squandered the only army worth the name on the Texian redoubts south of the city. Still quivering with anger, Herrera relented.

The question Zavala and his delegates had faced when it was clear Herrera was going to be forced to give in, was deciding how much to demand. It was easy enough to jettison any agreement regarding the struggling Republic of the Yucatan or limits on the Mexican navy in the Gulf of Mexico. Both Secretary of State Wharton and General Travis had assured him the Texas Navy would be able to maintain supremacy against Mexico for years to come. Giving in on those two issues allowed President Herrera to save enough face to agree to drop his demand to return Santa Anna to Mexico.

The negotiations hit a wall again when they talked about territory. Herrera reluctantly agreed to surrender any Mexican claim to the boundaries provided in the treaty of Bexar. But Texas now held an additional half million square miles of land. In truth, Zavala had considered it Crockett's folly when he had agreed to it the previous year, and he had half expected the former president to return to Texas defeated by the harsh land separating Santa Fe from Alta California.

He had been inclined to surrender all of California back to Mexico, knowing it would bring a close to the negotiations, but had been surprised when both Secretary of State Wharton and General Travis opposed it.

Wharton had argued, "Sir, if we keep California, we inherit several Pacific ports. If we can connect them to the east, it will make Texas a continental power. Spain had California for three hundred years, Mexico for twenty-five. Both Spain and Mexico had the opportunity to colonize it, but after all that time, maybe ten thousand Californios call it home. And according to Crockett's dispatches, folks were lining up in both San Diego and Los Angeles to swear allegiance to Texas."

But it was Travis' advice which gave him to the most to consider. It was, as the general was fond of saying, a game changer.

He had said, "Mr. President, the ports are no doubt valuable, but I have a strong suspicion there are rich minerals in the area that Mexico hasn't been able to exploit. Trying to hold all that territory could be a real challenge, although potentially very lucrative to our treasury."

Ever since Zavala had served as Crockett's vice president, he had seen the general had almost a preternatural sense about him. From anyone else, the idea of holding California seemed a pipe dream. "Let's assume we can get Herrera to negotiate a price, how in the name of all that is holy do we pay for it? We're neck deep in debt at the moment."

Travis' next words left him speechless. "This is just an idea, mind you, but we could keep a strip of land connecting Santa Fe to San Diego and Los Angeles and sell the rest of it. I think we all know a hungry neighbor to our north that is beating the drums for manifest destiny. An opportunity to acquire a few hundred thousand square miles would be hard for even a Whig to pass up."

It was an intriguing idea. After studying a map of North America, Travis had further refined it. He had suggested offering to the United States all the territory north of 36° 30 north, for the right price. In the territory held by the United States, the parallel of 36° 30 north was most commonly known as the Missouri Compromise.

The idea *was* appealing; he had asked, "You mentioned much of this land is likely rich in minerals, if that's so, why sell it to the United States?"

Travis' laughter had rung in his ears, "Most of us have given up our citizenship in the United States to make something of Texas. But we still have family and friends back east, and they are fixated on stretching from sea to shining sea, Mr. President. If we can arrive at an arrangement with Mexico for Alta California, our friends and family back east may decide we're a more tempting target for annexation than any of us can resist, and poof," he said, gesticulating with his hands, "we're gone."

Travis had used a pencil to draw a line cutting all of Alta California in half. The greater portion was to the north, but there was still a sizable section to the south. "Offer the United States this," he said, pointing at the northern portion, "and they will take a couple of generations absorbing it. All the while, we have around four hundred thousand miles between the gulf coast and the Pacific Ocean."

Zavala's mind returned to the present, still smiling as he recalled telling Travis, "That's the work of a couple of lifetimes."

The give and take between the two delegations had not been easy. Following the arrival of a courier from Mexico City, Herrera began signaling a change of heart. The final straw came when Wharton had asked, "would you rather have Texas as a neighbor or the United States?"

Zavala long suspected were it not for Texas, and the tens of thousands of Americans who now called the republic home, the United States would be eying the sparsely populated parts of northern Mexico. And if, as General Travis implied, there were riches in the northern reaches, then the United States would simply reach out and take it from Mexico. It appeared Herrera had reached the same conclusion. Compared to Texas, Mexico had many advantages. Against the United States, those advantages were turned around.

From there it was only a matter of negotiating the price for Alta California. The two presidents eventually settled on ten million pesos, payable over a ten-year period. The first payment was scheduled for the first of January 1844. Herrera had pushed for an earlier payment. Zavala suspected the recent news from Mexico City may have indicated another revolt. The sooner payment could be received, the sooner it could be used to put down the growing unrest in the central part of the country.

Now, as he was about to sign the treaty, he was confident he was giving Texas something they could be proud of.

The first article ended the war between Texas and Mexico.

In the second article, Mexico acknowledged Santa Anna's war crimes, and assented to his extradition to the Republic of Texas. It forbade Texas to use a military tribunal, and required the former dictator be given due process before, during, and following any trial.

The third article validated the 1836 Treaty of Bexar.

The fourth article ceded all of Alta California to Texas for the promised payment of ten million pesos, paid over a period of ten years. If Texas defaulted on payment, then the two nations agreed to a commission that would oversee the return of the province to Mexico. Zavala hated the last proviso, but it was necessary to obtain Herrera's signature.

The fifth article provided a path to Texas citizenship for all Mexicans living within Texas' newly defined boundaries and provided a one-year period for Mexicans living in Texas to choose Texas citizenship or sell their property and return to Mexico. Zavala was cautiously optimistic this article would provide a boost to the nation's population. Although there were perhaps ten thousand Mexicans living in California, there were upwards of fifty thousand living in what had once been Nuevo Mexico.

The sixth article guaranteed free travel between the citizens of both nations along the Rio Grande and provided a commission to survey the boundary between the two countries, from the town of Ysleta to the Pacific Ocean.

The seventh article required Texas police the Indian tribes within all its territory. Zavala worried about this provision. A commission was to meet annually between the two nations to adjudicate any claims resulting from Texas' failure to keep raids from crossing the international boundary. It was another provision Herrera had insisted upon. While Texas had maintained an uneasy peace with all the Comanche bands, those same bands had freely traversed parts of West Texas on their way to raid into Mexico. How he would keep them from violating this provision remained a mystery.

The eighth article made each nation responsible for any claims within their own borders regarding the costs of the war and passed Mexican liabilities to Texas regarding land disputes in the newly acquired territory.

The ninth article freed half of the Mexican officers not yet paroled upon the signing of the treaty. The remainder would be released once the treaty was ratified by both nations' deliberative bodies.

The tenth article allowed both nations to fortify any position on their shared boundary and to require citizens of each country to present themselves to duly authorized representatives of their host nation.

The eleventh article required Texas to remove all military personnel from Mexico upon the ratification of both nations' deliberative bodies.

Zavala stopped reading and took the quill lying beside the parchment and signed next to President Herrera's signature. With a stroke of a pen, the war was finally over.

The cantinas and bars of Saltillo were ringing with the sound of celebration as the town took on a carnival atmosphere. Will felt a little unstable on his feet as he left the building. He had to escape, every soldier with a couple of dollars in his pocket had tried to stand him for a drink. Had he remained, no doubt he would pass out on the floor before long.

Instead, now he just needed to put one foot in front of the other, as he made his way back to the government building. Apart from the Mexicans who called Saltillo home, the only people on the streets were other Texians, intent on having a good time. He saw a couple of men sitting under the veranda as he approached. President Zavala and Secretary Warton were in a pair of rocking chairs. The president had a rare cigar lit in his mouth. "If you tell Emily, I'll bust you down to a lieutenant and station you on some godforsaken border. After yesterday, I've got a lot more options available."

Still feeling the effects of cheap alcohol, Will held his hands up, "Your secret is safe with me."

Something had been bothering Will since the treaty's signing the previous day, "Mr. President, we pushed really hard, do you figure Herrera will be able to force the treaty through the Mexican congress?"

Zavala blew a ragged ring of smoke. "It's anyone's guess. I learned that he has some serious problems in Mexico City and it may be that a few heads will roll when he gets back there."

Will cocked an eyebrow, waiting for Zavala to continue. "Do you recall that post rider who came from Mexico City a few days ago? Turns out some of Herrera's Centralist allies have rebelled. You may have noticed that General Urrea disappeared the next day. He'll take charge of an army they have been reassembling in San Luis Potosi. It's not much, just a couple of thousand ill-equipped soldiers, but I suspect when he gets there, he'll be leading that army south."

Will asked, "Do you think Herrera can stay in office?"

"It's not a sure thing, but Mexico is tired of war. Herrera offers the best hope for peace. He has confirmed that whatever congress he pulls together, he will ram the treaty through." A sigh escaped Zavala's lips. "It's not ideal, and if things go too badly, we could find ourselves in another war with Mexico."

Will grimaced, "God, I hope not."

Zavala chuckled mirthlessly. "From your lips, Buck." He slipped into the familiarity that ran throughout the government. "But I don't think it will come to that. If Herrera can't hold on to the presidency, then Mexico is looking at a civil war. On the other hand, if he can hold on, in few months he's going to get a big boost from us when we make that first payment."

Will worried about that first payment, due at the beginning of the year. "Any idea where you're going to find a million pesos?"

He noticed Zavala's focus and attention shift. It appeared the president was looking beyond Will. Curious, he turned around and saw a man on horseback riding across the plaza. The rider approached the three men. "I've got a message for General Travis."

Will turned around and used his index finger to raise the brim of his hat. "You found him."

The rider casually saluted with a wave of his hand. He reached into his jacket and brought out an oilskin packet and handed it over. Will asked, "Do you know the contents?"

Reluctantly, the rider nodded. "It ain't good, General, sir. I'd druther you read it than hear it from me."

Was it Becky? Was there a problem back home? Will found the rider's reluctance to speak alarming. "Tell me, man. If you know something don't wait on a damned letter."

"Sweet Jesus, sir. President Crockett, I mean, the colonel. He's dead."

Will felt the color drain from his face. His mind screamed. But he managed to stammer, "What about my son? What about Charlie?"

"I'm sorry, sir. But he's been kidnapped."

The Texas Cession: A Short Story

November 1843; Washington, District of Columbia

He looked out the window of the coach, as the contraption rolled along the macadamized road. Clutching at the scarf, he pulled it tighter around his throat as a cross wind cut through the vehicle. It chilled him to the bone.

"Close the damned curtain, Beecher." Snapped the man beside him. Artemas Beecher drew the curtain closed. He eyed the middle-aged man beside him. Colonel William Ward wore the expensive clothing of a successful southern planter, although how long before he would be able to return to his plantation in East Texas was anyone's guess. The ink was still drying on the document appointing him minister plenipotentiary to the United States. President Zavala had appointed him to the position after his battalion's heroic defense at the Battle of Saltillo earlier in the year.

Artemas owed his own position of clerk to Colonel Ward. He had joined the 4th Infantry as a musician a couple of years earlier, while the battalion was still an ad-hoc collection of reserve companies. But it was during the fateful Battle of Saltillo that the seventeen-year-old drummer saved his colonel's life when the redoubts southern wall was nearly breached. Ward had been shot in the leg and had fallen on the parapet. As the soldados clambered over the wall, Artemas had pried a bayoneted rifle from the fingers of a dead rifleman and had forced his way in front of the colonel, slashing and swinging the bayonet's tip. Several men standing atop the steep, sloping wall leapt back the way they had come, sliding down the dry ditch.

Artemas sat on the padded bench, his face a mask, as the emotions of the battle, five months in the past, boiled within him. He had thought himself a goner, until other riflemen raced to fill in the void. Colonel Ward had survived with only a slight hitch in his leg. For his bravery, Artemas had been offered the role of clerk, once President Zavala had offered Ward the ambassadorship to the United States. It was a strange fate for a farmer's son from San Filipe.

The driver applied the brake, slowing the coach. Over the squeal of the brake, as wet wood gripped wet iron, Artemas heard voices from without. Ignoring the earlier command to leave the curtain closed, Artemas peered out. The imposing Treasury building of the United States filled his view. The entrance was framed by large, ornate columns. Stairs ran from the decorative wooden doors to the paving stones which stretched the from the building's base to the macadamized avenue.

Crowding the expansive sidewalk were men and women, holding signs. As the coachman swung the side-door open, Artemas read one of the signs. "No Slavery! No Compromise!" Another sign read, "Free Soil for a Free

People!" Another proclaimed "United States are a city on a hill.! No to expansion!"

He leaned back in the seat as the Texas Secretary of State, William Wharton stepped from the coach, followed by Colonel Ward. For the briefest of moments, Artemas was alone. He eyed the strident messages hoisted into the air by the protesters and as he stepped down, he hurried to catch up with Texas' envoys. Their shoes echoed on the slick paving stones as the small party of Texians strode purposefully by the middle-class Whigs who had taken time to protest the negotiations.

A doorman, whose face was dark as night, closed the richly carved door behind Artemas, silencing the crowd of protesters.

The Treasury department shared part of the gargantuan building with the Department of State. The party was escorted by a dapperly dressed young man. Artemas followed Ward and Wharton up a wide staircase and through a set of double doors embossed with the great seal of the United States. In gold lettering above the seal was stenciled "Department of State."

They were led into a room, with a long, mahogany table in the center. A dozen chairs lined the table. The young guide said, "Messieurs Webster and Randolph will be in directly."

Moments later, the American delegates for the conference strode through the door. Artemas studied the men. He had met Fletcher Webster a few months before in Austin, when President Zavala had first offered to sell a portion of northern California to the United States. Until then he had been the American minister to Texas. The twenty-five-year-old was the son of the American vice-president. The next man to enter was Thomas Randolph.

He was of middle years, hair graying at the temples. When he shook hands with Artemas' superior, he spoke with a soft Virginian accent.

After the men took their seats in the comfortable chairs arranged around the ornate table, Randolph, as Under-Secretary of State spoke first. "Allow me to extend our congratulations to your nation regarding your success against Mexico. There is something which stirs the heart to watch Anglo-Saxon arms victorious over our less able neighbors."

William Wharton raised his hand in a half-salute, "Providence blessed Texian arms, Mr. Randolph."

Artemas had traveled with Secretary of State Wharton since leaving Galveston, and recognized the gentle rebuke in the diplomat's words. The army of the republic had fielded an entire battalion of Cherokee and hundreds of Tejanos had served in the late war. Command of Texas' mounted force was under Brigadier General Juan Seguin, who Artemas considered the most famous Tejano in the republic. Referring to Texas' victory as a feat of Anglo-Saxon arms was impolitic.

Randolph smiled benignly in response. More perceptive, Minister Webster added, "On the wide world stage, our nations are brothers, and seeing you prosper in your late war, buoys our hearts as well."

As the two parties sat at the table, Wharton looked apologetic. "I confess, a year ago had I been told my adopted nation would reach from the Gulf of Mexico to the Pacific Ocean while the nation of my birth would still jointly administer the Oregon Territory with Britain, I would have labeled such a person a lunatic."

Artemas was not the only person at the table to raise an eyebrow. Wharton's oblique observation was a reminder Texas remained dissatisfied the Clay administration had rebuffed an offer by Texas to host a conference between Washington and London to settle their disagreement over Oregon. Even the British envoy, Henry Fox had sent informal word her majesty's government would view American acceptance of Texas' offer with favor. President Clay's silence over the matter the previous year had not gone unnoticed.

Artemas hid a smirk. Of course, the British had been in favor of a conference. Texas captured two modern steam powered iron-hulled warships from the Mexican navy the previous year and Mexico stopped payment to the British bankers who had financed the ships' construction. Those same bankers had been eager to reclaim the ships and had used their influence with the British Foreign Office to float the idea of accepting the offer from Texas.

Now, Texas held California and two new warships. President Clay's latest offer to host a conference in Washington to resolve the Oregon boundary dispute had gone unanswered by Whitehall. If anything, Artemas thought the American diplomats had done an admirable job hiding their reactions to Wharton.

Randolph forced a narrow smile. "I'm convinced John Bull will eventually come around. It's in their interest to settle the boundary in Oregon, too."

"Eventually," Wharton conceded. "But, enough about what the British may or may not do. If I may, let us discuss something we're both empowered to do something about."

He looked at Artemas, "Mr. Beecher, be so good as to unroll the map."

The young man jumped to his feet and uncapped a leather tube. He drew from it a large map and unrolled it. He took a few small stones from his pocket and weighted the map down. Detailed on the map was North American from the Mississippi to the Pacific Ocean. A cartographer had drawn new national borders, showing the boundary line of the Adams-Onis Treaty as Texas' northern limit.

Randolph stared at the map, his attention drawn to the western section, the Pacific coastal area, "There are some fine bays and natural ports along your newly acquired coastline."

Wharton allowed a half-smile, "Imagine what your government could do with them. I'm sure it's tiresome to base your Pacific Squadron out of roving supply ships instead of a modern port."

Minister Webster had been silent, deferring to Randolph's senior position in the State Department, but at the mention of the ports, he said, "I had heard President Zavala and General Travis had been interested in extending the line of the Missouri Compromise in any negotiations."

Artemas blew the lucifer out and turned the nob on the lamp until the shadows on the room retreated into the corners. He turned and watched Minister Ward kneel and light a fire in the room's fireplace.

As the room warmed, the young man took a seat at a desk, while the older men rested in two plush, comfortable chairs facing the crackling fire.

Wharton took a sip from a glass tumbler, "I bet Henry Clay is kicking himself for not agreeing to our offer last year. Had they settled the boundary with the Brits, they'd have more leverage today."

Ward snickered into his drink. "I ain't prone to saying anything bad about my fellow Southerners, but damned, how did Tom Randolph's star rise so high? And that pup of an ambassador, Fletcher Webster is still wet behind the ears, by God."

Wharton chuckled appreciatively, "When you're the grandson of Thomas Jefferson, it tends to cloud people's judgement, Bill. But don't misread young Fletcher. He's got more of his father in him than I'd like. If you've noticed, Randolph deferred to him several times today. I'd be surprised if he didn't make a beeline over to the Presidents mansion and report to his pa and Clay."

Forgetting his place, Artemas asked, "Isn't that a good thing, sir? If Mr. Webster is reporting directly to the president, seems Mr. Clay is really interested in your negotiations."

Ward's face creased into a frown, but held his peace when Wharton nodded in approval. "Your right, Mr. Beecher. But Henry Clay wouldn't have allowed the negotiations unless he was serious about buying part of California. No matter how long it takes or how much horse trading our American counterparts attempt, the major issues we'll settle are the price and the boundary. There's no doubt in my mind, we'll bring a treaty back to Austin."

He set the empty tumbler on the narrow table between the chairs and pulled a cigar from his jacket. He cut the end from the cigar and lit it. As he puffed on it, he turned thoughtful. "You know, Bill, Lorenzo and Buck gave us enough latitude to negotiate the best possible treaty."

Ward leaned over his chair, "You thinking of getting more money from Clay?"

Wharton waved the cigar, "I wouldn't turn up my nose at that, but no, Bill. That's not what I'm thinking. I'm mindful that a good fence makes a good neighbor. Texas is separated from Louisiana by the Sabine River, for the most part. Then we've got the Red River to our north and the Rio Grande to our south. If we set the thirty-six thirty meridian as our new boundary, we'll have more than a thousand miles of open borders with the United States."

Ward wore a confused expression, "But, there's not damn all west of the Red River. What's it matter?"

Artemas wondered the same thing. The land to the west was empty of civilization. Like a professor explaining a complex lesson, Wharton gently shook his head. "Not so much as we might like, Bill. There are more than thirty thousand men, women and children living in the Rio Grande basin around Santa Fe and Albuquerque. Word is, most of them are going to stay put and accept Texian citizenship. There's another ten thousand or so on the California coast. Add in the Indians and the land is hardly empty."

He took a final puff from the cigar and set it in a brass tray. "I've been looking at young Master Artemas' map, and I think we should use the natural rivers of our newly acquired territory to separate Texas from the United States. Both the Colorado and San Juaquin Rivers are natural boundaries, and if we offer those boundaries to Messers Webster and Randolph we need only worry about three hundred miles with no river between us and them, and that's through some of the most inhospitable land God ever made."

His face, Artemas decided, was devoid of emotion when he finished. It was as though he were hiding something. The young man ventured, "Is there anything else, sir?"

"If we offer these new boundary lines to the United States, we'll keep nearly one hundred thousand more square miles than under the thirty-six thirty offering."

Artemas looked at the map. Yes, he could see the benefit. There would need to be some accommodation regarding the bay at San Francisco. The boundary would run through the bay. It would provide the US Pacific squadron a couple of different options for good anchorage. His eyes rose as he studied the map. Texas would retain Monterey, Los Angeles and San Diego.

Outside the window snow eddies swirled. Artemas shivered despite the heat radiating from the franklin stove. November would be giving up the ghost within the next couple of days, and already old man winter was covering the American capital in a white blanket. He turned his back on the window and saw the other men in the room were all smiles.

Well they should be, he thought. All that remained was for the two sides to sign the treaty. That, and get both countries' senates to ratify it. He walked over to the conference table and looked at the map spread across it.

An army cartographer had redrawn the map Artemas has brought to the conference, and the proposed boundaries were clearly marked. Texas would retain everything south of the San Juaquin River in the western portion of the territory and everything south of the Colorado River in the east. The territory to be transferred was close to three hundred thousand square miles. The agreed upon price for the territory worked out to a bit more than four and a half cents an acre, or nine million dollars, paid out over the course of six years.

The treaty which ended the Texas-Mexican War required Texas pay ten million pesos for all of Alta California, but it was to be paid over ten years. Artemas didn't envy the Treasury Department. It would be their responsibility to manage the receipts and payments.

The young man turned, as he heard Thomas Randolph laughing. The Undersecretary of State was leaning over the table, examining the new markings on the map. Next to him stood Artemas' superior, William Ward.

Ward said, "Nice touch, calling your part of California, 'Jefferson.' I like that."

"It only seems fitting. Thomas Jefferson gave us the Louisiana Purchase, doubling the size of our nation. Naming our newest acquisition in honor of our third president strikes me as a singular honor."

The door opened, and a man entered, carrying a contraption over his shoulder. The young man's eyes lit up when he saw it was one of the new daguerreotype machines. He had seen several studios offering pictographic services around the American capital.

Fletcher Webster raised his voice, "Gentlemen, I thought it would be fitting to capture such a momentous moment for both of our nations so that a likeness of this occasion could be kept for posterity."

The signatories, Randolph and Wharton stood next to the treaty, holding the pens which they had used to sign the document. Webster and Ward stood to either side. As the photographer slid the plate used to capture the image into the contraption Wharton waved to him. "Mr. Beecher, stand beside Mr. Ward. I've a feeling this is a moment for the history books."

Summer 1844

He scratched at his beard as his sure-footed mount crested the hill. Artemas sucked in his breath when his eyes fell on the valley below. A river snaked through the valley, meandering from north to south. He recalled the name, having studied the map of the area more times than he'd care to remember. It was the Rio de los Americanos. As he followed one of his traveling companions down the hill, he wondered if the Yankees would keep the name or change it.

He wiped sweat from his brow and eyed the midday sun. Even though the party had traveled only a hundred miles from San Francisco, the temperature had spiked as they moved away from the coastal plain and entered the interior highlands. "At least it's not as hot as it is in Austin," he thought.

He let his mount pick its route down the hill while he ran his eyes up and down the valley. Logging the old growth trees would be profitable, but that wasn't the reason he and his traveling companions had spent four months traveling by sea around South America. Further down the hill rode the party's leader. Major Jack Hays gripped the reins with his one arm, as he led a dozen men into the valley.

Artemas, like the others following behind the former Ranger, had received a land grant following the war with Mexico. At that time, he had given it little thought. He had joined Colonel Ward's trip to Washington, DC as his clerk. He shook his head at the memory. Ward's appointment as minister to the United States was payback for his service in the war, and Artemas had learned by the end of the negotiated treaty that Ward was ill suited to the role. This realization demoralized the young man and he had returned to Texas with Secretary of State Wharton.

When he arrived back in Austin, Major Hays made a point of meeting him because his land grant was in the recently sold territory of Jefferson.

His horse neighed when the party reached the river, tearing his mind away from the past. Major Hays climbed from his mount. "Alright boys, let's set up camp here. Time to find out if the rumor of gold is true."

Stay tuned for the continued adventures of the Lone Star Reloaded Series, book 5 at the end of 2018.

Thank you for reading Down Mexico Way

If you enjoyed reading Down Mexico Way please help support the author by leaving a review on Amazon. For announcements, promotions, special offers, you can sign up for updates from Drew McGunn at:

https://drewmcgunn.wixsite.com/website

About the Author

Drew McGunn lives on the Texas gulf coast with his supportive wife. He started writing in high school and after college worked the nine-to-five grind for many years, while the stories in his head rattled around, begging to be released.

After one too many video games, Drew awoke from his desire for one more turn, and returned to his love of the printed word. His fascination with history led him to study his roots, and as a sixth generation Texan, he decided to write about the founding of Texas as a Republic. There are many exceptional books about early Texas, but hardly any about alternate histories of the great state. With that in mind, he wrote his debut novel "Forget the Alamo!" as a reimagining of the first days of the Republic. Down Mexico Way is the fourth in the series.

When he's not writing or otherwise putting food on the table, Drew enjoys traveling to historic places, or reading other engaging novels from up and coming authors.

Made in the USA
Columbia, SC
24 December 2018